Books
by Jerome Weidman

NOVELS
I Can Get It for You Wholesale
What's in It for Me?
I'll Never Go There Any More
The Lights Around the Shore
Too Early to Tell
The Price Is Right
The Hand of the Hunter
Give Me Your Love
The Third Angel
Your Daughter Iris
The Enemy Camp
Before You Go
The Sound of Bow Bells
Word of Mouth
Other People's Money
The Center of the Action
Fourth Street East
Last Respects

SHORT STORIES
The Horse That Could Whistle "Dixie"
The Captain's Tiger
A Dime a Throw
Nine Stories
My Father Sits in the Dark
The Death of Dickie Draper

ESSAYS AND TRAVEL
Letter of Credit
Traveler's Cheque
Back Talk

PLAYS
Fiorello!
Tenderloin
I Can Get It for You Wholesale
Asterisk: A Comedy of Terrors
Ivory Tower (with James Yaffe)

Last
Respects

Last Respects

by
Jerome
Weidman

Random House

New York

All rights reserved under International
and Pan-American Copyright Conventions.
Published in the United States by
Random House, Inc., New York, and simultaneously
in Canada by Random House of Canada Limited, Toronto.

ISBN: 0-394-46551-2
Library of Congress Catalog Card Number: 77-156966

Manufactured in the United States of America
by The Book Press, Brattleboro, Vermont

9 8 7 6 5 4 3 2

FIRST EDITION

To
the memory of
Annie Falkovitz

"Happy he with such a mother!"

The Princess,
Alfred, Lord Tennyson

Last
Respects

1

MY MOTHER'S BODY disappeared three weeks ago from the Peretz Memorial Hospital in the Borough of Queens. The event took place sometime between 8:25 A.M. and 11:40 A.M. on the morning before Christmas Eve. It was a Sunday. At 8:25 on that morning I received a phone call at my home from Dr. Herman Sabinson.

"It's all over," he said. "She went in her sleep sometime during the night. There was no pain. She just went quietly. Did you hear me? I said she had absolutely no pain. Did you hear me?"

"Yes, sure," I said. "I heard you."

I also believed him. Or wanted to. Herman Sabinson and I are old friends. Just the same, I could not help wondering. How did he know? How could anybody know?

"Now, I want you to do me a favor," Herman said. "For me as a doctor, I mean. Are you listening?"

I said, "I'm all ears."

A phrase I have never understood. Who has more than two?

"Not only for me as a doctor," Herman Sabinson said. "You'll be doing it for the family as well. Not to mention for yourself."

"What do you want me to do?" I said.

"I want you to allow me to perform an autopsy," Dr. Herman Sabinson said.

The word slid through my mind like a politician's campaign promise. I had heard it before, many times. Hearing it again made no special impression. It was just a word. It seemed appropriate to the conversation of a man who was intimately concerned every day with a subject about which I knew very little: death.

"All right," I said.

"You'll have to do more than just say all right," Herman Sabinson said. "You'll have to give your written consent."

This did not seem unreasonable. I had been signing papers for almost a month. Ever since I found my mother on the floor of the foyer in her three-room apartment on 78th Avenue in Queens. I had signed the papers admitting her to the Peretz Memorial Hospital. I had signed a form giving the surgeon permission to operate on her fractured thigh bone. There had been a number of other documents. They covered her Medicare registration; the activities of a firm of anesthesiologists who serviced the operating room in the Peretz Memorial Hospital; the corporation that owned the ambulance in which she was carried to the hospital; and two or three other printed forms with blank spaces that in one way or another touched on the complicated process of attempting to bring back to normal health an ailing citizen of New York City who had almost no financial resources of her own.

"You want me to go somewhere to sign a paper?" I said into the phone.

"That's correct," Herman Sabinson said.

"All right," I said. "Just tell me where."

"Here at the hospital," Dr. Herman Sabinson said. "I'll leave the form with Mrs. O'Toole in the Admitting Office. Any time this morning will be okay, so long as it's before noon, and then you'll be in the clear."

I wanted to laugh, but I didn't. Herman would have thought it unseemly. He would not have understood that he had just said something funny. He had no way of knowing that so far as my mother was concerned, I had never been in the clear. My mind refused to accept the statement of a comparative outsider that I would achieve this state by signing yet another piece of paper.

My mother had been a burden to me for many years. Not only financially. The money she had cost me had merely been an irritant. What had bothered me more and more during the last decade of her almost ninety years was that I did not know what to do about her.

This was caused in part by the fact that I felt she did not know what to do about herself. Life for her had never been something you lived. It was something you got through.

She seemed to get through her first eighty years in a manner that satisfied her. At any rate, I was unaware of any dissatisfaction on her part. Perhaps because I wasn't paying any attention. Why should I? I had my own problems.

Then my mother moved into her eighties and I became intensely aware of something she apparently did not herself understand. She was dissatisfied with the scheme of existence. Not her existence. That had always seemed to her to be perfectly sound. When she became a problem to me, and in my efforts to solve it I started paying attention to her, I began to grasp that she felt the world she had always been able to manage had suddenly become unmanageable. It annoyed her.

"I'll sign it," I said into the phone to Herman Sabinson. "I'll be there in half an hour, if I can get a cab."

I couldn't get a cab. Not at once, anyway. I live in a part of Manhattan that is unpopular with taxi drivers. The subway and several bus lines solve most of my transportation problems, but my mother had died in a part of the Borough of Queens that I was not sure I knew how to reach by subway or bus. Besides, it was Sunday, and it was the day before Christmas, and I could not remember how the mayor was making out in his annual negotiations with the Transport Workers Union to avert the strike that always seemed to be threatened for, or actually came on, Christmas Day. Or perhaps it was New Year's Eve? I had a feeling that I was somewhat confused about the hard facts of day-to-day life with which most of my neighbors were coping. A taxi seemed a sensible extravagance.

Even on sunny days in the summer I have to walk several blocks downtown, and move east toward the river, before I can get a taxi to stop for me. The day my mother died was not sunny. It was gray and cold. The sort of day in which the Brontës seem to have spent their lives. The sky was sullen. I remembered skies like this during the bad days of the blitz in London. I remembered that in those days these skies reduced even my pleasant thoughts to vague, shapeless fears. My thoughts were not pleasant as I moved downtown and eastward, keeping my head down against the wind. How could they be? A man who wants to laugh when he receives word of his mother's death is at least a son of a bitch, probably worse. Pleasant thoughts indeed.

At the corner of Lexington Avenue and 77th Street, on my way toward Third, the traffic light changed to red. I stopped. So did a taxi heading down Lexington. I stepped quickly down from the curb, wrenched open the taxi door, plopped onto the rear seat, and pulled the door shut with a bang.

"Merry Christmas," said the driver. "Where to?"

"Merry Christmas," I said. "The Peretz Memorial Hospital."

"You mean in Queens?" the driver said.

The tone of his voice told me at once I had not made a friend.

"Yes," I said.

"Jesus," the driver said.

"What's the matter?" I said.

"What's the matter?" the driver said. "It's an empty ride back, for Christ's sake, that's what's the matter."

"I guess you haven't been there for a long time," I said. "I've been there every day for the past four weeks. Every time I get there, on the front steps there are a dozen people fighting to get a cab back into Manhattan. You won't ride back empty."

"That's what you know," the driver said.

"I tell you I've been there every day this whole past month," I said.

"Yeah," the driver said. "But it's pretty damn early in the morning, and besides, this is the day before Christmas, buddy."

"What difference does that make?" I said.

I could hear the cutting edge in my own voice. I did not feel we were buddies.

"People don't go bucking visiting hours in hospitals the day before Christmas."

The light changed. The cab lurched forward.

"Hoddeyeh wanna go?" the driver said.

I didn't answer. My mind had been absorbed in controlling

the hatred for this stranger that I could feel mushrooming inside me. Now my mind had been jolted into an examination of his remark about the times when people visit hospitals.

"Hey," he said. "You hear me?"

"Sorry," I said. "I wasn't listening."

"I asked which way you want to go?" he said.

I looked out the window. The street sign indicated we were passing 76th and Lexington.

"As long as we're heading downtown," I said, "how about across the 59th Street bridge, then out Queens Boulevard to Union Turnpike? The hospital is two blocks further down."

"I know," the driver said. "One thing a taxi driver learns in this town. You learn the places people get sick in. Christ, this is one hell of a long trip."

It was longer than he thought, but of course he had no way of knowing that. Even I had not known, until early that same year, when my father died, that my mother had been born in Soho. I had always assumed she had been born on the farm in the Carpathian mountains of Hungary from which she had come to America shortly before the First World War.

A month before this day before Christmas on which my mother had died, when I was filling out the forms in the Admissions Office of the Peretz Memorial Hospital, it had seemed wise to me to forget about Soho. I listed my mother's place of birth as Berezna in Hungary. This checked with the records of the Department of Justice in Washington.

Only I, and the government, of course, knew that my mother had a police record. It was almost half a century old. There was probably very little chance that the Peretz Memorial Hospital would have been interested in the information. But Medicare, which was going to pay her bills, is a federal organization. So is the Justice Department. Even though my common sense told me one could not possibly affect the other, I had learned my common sense from the woman whose dead body was now waiting in Queens for the authorization that would permit Herman Sabinson to perform an autopsy. I knew what my mother would have wanted me to do. She had spent her life in the shadow of an adage of her own invention: "If you keep your mouth shut, nobody will know as much about you as you know yourself." After half a century I suddenly found myself wishing I knew less about her than I did.

"So where the hell are they?"

I came up out of my thoughts. The irascible voice had come from the front of the cab.

"Where the hell are who?" I said.

"These dozens of people," the taxi driver said. "That you say they're all the time standing around here, fighting to get a hack back to Manhattan."

I looked out the window. The cab had stopped at the top of the low concrete rise that surmounts the crescent driveway in front of the Peretz Memorial Hospital. My first reaction was a sense of astonishment. The trip by cab from Manhattan takes approximately forty minutes. Two or three times during the past my taxi drivers had made it in thirty-five minutes. One giddy afternoon, in half an hour. The driver, a bit giddy himself, had said it was the Pope. His Holiness was on a brief visit to the United States and every automobile in the Borough of Queens, the driver had said, was chasing the Pontiff's entourage, which was heading for God knows what, but happily the what seemed to be in the opposite direction from the Peretz Memorial Hospital. It seemed to me now that I had stepped into this taxi at Lexington and 77th only minutes ago. Yet here I was at the Peretz Memorial Hospital. At least a half hour must have gone by. I did not understand how I could

9

have been unaware of the passage of this amount of time. It was obviously due, I felt, to my feelings about my mother's death. Which made me suddenly wonder what my feelings were.

I knew with certainty only one: a feeling of relief that it was all over. But there were other feelings. There had to be. Even if I didn't know my mother as well as I should have, I know myself better than I would like. I could feel the worry about those other feelings mounting slowly and inexorably inside me.

"They must have heard you were coming," the taxi driver said.

"What?" I said. I said it irritably. By now I hated him.

"See—I was right. Those people you say they're all the time out front here fighting for cabs," he said. "They must have heard you're coming. Let's make this guy look like a liar, they must have said. And they all beat it back to Manhattan by subway so I'll have to ride back empty."

I wondered. Could the driver have been right when he'd said nobody goes to hospitals on the day before Christmas? On East Fourth Street, where I had been born and raised, we had never done much about Christmas. It wasn't exactly an East Fourth Street holiday. But we always went to see sick people on the day before Yom Kippur. I remembered vividly being sent by my mother to deliver jars of chicken soup to ailing neighbors on the day before Passover. The recollection thrust me into a moment of witless generosity.

"What does it say on the clock?" I said. "I can't read it. I forgot my glasses at home. Three seventy-five?"

"Three eighty-five," the driver said. "And a quarter for the Triboro toll."

"Here's ten," I said. "If you do have to ride home empty, don't be sore at me."

The driver, taking the ten-dollar bill, looked pleased but also uneasy. As though he felt he was getting the money not because he deserved it but because his sullen remarks had blackmailed a nervous passenger into doing something the passenger would not have done ordinarily. Which was exactly what had happened.

"You don't have to do this," he said. There was not much conviction in his voice. "I'm what they call every year during the transit strike negotiations a common carrier. You want to go to Queens, I gotta take you to Queens. All you have to pay is what it says on the clock."

"It's Christmas," I said. "Buy something for your wife."

"I'm not married," he said. I laughed. The driver said, "What's funny about that?"

"It's the sort of thing my mother would have said."

It was, too. Among the things about her that were unexpectedly appearing in my consciousness like litmus-paper tests was the realization that I had never heard my mother tell a joke. Yet I was all at once intensely aware that she had always been able to make me laugh. Her humor had obviously been unintentional. It occurred to me, as I walked into the Admissions Office of the Peretz Memorial Hospital on this dismal morning before Christmas, that the same word applied to my mother's whole life. She had been too shrewd to arrange the almost nine decades of her existence the way she had been forced to live them. Given a chance to control things, I felt, she would almost certainly have done better. Unintentional was the word, all right.

"Can I help you?" said the girl in nurse's uniform at the desk behind the Information window.

"Mrs. O'Toole?" I said. "I'd like to speak with her."

"About what?" the girl said.

11

I examined the several ways I could have answered her question. A darling little old lady who has just cashed in her chips after exceeding by almost two decades her biblical allotment of three score years and ten? Or: a savage old bitch who has finally, thank God, fallen off my back? Or: the Jewish Eleanor of Aquitaine?

"Some papers I have to sign to authorize an autopsy," I said. "Dr. Herman Sabinson called me about an hour ago. He said Mrs. O'Toole would be expecting me."

The girl up to now had looked bright, intelligent, and sexy. Now she changed abruptly and completely. She looked exactly like the young nurse behind the Information window of a hospital in a TV soap opera who is confronted by the middle-aged son of an elderly lady who has just Gone to Meet Her Maker. I restrained my desire to reach in through the window and slap her.

In a sympathetic whisper she said, "One moment, please."

It is a phrase to which during the past many years I have, now and again, given a certain amount of thought. Do people who use it really mean one moment? I own a wristwatch presented to me by my two sons on my last birthday. They chipped in and bought it in Switzerland for a modest sum. It tells what time it is now in Calcutta and, among many other things, how long you should wait before taking the second pill. As the once sexy but now loathsome girl left her desk to find Mrs. O'Toole, I pressed the appropriate knob on my sons' birthday gift. Seven minutes and fourteen seconds after the *One moment, please* I had been asked to wait, the girl came back. Not alone.

"This is Mrs. O'Toole," the girl said.

It was like hearing a cicerone on a bus in the nation's capital say, "This is the Washington monument." What else—no, who else—could Mrs. O'Toole be? She was tall. She was slender. She had white hair doctored by a blue rinse. She wore the uniform of a Red Cross Gray Lady. She had the emaciated, elegant face of a once famous but now forgotten actress who had been sent over by Central Casting to play the cameo role of Edith Cavell in a documentary about the First World War. She held her hands clasped in front of her as though she were trying to prevent the escape of a rebellious butterfly. She had not even the hint of breasts.

"Dr. Sabinson told me you were coming," she said.

The possibility that he would not tell her had not previously crossed my mind. Crossing it now, it brought me a moment of panic. Suppose I had been forced to explain to this creature why I had come to see her? All at once I was grateful for the network of intermediaries among whom I spent my life. The dentist's assistant to whom I didn't have to say, "I've come to have my teeth cleaned." She had sent me the card. She knew why I had come. The clerk in the grocery store to whom I didn't have to say, "My wife said to pick up the asparagus." The paper bag is already marked with my name, which he scribbled when my wife called.

"If you'll give me the paper," I said, "I'll sign it."

The center of Mrs. O'Toole's smile moved. It was as though the commander of the German firing squad had said to Miss Cavell, "There's been a small change in plans. Instead of executing you, the High Command has instructed me to present you with the Iron Cross First Class."

"One moment, please," Mrs. O'Toole said.

This time it didn't take much longer than that. She opened the door next to the Information window, came out into the reception room, and closed the door carefully behind her. Except for the belligerently compassionate look from the girl behind the Information window, Mrs. O'Toole and I were alone in the room decorated with beige monk's-cloth sofas and framed photographs of Chaim Weizmann, David Ben-Gurion, and General Evangeline Booth.

"About those papers," she said.

"Yes?" I said.

"The papers Dr. Sabinson wanted you to sign?" Mrs. O'Toole said.

"Yes?" I said.

"Actually it was only one paper," she said.

"Was?" I said.

Mrs. O'Toole shifted her imprisoning grip on the invisible butterfly. "What I mean," she said, "I mean it is no longer necessary for you to sign the paper."

"Why not?" I said. "Dr. Sabinson told me he could not perform the autopsy unless he had my written permission. He said you'd have the form or paper or whatever you call it, he said you'd have it ready for me. He told me that on the phone this morning."

"Yes, well," Mrs. O'Toole said. "But—"

Her voice stopped without any diminution in the decibels of sound she was uttering. It was as though we had been talking on the phone and a switchboard operator had inadvertently pulled the plug that connected us. Mrs. O'Toole looked troubled. It came to me with a sense of guilt that she looked more troubled to me than I probably looked to her. I could suddenly see the faces of people I knew. Dozens of them. The faces all reflected horror. My mother had just died and, to them, the way I was taking it branded me a son of a bitch. Some of them, of course, had always thought I am a son of a bitch, so I could dismiss those. I could not dismiss the others. They were men and women I respected. All I could do was say

14

to myself that they did not know how I was taking this. They had not known my mother.

"Mrs. O'Toole," I said. "Has anything gone wrong?"

The idiocy of the question caused my own voice to falter. How could anything go wrong? Death, Rabbi Goldfarb used to say on East Fourth Street, was the end of all our journeys. My mother had come to the end of hers. Herman Sabinson had told me so only this morning. Nothing more could happen to her.

"Well, not exactly," Mrs. O'Toole said. "It's just that, well, the necessity for signing the paper, the authorization for the autopsy, it's no longer necessary."

"You mean," I said, "it is no longer necessary to obtain the written consent of a member of the family before an autopsy can be performed? You mean that rule has been changed between now and the time Dr. Sabinson called me early this morning?"

"Oh, no," she said. "No, no, no. It's merely that, well, it's not necessary for you to sign."

"Did Dr. Sabinson tell you it's not necessary?" I said.

He had seen me through my first contact with death. Burying my father the year before had been made easier for me by the intelligent sympathy of Herman Sabinson. I was not going to stop leaning on him now.

"No," Mrs. O'Toole said. "I have not been able to get in touch with Dr. Sabinson since he called you. He called from my office here at the hospital. Then he went out on house calls. He doesn't know what happened."

"What did happen?" I said.

Mrs. O'Toole's hands crushed together. Oh, God, I thought. That poor bastard of a butterfly. He ain't coming home for dinner tonight.

15

"Nothing happened," Mrs. O'Toole said sharply. Then the sharpness in her voice seemed to come back and hit her. She blushed. I thought with almost insane irrelevance that I had never before realized how much a blush can do for a woman. For a moment or two this bloodless old do-gooder looked almost pretty. "The signing of the paper is no longer necessary," Mrs. O'Toole said. "That's all. You don't have to sign the paper."

I thought that over for a couple of minutes. The thinking did not help. Something had obviously happened after Herman Sabinson had called me. It was pretty obvious that I would not learn what it was from Mrs. O'Toole. It was even more obvious that it couldn't possibly make any difference. My mother was dead. Nothing more could happen to her. Except, of course, the funeral arrangements, which were my next chore. It was the day before Christmas. I had just given a sullen taxi driver a six-dollar tip. A moment of generosity to this Red Cross Gray Lady did not seem inappropriate.

"Look," I said. "If it's no longer necessary to sign a paper authorizing an autopsy, okay. But as long as I'm here, why not let me sign it? The worst that can happen is that you'll just have to throw the paper away. If it turns out later that the rules have changed again, and I do have to sign it, then I won't have to make another trip back here. This will be a great convenience for me because I have to go over to the undertaker now and make the funeral arrangements."

I did not add that it would also make me feel better about Herman Sabinson. I had made him a promise. I wasn't feeling my best. I knew it would make me feel better if I did not break my promise to him. I wished all the people who thought I was a son of a bitch were in a position to make a note of that.

16

"Well, all right, yes, very well," Mrs. O'Toole said. "That makes sense."

She went back through the door beside the Information window. I stared at the pictures of Chaim Weizmann, David Ben-Gurion, and General Evangeline Booth. I hoped Rabbi Goldfarb, who died the day Sacco and Vanzetti were executed, would forgive me for thinking General Booth was the best-looking of the three.

Mrs. O'Toole came back with a printed form and a ball-point pen. "Here," she said.

I signed below her pointing finger. The nail was painted blood-red. The color gave me a small stab of pleasure. All at once Mrs. O'Toole was part of the world of the living rather than the world of the dead.

"Thanks," I said.

Mrs. O'Toole took the paper. She retracted the ball point. And my pleasure fled. I could tell from her face what she was going to say.

"I'm sorry for your trouble," she said.

For a startled moment I wondered why the pain seemed to ease somewhat. The line from A. E. Housman's poem, "Others, I am not the first," was suddenly running through my mind. The problem of facing the undertaker, whom I had faced so short a time ago when my father died, all at once seemed no more than an unpleasant chore. A chore I was capable of handling.

"Thank you," I said.

Mrs. O'Toole touched my arm, gently, exactly as the director, beyond the camera's sight lines, would have instructed her to do it, thus destroying the moment of dignified understanding we had shared. But I walked out of the Admissions Office with the feeling that I had no right to dislike her. She could not help being what she was: a pain in the ass to a middle-aged man who had wanted to laugh on learning that his aged mother had just died.

Out on the street, at the top of the low concrete rise that surmounts the crescent driveway of the Peretz Memorial Hospital, I forgot about Mrs. O'Toole. There were no taxis. There were no people waiting for taxis. There was only a scene of desolation that it occurred to me was typical of the Borough of Queens. I decided to walk up to the Battenberg Funeral Home. It was a journey I had made before.

My father had died nine months earlier. On an ordinary Tuesday in April. Warm but not too warm. Sunny but not bright. The casualties in Vietnam, announced on the kitchen radio as I boiled my egg, were lower than those announced for the previous week. Horst the elevator operator said, "Have a nice day, sir." In a way, I did. My father had died in a manner that I knew would have pleased him. Neatly. No fuss. He rose from the breakfast table, holding his copy of the *Jewish Daily Forward,* and he fell down. Eleven minutes later, when Herman Sabinson called me, he said my father had been dead for ten and nine-tenths minutes.

"Possibly longer," Herman said. "I was in there no more than ninety seconds after your mother rang my bell." Herman Sabinson lives in the apartment next to the one my mother and father occupied for over twenty years. "He'd been dead for at least three-quarters of a minute. My analysis indicates he was dead before he hit the linoleum. It was instantaneous. Not a split second of pain. Meet me at the Peretz Memorial Hospital as soon as you can."

I did, but it had taken almost an hour. There had been a taxi strike and I had taken the wrong train when I changed at

Queensboro Plaza. But Herman Sabinson had been waiting when I got there.

"Forget it," he had said in answer to my apology for tardiness. I wondered if he knew what he was saying. Forget what? "I've got a dozen patients here at Peretz Memorial," Herman Sabinson said. "While I was waiting for you I filled in the time checking them out. Sign here, and then you can go on and make the funeral arrangements."

Nine months later, I was going again. On a gray, unpleasant day that I felt must be making everybody in the neighborhood feel as terrible as I did. "Come all ye faithful," Miss Kahn had led us in song in P.S. 188 when I was in kindergarten, on the day the New York City public school system had thrust us into making cardboard cut-outs of the Three Wise Men to be pasted on our classroom windows. The feelings of those days, in another time. another world, were suddenly as real as a toothache. My mother had never shared those feelings. The Christian faith was for her an important segment of enemy terrain. Gentiles had created her police record. The followers of Jesus had snapped at her heels all the days, hours, and minutes of her long and bitter life. They would not even allow her to live with the minor fiction that apparently meant more to her than the well-being of her son: her passionate belief that she had been born in Berezna, Hungary.

"Not true," my Aunt Sarah had said to me after my father's funeral. "Mama was not born in Hungary."

We had come back to my mother's apartment from the cemetery. A distant but well-intentioned cousin was busy in the kitchen and the living room, serving sandwiches and coffee to our relatives. I had set up a bar in the foyer. I waited until everybody had a drink before I went looking for my Aunt Sarah. Among all my relatives, Aunt Sarah, who lived in New

Haven, had always been my favorite. The reason is embarrassingly simple. I had always been her favorite. My feelings about people are primitive but firm. I like people who like me. I dislike people who dislike me. Aunt Sarah always liked me.

I made her a good strong highball and took it into the bedroom. She was reclining on my just deceased father's bed. I use the word reclining because I think it is the way Aunt Sarah would have wanted me to describe her position. She was almost eighty, and her weight had been going up steadily for several years, but she did not like to be reminded of either. My father's funeral had tired her. The noises the other guests were making in the living room annoyed her. Here, in the bedroom, she had taken off her shoes, released some of the complicated fastenings of her undergarments, and eased herself into a half-sitting position against the pillows on my dead father's bed. My Aunt Sarah was definitely not lying down. I had taken the precaution to bring along a drink for myself.

"If she wasn't born in Hungary," I said, "where was she born?"

It was like discovering that the wife of Menelaus had never been near Troy. What in God's name were you going to write in on the government form?

"Soho," my Aunt Sarah said.

I had a moment of shock. Soho was Dickens. My mother was Sholem Aleichem.

"You mean Soho in London?" I said.

"If there's two Sohos," my Aunt Sarah said, "nobody ever told me."

She started to tell what I suppose she would have told twenty, thirty, even forty years earlier. That is, if I had asked. Crucial information—the bits and pieces that add up to a life, change it, and in the end destroy it—is always lying around waiting to be picked up. The trouble is that somebody has to be near enough to tell you to bend over.

"But what was Mama doing in Soho?" I said.

"What were you doing on East Fourth Street?" my Aunt Sarah said. "Getting born."

"Yes, but I know how I got to East Fourth Street," I said. "I don't know how Mama got to Soho."

My Aunt Sarah took a sip of her drink and said, "It was this good-looking louse Yeedle Yankov. Our Aunt Sheindle, she was your grandmother, she fell in love with the bastard."

I had never seen my mother's mother. Aunt Sarah snapped open a small golden locket and showed me a picture of her. I don't know how things were in Berezna, Hungary, in 1877, but in at least one respect I think it is safe to assume they were not much different from the way they had been in the Garden of Eden. My grandmother, Sheindle Baltok, had clearly been a knockout. Not a very unique knockout. When you've seen one golden-haired Hungarian beauty, you have seen them all. What startled me was the sudden realization that my mother's mother had belonged in this great tradition. It made me wonder about my mother.

"Was my mother as beautiful as my grandmother?" I asked.

"You wouldn't have to ask," my Aunt Sarah said. "If you had known her as a child."

"In Soho?" I said.

"Before Soho," my Aunt Sarah said, "a lot happened."

What happened was this. The Baltok family owned the most prosperous dairy farm in Berezna. The heir to the farm was the Baltok's only child, my Grandmother Sheindle. At seventeen she fell in love with one of the town's most distinguished bums. The word is my Aunt Sarah's.

21

"By Hungarians," she said, "to be a bum is like by a butcher to be a lamb chop. There's too many of them around to make any one of them something special. But Yeedle Yankov was even by Hungarians an extra-special lamb chop. He came from somewhere in the hills above Berezna. Nobody knew his family. They could have been sheep. He never did a day's work, but he had a smile like in the morning the sun. When your Grandmother Sheindle fell in love with this bastard, and when her father said he would drop dead before he let her marry the bum, Sheindle and Yeedle ran away. Nobody knows if they ever got married but everybody knows they arrived in London without a penny because Yeedle never earned one and Sheindle's father wouldn't give her one. Well, one thing Hungarian women know how to do, even the ugly ones, they know how to cook. So Sheindle opened a small restaurant in Soho, where she did very well, and Yeedle started doing what all Hungarian men do very well. He started kitzling the lady customers. By the time your mother was born, even Sheindle knew she had a first-class prize bum on her hands, and by the time your mother was three years old, and Yeedle ran away with one of the lady customers, your Grandmother Sheindle was not surprised."

Neither, according to Aunt Sarah, was she disheartened. My grandmother was apparently a tough customer. She sold the Soho restaurant. With the proceeds and her three-year-old daughter, she followed Yeedle Yankov to Trieste, where he had settled down with his new consort.

"Don't ask me why in Trieste," my Aunt Sarah said. "Except we always understood in the family that's where Yeedle's new girl friend owned some property. Another thing don't ask me is how your Grandmother Sheindle found out where they were living, except when she made up her mind to do something, Sheindle did it. What she did in Trieste, when she got to the house where Yeedle Yankov and his new girl friend were living, your grandmother didn't go upstairs herself. She sent your mother."

"Three years old?" I said.

"By then three and a half," my Aunt Sarah said. "Your mother went upstairs and she knocked on the door where Yeedle Yankov was living, and when Yeedle Yankov opened the door, and he saw standing there on his doorstep in Trieste the little daughter he had left behind in Soho, guess what happened?"

"He dropped dead," I said.

My Aunt Sarah gave me a sharp look. "How did you know?" she said.

I didn't, of course. I had merely responded, as any conscientious actor would, to the role that had been assigned to me in my Aunt Sarah's narrative.

"You mean he really did?" I said.

"You mean you were only guessing?" my Aunt Sarah said.

"I meant it as a joke," I said.

"Some joke," my Aunt Sarah said. "For the first time in six months a man sees his little three-and-a-half-year-old daughter, and it makes him drop dead. Go laugh."

I did, somewhat uneasily. Aunt Sarah had the delivery of a natural-born comedian. When she paused after her punch lines, it was difficult not to laugh. But the man who had dropped dead in Trieste, this Yeedle Yankov of whom I had never before heard, had been, I suddenly realized, my grandfather.

"What did my grandmother do?" I said.

"What did you expect her to do?" my Aunt Sarah said. "She had come to Trieste to get back the man she loved. What did she find? A dead Hungarian. Did you ever love a dead Hungarian? Your Grandmother Sheindle took her little daughter, that's your mother, Sheindle took her daughter and they went back to Berezna."

I tried to imagine what Berezna was like. I couldn't. The word did not sound like a place. It sounded like the name of a hard, sharp cheese sold in small shops on Second Avenue.

"I suppose her family was glad to see her," I said.

My Aunt Sarah's reply was a Hungarian phrase I remembered from my youth. It can be translated into English only as "In the pig's ass."

"What happened?" I said.

"When they came back to Berezna," my Aunt Sarah said, "Sheindle thought she was coming home, but she wasn't. Everything had changed in Berezna since she ran away with Yeedle Yankov. For one thing, Sheindle's mother had died. For another, her father had married again. A very young girl, younger than Sheindle. And they had two brand-new children, younger than Sheindle's daughter, your mother. I was one of those children. Can you imagine?"

For several moments, sipping my drink and listening to the guests out in the living room celebrating my father's burial, I tried. But my imagination did not clarify anything. All I could see was a young girl, with a daughter not quite four, coming home to her father's house in a Hungarian town the name of which sounded strange to me.

"The new wife?" I said. "My grandmother's stepmother? She didn't like Sheindle?"

"Nobody liked Sheindle," my Aunt Sarah said. "Not even her father. You have to remember she ran away with a bum. So when she came back, plus now she's got a daughter yet, a daughter that nobody knew if the baby's father and mother they ever married, everybody said what you expect people to say in such things. They said she deserved it. Sheindle."

I took another sip of my drink and thought about my unknown grandmother. My thoughts were not very complicated. It seemed to me she had been given a raw deal. But thoughts don't usually stop at logical punctuation marks. They tend to run on like dripping faucets. With a certain amount of embarrassment I realized that my thoughts about my Grandmother Sheindle were derived from recollections of Nathaniel Hawthorne. *The Scarlet Letter* had moved me deeply in Miss Marine's English II class at Thomas Jefferson High School.

"Listen," I said to my Aunt Sarah. "You trying to tell me when she came home from Trieste, her father wouldn't take her in?"

"It wasn't Sheindle's father," my Aunt Sarah said. "It was his new young wife. That was my mother. And where do you get things like they wouldn't take her in? They were all Hungarians, sure. But they were also Jews. Jews never close a door on *mishpoche*. They could hate them, but they never keep them out. If you don't take care of your own, who's going to do it? Nasser?"

"Let's keep him out of this," I said. "I'm trying to find out about my mother."

"If you don't interrupt so much, you will," my Aunt Sarah said. "It wasn't Sheindle's father that hated her. It was her father's new young wife. *My* mother. You have all this straight?"

I did, and I didn't. It was simple enough to follow the relationships. By comparison with what I read in the society columns of my daily newspaper every morning, grasping this was as simple as grasping an overhead strap in the subway. What I didn't grasp was how all this had led to the bedroom of a three-room apartment in Queens on this day when I had just buried my father.

"She hated Sheindle so much," my Aunt Sarah said, "she said there was no room for them in the house, and she made them live upstairs in the hayloft over the cows in one of the three barns. Sheindle and her daughter. How this made Sheindle feel, you can imagine."

"She must have hated it," I said.

My Aunt Sarah nodded again. "She hated it so much, four months later she was dead."

"That means the little girl, my mother," I said, "the four-year-old girl, she was now an orphan."

My Aunt Sarah said, "On the ball nobody is ever going to say you're not."

"What did she do?" I said.

"You mean what did her grandfather do," my Aunt Sarah said.

"No," I said. "I mean his new wife. The young one. Your mother. What did she do?"

My Aunt Sarah gave me an odd look. It could have been appreciation. It could have been annoyance. I had either shown a degree of understanding of which my Aunt Sarah had not thought me capable, or I had stepped on one of her punch lines.

"My mother," she said, "my father's new wife, what I heard later, she said if they had to support a bastard, then the bastard would have to do some work to earn her bread, the bastard."

Thus, at the age of four, or a few months short of four, my mother learned on a dairy farm in Hungary what, half a century later, her son learned during the Great Depression on the sidewalks of New York: eating is not one of the human rights

Thomas Jefferson believed were self-evident. My mother managed to eat. As, half a century later, did her son. By somewhat different methods. My mother, at the age of four, became what my Aunt Sarah called "the waker up of the goyim" on her grandfather's farm.

"You have to remember one thing," my Aunt Sarah said. "Here, in America, they have a thing they call anti-Semitism. It means if you're a Jew, do me a favor and drop dead. Jews are so used to this, especially in America, they forget there are places where it's different. Anyway, where it used to be different. One of those places was Berezna. In Berezna, if you were a goy, it was *you* do me a favor and drop dead, you goy. In Berezna there was anti-goyism. All the big dairy farms, like my father's, they were owned by Jews like my father. You own a big farm, you want it to work, you want to make money, you have to have labor. Cheap labor. In Berezna the cheap labor was goyim. They were glad to get the work. If they didn't get the work, they were hungry. But their gladness to get the work didn't change how God had made them. God made them slobs. So every morning, before the sun came up, somebody had to go out to wake them up they should be on time to milk the cows. That somebody, my mother, my young mother who married my old father, after Sheindle died my young mother said the person to wake up the goyim every morning for milking the cows it should be Sheindle's daughter."

There is nothing in the record to indicate that my mother objected. Perhaps she didn't remember. I have tried many times to remember what the world was like when I was four years old. No luck. I can get back to six, when I was in kindergarten and I had trouble with clay and colored chalk. I can remember watching soldiers unload from troopships at the East Third Street docks. That must have been between 1917, when we got into what my father called Woodrow Wilson's War, and 1918, when we got out into what my father called Woodrow Wilson's Fourteen Points. I was more than four then. Not much more, but more. Four and a half, perhaps. But I can't work my way back to four or less than four, the age at which my mother started out every morning before sunrise to wake the goyim on her grandfather's farm in the Carpathian mountains so that the cows would be milked on time.

"She did a good job," my Aunt Sarah said. "I never heard a word of complaint."

But there must have been words of complaint. Even if un-spoken, in my mother's heart. Otherwise, what would I be doing, eighty years later? On the morning before Christmas Eve? Trudging through the gray, dismal, bone-cold streets of Queens? From the Peretz Memorial Hospital on Main Street to the Battenberg Funeral Home on Queens Boulevard? A Jewish boy from East Fourth Street? Wearing a Brooks Brothers overcoat? Carrying a head stuffed full of long division from P.S. 188 on Houston Street? Algebra and Nathaniel Hawthorne from Thomas Jefferson High School on Tenth Avenue? The Rule in Shelley's Case from New York University Law School on Washington Square? In short, if my mother had been content with her life in Berezna at four, what was I doing three thousand miles away an hour after her death in the Borough of Queens?

Well, for one thing, I discovered when I got to the Battenberg Funeral Home, I was trying to choose the appropriate coffin.

"It all depends on the family," young Mr. Smith said. "Not

only how they feel about the deceased, but also their economics."

I was no longer inexperienced in these matters. When I had buried my father out of, as the phrase goes, this same funeral home, in what had been for me then a totally new and somewhat jolting experience, I had learned a couple of things. One was this: when you are negotiating the price of a coffin, it is less disturbing for the buyer if the man at the selling end of the negotiation is named Smith rather than Dinkelhelmwurster. A mind distracted into wondering how anybody came to be named Dinkelhelmwurster might also be distracted into wondering why a pine box should cost seven hundred and fifty dollars.

"Look, Mr. Smith," I said. "My mother was a very simple Jewish woman."

I paused. I had just realized, from hearing my own words, that the statement was as totally preposterous as a War Department press release about Vietnam. For several moments I sat in silence, listening to the echoes of my own foolish words, and then a curious thing happened. It happened inside me. I made an effort to remain motionless. I did not want young Mr. Smith, who was obviously an heir to the Battenberg family business, to sense that the man to whom he was trying to sell a coffin had just had a moment of revelation. My mother had never been anything more to me than one of the many irritations and nuisances with which daily life is strewn: tax returns, physical check-ups, dentists' appointments, drivers' license renewals, supplications for worthy charities. Now, all at once, facing young Mr. Smith in his glistening black Italian silk suit across the table in the Arrangements Room of the Battenberg Funeral Home, I realized that I was doing something much more important than discarding a nuisance. I suddenly realized that my irritating mother had been a very important person. Not because of her police record. But because of the way she had been forced to live her life.

"The best pine?" I said. "How much will that cost?"

Young Mr. Smith's face did not exactly brighten. The trick in the funeral parlor business is never to vary your expression. But I could tell that young Mr. Smith felt he had made a score.

"Why don't we go downstairs and take a look at what's available?" he said.

What was available had a grisly fascination. The room in which only a few months ago I had selected my father's coffin had been redecorated. Or rearranged. I stepped through the door held open by the obsequious Mr. Smith, and paused.

"Is something wrong, sir?" he said.

I hesitated, forced myself to concentrate, and had it. "The hand-carved walnut job," I said. "The twenty-two-hundred-dollar number. It used to be on this side."

Mr. Smith looked startled. He surveyed the room. His face cleared. "Oh, yes," he said. "We moved it because the sunlight from the center window was fading the grain."

"It looks better over here," I said.

"Thank you, sir," Mr. Smith said. "By the way, there's been a slight increase in price for the walnut. It's now twenty-three hundred fifty."

"Well," I said, "I didn't have the walnut in mind." I was aware that I was speaking quickly. I wanted to forestall the inevitable speech about inflation and how everything was going up. "I want something appropriate but not expensive."

I was pleased by the sound of my own voice. Relaxed. A

man in control. Why not? I knew the dialogue. I had spoken it all once before, nine months ago.

"Yes, sir," Mr. Smith said. "Here, then, to begin, this is our most inexpensive item."

The Battenberg Funeral Home's most inexpensive item was a pine box in which the citizens of Pompeii, fleeing the encircling lava, would have been ashamed to pack their lares and penates.

"Is it still seven hundred and fifty dollars?" I said.

"No, I'm sorry, it's eight hundred now," young Mr. Smith said. "It's this inflation, you know. Everything is going up."

Everything, apparently, except Mr. Smith's voice. It had sunk to his lowest register. The sounds reminded me of Orson Welles when I first encountered that extraordinary talent.

"All right," I said. "I'll take it."

"There's only one point, sir," Mr. Smith said.

"What's that?" I said.

"Your mother, I take it, sir, was of the Orthodox Jewish faith?"

I gave him a sharp glance. "What about it? So was my father. And that's the coffin I got for him," I said.

"Then you must know," Mr. Smith said, "that a person of the Orthodox Jewish faith is not allowed to be buried in a casket fastened together by nails or any other kind of metal."

"But the one I got for my father less than a year ago didn't have any metal in it."

"What can one do?" Mr. Smith said. "It's a matter of rising labor costs. To comply with the Jewish faith, to fasten a casket with wooden pegs, that costs money. Nails are cheaper because driving them in is quicker."

"The Romans made the same discovery," I said.

31

Mr. Smith looked puzzled. "I beg your pardon," he said.

"Nothing," I said. "Just show me the lowest-priced pine casket that's fastened with wooden pegs."

Mr. Smith led me to an imitation "mahogany" casket. On it was a discreetly lettered price tag: $1,250.

"Please don't go any further," I said. "I'll take it."

Mr. Smith bowed slightly and led the way back upstairs to his office. Mr. Smith's office was small and had no windows. The door did not open and close on hinges. It slid back and forth on a chromium track. The bare walls were the color of a Hershey bar. The long polished table that filled almost all of the floor space was somewhat darker. The six chairs that surrounded the table were made of the same wood. They had high backs. I wondered where the light came from. Then I remembered I had wondered the same thing nine months ago. I glanced up at the ceiling paneling which concealed the sunken fluorescent bulbs. It was the sort of room in which Gestapo officers used to interrogate their victims in movies.

"Please sit down," Mr. Smith said.

I took the chair in which I had sat last time I was there. I knew the chair Mr. Smith was going to take. He did. The one that faced me directly across the table. From a concealed drawer he brought out a pad of yellow forms. From his breast pocket he drew a ballpoint.

"Name, please?"

I told him. He wrote it down.

"Address?"

I gave him my address. He wrote it down.

"Is this where the bill is to be sent?"

I wondered if Mr. Smith would think me irreverent if I answered the way I knew my mother would have answered:

"No, send the bill to the cemetery." I wondered. But what I said was, "Yes."

Mr. Smith made a note on his pad. "How many limousines will be required?" he said.

I had forgotten about the limousines. Or rather, their contents. I was reminded now of another unpleasant chore: the people, mostly relatives, who would have to be called.

"Well," I said, and I tried to remember my father's funeral. Had there been three limousines? Or four? The number of cars depended now, as it had depended then, on the number of people I would have to call and invite to the funeral. But at the moment the only person I could think of was my Aunt Sarah in New Haven. Surely three limousines would be enough for even a favorite aunt?

"Let's say four," I said. "Just to be on the safe side."

"Four," Mr. Smith said, and his ballpoint nailed the number down into the proper blank space on the yellow pad. "Now about the shrouds."

I knew about the shrouds. When I had been preparing for this visit in connection with my father's funeral, the rabbi of my father's synagogue had come to my parents' apartment to instruct me.

"Don't let them rook you," the rabbi had said. "These wise guys, they're always tryna runyuppa bill. What you want, and you tell it to him plain, I mean don't let them push yirround, you tell this guy this is an Orthodox Jewish funeral, you tell him. What you want is plain, simple, ordinary linen shrouds. The cheapest."

"This is an Orthodox funeral," I now said to Mr. Smith. "I want plain, simple, ordinary linen shrouds."

Mr. Smith muttered to his darting ballpoint, "Plain, simple, ordinary linen shrouds." He looked up. "How about somebody to sit with the body overnight in the chapel?"

I hesitated. When I had been asked the same question about my father, I had unhesitatingly said yes. I had known then that my mother would have been annoyed if I had said no. Not to have paid for someone to sit up with my father's body would have been an advertisement to her neighbors that her son was a cheapskate. My mother didn't really care if I was a cheapskate. What she cared about was that her neighbors should not be aware of this degrading fact. Now, however, the situation was different. I didn't give a damn about what my mother's neighbors thought of me. Furthermore, I didn't see how they could possibly learn whether I had or had not paid for someone to sit up with my mother's body. Most important, however, was my recollection of my mother's feelings. She had never liked people peering over her shoulder.

"No," I said. "Let's skip somebody sitting up with the body in the chapel."

Mr. Smith studied the yellow sheet. He was silent for a couple of moments. "Now the honorariums," he said.

I already knew what this meant: the tips to the drivers of the limousines and the various cemetery employees.

Mr. Smith went on, "We can place a round figure on the bill, or would you prefer to handle this yourself?"

"No," I said. "Put the round figure on the bill. Anything else?"

"The date," Mr. Smith said. "Tomorrow being Christmas Day, the cemetery employees will not be working, so the funeral can't take place until Tuesday, the earliest."

"Tuesday will be fine," I said.

"Eleven o'clock?" Mr. Smith said. "Or the afternoon? Two? Three?"

"Better make it three," I said. Aunt Sarah would have to come down from New Haven.

"Three o'clock," Mr. Smith said to his moving ballpoint. He paused, and again he studied the yellow sheet. "I think," he said finally, "yes, I think that covers it."

I stood up and said, "Thank you."

Mr. Smith stood up and said, "There's just one more thing."

The sound of his voice made me look at Mr. Smith more closely. He had suddenly reminded me of Mrs. O'Toole in the Peretz Memorial Hospital. "What's that?" I said.

"Tomorrow morning at eight o'clock," Mr. Smith said, "you will have to appear at the morgue in the Queens County General Hospital to identify the body."

My reaction to this statement reminded me of a moment during the war. I had been sailing in a British convoy from Halifax to what was then always identified on travel papers as "a U.K. port." This always proved to be Liverpool. I was on a small freighter that had been built before the First World War. It had been put out to pasture on the Mersey after the Treaty of Versailles, but recalled to service when the German submarines in the early days of World War II were sinking British hulls faster than the shipyards on the Clyde could build them. The small vessel could just barely make seven knots. Since a convoy takes its speed from the slowest vessel in it, our eighty-five vessels went lumbering across the North Atlantic at seven knots. A week out of Halifax the convoy was caught by a German submarine pack. We were under attack for three days.

At first, it was like watching a movie. From my gun pit, a makeshift box that had been built hastily on top of the wireless room, I grew accustomed to seeing, in the distance, a ship that had been plowing along as a heaving silhouette on the horizon suddenly erupt into the air, fanning out in a shower of countless scraps, like a handful of sand flung to the sky by a child on a beach. I was frightened, of course, but in a few hours I had become anesthetized by the distance. It was happening to other ships, not mine. Then, on the second day, it happened to a ship on our port side, perhaps a quarter of a mile away. The impact of the explosion rocked our small vessel. I was flung across the gun pit and slammed into the twin Marlins I was supposed to be manning. It was as though the actors in the movie had come off the screen and started to belabor the people in the theater. I remember the indignant words that flashed through my mind: "What the hell do these bastards think they're doing?"

Years later, in the Battenberg Funeral Home, I had the same reaction. I stared at Mr. Smith. "What did you say?" I said.

"I'm sorry," he said nervously. "But you will have to show up at the morgue in the Queens County General Hospital tomorrow morning at eight o'clock to identify your mother's body. Until you do that, we can't go ahead with the preparations for the funeral."

"There's something wrong," I said. "My mother can't be in the Queens County General Hospital. She died less than two hours ago three blocks from here, in the Peretz Memorial Hospital."

Mr. Smith put his palms together. I thought: Oh, God, he's got a trapped butterfly, too.

"I'm sorry," he said. "I don't know what happened. All I know is that we had a call from Peretz Memorial, and they said your mother's body is in the morgue at Queens County General."

I remembered Mrs. O'Toole's uneasiness when she told me

it was no longer necessary to sign the document Herman Sabinson had said he would leave for me in her office. "How did my mother's body get there?" I said.

Mr. Smith looked as though he was about to burst into tears. "I don't know," he said. "All I know is what they told me."

I hesitated, staring across Mr. Smith's head at the Hershey-bar wall. Slowly, through my confusion, came a curious feeling of rightness. This, I began to grasp, was precisely the sort of thing that would happen to my mother. All the streets down which she had walked during her lifetime had taken unexpected turns. She had never ended up in the places toward which she had started.

"May I use your phone?" I said to Mr. Smith.

"There's a booth out in the hall," he said.

Phone calls were obviously not like honorariums. There was no line for them on the yellow pad. "Excuse me a minute," I said.

I went out into the hall and into the booth. The *ping* from the instrument when my dime dropped into the slot was reassuring. It had nothing to do with death. The sound would have been the same if I had been making the call from a cocktail lounge.

"Dr. Sabinson's wire."

"Is this Dr. Sabinson's office?" I said. "Or his answering service?"

"This is his service," the female voice said. "Can I help you?"

"I wanted to talk with Dr. Sabinson."

"He's out on house calls. If you'll give me your name and number I'll have him get back to you when he checks his messages."

"How long will that be?"

"Dr. Sabinson usually calls me about once every hour. Is this an emergency?"

For a few moments I didn't know how to answer the question. I knew what the girl at the other end of the phone meant by an emergency. I was suddenly wondering if she would understand what the word emergency now meant to me.

"Yes, it is," I said. "But Dr. Sabinson won't be able to call me back because I'll be moving around."

All at once I was less confused than I had been for an hour. I knew what my next move was going to be.

"I'll try him later," I said and hung up. Fed another dime, the instrument *pinged* again. I dialed the Peretz Memorial Hospital. "Mrs. O'Toole," I said. "Admissions Office."

"Admissions Office, good afternoon."

I looked at my watch in surprise. It *was* afternoon. "Mrs. O'Toole, please."

"She's not in at the moment. Can I help you?"

The girl at Dr. Sabinson's answering service had asked the same question. God helps those who help themselves, my mother used to say. And repeat. She never said anything only once.

"When will she be back?"

"Not until Tuesday. Mrs. O'Toole has gone for the day, and tomorrow is Christmas, so she won't be in until Tuesday."

"Okay," I said. "Thank you."

I would have to do this on my own. I hung up and went back into Mr. Smith's room.

"Is there any reason why I can't go out to the morgue now?"

"I don't understand," Mr. Smith said.

Why should he? It was not his mother.

"I'm out here in Queens," I said. "Why can't I go over to

38

the morgue and identify the body?" Mr. Smith didn't seem to understand. He looked confused. It occurred to me that he was upset by what he apparently considered my unseemly haste. I said, "What I mean is, there's no point in my coming all the way back from Manhattan tomorrow morning at eight to do something I can do now, while I'm out here in Queens."

Mr. Smith's face cleared. "You know," he said, "that might be a good idea. You'll get it out of the way and we . . . we'll be free to go ahead with the funeral arrangements. In these situations, we see it happen every day, there's so much to do, a person never knows where to begin."

2

T HAT'S WHERE I WAS one up on Mr. Smith. I knew exactly where to begin. The night the Manhattan Council of the Boy Scouts of America staged the eliminations finals for the 1927 All-Manhattan rally.

At the time the trouble seemed no more than a laundry problem. The Council had scheduled the eliminations for a Wednesday night. But the regular weekly meetings of Troop 244, of which I was senior patrol leader, took place on Saturday nights. Every Friday, therefore, my mother laundered and pressed my uniform. Not because she approved of the Boy Scouts of America or my participation in their program. On the contrary. My mother hated all uniforms, whether they were worn by Cossacks, ushers, Babe Ruth, or her son. But the weekly meetings of Troop 244 took place in the Hannah H. Lichtenstein House on Avenue B between Ninth and Tenth Streets. This was pretty far uptown from our tenement flat on East Fourth Street at the corner of Lewis, where my mother felt safe, and uncomfortably close to what my mother thought of as gentile terrain, where she would not have ventured without a police escort. Also, the scoutmaster of my new troop was an uptown goy named Mr. O'Hare. While my mother continued to ignore my activities as a boy scout, even though I had been one for over two years, she was not going to allow her oldest son to show up on the fringe of enemy territory, and appear in front of a *shaygitz* scoutmaster, looking like a slob.

So, as I said, every Friday she laundered and pressed my uniform, and every Saturday, when the senior patrol leader of Troop 244 showed up at the Hannah H. Lichtenstein House, his profile may have looked somewhat different from that of Sir Robert Baden-Powell, the commander of the garrison at Mafeking who founded the Boy Scout movement after the Boer War, but the starched khaki breeches, the immaculate khaki shirt, and the beautifully ironed blue neckerchief would have done credit to the snub-nosed, apple-cheeked little Norman Rockwell type whose picture adorned the cover of the B.S.A.'s national handbook.

"Wednesday?" my mother said when I asked her on Tuesday if she would launder and press my uniform in time for the eliminations contest. "Every week I wash on Friday. What's all of a sudden Tuesday?"

"This is something different," I said.

"Different how?"

My mother spoke only Yiddish and Hungarian. My Hungarian was weak, but Yiddish was to me what Greek had been to Homer. Until this moment I had assumed I spoke it with the same sort of ease. This moment, however, involved an explanation of why the Manhattan Council had scheduled its rally for Wednesday night. Words didn't exactly fail me. I have always had a capacity for keeping them coming under pretty nearly all conditions. But Yiddish, I saw soon enough, was in this instance proving inadequate. Besides, there was this curious game in which my mother and I were both involved: her pretense that the scout movement did not exist, and mine that I went off in uniform every Saturday night to some sort of vaguely defined social activity. My mother gave me the look she usually reserved for my father at all times, and for any shopkeeper's first quotation of a price for anything.

"Let me get this straight," she said. Her tone implied clearly that if she got it any straighter her comprehension could be used as an architect's plumb line. "You want me to wash and press the khaki shirt and pants on Tuesday?"

"Yes," I said. "You see, Ma, I gotta have it for Wednesday."

"And Friday?" my mother said. "You'll want I should wash and press it again so you can wear it on Saturday?"

"That's right," I said. "You see, Ma, this Wednesday thing, the eliminations contest, that's something special. It's extra. It has nothing to do with the regular Saturday night meeting."

"It has nothing to do with me either," my mother said. "A slave over the washtub for uniforms, this I did not come to America to be."

It was her constant refrain, her endless quest. Why she had come to America. It was also her exit door from everything she did not want to do.

"But, Ma, I'm the captain of the signaling team," I said. "You want I should go looking like a slob?"

"Tell them to hold these alimations on Saturday."

"Eliminations," I said.

"Whatever they are," my mother said, "tell them to do it Saturday, so you'll have the clean shirt and pants I wash on Friday. On Tuesday, no. I'm busy."

This was preposterous. How could she be busy? All she did was cook and clean and wash for my father and me, my sister and brother. If she was able to wash my uniform on Friday, why couldn't she also do it on Tuesday?

42

"Ma, I could get a medal for this."

"For what?"

"For signaling," I said. "Morse Code. With a flag. I'm the best in the troop. If we win these eliminations, our troop, we go on to the finals. Everybody who wins in the finals, they get a medal."

"So you be different from everybody," my mother said. "You win in a dirty uniform."

I didn't doubt that I could. According to Mr. O'Hare I handled a Morse signaling flag with more skill than anybody he had ever known. Not to be dishonestly modest about it, the main reason Troop 244 had managed to get as far as the eliminations finals in the 1927 All-Manhattan rally was my dexterity with a Morse signaling flag. I was secretly convinced I could carry the troop into the *final* finals and go on to win the rally. But somehow, I don't know why, I didn't want to get up there in a soiled, unpressed uniform. So I took my problem to George Weitz, my teammate.

"You are a *shmendrick*," said George. "But you are one hell of a signaler."

At fourteen, I thought I was pretty grown up. I did not think I was a *shmendrick*. But I did not think I was St. Francis of Assisi, either. On East Fourth Street in those days, I was trying to do what everybody else was trying to do: hang in there. I did not know this, of course. Years went by before I realized what had been wrong. I was bucking a tide without even being aware that I was immersed in water. Every adult on the block was an immigrant from some part of Central Europe, and every child was, like George Weitz and myself, a first-generation American. We talked to each other like illiterate diplomats. The simplest communications were papal encyclicals in garbled syntax. But not when I was talking to someone like George. George was on my side. I liked George, but I did not like being called a *shmendrick*.

"You say I'm a *shmendrick* because I beat you for senior patrol leader," I said. "If you'd beat me, I'd say you're a *shmendrick*. But never mind that. I want you to do me a favor."

"Like what?" George said.

George was a funny one. He didn't really live on our block. He lived one block west, in a brownstone between Avenue C and Avenue B. There were no brownstones on our block, Fourth Street between Avenue D and Lewis. Ours was a block of tenements, and they were all pretty much alike. The tenement we lived in, for instance, at the corner of Lewis Street, was typical: thirty-two flats in the six-story "front house" which faced Fourth Street, and thirty-two flats in the "back house" which faced a courtyard full of ash cans. But George Weitz lived in a small narrow house, all four floors of which were occupied by the Weitz family. Nobody thought this odd. George's father was a doctor. The Weitz family had moved in a short time ago, after Dr. Gropple died. Doctors were different. They were rich. They had servants. One of the servants the Weitz family had was known on the block as a "fat stupid Polish slob," who was in fact their only servant. She cooked, she cleaned, and scrubbed—there were some smart alecks on the block who said she did other things for Dr. Weitz—and she did the Weitz family laundry.

"Could you get your girl to wash and iron my uniform?" I said.

"What's the matter with your old lady?" George said. "She's all of a sudden a cripple?"

"No, but she's busy on Tuesday," I said.

44

"Doing what?" George said.

"What difference does it make?" I said. "She washes my uniform on Friday for the Saturday meeting. But this is for Wednesday. She can't do it. She's busy on Tuesday."

"Doing what?" George said again. "Putting double hem-stitches on the new Passover line at Meister's Matzoh Bakery?"

It was the sort of thing George Weitz was always saying. He was known on East Fourth Street as a smart-ass. I'd never heard of Meister's Matzoh Bakery. My guess was that neither had George. But things went on inside his head. Whatever they were, he enjoyed them. George made up those things in-side his head, then he said them out loud. But he was not a bad guy. Besides, he was my reader-receiver on the Morse team.

"It's just the breeches and the shirt," I said. "My necker-chief is still clean. I could bring them over after school and you could put them in your family laundry. What the heck, George, your girl won't know the difference." It seems odd to me now that on East Fourth Street we said heck when we meant hell.

"Okay," George said. "But don't tell the Feds."

It was a George joke. Not funny, perhaps, but part of what a stand-up comic would call his routine. It was the sort of thing he always signed off with. Don't take any wooden nickels. See you in church. Don't do anything I wouldn't do. Keep punching. Now it was don't tell the Feds. I didn't tell anybody. I just went home after school and dug out my khaki breeches and shirt, and my mother caught me.

"What are you doing?" she said. I told her. "No, you're not," she said. "In my family, if anything has to be washed, I'm the one that does it."

Even now I wonder if she said it with irritation or with pride. Anyway, she did it. On Wednesday night, therefore, when I met George Weitz on the corner of Avenue C and

Fourth for the walk to the Hannah H. Lichtenstein House, the crease in my breeches moved crisply an inch or two ahead of my legs, the starch in the collar of my khaki shirt was eating away at my Adam's apple, and my blue neckerchief looked like the sky over East Fourth Street on a hot summer day.

"I thought you were bringing over your uniform for our girl," George said as we started up Avenue C toward Ninth. "What happened?"

"My mother changed her mind," I said. "She found the time yesterday to wash it."

"Meister's Matzoh Bakery probably gave her a day off," George said.

I could see where Meister's Matzoh Bakery, whatever that was, had moved into George's head and settled down for a long stay. It was going to be the joke of the week, maybe month.

"Be funny later," I said. "Now just please concentrate on Morse. We gotta win this thing."

"We'll win it," George said. "None of these shmohawks from uptown can handle a Morse flag the way you and I can."

The "you and I" did not send me. George Weitz was not in my league. But I decided to let it go. He had more than a cockamaymey sense of humor. He had a temper. This was no time for a fight. Besides, let's face it, George was the second best reader-receiver in the troop. He was entitled to say "you and I." Suppose he had said "I and you"?

"Maybe they can and maybe they can't," I said. "We still have Mr. Krakowitz to worry about."

"You're not kidding," George said. "That jerk. Jesus."

I wondered about George's vehemence. I was not so sure that Mr. Krakowitz was a jerk. I mean, I'd never seen him do anything real rotten. There was no doubt, of course, that he was a pain in the ass. You didn't have to be rotten to be a pain in the ass. Not in 1927 anyway.

Mr. Krakowitz owned a men's clothing store on Avenue B, between Fourth and Fifth, four blocks down from the Hannah H. Lichtenstein House. Some of the guys, guys like George Weitz, for instance, said Norton Krakowitz didn't give a damn about the boy scout movement. He was in it for business reasons. He wanted to draw attention to his clothing store by posing as a public-spirited citizen. Norton Krakowitz? Owner of Krakowitz Men's and Boys' Clothes on Avenue B? A very good man. Works on the Boy Scouts. Some kind of executive on the Lower Manhattan Council. Spends a lot of time with the youngsters. Because he wants to help boys to grow up to be good men. Your son needs a suit for the High Holidays? Buy from Krakowitz. He deserves your patronage.

Anyway, that's how some people felt. If I didn't, or if I wasn't sure I did, it was because it wasn't till my bar mitzvah that my father bought me the one suit I had. I mean a whole suit. Pants and a jacket. Before that I even went to *schul* on Rosh Hashanah and Yom Kippur in the pants my father sewed for me himself and the sweaters my mother knitted for me. My feelings about Mr. Krakowitz were based mainly on the way he discharged his duties as a member of the Executive Committee of the Lower Manhattan Council. He enjoyed himself. It does not seem now to be a valid reason for disliking somebody, but now is different from 1927. I was fourteen in 1927.

Norton Krakowitz liked to sing in public, and he was crazy about Shakespeare and the Bible. On Saturday nights, after he shut up shop, he roamed the Lower East Side, from Delancey Street to Avenue B, dropping in for a few minutes each on all the settlement houses that housed boy scout troops under

47

his jurisdiction. I have no doubt, even though I cannot substantiate my certainty by actual eyewitness evidence, that Mr. Krakowitz filled each one of these few-minute sessions in exactly the same way that he filled the few minutes he spent with us every Saturday night in the Troop 244 meeting room at the Hannah H. Lichtenstein House.

Somewhere around nine-thirty there would be a sharp knock on the door. No matter what we were doing—laying out the itinerary for a Sunday hike, burning gauze pads to make tinder for our flint-and-steel sets—we would stop doing it. Mr. O'Hare, our scoutmaster, would go to the door, open it, and admit Norton Krakowitz. It was like admitting a Japanese trade delegation to a postwar parley. There were a lot of parleys in 1927.

Much smiling. A joke or two. Hearty laughter, mostly, as I recall, from Mr. Krakowitz. Then the speech. Thirty seconds to a minute and a half on Scouting as the Road to a Better and More Prosperous America. Then the song. It was always "Me And My Shadow." Norton Krakowitz sang it the way my father ate noodle soup: as though he would never again get a crack at another helping. End of song. Applause. Followed by the senior patrol leader (me) jumping to his feet and yelling, "How about three cheers and a tiger for Mr. Krakowitz?" No dissent. The troop came through with a "Rah Rah Rah, Siss Boom Bah, Mr. Krakowitz! Mr. Krakowitz! Mr. Krakowitz!" The recipient of this noisy adoration smiled, bowed, raised his hand, and announced: "One final word." It was never one, but it sure as hell—no, sorry, sure as heck—was final. Like: "Vanity of vanities, sayeth the preacher, all is vanity." Or: "How sharper than a serpent's tooth it is to have a thankless child." Another wave of the hand, and Norton Krakowitz was off to the Clarke House on Rivington Street for a repeat per-

formance. On East Fourth Street the Clarke House was pronounced the "Clock House." There was a huge clock over the
wide gray stone entrance.

"This bastard could ruin us," said George Weitz. We had
turned up Ninth Street toward Avenue B. "Where the hell
does the Manhattan Council get off appointing a crap artist
like that to be one of the referees?"

Crap artists are, of course, familiar decorations of all civili-
zations. Look at Caligula. Look at Hitler. On the other hand,
they are not all so vicious. Look, as long as we're looking, at
Jimmy Walker. I think Norton Krakowitz was closer to Jimmy
than to Caligula. I think that's why I understood but was not
terrified by the thoughts of George Weitz.

Similar thoughts had been running through my mind during
the past few days. The referees of the eliminations contests performed a variety of functions, depending on the events they
supervised. The main duty of the One-Flag Morse supervisor
was to compose the messages that the competing teams would
be wigwagging to each other. My thoughts had clustered
around a central uneasy question: What kind of message could
you expect to be cooked up by a referee who even before a hat
was dropped broke into "Me and My Shadow"?

"Don't worry about it," I said to George. "Whatever this
slob cooks up, you and I can send it. Good evening, Mr.
O'Hare."

The scoutmaster stopped and turned. He was two steps
ahead of us on the way up the white marble stoop that led to
the front doors of the Hannah H. Lichtenstein House.

"Ah, good evening, young men," said Mr. O'Hare.

Mr. O'Hare was very fond of all the members of Troop 244.
At any rate, he certainly acted that way. But Mr. O'Hare had a
very poor memory. He could not remember our names. So he

49

called us all young men. I must say, in view of what I was called all the rest of the week, especially by friends like George Weitz, I enjoyed being addressed as "young man." It was like coming up out of a sewer and finding yourself in the middle of a Frank Merriwell novel.

"Bright and early, I see," said Mr. O'Hare.

That was another thing I liked. The way Mr. O'Hare talked. It was as though he had learned English not from Miss Hallock at J.H.S. 64 but by committing *David Copperfield* to memory.

"We were sort of worried about what Mr. Krakowitz is going to cook up for the One-Flag Morse message," George said as we trotted up the marble steps together. I ran on ahead to pull open the heavy door for Mr. O'Hare. Thus I was facing him and George when George said, "We thought, you know, he might come up with, you know, something out of Shakespeare or something."

George made it sound as though coming up out of Shakespeare was not unlike surfacing from a septic tank.

"I shouldn't worry about that if I were you," Mr. O'Hare said. "It doesn't really matter if it's out of Shakespeare or the New York *Daily News,* does it? Words are words. They're composed of letters. All you have to do is wigwag the letters one at a time and the words will take care of themselves, won't they?"

"Yes, sir," George said. Softly, as he followed Mr. O'Hare into the lobby, he added, "You stupid jerk."

"Shut up," I whispered, then fell in beside Mr. O'Hare. I did not like what George was doing. Even then I grasped the wisdom of keeping one's eye on the ball. The ball was the One-Flag Morse signaling medal. "What George means, Mr. O'Hare, he means maybe Mr. Krakowitz, you know how he is, he could hit us with a surprise."

"Oh, now, really, young men, I doubt that," Mr. O'Hare said.

It seemed to me Mr. O'Hare's voice lacked conviction. Moving along between him and George Weitz down the marble lobby of the Hannah H. Lichtenstein House, I sneaked a look at our scoutmaster. I did it quite often. Not because Mr. O'Hare was a man so fat that he didn't seem to walk so much as shake himself forward, like the jelly quivering around a piece of gefüllte fish when my mother brought the plate in from the kitchen. Or even because his face looked like that of the man in the Admiration cigar ads. What fascinated me about Mr. O'Hare was his total lack of reality. He could have been a specimen in a museum or an animal in the zoo. I always expected to find, somewhere over his head, a small sign identifying his species and native habitat. Mr. O'Hare was a creature from another world: uptown. A goy in a double-breasted blue serge suit, just like the Rogers Peet man, who came down to the Lower East Side three times a week after work. Why? To conduct Jewish boys like me and George Weitz with painstaking care through the absorbing intricacies of the Scout Handbook? Hmmm.

Years later, whenever he crossed my mind, Mr. O'Hare always left great big fat muddy footprints. They all oozed question marks. Had the fat man been a male Jane Addams? A henpecked husband of limited income driven not to the card table or the bottle but to a virtuous dedication that got him out of the house at night for no greater expense than the carfare down to Avenue B? A closet fairy, maybe, who liked to hang around boys? Or just a plain, ordinary, garden variety uptown dumbbell?

I don't know. The question marks remain. So does the shining memory of the man who had said in front of all the members of Troop 244 that he had never seen anybody handle a Morse flag the way I did. I liked Mr. O'Hare, jerk or no jerk.

"Okay," I said. "Whatever Mr. Krakowitz gives us to send, sir, we'll send it."

Humble. Resigned. Accepting the inevitable without protest. Even with a touch of grace. After all, was not a scout, in addition to trustworthy, loyal and so on, also courteous? It worked. There are things you can do with your voice when you are fourteen that Demosthenes could never have achieved with a mouthful of pebbles at sixty. Mr. O'Hare's round, unbaked apple-pie face creased in a troubled frown. He wanted to win even more than George Weitz and I did.

"Why don't you young men just pop on to the gym," Mr. O'Hare said. "Mr. Krakowitz is well aware of his duties as a referee. I am absolutely certain nothing of a surprising nature is in store for you."

I was unaware then that Mr. O'Hare had uttered one of the more foolish statements the human animal is capable of making.

The message Mr. Krakowitz wrote for me to signal was: *We have left undone those things which we ought to have done, and we have done those things which we ought not to have done.* Twenty-five words from the Book of Common Prayer.

I did not know this at the time. In fact, at the time I didn't even know there was such a thing as the Book of Common Prayer. All I knew, when the starting gun went off and my reader-receiver tore open the sealed envelope, was that if Troop 244 was going to make it into the All-Manhattan finals, we would have to break our collective rear ends. The four teams we were competing against were hot. They had a reputation that had preceded them all the way uptown to Avenue B.

This did not worry me. I had assumed they would be hot.

If they weren't, how had they come up as far as this phase of the eliminations? The reason their reputations did not worry me was that I had a feeling about Morse Code. A sort of green thumb, you might say, for sending and receiving dots and dashes. I don't know where I got it. When Mr. O'Hare had told the troop I handled a Morse flag better than any scout he had ever known, I accepted the compliment without any of that digging-my-toe-into-the-hot-sand nonsense. So far as the denizens of the Hannah H. Lichtenstein House were concerned, false modesty had not yet been invented. Mr. O'Hare's compliment seemed to me no more than just.

I was pretty good at knot-tying. I could whip up a spiral reverse bandage as well as most members of the troop. I could without too much effort get a spark and then a bit of fire out of a piece of flint, a slab of broken steel file, and a wad of singed surgical gauze. But it was my skill with the Morse flag that had bumped me up to senior patrol leader of Troop 244, and it was this skill that made me feel that night we were going to win, no matter how fancy Mr. Krakowitz got.

What I got, when I whipped out the last letter of the last word in my message, was a tap of approval on my tail from Chink Alberg. His real name was Morris, but on East Fourth Street, Morris Alberg was known as Chink because he had slant eyes. He was squatted down on the shiny yellow wood of the gym floor, about three feet to the left of my widespread legs. This kept him clear of my wigwagging flag, which was mounted on an eight-foot bamboo pole, and yet close enough so I would have no trouble hearing him call out the letters of the message from the sheet that had been handed to him in a sealed envelope by Mr. Krakowitz just before the starting whistle blew.

"Two minutes ten!" Chink said from somewhere down

around my knees. I could hear the excitement in his voice. It made my heart jump. Two minutes ten for twenty-five words, averaging out to six letters each, was better than I had done even in my best practice sessions. "We're ahead!" Chink said. "Jesus, we must be! Two minutes ten is—!"

"Shut up!" I said without moving my head or shifting my glance. At the other end of the gym George Weitz had set his flag in motion. I could see Hot Cakes Rabinowitz, squatting at George's feet, moving his lips as he called the letters from the sheet of paper fastened to the clipboard in his lap.

"Start writing!" I hissed at Chink. Inside my head the wig-wags of George's flag recorded dot, dot, dash. "U," I yelled. Dash, dot went the flag. "N," I yelled. George's flag dropped to the left in a single dash. "T," I yelled. Three flips to the left. "O," I yelled, and even though Mr. O'Hare had cautioned us over and over again that a receiver must never worry about the words but merely call the letters, I could not stop myself from putting these first four together and yelling, "Unto!"

Thus I knew that for the second half of the Troop 244 segment of the flagged Morse eliminations contest for the 1927 All-Manhattan rally, Mr. Krakowitz had chosen something from either the Bible or Shakespeare. At that time these were the only two areas of printed material in which I had encountered the word "unto."

Later, at Mr. O'Hare's post-mortem analysis of our performance, I learned that the message George Weitz had started to wigwag to me was from Matthew XXV:29: *Unto every one that hath shall be given, and he shall have abundance; but from him that hath not shall be taken away even that which he hath*. At the time, however, I knew as much about Matthew as I knew about the Book of Common Prayer, which was nothing.

I did, however, know two things: Chink's excited analysis was probably correct, we were ahead; and I was receiving George Weitz so clearly and easily that the odds were good we would finish ahead.

After all these years I am still uncertain about how many words of Matthew XXV:29, George Weitz managed to wig-wag at me across the gym, but I am absolutely certain about my performance at the receiving end. I never got beyond that first word "unto."

A split second after I yelled the letter "O" down to Chink at my feet, I saw my mother.

There are those who may not consider this startling. Or even interesting. After all, sons and daughters have been seeing their mothers since Cain and Abel began to notice that the Garden of Eden was becoming a bit cramped. And while it is true that Cain and Abel would undoubtedly have raised an eyebrow if they had caught sight of *my* mother, the reason for their surprise would have been considerably different from mine. In a manner of speaking, until that moment in the Hannah H. Lichtenstein House, I had never before seen my mother.

Let me clarify that.

The first five years of my life had been lived in our tenement flat about two hundred feet from the docks that jutted out into the East River to accommodate the coal and lumber barges. More accurately, those first five years had been spent in that railroad flat and in the shadow of my mother's slender and almost tiny figure: she put on only a little flesh in her middle years; she weighed a hundred and five pounds the day I was born, and she was still almost exactly that the day she died.

When I say I lived in that flat, I do not mean what most people mean when they say they live in a certain place, a geographical point from which they leave daily, let us say, to go to work, and to which they return nightly to be fed, have some entertainment, and then go to sleep. When I say I lived in that flat on East Fourth Street for the first five years of my life, I mean it the way Edmund Dantes would mean it if he were describing his residence in the Chateau d'If.

I never went down into the street without my mother. I never met a human except in her presence. I don't recall that I wanted to. It never occurred to me to question my way of life. I hope Dr. Spock is not listening, but I have a strong feeling that very few five-year-olds do. I just jogged along from day to day, doing what I was told, trying to stay out of trouble, and listening quite a lot. What I heard was not very exciting. The adults who lived on our block were almost all, like my mother, immigrants from Hungary or, like my father, immigrants from Austria. They spoke what my parents spoke: Yiddish and Hungarian. So did I.

Then, in the middle of my sixth year, the laws of her new country penetrated to my mother's consciousness. I don't know how. Perhaps a neighbor warned her that by keeping me in the house she was doing something that would bring down on her the retaliation of authority. This seems to me a reasonable guess. My mother's whole life, as I look back on it, was directed by a ceaseless effort to avoid tangling with the law. Anyway, she took me around the corner to P.S. 188 and registered me in kindergarten class. The English language exploded all around me.

The immediate result was to force on me a double life. It lasted for six years, and I loved every minute of it. Every minute of my double life, I mean. For those six years it was Yiddish on the fourth floor of 390 East Fourth Street; English in P.S. 188 and on the surrounding pavements. I'm pretty sure my mother was aware of my double life. But she pretended she knew nothing about it. Which leads me to conclude that she was afraid of my life in P.S. 188 and on the surrounding pavements, because I learned as I grew older that her way of treating anything terrifying was to turn her back on it. What didn't exist could not hurt her. Or so she thought. All I thought about was the fun I was having.

Then one day I was summoned from my 6-B class to the office of Mr. McLaughlin, the principal.

"A great honor has been conferred upon you," he said. Mr. McLaughlin looked like a British officer in one of those steel engravings that illustrated *Vanity Fair*. Perhaps he was aware of this and tried, when he spoke, to underscore the image. The word honor, when he pronounced it, came out as un-oar. "You are going to be transferred from P.S. 188 to a rapid advance class in Junior High School 64 on Ninth Street," he said. "This is being done because of your brilliant scholastic achievements."

I did not understand what Mr. McLaughlin was talking about, and no wonder. The truth probably was P.S. 188 was becoming unmanageable because of overcrowding. To solve the problem Mr. McLaughlin had undoubtedly solicited the help of friendly principals in nearby junior highs. Their help enabled Mr. McLaughlin to transfer a number of students out of P.S. 188 to less congested schools. I think I was one of the few boys from P.S. 188 who landed in J.H.S. 64 on Ninth Street.

At first I was apprehensive about the transfer. Ninth Street was five blocks uptown from the block where I had thus far spent all of my life. It doesn't sound like much. What's five blocks? Well, in my day, which was half a century ago, it could be half a world. To a boy, anyway. At that time the Lower East Side was not so much a crisscrossed network of streets and blocks, as it was a cluster of different villages with totally different populations.

Ninth Street was almost exclusively Italian. I remember the feeling, on that first morning when I walked up to J.H.S. 64, that I had entered a strange country. It was. I had never known any Italians. Naturally, I was worried. My concern was short-lived. Aside from the fact that they bought strange foods displayed in store windows that did not look like Mr. Deutsch's grocery on our block or Mr. Shumansky's chicken store on the Avenue C corner, the Italians of Ninth Street seemed after a few days no different from the Hungarians and Austrians of my block. In relation to me, that is. They didn't seem to know I was alive. This suited me fine. I didn't want anybody staring at me during the settling-in process. This process ended the day my teacher announced that Mr. O'Hare, the scoutmaster of a newly formed scout troop, was looking for recruits, and any boy interested in joining could meet Mr. O'Hare for a talk after school in the gym of the Hannah H. Lichtenstein House around the corner on Avenue B.

I had, of course, belonged to Troop 224 for about two years in the Hamilton Fish Park Branch of the New York Public Library until the scoutmaster died and the troop disintegrated. I missed it. I welcomed this opportunity to become involved again with knot-tying and Morse Code. Once more my mother pretended she was unaware of my involvement in the scout movement. She was dedicated to this pretense with a fierceness that still impresses me. Look at the things she had to pretend she did not see. The signaling flags I brought into the house. The flint-and-steel sets. The knot-tying equipment. The merit badge pamphlets and other technical literature that began to appear after supper on our kitchen table along with

my schoolbooks when I was supposed to be doing my homework. My mother never saw any of it. She was determined
not to see any of it. She laundered that uniform for me every
Friday. She pressed it. She removed grease spots from the
breeches with Carbona. She sewed my insignia and, as I earned
them, my merit badges on the shirt. She did all that, but she
never acknowledged the fact that her son disappeared every
Saturday night at six o'clock wearing a khaki uniform and did
not come home until almost midnight.

Looking back on it, the only thing that seems strange to me
about the whole business is that I did not find it strange. Some
instinct told me it was crucial to my mother's existence for her
not to acknowledge my participation in any life outside her
own orbit. Out of this same instinct came my total acceptance
of the structure she had created, as well as my skill at maintain-
ing my role in it.

That is why I could not believe my eyes on the night when
I wigwagged twenty-five words with a single red and white
Morse flag across the gym of the Hannah H. Lichtenstein
House in two minutes and ten seconds flat.

"Come on!" Chink Alberg barked from somewhere down
near my left knee. "All I got is u, n, t, o!" I didn't answer. I
was staring with astonished disbelief at my mother's figure at
the other side of the gym. "For Christ's sake!" Chink yelled.
"What the hellzamatter with you?"

"It's my mother," I said.

"To hell with your mother," Chink snarled. "Start calling,
for Christ's sake. Them other bastids, they're getting ahead
of us!"

I was aware of this. I could see George Weitz at the other
side of the gym. His flag was whipping left and right. I could

59

see Hot Cakes Rabinowitz kneeling to the left of George, calling the letters from his clipboard. I could even see the four rival teams, two on each side of George and Hot Cakes, wig-wagging away like crazy, wiping out the lead I had gained with my two minutes ten, and pulling ahead. But I saw them all only peripherally. Like the clouds around the edges of a portrait in a museum. Or the grass under the feet of the painted main subject. My eyes were nailed to the stranger in the center.

My mother had never been inside the Hannah H. Lichtenstein House. During the months of my involvement with Troop 244 she had never acknowledged its existence. I had every reason to believe she did not even know its location. It could have been in her native land. Which was where? Hungary? Far Cathay? The Mountains of the Moon? When you got right down to it, how did I know where she had come from? She could not possibly be here. Therefore she wasn't. This creature who had erupted in the middle of my signaling triumph and was now destroying it, was somebody else. Not my mother. Who? Across the length of the gym I examined her.

A skinny little woman. With blond hair pulled back into a neat knot on top of her head. Her little head. Everything about her was little. Especially her face. A fierce little face. But out of that little face two big blue eyes shone like lights. The whole thing—I had the impression of a force, not a human being—sheathed in something black. Not dressed. Wrapped. What she was wearing could have been painted on her body. High neck. Long sleeves. Skirt sweeping the yellow boards of the gym floor. She—no, it!—reminded me of something. I could hear Chink snarling furiously at my feet. I knew I was losing for Troop 244 the right to participate in the All-Manhattan rally. I felt in my sinking gut the waves of contempt and rage I was earning from my fellow scouts. But my mind had room for nothing but the desperate question: Who in God's name was this stranger?

The answer surfaced abruptly out of my life at school. More accurately, out of my American history textbook. Coming across the Hannah H. Lichtenstein House gym was Molly Pitcher, moving firmly to take over the gun in the middle of the Battle of Monmouth at which her husband had fallen from a heat stroke. The fact that she looked like my mother didn't matter. Nobody was fooling me. This was Molly Pitcher.

"What the hellz she think she's doing?" Chink Alberg screamed.

"How should I know?" I screamed back.

"She's your mother, ain't she?"

This regrettable fact now came crashing down on me like a toppling wall. Because at my mother's side, moving along beside her across the gym, I saw Mr. O'Hare.

The scoutmaster was swung slightly to one side and bent over, so the words he was uttering as he moved dropped into my mother's left ear. It was about two feet below his mouth. I could not, of course, hear Mr. O'Hare's words, but I knew they were angry. I could tell from his gestures. Great chopping swirls at the air, like an untrained swimmer plunging ahead with a primitive breaststroke. And the color of his face. Like the skin of a tangerine. I knew something else. Mr. O'Hare's words did not matter. Not to my mother, anyway. Mr. O'Hare was unaware of this. Why should he know that my mother did not understand English?

"You can't do this," Mr. O'Hare was saying as he and my mother reached me and Chink. This was not the first time I had been impressed by the lack of logic, if not intelligence, in the remarks uttered by grownups. It was no time, however, to make notes on mental scoreboards. The fact remains that my

61

mother *had* done it, and what she had done I found incredible. She had just brought the whole 1927 All-Manhattan rally eliminations finals to a halt.

"You come with me," she said to me.

"What is she saying?" Mr. O'Hare snapped.

"Listen, Ma," I said desperately in Yiddish. "For Christ's sake," I added angrily in English. "What the heck are you doing?" I concluded hysterically in a combination of both.

"God damn that bitch," Chink Alberg said from somewhere around my knees. "She's messing us up!"

"Morris, we'll have none of that language, if you please," said Mr. O'Hare.

He had once explained to the troop that to call a fellow scout Chink was like calling the king of Italy a wop. I didn't quite grasp the comparison. Everybody I knew called Victor Emmanuel a wop. Everybody who talked English, anyway. Mr. O'Hare, who talked nothing else, grabbed my arm and said, "If this lady is your mother, will you please ask her to listen to me for one moment?"

"Ma," I said, "Mr. O'Hare wants to tell you something."

"You tell this pudding-headed goy to get out of my way," my mother said.

She grabbed my arm and started to hustle me across the gym floor, toward the doors behind George Weitz and Hot Cakes Rabinowitz. Mr. O'Hare loped along.

"My good woman," he said.

"Get dead," my mother said.

I swallowed my gum. She had said it in English. Not very good English. In fact, I wasn't sure my mother had spoken English. I allowed her to drag me along. My mind seemed to follow like a reluctant dog on a leash. An astounding thought had erupted in my mind: Maybe I wasn't the only one who had been leading a double life?

"I must say, madam," Mr. O'Hare said.

He didn't say any more. We had swung around George Weitz and Hot Cakes Rabinowitz and reached the doors to the lobby. My mother put her free hand up to Mr. O'Hare's bulging belly. One hundred and five pounds, remember. And she shoved. What she shoved, remember, was at least two hundred and twenty pounds of solid suet, maybe more. And Mr. O'Hare toppled back.

Not exactly into the arms of George Weitz. He couldn't. There was that eight-foot bamboo pole between them. It was in a relaxed position because George had forgotten all about Matthew XXV:29, and was staring at my mother in astonishment. As a result, the red and white Morse flag at the top of the pole clearly marked for all observers in the gym of the Hannah H. Lichtenstein House the precise spot where the bamboo pole and Mr. O'Hare made contact. William Tell, aiming for the apple on his son's head, couldn't have done better. Bull's-eye. Mr. O'Hare screamed. My mother—still one hundred and five pounds, remember—punched open the swinging doors and dragged me through them into the Hannah H. Lichtenstein House lobby.

"Ma," I said. "Do you know what you've just done?"

"Come on, come on, come on," she said. "There's no time."

"Ma, they're waiting for me," I said. I was talking to her back. The dragging process had resumed. Across the marble floor of the Hannah H. Lichtenstein House lobby. Through the great big double doors. Out into Avenue B. "It's my team," I said. "Ma, we were winning. I wigwagged twenty-five words in two minutes and ten seconds flat."

"You can do it again," my mother said, dragging me down Avenue B. "Some other time."

"But there won't be any other time," I wailed. "This is the eliminations, the semifinals. You just got us eliminated, Ma."

"What's eliminated?"

The English word, imbedded in my hysterical Yiddish complaint, had captured her attention.

"It's like, you could say, like lost," I said. "It means we lost."

"So if you lost, what are you complaining about going back? What's there to go back for? You can't be—What did you say —ellimated?"

"Eliminated."

"You can't be eliminated twice," my mother said.

She led me around the corner of Tompkins Square Park into Seventh Street. Halfway up the block toward Avenue A she released my wrist. It was though she had decided the reluctant dog had been dragged so far and around so many turns from the place where he wanted to be, that there was no longer any chance of his escaping from her side. The poor pooch was no longer capable of finding his way back. My mother was almost right. Not in the sense that I couldn't have found my way back to the Hannah H. Lichtenstein House. My mother was right because I wouldn't have tried. I was too ashamed of what had just happened to face Mr. O'Hare and the members of my troop. I wondered if I would ever be·able to face them. I also wondered if my mother had gone crazy. Not only because she had just told Mr. O'Hare to "get dead," but because of where she was heading.

To my knowledge my mother had never been further west of the East River than Avenue C. Yet tonight she had come as far west as Avenue B to drag me out of the Hannah H. Lichtenstein House gym, and now we were crossing Avenue A on our way to First Avenue. I had, of course, done a certain amount of roaming away from Fourth and Lewis streets during the six years of my double life, and when Mr. O'Hare took the troop out on a Sunday hike, we always met him at the subway station in front of Wanamaker's on Astor Place. This was quite a distance from the corner of Fourth and Lewis streets. I was an explorer. But all my roaming had always been done in the company of other Magellans like George Weitz and Chink Alberg or another friend from the troop. Also, all of our roaming had been done during the day. Now it was night.

Night was to the greenhorns what Lent is to the Catholics. Watch out. Forbear. Don't do. Stay home. They did, including my mother, and so did their sons, including me. Yet here we were, both of us, like hypnotized converts to the dictates of Horace Greeley, heading west. Under the El tracks of First Avenue. Across the cracked but brightly lighted pavements of Second Avenue. Into the frightening gloom of Third Avenue.

Frightening, I grasped in a few moments, only to me. My mother plowed ahead, around the shadowed butt end of Cooper Union, into the ominous open terrain of Astor Place, and swung left into Lafayette Street. She moved with a puzzling kind of leaning-forward directness, as though impatient to reach her destination, but also with an even more puzzling familiarity. My mother, plunging into the semi-darkness of Lafayette Street, could have been crossing our kitchen on East Fourth Street with a paper bag full of pushcart apples toward the cut-glass bowl in our front room. She wasn't frightened. She had made this journey before. I could tell. No, I could feel it. I could feel it, and I couldn't believe it. Where were we going?

"Here," my mother said.

She had stopped in front of a dark brown building. In the

light from the lamppost it was easy enough to make out the gold lettering spread in an arc like a movie star's eyebrow across the street-floor plate-glass window: *Meister's Matzoh Bakery, Inc.*

My stomach jumped. Twice, the day before and tonight, George Weitz had made cracks about my mother and Meister's Matzoh Bakery. He obviously knew something I didn't know.

"What are we doing here?" I said.

"They talk English," my mother said. "I want you to talk for me."

"Yeah, sure," I said. "But who are they?"

No answer. She had moved up onto a sandstone step in front of a dark door to the right of the plate-glass window. She was peering at a panel of black bell buttons set like polka dots in a rectangular brass plate. There were no markings under the buttons. This did not seem to bother my mother. She worked at them as though she were doing a puzzle. Muttering to herself in Yiddish, she ran her forefinger horizontally across the black buttons, then down, and making a sharp left, she finger-walked back the way she had come. The muttering stopped. She pressed a button.

Far back inside the house, and it seemed to me above our heads, a bell rang. It sounded somewhat like one of the bells in J.H.S. 64 if you happened to be in the toilet when it went off on the staircase at the far end of the hall. The effect was somewhat the same, too. The sounds of movement behind the dark door. Sounds coming closer, sounds that were unmistakably heel taps. They stopped at the other side of the door.

In the sudden silence, I became aware that I was being watched. I turned nervously. Nobody was in sight. My mother and I were alone on that dimly lighted stretch of Lafayette Street. When I turned back, the dark door was opening. A young man squinted out at us. I was struck by two things. He was wearing the sort of suit Mr. O'Hare wore, and he looked familiar.

"Okay," he said. He sounded familiar, too. He held the door wide. My mother stepped in. When I followed her, the young man said sharply, "Who's he?"

"What did he say?" my mother said in Yiddish.

"He wants to know who I am," I said.

"So why don't you tell him?" my mother said.

"I'm her son," I said.

"What does she want to bring her son for?" the young man said.

I translated for my mother.

She said, "I'll tell his father."

I translated for the young man. He did not seem pleased, but he closed the door behind us and started to fuss with a complicated metal arrangement that was obviously some sort of locking device. While my mother and I waited for him to work a set of double blue-black steel bars into their slots, I saw why out on the street I'd had the feeling I was being watched. Two thirds of the way up on the door there was a peephole.

"I'll go first," the young man said, and he did.

"What did he say?" my mother said as she started to follow and I started to follow her.

"He said he'll go first," I said in Yiddish.

"From brains this particular son will never die," my mother said. "The stupid idiot, he always goes first."

So my guess was right. She had been here before. When? Obviously during the day. What day? "Always" meant more than once. So she had been here several times. How many? When I was battling plane geometry in J.H.S. 64 and my father was sewing pockets in the pants factory on Allen Street.

For the first time since my mother had erupted into the middle of George Weitz's attempt to wigwag a section of Matthew XXV:29, across the Hannah H. Lichtenstein House gymnasium, I stopped being furious about the elimination of Troop 244 from the All-Manhattan rally and I became interested in my surroundings.

These seemed to be a long, dark hall. Then the young man turned right, my mother and I followed, and we were crossing what looked like an enormous storage room. It was stacked from floor to ceiling with long white boxes, each one tied with string. The room was poorly lighted, but when we passed a spot under one of the bulbs that hung from the ceiling on lengths of long black wire, I saw that all the boxes were marked in the same way as the plate-glass window out in front: *Meister's Matzoh Bakery, Inc.*

I had never heard of Meister's matzohs. My mother was partial to Horowitz Bros. & Margareten. Anyway, that's what she always bought when Passover rolled around. Could it be that my mother was shifting her matzoh allegiance? It could be, but I doubted it. My mother may have been illiterate, but she was loyal. Also, how did George Weitz hear about it?

"Easy going through this part here," the young man said. "The ovens are hot."

"He said . . ." I started to say to my mother in Yiddish.

"I know what he said," my mother said. "The idiot always says the same thing. He thinks I'm an idiot like him who wants to get burned."

We were moving single file through a long room that smelled vaguely of fresh bread. It seemed to be lined on both sides with a series of shoulder-high tin boxes about ten feet wide. There were spaces between the boxes almost as wide as the boxes themselves. On these spaces lay strips of metal belting that seemed to be made from woven bicycle chains. It was like moving past Mr. Pollock's blacksmith shop on East Fourth Street when his forge was going. You could feel the heat from the tin boxes. The young man led us out of this room into a hall colder and darker than the one we had entered from the street. Here the smell was different. Sharp and odd but not unpleasant. Like fresh wrapping paper. The young man snapped on a flashlight. He turned the beam on my mother's shoes.

"Watch the corners," he said. "These bundles sometimes have sharp pieces of wire sticking out."

"He said . . ." I started to say to my mother in Yiddish.

"I know what he said," my mother said. "*You* watch the sharp pieces of wire sticking out."

The flashlight beam sliced up and across the wall on my left. I caught a brief glimpse of stacked burlap bundles. The smear of light picked out some of the wires that held the burlap tightly cinched in, the way my father's belt held his belly.

"Now he's going to say watch the steps," my mother said in Yiddish.

"What did she say?" the young man said.

"What did he say?" my mother said.

"He said what did you say," I said in Yiddish.

"Don't tell him," my mother said.

"You heard me, kid," the young man said. There was no mistaking the threat in his voice. "What did she say?"

"She said was I okay," I said.

"She sure worries a lot about you," he said.

"She has to," I said. "I'm the only one in the family talks English."

"Well, watch the steps," the young man said.

They were worth watching. They looked like the floor of the toilet in the American Movie Theatre on Third Street. Black and white marble tile. At the top of the stairs the young man shoved the flashlight into his pocket and opened a door. He held it wide for me and my mother and, as we entered, yelled across our heads, "Hey, Pa!"

In through a door at the other side of the room came a tall, heavy man with almost white hair. He was yawning and rubbing his eyes with one hand. In the other he carried a steaming white kettle from which the enamel was chipped here and there like small blue bruises. He wore carpet slippers and a quilted bathrobe, both not unlike my father's, but newer. My father never bought anything new. Everything he owned he had already owned the day I was born. The heavy man needed a shave. So did the young man, but it wasn't this similarity that made me realize why, when he opened the street door, the young man had looked familiar. It was the way he had yelled, "Hey, Pa!" Alone, he had been a tough-looking wise guy in an uptown suit. In the same room with his father, he became part of a team. They looked like all the Italians who lived on Ninth Street.

"Look who's here," the young man said.

The old man looked, then said, "Who's the kid?"

"Her son," the young man said.

"Oh, Jesus," the old man said. "That means she wants to talk."

"I told you last year you better learn Yiddish," the young man said. "You want me to get her out of here?"

"No, no," the old man said. He sounded tired but not unfriendly. "She's the only one we got on Fourth Street."

"We got that other one," the young man said. "You know. The fat Polack with the hair."

"Yeah, but she don't go no further east than Avenue B," the old man said. "I'll talk."

"You want me to wait?" the young man said.

The old man said to me, "Ask your mother, kid, ask her if she wants to talk to me alone, or is it okay my son hears?"

I translated for my mother.

"I don't care," she said.

"My mother doesn't care," I said.

"Maybe then you better stay," the old man said.

"Okay," the young man said.

He pulled out the four chairs that surrounded a table in the middle of the room. He did it slowly, with great care, as though he were one of those butlers in the movies preparing the places for a conference of diplomats.

"Sit, please," the old man said.

My mother and the old man sat down facing each other. He set the steaming kettle in front of him and dipped down toward the spout. As I took the chair on my mother's left, and the young man took the chair on her right, the old man pulled a thick towel from around his neck and put it over his head to form a hood.

"Jesus," the young man said. "I never realized before, Pop, she's pretty good."

"Shut up," his father said, sucking in gulps of steam from the kettle spout. "The kid."

The young man took his eyes from my mother and said, "Yeah, I forgot."

"People who forget," the old man said, "they go early."

"I'm sorry, Pop."

The old man said to me, "What are you looking at, kid?"

I was looking at the kettle and the towel hood from under which he was speaking, but I thought my staring had annoyed him, so I said, "That thing."

I pointed to a huge white enamel box against the wall

71

behind him. On top of the box a flywheel as big around as a basketball was humming. The wheel was attached by a leather strap to a motor on the floor as big as an automobile tire. The sounds from the motor were louder and more irregular than the smooth hum from the flywheel.

"It's a refrigerator," the old man said. "Give the kid a drink."

The young man stood up, went to the white enamel box, and with a grand double-handed gesture, opened the two doors the way Mr. Seaman, the undertaker on Avenue C, opened the back of his hearse. The inside of the box was lined with wire shelves. They were loaded with bottles and the kinds of strangely shaped and oddly packaged foods that hung in the windows of the Italian groceries on Ninth Street. The young man lifted out a dark bottle. He slammed the white enamel doors shut. He pulled the cork from the bottle by hooking it into and twisting it out of a gadget fastened to the wall near the refrigerator. He took three glasses from a cupboard. He emptied the contents of the bottle into them. He did all this like a juggler. No pause between steps. I had the feeling he thought of us as an audience. He slipped the empty bottle into a wooden box between the cupboard and the refrigerator. He brought the glasses to the table. He set them before me, my mother and himself. He sat down. I wondered if we should applaud.

"What is it?" my mother said.

The old man clearly understood the Yiddish question. He did not ask for a translation. He pulled the bathrobe up around his neck, hunched himself more deeply into the towel hood, and said to me, "Tell her not to worry. It's Moxie."

Go explain Moxie to my mother. A woman who had never put anything on her table except milk and sink water.

72

"Ma," I said, "it's like milk or sink water."

"Milk is white," my mother said. "Sink water is no color."

The old man obviously sensed from the tone of my mother's voice that she had no confidence in the refreshment his son had served us.

"Tell her to take a taste," he said to me. He took a deep, heaving, sucking inhalation of steam from the kettle spout. In a choked voice he said again, "Tell her to take a taste."

I told my mother to take a taste. Cautiously she lifted her glass and took a sip. Her opinion was obvious from the way she set down the glass. I did not bother to translate her one-word comment: "*Pishachgst!*"

"Well, anyway, all right," the old man said. He sounded as though he were talking underwater. "I've got this thing in my chest," he bubbled. "The doctor says I should stay in bed. Tell her to say what she has to say. I have to get back in bed."

He coughed into his cupped hands while I translated for my mother.

She said, "Ask him what it is with the Shumansky wedding."

I did as I was told. The old man nodded and rubbed his eyes as he wiped his cough-spattered palms on the bathrobe.

"I know," he said. Again tired. But also again friendly. "It's a big order," he said, sucking in steam. "Eighteen quarts. My sons and I, we must fill the order direct ourselves."

"Why?" my mother said.

The old man sighed. A wheeze, really. It started him coughing again. He clutched the towel over his head with both hands. I had the feeling my mother was annoying but not surprising him. It was as though, in spite of his illness, he had been induced to go to the theater, perhaps because his family had said getting out of the house would do him good, and when he got to the play he found he knew all the jokes before the entertainers uttered them.

73

"It's like this," he said. "Small orders, a bottle here, a bottle there, fine. This you can handle. And you've handled it for us very good. But the Shumansky wedding. Eighteen bottles. For a woman it's too much."

"Why?" my mother said again.

"Why?" the old man said. "Think why. It's eighteen bottles. Just to carry alone, it's impossible for a woman."

"I have a son," my mother said.

The old man parted the flaps of the towel to look at me. I had a feeling I should stand up and flex my biceps. Or push out my arms to show the spread I could achieve. He was looking at me as though he had just become aware of my presence. I found this embarrassing. I had been talking my head off, translating like crazy. I thought he had grown accustomed to my presence. All of a sudden I felt like an intruder.

"He's a kid," the old man said finally. He paused to inhale a large gulp of steam. "I can't take a chance," he said. "He's a nice boy. I can tell. I know nice boys. I'm glad you got one. But I can't take a chance on a kid. He—" The old man's voice stopped. His chest went on working. As he caught the explosions of phlegm in his palms, he huddled deeper into the towel hood and examined me more closely. Finally, on a series of low gasps, he said, "What's that he's wearing?"

"My scout uniform," I said. "I'm senior patrol leader of Troop 244 in the Hannah H. Lichtenstein House."

"Jesus," the old man said. He turned to his son. "Like the cops?"

"No, no, no," said the young man. "It's like—oh, Christ." He scowled at the glass of Moxie on the table in front of him, then said, "Like the Boys' Club? On Avenue A and Tenth?"

"The Hannah H. Lichtenstein House," I said, "is on Avenue B and Ninth."

"I know, I know," the young man said irritably. "I'm just trying to explain." He turned back to his father. "It's like to keep them off the street, Pop. They play games. They make bandages. They tie knots. It has nothing to do with the cops."

"You sure?" the old man wheezed.

"Positive," the young man said. "You want more hot water, Pop?"

The old man shook his head. He reached out and patted my hair. He did it as though he was testing it for springiness. It was springy enough. In those days I grew a skullcap of tight little kinky black curls.

"A nice boy," the old man said. "He's working yet?"

I translated as though he were talking about Chink Alberg or Hot Cakes Rabinowitz.

"After school," my mother said. "In Lebenbaum's candy store on Avenue C."

"Very nice," the old man said. "Very good. How old?"

"Fourteen," my mother said.

"Good," the old man said. "Very good. All of mine, the whole four, I started them the same age. It makes them understand."

"He understands," my mother said.

"What?" the old man said.

"He understands it's a family," my mother said. "Everybody has to help. If I tell him to carry, he'll carry."

"He's carried before?" the old man said.

"No," my mother said. "Up to now I didn't need help. One bottle, two, anybody can carry. But the Shumansky wedding, eighteen bottles, he'll help me."

The old man was taken by a yawn. His body shook. The shaking ended in a belch.

"Excuse me," he said. "It's this thing in my chest. Like a

75

load of cement. I have to go to bed. Listen. About the Shumansky wedding, I'm sorry. We'll fill the order ourselves. Other
things, you can do like always. All right?"

Before I finished translating, my mother stood up.

"No," she said.

"What?" the old man said.

Not a question. Another explosion.

"She said no, Pop," his son said.

"You shut up," my mother said to the young man. "To
talk for me, I brought my own son." She shoved my shoulder.
"Tell him, the stupid idiot."

Something told me something else: it was wiser not to tell
this old man what my mother had said.

"My mother says," I said to the young man, "you should
she says please let me do the saying of what she says."

"Jesus, all right," the old man said. "But what's there to
say?"

I translated with nervous care. The low hum from the flywheel on top of the refrigerator, and the louder noise from the
motor on the floor beside it, suddenly seemed to be filling the
room like the raging waters in the picture of the Johnstown
Flood that hung on the wall of Mr. McLaughlin's office in
P.S. 188.

"There's this to say, Mr. Imberotti," my mother said. The
name came as a relief. I had not realized until now that I was
troubled by the gap between what it said on the window
downstairs and the fact that this father and son looked like all
the Italians on Ninth Street. Italians were not called Meister.
Imberotti was more like it. "A bottle for a bar mitzvah," my
mother said, "two bottles for the *schul* on Purim, for this I'm
good enough. But for the Shumansky wedding, because it's
eighteen bottles, where a person could make herself a dollar,
for this I'm not good enough."

76

The old man waited patiently for my translation, then said, "That's not the way to look at it."

"I work for you to put bread on the table for my husband and son," my mother said. "Now there comes a piece of cake, so you take it away from me. How should I look at it, Mr. Imberotti?"

"Like this," the old man said. "You're a person we like. You're a person we trust. For three years we've worked together like friends. Why should we stop being friends?"

"We shouldn't," my mother said. "To stay friends, all you have to do is let me take care of the Shumansky wedding. I'm entitled to it."

The old man shook his head sadly. The towel flapped. Mr. Imberotti caught the ends. "I can't," he said. "The order is too big."

"You mean the profit is too big," my mother said.

"Listen, Pop," the young man said. "This broad is getting off base."

I didn't translate that. I pretended I hadn't heard it. I was beginning to worry.

"No, she has a right," the old man said. "But her right doesn't change that she's wrong." He patted my head again. "Tell that to your mother."

I did, and my mother did a surprising thing. She also patted my head. Exactly the way the old man had patted it.

"It's time to go," she said.

I stood up and came to her side.

"You're angry?" the old man said.

"No," my mother said. "I'm going home to bake you a *lekach*."

"Will you still be working for us?" the old man said.

"You'll find out," my mother said.

She took my hand and led me toward the door.

"Don't do anything stupid," the old man said.

My mother gave him the kind of look I'd seen her give my father every day of my life, but she didn't give him the dialogue that usually followed that look.

The old man came up out of his chair on an explosion of wheezing. "What are you going to do?" he gasped.

"You'll find out, you Italian bastard," my mother said.

I didn't translate that, either.

"Help them get out," Mr. Imberotti said to his son.

His voice rasped. I wasn't surprised. The word "bastard" needs no translation. Its meaning wallops around for all to understand in the sounds that send it out into the world. What little I could see of the old man's face through the towel hood indicated he understood. The sounds he made in reply made my stomach churn. My mother, I knew, had made a mistake.

"Mario," the old man said, and that's all he did say before the coughing fit hit him. But at least I had finally learned the name of the young man in the Rogers Peet suit. "Mario," the old man said again, and before the coughing fit floored him, Mr. Imberotti managed to get this much out to his son: "We got a bad one on our hands, Mario."

3

ERHAPS THEY HAD. I say perhaps because the words had no precise meaning for me. I'd never thought of my mother as a bad one. Perhaps she even was a bad one, whatever the words meant to Mr. Imberotti. Whoever *he* was. But none of it held my attention for very long. I had other things on my mind. More precisely, one thing: what had happened in the gym of the Hannah H. Lichtenstein House the night before.

Catastrophe. It was for me a totally new experience. My first earthquake, so to speak. I didn't know what to think about it, so I didn't think. I stewed. I don't recall that I had ever until then had a sleepless night. Perhaps that one wasn't actually sleepless. But I did an awful lot of tossing and turning. In the morning, when I left the house for school, I felt rotten. As though the earthquake had ended but the threat remained. The rumbling underfoot had stopped. Masonry and shattered glass had ceased falling. But what was I going to do about the fires crackling all around me? What was I going to say to George Weitz and Chink Alberg and the others?

Luckily, the first one to whom I had to say anything was

Hot Cakes Rabinowitz. I met him near the Avenue C corner
as he came out of his tenement with his schoolbooks.

"Hey," he said, "you missed it."

I had a sudden vision of a lynching party setting out to find
me and coming back empty-handed. Should I sigh with relief?
Turn and run? Or brazen it out?

"Missed what?" I said.

"We won," Hot Cakes said.

I didn't believe him, of course. But it seemed sensible at
the moment not to say so. Calling Hot Cakes a liar could lead
to only one thing: a denunciation for the role I had played in
the troop's defeat. Besides, Hot Cakes was not a wiseguy like
George Weitz. Hot Cakes was a quiet kid with thick glasses
and no sense of humor. He never laughed unless he was tickled.
Hot Cakes was what we then called a *yoineh*. Today the
nearest equivalent to a *yoineh* is a square. I did not think then,
and I do not feel now, that either word is pejorative. It is a
label. Hot Cakes did not make jokes. They were made about
him. Mainly because his real name was Ira. The name vanished from East Fourth Street the day his mother, on her way
out to the Avenue C pushcart market, left her son doing his
homework at the kitchen table with instructions to keep an eye
on two honey cakes Mrs. Rabinowitz had going in the oven.
Ira forgot his mother's instructions. The honey cakes burned
to a couple of inedible crisps. And to the kids of our block,
Ira Rabinowitz became Hot Cakes Rabinowitz.

"We won what?" I said.

"The eliminations," Hot Cakes said. "You should have
been there."

"My old lady pulled me out," I said. This was hardly news
to Hot Cakes. He was George Weitz's reader-receiver. He had
seen it happen while squatting at George's knee the night

before. I tried harder. "My aunt got sick," I said, and then my powers of invention stalled. In those days I had trouble telling lies. Not because of any moral convictions. It was simply that I had not yet learned how to fit the pieces together. It is a simple art. Simple and degrading. I learned how to manage it as I grew older. At that time, however, I merely tried. "My aunt from New Haven," I said. "She came down to visit us." No, I thought, hold it. If she came down to visit us, and she got sick, she would now be in our house, which she wasn't. Try again. "She started out to visit us," I said. "But she got sick on the way and my mother needed me to go along with her to the place where my aunt was sick so I could talk English for her." This would go down, I felt. Hot Cakes, like almost every kid on the block, also had to talk English for his mother. "So she came and got me," I said with more confidence. "My mother." Here I stalled again. I could see what was coming up next. The place where my mother had taken me to talk English for her about my sick aunt. I suddenly knew I could not negotiate that hurdle. My powers of invention, limited at best, are at their worst when I am desperate. Instead, I said, "How'd we win?"

"We took three firsts," Hot Cakes said. "Bandages with arterial pressure points. Then the knot-tying, and also the flint-and-steel. We got a second on bridge-building. We got a third on camp hygiene, and we got a second on basket-weaving. The only thing we got nothing on was One-Flag Morse."

How could we not? With the troop's ace wigwagger not at his post but heading across town to Meister's Matzoh Bakery?

"My aunt," I said nervously without conviction. "She got sick. My mother, she had to go, so she needed me to come along and talk English for her."

But Hot Cakes was not interested. We had reached the

school. Hot Cakes disappeared into the crowd waiting for the first bell. I was left alone with something new: a feeling of resentment. I had assumed my skill with a Morse flag was the core around which Mr. O'Hare had built his hopes for the troop's success. It had never crossed my mind that without me Troop 244 had a prayer. Yet without me my friends had won. Anyway, I had always thought of them as my friends. Some friends. My feeling of resentment gave way to a sense of betrayal. You couldn't trust anybody. Your own mother. Your fellow scouts. Even the man who had stated in public that you were the best Morse wigwagger he had ever known. Bitterness seized me. It is not a good thing to be seized by.

I spent the morning inventing plans for murdering my mother, and ducking George Weitz. This was easy enough between first bell and lunch because George and I were not in the same class. Once the lunch bell rang, however, it was not so easy. George was a pig. I do not mean that he looked like a pig. Actually, he was tall and slender and quite handsome. George was a pig about food. He couldn't stop eating.

The lunch he brought every day from home was always much larger than the lunch any of the rest of us brought. This was only natural. Since his father was a doctor, we took it for granted the Weitz family was rich. Rich people ate more than poor people. What was unnatural was the way George disposed of these substantial lunches.

He always started eating on the staircase while the classes filed down from the classrooms to the yard. By the time the rest of us had found places to squat—there were no chairs, tables, or benches in the schoolyard—and began opening our paper sacks, George had finished the meal he had brought from home. He would then spend the rest of the lunch hour moving from group to group, begging for food. Very few boys refused him. I know I never did. Not because I had too much, or because I wasn't hungry, but because I rarely liked what I had in my paper bag.

My mother was a rotten cook. As a result, what we didn't finish at our evening meal had to be thrown out. There were never any tasty leftovers to put in my lunch bag the next day. Furthermore, my mother never seemed to get the hang of making a sandwich. I don't mean fancy three-deckers, or the tricky four-color inventions that now separate the short stories from the sanitary-napkin ads in our national magazines. I mean any old sandwich. Occasionally, when I offered to show my mother how the mothers of the other boys in my class made their sons' sandwiches, she told me to hold my excessively overgrown mouth. I translate literally. In Hungarian the admonition doesn't sound so awkward. Merely nasty.

Nobody ate sandwiches in Hungary, my mother said, and she had not come to this country to learn stupid tricks. Anything she did not know how to do was stupid. As a result my lunch usually consisted of a big *toochiss* roll cut down the middle and smeared liberally with butter or chicken fat, a couple of pieces of fruit, and a pale green empty Saratoga #2 bottle refilled with milk. My father always kept a case of Saratoga #2 mineral water under his bed. He drank a pint bottle every second morning of his life. My father worried constantly about his *moogin,* Yiddish for bowels.

My worry on that morning after the All-American semi-finals remained just as constant. What was I going to tell George about what had happened the night before? As he headed toward me, I saw George was munching a cabbage leaf. He had just chiseled it from Chink Alberg. Chink's mother used cabbage in his sandwiches the way, I learned years later, uptown women use lettuce. It was obvious that if

I wanted to hold George off, I would have to do better than cabbage leaves. I examined my lunch bag. I had finished my roll and milk, but I still had a banana and an orange. I pulled them from the paper bag.

"Here," I said, holding out the fruit. "You can have these."

"And you can have this, you little louse," George said.

A few stunned moments had gone by, and I could actually see George walking away from me, back across the yard toward Chink Alberg, before I realized that my banana had joined George's fist in delivering the belt in the kisser.

I don't feel I should go into my character as of today. Anyway, I don't want to. The years take their toll. But in those days I was not a coward. Until that day in the J.H.S. 64 schoolyard, nobody had ever laid a hand on me without getting paid back. George was the exception. I stood up and went across the yard to the toilet, turned on the tap, and washed the squashed banana from my face. I did it without resentment. The night before, George had been within sight of a medal. I had kicked it away from his outstretched hand. I had earned my humiliation.

Earned it, yes. But liked it, no. Before the bell rang summoning me back upstairs to class, I had taken care of my face by washing it, and I had pulled together the cracks in my ego by adding George Weitz's name to what my mother called her *verbissennah* list. Some day, I didn't know when or how, I would pay him back for that shot in the mouth.

Until that day came, however, I had to cope with my mother. What was I going to do with this stranger who had come out of the woodwork in the Hannah H. Lichtenstein House gym to lose me a medal, lead me into a crazy conference with a couple of Italians behind a window that said

84

Meister's Matzoh Bakery, Inc., and earn me a belt in the kisser from George Weitz? Answer: stall.

This seemed easy enough. Several clearly defined opportunities presented themselves. My weekdays were broken up into neatly defined units.

Morning to three P.M. belonged to J.H.S. 64. From four to six I was in the hands of Rabbi Goldfarb in his *cheder* on Columbia Street. Six-thirty to about seven-thirty was what my mother called "sopper" time. After that, until ten-thirty, I worked in Mr. Lebenbaum's candy store around the corner on Avenue C. The rest was not exactly silence, but close enough: on East Fourth Street you learned very early how to sleep surrounded, like the seed in an avocado, by a fatty layer of outside noises.

As an opportunity for stalling my mother, I saw at once that supper didn't count. My father would be there, at the kitchen table, as he always was. It would be simple enough to avoid my mother merely by concentrating on him. Well, maybe not simple. My father was silent most of the time. The rest of the time, when he came edging timidly into the silence with a remark, what he said was not exactly stop-press news. But he got through his evening meal, as he got through the rest of his life, without creating any tensions around him. No, stalling my mother at that time would not be too difficult.

There was, then, only one danger spot. The hour between my departure from J.H.S. 64 on Ninth Street and my arrival in Rabbi Goldfarb's *cheder* on Columbia Street.

This time was always spent in hurrying from Ninth Street to Fourth, dumping my schoolbooks, downing the glass of milk and slice of honey cake or plate of *eierküchel* my mother had set out for me on the kitchen table, and then either hotfooting it or hitching a wagon ride to Columbia Street. This interlude should have been pleasant. My mother was a rotten cook, true, but at that time I didn't quite appreciate the fact that good cooks were preferable to bad. Food was food. My mother's *eierküchel* sopped up milk satisfactorily, and her honey cake, like anybody else's honey cake, was sweet. Unfortunately, she acted about them the way a gold miner in a Jack London story watched the assayer test the ore the weary prospector had managed to bring back to civilization.

First bite. My mother: "It's good?" Me: "Wait till I chew it." I chew it. My mother: "Well?" Me: "Yeah." My mother: "Yeah what?" Me: "Yeah, it's good." My mother: "That's all you can say?" Me, in English: "No, but that's all you're going to hear." My mother: "Speak so I can understand." Me: "I said it's the best honey cake you ever made." My mother: "So why do you take such small bites?" I take a big bite. My mother: "Don't eat so fast. You'll get sick."

I never had. But this just might be the day. It was a risk I decided not to run. When the three o'clock bell rang, I did not go home. Carrying my schoolbooks, I headed down Avenue C. I got as far as Second Street before an ice wagon came clopping along, heading my way. In those days ice wagons were the only vehicles in the neighborhood that had a nice low-slung wooden step on the back. I hopped on. The horses made good time. Too good. When I hopped off in front of Rabbi Goldfarb's *cheder,* I was early. I could tell by the garbage cans on the sidewalk.

Today, of course, I own a wristwatch. If I forget to wind it, I can always, as I move around town, learn the time of day by looking up at the Paramount clock or at the jittery little device in front of the IBM Building on Madison. Even in those days the clock atop the Con Edison tower on Fourteenth

Street was considered pretty accurate. But to see the Con Edison tower from the arena in which I spent my early years you had to go up to Avenue A for a clear view north, and that was going a bit far to learn it was suppertime. Aside from the J.H.S. 64 school bells, therefore, which were as inexorably accurate as the East River tides, the only reliable timepiece to which I had access were the two garbage cans in front of Rabbi Goldfarb's *cheder*.

The *cheder* was located on the top floor of a three-story faded red brick building. It looked a little peculiar, to me anyway, among the crumbling, crowded, leaning-against-each-other six-story dirty gray tenements of Columbia Street. The street floor was occupied by a stable. Here were housed the horses used by local distributors of ice and coal and by the many undertakers who did business in the area.

Above the stable, on the second floor, a heavily bearded scroll writer and his wispily bearded assistants worked on lettering the Torahs that were ordered for presentation to different synagogues on special occasions, and the prayer cloths, embossed prayer books, and phylacteries that were the traditional gifts from parents to sons at their bar mitzvah ceremonies. The top floor of the building was used as a synagogue on Saturdays and special holidays by a burial society composed of immigrants from a small town in the Ukraine, who were held in contempt by my mother. Russian Jews? *Pfeh!* She didn't exactly spit. After all, she did all the cleaning around the house. But she made her point.

Years before I met him, Rabbi Goldfarb, who may or may not have come to America from this Ukrainian town, seemed to have grasped the fact that six days a week, not counting weeks containing special holidays, the burial society's top-floor synagogue was not used. He made some sort of rent deal with the burial society, and established his afternoon school in their quarters. When my mother enrolled me, Rabbi Goldfarb had a reputation on East Fourth Street as one of the best *melameds* in the business.

This meant his teachings took hold. He could be counted on to turn a "nice Jewish boy"—a term employed by all parents for all sons even if the little bastards had already displayed the interests of Jack the Ripper and the proclivities of Boss Tweed—into a "good Jew," a term that didn't exactly defy definition but certainly resisted it. More accurately, nobody bothered to make the definition. Why bother? Who wasted time defining Mt. Everest? There it was. A great big fat mountain. There we all were. Good solid unimpeachable Jews.

During the day, while I and the rest of his pupils were soaking up America's gentile culture in schools like J.H.S. 64, Rabbi Goldfarb moved through the neighborhood, the way veins of fat marble a good steak, performing good works. He presided at funerals. He cemented friable marriage relationships. He advised troubled mothers. He read the riot act to troublesome sons. He helped arrange the bringing over of relatives from Europe. For all these services he received a fee, of course, but he was famous for leaving the size of his emoluments to the discretion of the people he served. Not so with his fees for teaching in his *cheder*. These were fixed as strictly as his rules about punctuality.

Rabbi Goldfarb always arrived at his *cheder* sometime between three-forty-five and four o'clock. His pupils were due at the same time. It was not essential that he get to class ahead of them. There was nothing to prepare. Whatever it took to transform a nice Jewish boy into a good Jew, Rabbi Goldfarb had it all in his head. The few minutes between his arrival and the time his big silver onion watch showed four o'clock, he spent in hanging up his coat, visiting a hall toilet that would have been spurned by the men and women imprisoned in the Black Hole of Calcutta, and polishing up his chair rung.

This piece of wood, about twenty inches long, was to Rabbi Goldfarb's life as a pedant what Excalibur was to Arthur as a king. Rabbi Goldfarb twirled it as a badge of office. He used it as a pointer. He polished it as a tension reliever. And he employed it as an instrument of punishment.

The causes for punishment were two: stupidity and tardiness. A few moments before four sharp, Rabbi Goldfarb emerged from the toilet, buttoning his fly, and started the day's lesson with whatever pupils were present. Whenever the door opened, after his watch showed four o'clock, Rabbi Goldfarb would dart forward, and without listening to the inevitable explanation or even giving the offender an identifying glance, begin to swing his chair rung. He always aimed for the ankles. He rarely missed. When he did, Rabbi Goldfarb took another cut at the offender. He never missed twice. It hurt like hell, but he made his point: nice Jewish boys who expect to grow up to be good Jews get to *cheder* on time.

I always did. After my first experience with Rabbi Goldfarb's chair rung, anyway. In fact, after that I was always early. It was easy enough to tell just how early by a glance at the two garbage cans on the sidewalk near the entrance to the building.

It was a time when few people in that neighborhood used tinned foods. And most bottles were returnable for the deposit. Nobody threw them out. So that garbage cans usually contained mostly soft materials. Almost everybody, however, used coal for heating. So did the owner of the stable on the ground floor of this building. As a result, on top of most garbage cans there was usually a mound of ashes. East Side ashes in those days always contained pieces of black rock that had been dumped into the coal by the seller to fatten his profit and, naturally, had refused to burn for the customer. Every boy who arrived early for Rabbi Goldfarb's *cheder* paused at the garbage cans to pick through the ashes for one or more of these black rocks before he went upstairs. These rocks were our only protection against the rats.

On the afternoon following the All-Manhattan rally eliminations, when I hopped off the ice wagon in front of Rabbi Goldfarb's *cheder* on Columbia Street, the ashes on top of the garbage cans were two symmetrical mounds. The conical grayish-white masses had not yet been disturbed. So I knew I had arrived first, and knew it was not yet a quarter to four. I pawed through the ashes at the top of both garbage cans and selected four black rocks. They were the best I had ever found. The smallest was as big as a baseball.

I shoved three of them under the straps of my schoolbag the way a Cossack might have shoved bullets into his bandolier. Holding the fourth rock in my hand, I started up the stairs. I always felt, when I did this, as though I were a character in a novel by James Fenimore Cooper stalking Indians through the Primeval Forest instead of rats up a flight of Columbia Street stairs. The stairs were so decayed that the wood sank under my feet. I always hopped my way up fast, from step to step, afraid that if I remained in one spot too long, my weight would tear through the step below. This gave me the feeling I was climbing a rope ladder. I moved upward as though I were tunneling through a layer cake from the baking pan to the top layer of icing. Up through the ground-floor smell of manure. Up through the second-floor smell of unwashed Talmudic scholars. And finally out into the complicated stink of Rabbi Goldfarb's domain. I tiptoed across the rotted wood of the landing and put my ear to the *cheder* door. Like Chingachgook with his ear to the ground, I could feel my heart respond with a leap of excitement. At the other side of the warped and cracked plywood slab I could hear the rustling sounds of my quarry. There was no doubt about it. I had arrived first.

Crouched low, my ammunition at the ready, I eased the door open and peered in. The synagogue in which Rabbi Goldfarb conducted his *cheder* was a single large room. It looked like the illustration in my school history book that showed the log cabin birthplace of Abraham Lincoln. Whatever had been done to the rough wooden boards since they had been put up to form these walls had been done not by paint but by the weather. The floor could have been brought untouched from the prairie. It was as full of holes as a Swiss cheese.

One hole slowly gathered my roving glance like iron filings drawn to a magnet. It was near the gold-embroidered purple curtains that shielded the closet or ark in which the Ukrainian burial society kept its two Torahs. At the edge of this hole crouched a big rat, who was nibbling away at the edges of the hole as though the floorboards were Mary Jane candy bars. Who could blame it? Nothing else in the building was edible.

Gently I pulled the door wide enough to give me a free, full swing. I took aim and let go. I did not achieve the success George Weitz had scored the night before with the tip of his Morse flag when my mother's shove sent Mr. O'Hare tumbling backward in the Hannah H. Lichtenstein gym. But it was not a bad shot. I winged the bastard. He squealed, leaped, and disappeared down the hole. All his pals went with him down their own holes.

Stepping through the door, I could hear them slithering underfoot and through the walls, playing what sounded like a pretty fast-paced basketball game on their way back to wherever they came from so they could rest up until Rabbi Goldfarb's class left for the day and they were free to come back and start feeding again.

To encourage their departure, I fired two of my remaining three rocks into different corners of the room. They hit nothing but the walls. The booming noise, however, was very satisfactory. The door behind me opened. Rabbi Goldfarb came in as I was winding up for my last shot.

"All right, enough," he said. "Get the *Chimish*."

The *Chimish* was a set of battered texts from which Rabbi Goldfarb taught Jewish history by leading his pupils in chanting aloud every day a new section of Our Heritage. The books were kept in an old Sheffield Farms milk-bottle crate on top of the gold-embroidered curtains so they would be out of reach of the rats. By the time I brought the crate down, Rabbi Goldfarb had disappeared into the toilet and about a dozen other pupils had arrived. Each boy carried at least one or two rocks. These were fired against the walls, even though no rats were visible, while I set out the *Chimish* texts on the three long tables that formed the instruction area of the *cheder*.

Except by sight, I did not know any of my classmates in Rabbi Goldfarb's *cheder*. They came from below Delancey Street or east of Goereck Street, and they went to schools like J.H.S. 97 on Mangin Street and to settlement houses like the Educational Alliance on East Broadway. I had nothing against "97" or the "Edgie," but between J.H.S. 64 and the Hannah H. Lichtenstein House, my life was pretty full. I had no desire to enlarge my horizons, or dilute my pleasures in what I did have. These kids were not friends. They were just a group of voices with which I did a little chanting every day in a Columbia Street outpost of my world because my mother thought it was good for me. I had never even bothered to learn the names of my fellow chanters. In a vague way I identified them in my mind by their physical characteristics. Sweat Nose. Wart Face. Four Eyes. Fat Ass. Knock Knees. It came as no surprise to me one day to learn that I was known as Wishbone. I was tall for my age, thin for any age, and bow-legged.

I slapped down a copy of the *Chimish* in front of each boy, piled the rest at the head of the table, and slipped into my seat as Rabbi Goldfarb came in from the toilet buttoning his fly. He picked up his chair rung, hit the edge of the table, and we were off.

I don't remember how long we were at it. You didn't have to think about what you were chanting to keep Rabbi Gold-farb at bay. What he wanted was noise. I remember only that Rabbi Goldfarb had taken his cut at the ankles of three late-comers, and we were all bellowing our way into "*Ah-ahl kayne, ibber dehn, arroll siffisoyim, ungeshtuppte leftzin,*" when my mother came in.

The chanting stopped. Rabbi Goldfarb smiled. Anyway, I think he did, because he was always obsequious to parents. But you couldn't prove it, because smiling is done with the face and Rabbi Goldfarb had no face. What he had was a furry black fedora with a greasy band that seemed to start somewhere near the ceiling and came down to his eyebrows, and a thick black beard that started under his eyeballs and came down to his plump little belly. In between could be seen a blob of pink. It didn't look like anything I had ever previously seen attached to a human body by natural growth, but it must have been a nose because Rabbi Goldfarb was constantly blowing it into a red bandanna with dirty gray polka dots that suggested they had once been white. Above the blob of pink were two watery fried eggs with tiny black yolks that were undoubtedly his eyes.

"I'm sorry to interrupt," my mother said. "I came to see if my son is here."

Rabbi Goldfarb pointed the chair rung at me. He could have been the owner of a famous collection of paintings who at the end of a guided tour for a distinguished visitor had paused at last in front of his most prized possession.

"Today," Rabbi Goldfarb said, "your son was the first."

My mother came across to the table and said, "You didn't come home after school."

There was no accusation in her voice. Nor was there even the hint of a question. She had simply stated a fact. I was unaccustomed to this. My mother never stated facts simply. When she got her hands on one, she reissued it to the world, meaning me and my father, like a papal bull framed in electric lights.

"I couldn't," I said. "I got kept in after class. If I'd gone home to leave my books I would have been late for *cheder*."

"He wasn't late," Rabbi Goldfarb said. "He was first."

My mother smiled as though he had told her I stood at the head of the class. "I'm glad," she said. "I don't like he should be late for *cheder*."

The tone of her voice bothered me. I had never heard her sound like this. Like what? I thought. I concentrated. I strug-

gled. Friendly? Relaxed? Gentle? The words all fit, and yet
they didn't even come near what I felt. I was confused the way
I had been confused the night before. The night before, she
had been an astonishing stranger, determined, hard, implac-
ably embarked on a single-minded course of action from the
path of which she swept all opposition with a ruthless hand, a
dose of startling English, and a total disregard for consequences to others. Now, a day later—no, eighteen hours later
—she was another kind of stranger. A feminine creature in a
male world, a little blond thing with bright blue eyes, uneasy
about intruding, hoping for no more than the answer to a question that had been troubling her.

"If all my boys were like yours," Rabbi Goldfarb said, "I
would have no troubles."

My mother smiled again. My stomach jumped as though it
had received a dose of something indigestible and was taking
action to get rid of it before the trouble started. Blond little
thing or not. Big blue eyes or not. She was still my mother.
What was my mother doing in the late afternoon vamping a
hill of greasy fedora and bellybutton-length beard who smelled
like his own toilet?

"Would you do me a favor?" she said.

"A question to ask!" Rabbi Goldfarb said. "Just say what."

"He came here straight from school," my mother said. "The
glass of milk, the plate of *lekach,* I just baked it this morning,
they're standing on the kitchen table. When you finish with
him here, you could maybe tell him he shouldn't go any place
else? He should come right home straight?"

The notion that I would even dream of doing anything else
was astonishing. I mean, to me. Then I saw that it was equally
astonishing to Rabbi Goldfarb. She simpered at him. I know
it sounds foolish, even insane. But I saw it happen. My mother

simpered. And she got what she obviously wanted. Rabbi Goldfarb swung the chair rung at my ankles.

"Ouch!" I yelled.

"You heard your mother!" he thundered.

4

NOBODY HEARD HER more clearly than my father. And nobody seemed more indifferent to what he heard. Not rude. I don't believe he would have dared that. Come to think of it, I believe he would have been incapable of it. My father was polite the way other people are short or tall or red-headed. He couldn't help it. But he managed in his own way to scurry through my mother's fusillade without being gunned down. I did not appreciate his skill, or even understand it, until one day years later, when East Fourth Street was far behind me, I saw some sandpipers on a Pacific beach.

I had never before seen sandpipers. I was lying on the beach, pleasantly dazed by the afternoon sun, watching the surf roll in and wash out. All at once I became aware of these tiny birds, sitting high as lollipops on their matchstick legs. As the surf came in, they raced swiftly toward me up the sand, without fear, their matchsticks twinkling industriously, keeping their feet clear of the water. The foaming edge of the surf rolled slowly to a halt, hesitated, and started washing back to sea. Without pause or hesitation the sandpipers turned and, on perkily hurrying legs, sped after the receding crest of foam. Back and forth, back and forth, like a metronome, without excitement or relief or, so far as I could see, even interest. As though that was all they had to do in life.

My father, of course, had to do more. He had to get up at five in the morning because he was due in the pants shop on Allen Street at seven. The walk took at least a half hour. Between his bowels and his other preoccupations, the hour and a half between five, when he got out of bed, and six-thirty, when he got out of the house, was just about adequate for him to touch all the bases of his routine. If he put his back into it, that is, and pushed. Consider what my father had to do every morning in those ninety predawn minutes.

First, get out of bed without waking my mother. Easy enough, perhaps, for Dolly Madison in the White House. Not on East Fourth Street. Each of the four legs of the bed in which my parents slept was set in an empty Heinz pickle jar full of kerosene. Fourth Street bedbugs were tough. I've seen them come at you as big as olives. I've known them to get up after being whacked with the heel of a shoe, shake themselves, and start coming at you again. But I've never seen one survive my mother's traps. Up the side of the jar, over the edge, down into the moat of kerosene, and it was curtains for the bedbug. The only trouble with this device was that the slightest movement by anybody in the bed made the four jars start tinkling like a carillon. My father didn't weigh much, true. But what got him noiselessly off the nuptial couch every morning was not his weight, or lack of it, but his skill as an avoider. He twinkle-toed his way out of that bed every morning like a sandpiper on a beach skittering away from the edge of rolling surf.

But that was only the beginning. Now he sneaked his dose of Saratoga #2 from the case under the bed, got it out into the kitchen, and drained the bottle. All this had to be done fast. If the stuff didn't work by the time he left the house, he got caught on the walk to Allen Street. That's why my father always cut across Hamilton Fish Park on his way to work. The free toilets were open twenty-four hours a day.

So, he obviously felt, were my mother's eyes and ears. Everything he did was done with one foot poised in the direction of escape from her. After the bottle of Saratoga #2 went down, he prepared his breakfast: a cup of hot water into which he poured two tablespoonfuls of honey, and a tumbler full of "sweet" cream, which he purchased every evening on his way home from work and kept overnight on the window sill outside the kitchen to prevent it from going bad. The hot water and honey and the cream were for his *moogin,* the top of his intestinal tract, as the Saratoga #2 was for its bottom. He had no fears for the sections in between. It was not unlike taking care of a transcontinental railroad by every day industriously polishing the furniture in the New York and San Francisco terminals without paying the slightest attention to the three thousand miles of track in between.

I don't think my mother ever thought about my father's preoccupation with his bowels. He bought his own cream and honey and Saratoga #2 out of the meager sum she allowed him as pocket money each week from his wages. Once the stove was going, it cost nothing to heat water. Financially, my father and his internal organs were self-supporting. They were no concern of hers.

Yet my father lived his life as though convinced that if my mother caught him preparing his breakfast, she would at once notify the immigration authorities and have him deported. The slightest sound from the bedroom would send him scurrying from the stove, where he was waiting for the water to boil, into the front room, where he pretended to be busily lacing his shoes, until the sounds out in the bedroom died down.

With the Saratoga #2, the hot water, the honey, and the sweet cream inside him, he would twinkle-toe out of the house, pumping his skinny legs desperately, like a sandpiper racing up the beach away from the pursuing surf. How he walked the pavements to Allen Street—fast? slow? head high? crouched over?—I don't know. I had never paid much attention to my father outdoors. He came alive for me only in the evening. I use the word "alive" advisedly. After all, he did breathe. Rather noisily, in fact. You could hear him coming up the stairs. Not because he panted. I don't recall that there was ever anything wrong with his lungs. But as he climbed he helped himself along with a sort of gasping singsong: "Puff-puff-puff," he chanted. "Puff-puff-puff. Puff-puff-puff." It sounded somewhat like a prayer. As though he were seeking divine help to get him through another "sopper" time. God knows (I'm told He does) my father needed it.

Not that anything overtly unpleasant ever took place between the time my father came home from work and I came home from Rabbi Goldfarb's *cheder,* and when I went off to my job in Mr. Lebenbaum's candy store. It was merely that my mother ran our home the way Charles Laughton ran the *Bounty.* Nobody had to be flogged or put on bread and water. The captain's authoritative presence was always around you.

It kept my father moving. If my mother approached the kitchen sink as he was washing up, my father swayed out of her reach toward the window. When my mother brought a dish from the stove to our table, he swayed away from her toward the wall. When she came back to clear away the dishes, he went to the front room to get his *Jewish Daily Forward.* The performance was not without grace. It was a little like being caught for an hour and a half in a ballet choreographed not to music but to invisible steel runners to which the participants were lashed inexorably until the end of the performance.

This always came, for me anyway, when I left for Mr. Lebenbaum's candy store. There was, however, one exception on the nights when my father attended the regular monthly meeting of the Erste Neustadter Krank und Unterstitzing Verein. Translation: First Neustadter Sick and Benevolent Association.

This was a burial society the members of which were all men who, like my father, had come to America from the environs of Neustadt in Austria. I had no idea at the time about the purpose of the organization. Almost half a century later, when my father died and I paid my first visit to the Battenberg Funeral Home in the Borough of Queens, I learned the function of a burial society: to defray the cost of the funeral of one of its members to the extent of fifty dollars.

My father paid monthly dues to the First Neustadter Sick and Benevolent Association for sixty-six years. His funeral, a modest one, set me back about fifteen hundred dollars. It would have cost me closer to sixteen hundred if the First Neustadter Sick and Benevolent Association had not come through with the aforementioned fifty dollars. For anybody who is not near the top of his class in long division, I have worked out the arithmetic. Fifty dollars divided by sixty-six years of contributions comes to roughly seventy-five cents a year. I say roughly, because I have worked it out to only four decimal points: seventy-five cents and .7575 of the seventy-sixth cent.

Seventy-five and three-quarters cents a year are, as the phrase makers put it, better than nothing. I know some phrase makers who would say seventy-five and three-quarters cents a year are not to be sneezed at. I am not sneezing at them because this small statistic—the result of dividing fifty dollars by sixty-six years of contributions—gives a remarkably accurate picture of my father's grasp of fiscal matters. He felt about his visits to the monthly meetings of the First Neustadter Sick and Benevolent Association as the devout Moslem thinks about his pilgrimage to Al-Medinah and Mecca. Only death could have stopped him from making the journey.

Only death or my mother.

What makes that evening memorable, the evening after the semi-finals for the 1927 All-Manhattan rally, is that my mother did something as odd in our own house as she had done the night before in the Hannah H. Lichtenstein House gym.

Supper was finished. My mother came to the kitchen table to collect our dishes. My father swayed away toward the wall, and in the same graceful movement, up out of his chair and into the bedroom.

"What are you doing?" my mother said.

"Getting dressed," he said.

"Dressed for what?" my mother said.

"The society meeting," my father said from the bedroom. "It's First Neustadter tonight."

"Not tonight," my mother said.

My father appeared in the bedroom doorway. "Sure tonight," he said. "The postcard came last week."

He disappeared into the bedroom and came back with a postcard. I don't know if second-class mail had at that time been invented. If it had, no examples of it had yet penetrated to East Fourth Street. Aside from occasional letters sent by my mother's relatives in Hungary and my father's *mishpoche* in Austria, only three things came out of our mailbox in the hall downstairs every month: the gas bill, my copy of *Boys' Life,* and the postcard reminding my father of the monthly First

Neustadter Sick and Benevolent Association meeting. He waved it at my mother.

"No," my mother said.

"What do you mean no?" my father said. It is a difficult question to ask in the sort of tone one gathers Oliver Twist used when he held up his bowl, but my father swung it. He said, "It says here on the card tonight is the meeting."

"What it says on the card you can forget," my mother said. "What you should remember is what I'm telling you. No meeting. Not tonight. Tonight you're staying home."

"But I have to go to the meeting," my father said.

"Next month you can go twice," my mother said. "Tonight you're staying home."

"Why?" my father said.

"I want somebody here at home," my mother said. She jerked her head in my direction. "Something might happen tonight while he's at Lebenbaum's."

5

MY MOTHER'S CONCERN for what might happen while I was at Lebenbaum's was as puzzling as her appearance earlier that day in Rabbi Goldfarb's *cheder*. What could happen at Lebenbaum's had been happening with unexciting regularity day after day during the eight months I had been working in the candy store. Aside from the dollar a night Mr. Lebenbaum paid my mother for my services, I did not see how anything that went on in the store around the corner could interest her. Certainly none of it seemed to offer even a remote reason for keeping my father from attending his monthly meeting of the Erste Neustadter Krank und Interstitzing Verein.

Not because Mr. Lebenbaum had confided in me, but because after eight months certain aspects of a situation in which you are imbedded tend to become clear, I knew that my boss was disappointed in his candy store.

Abe Lebenbaum was a bachelor in his late thirties. He lived with his mother on the top floor of the Avenue C tenement in which his candy store shared the street floor with Baltuch's Hardware Store. Abe Lebenbaum's personal history was not unlike that of my father. He, too, had come to America shortly before the First World War from some town in Austria. Both men had evaded the draft. My father by getting married and producing me. Abe Lebenbaum by hacking off his left thumb with a meat cleaver borrowed from Shumansky's chicken store. Like thousands of other immigrants, both men had been hustled—nobody went voluntarily; everybody was steered into the shops by other immigrants who were already enmeshed—into the men's clothing sweatshops of Allen Street. Here the similarity between Abe Lebenbaum and my father grows fuzzy.

With the savings from his first American wages Abe sent for his Austrian mother. I think my father would have done the same but he didn't have a mother. Abe began to be dissatisfied with his long days over a sewing machine in the Allen Street pants factory. My father may have been dissatisfied, too. But he had a wife and a son. He was forced, or felt the compulsion, to bring home a few dollars at the end of every week to get the family food on the table. Abe Lebenbaum obviously had to do the same. He had a mother up there on the sixth floor of his tenement. But he had something else, something my father did not have: a feeling that this was not the way things should be.

Abe Lebenbaum's view of America, as I heard him express it many time to cronies in the candy store, started where every immigrant's view started: it was the *goldene medina*. Streets paved with gold. Public fountains spouting milk and honey. Every man a millionaire. Every man, that is, who was serious about becoming one.

Nobody was more serious than Abe Lebenbaum. It did not take him long to appraise the gap between his seriousness and his achievement. He took a good hard look around him. Between East Fourth Street and Allen Street there was a surprising amount to see. What Abe saw most clearly was that the people who came closest to his notion of a millionaire were those who did not work for others, as he was doing, but owned their own businesses. The achievement of this clarity of vision coincided with the death of the owner of the candy store on the street floor of the tenement in which Abe and his mother lived. The widow wanted to get out. By borrowing the purchase price from several relatives, Abe got in.

He didn't exactly get in over his head, but he got in deep enough to make breathing difficult. The hard breathing provided a lesson in economics. Abe had not earned much in the pants shop on Allen Street, but what he had taken in had been his to carry home, and once he got home he could stop thinking about the shop until he had to show up for work the next morning. Now that he owned his own business, things were different.

Abe had no way of knowing what he earned. He learned soon enough a lot of things he wished he did not have to learn. When he took in a penny for a Tootsie Roll, for example, or a nickel for a malted, or eleven cents for a pack of Sweet Caporals, Abe knew that a piece of that penny or nickel, a part of those eleven cents, had to go to the jobber who had sold him the candy, the malted powder, the chocolate syrup, and the cigarettes. Fair enough, of course. Why should a jobber give Abe Lebenbaum free Tootsie Rolls? He didn't expect charity. He was a businessman. An American businessman. Abe expected to be treated like every other American businessman. He was. And that was the trouble.

Like every other businessman Abe had to pay rent for the place in which he did business. He had to pay for the electricity that enabled him to display his wares. For a charwoman to come in and sweep. For a janitor to cart away his rubbish. For things Abe did not understand and so had to pay a bookkeeper who came in once a week to write the details into complicated forms that were then mailed to City Hall.

If all this added up to a lesson in the economics of the *goldene medina,* it also provided a lesson in what happens to the human body when it is transplanted from a small town in Austria to Avenue C in New York. Making a living by working from seven in the morning to six at night in an Allen Street pants factory was tough. Making a living by opening a candy store at six in the morning, so men on their way to jobs in Allen Street could buy their cigarettes, and keeping the candy store open until one in the morning, so the local whores would not be deprived of the only telephone in the neighborhood through which they conducted their business, was something else again. In fact, it was impossible. About a year after he stopped being an American sweatshop slave and became an American businessman, Abe Lebenbaum collapsed.

That's how I got my job.

Walking toward it the night after my mother caused Troop 244 to lose the elimination finals in One-Flag Morse for the 1927 All-Manhattan rally, I was not so scared as I had been in the morning on my way to school. My big worry then had been what I was going to say to George Weitz, and George had solved that during lunch hour in the schoolyard by giving me the shot in the mouth that had landed him on my *verbissenneh* list.

I never worried about people on that list. Once they were on it they became, in my mind, immobilized. There was nothing more they could do to me. They were now on a shelf, waiting their turn for whatever it was I could one day do to them.

With George out of the way I was free, as I walked up Fourth Street toward Avenue C, to try to make some sense out of three events that made no sense to me at all. One, the visit

107

to Mr. Imberotti and his son the night before in Meister's
Matzoh Bakery. Two, my mother's appearance that afternoon
in Rabbi Goldfarb's *cheder*. And three, her refusal to allow my
father to attend his monthly burial society meeting tonight.
The sequence made no sense. But my mother always made
sense. I had my Aunt Sarah's word for it.

"Inside her own head, I mean," my Aunt Sarah from New
Haven said to me years later. "The trouble was she never
bothered to explain where she was going. When your mother
made up her mind to do something, she figured out the steps
she had to go through to do it, and then she started out. If you
were lucky, you didn't get in her way."

Well, on that evening I was still lucky. I had not yet got in
her way. She had merely ruined my chance at the All-Manhattan One-Flag Morse medal, and then made me look like a
horse's ass in front of the *yoinehs* in Rabbi Goldfarb's *cheder*.
My father, on the other hand, had not been so lucky. She had
just switched signals on the subject of his First Neustadter Sick
and Benevolent Society meeting. Well, that was his lookout.
Life with my mother might have proved interesting to Clar-
ence Day. To me it was a matter of every man for himself.

"Hello," I said when I came into the candy store.

"You're late," Mrs. Lebenbaum said.

Abe Lebenbaum's mother would have said the same thing
if I had arrived in midafternoon. "You're late" were the only
two English words she could pronounce.

"No, I'm not," I said to her in Yiddish. I pointed to the
twenty-four-inch-in-diameter octagon-shaped walnut-framed
Seth Thomas on the wall under the Moxie sign. "It's not even
seven-thirty," I said. "I'm early."

"A brightly lighted and gloriously glowing blessing on your
shining head," Mrs. Lebenbaum said in Yiddish. "That a boy

your age should understand in his heart how much my Abe needs his sleep, it's *tokke* a miracle."

The miracle was not that I understood how much Abe Lebenbaum needed sleep. The miracle was that his mother did not seem to know how little he got. If Abe Lebenbaum had been born forty years later, he could have thumbed his nose at the economics of the candy store business. Let the jobbers take their Tootsie Rolls and drop dead. Or, preferably, their O. Henrys, which in those days cost a dime and were as big as a stunted Hebrew National salami. If fate had been a little more kind with the calendar and made Abe Lebenbaum a young man of today, he could have had his choice of the hero's role in almost any current Swedish movie or American best-seller. The tragedy of Abe Lebenbaum's life was that he hit the scene before his time. Think of it. This was only 1927, and already he was a full-fledged, in-there-pitching, totally dedicated sex maniac.

His physical collapse, which brought me onto Abe Lebenbaum's payroll, was attributed to inhumanly long hours of overwork behind the cracked marble counter of his candy store. No man can make chocolate malteds and sell Sweet Caps nineteen hours a day and remain on his feet. Or so East Fourth Street was led to believe. Hiring me as his assistant did get Abe Lebenbaum off his feet, but not quite in the manner the people of our neighborhood thought.

After I appeared on the scene, the schedule in the candy store went like this. Abe opened up at six in the morning. He remained on duty until eleven. His mother came down to the candy store at eleven and relieved him. He went upstairs for a snack and a nap. At one in the afternoon he came down and relieved his mother. Abe remained on duty until about six-thirty, when his mother came down to take over until I arrived, then he went back upstairs for supper and his second nap. At ten he came down so I could go home, and he stayed on the job until one in the morning, when he closed up shop.

That was the schedule.

Now to put this schedule together with the sources of income that kept the candy store going. These were three. First, of course, there was the sale of candies, malteds, soft drinks, cigarettes, and an occasional nickel cigar. Second, the slot machine in the back room. And third, the telephone booth in the far corner near the back door.

The relationship of the sale of Tootsie Rolls, malteds, and cigarettes to Abe Lebenbaum's profit was not unlike that of a dripping faucet on Riverside Drive to the water level of the Hudson River up at Poughkeepsie. The slot machine, on the other hand, was very important. When the collector came around every Saturday morning and unlocked the steel drawer at the bottom, Abe Lebenbaum received one half the nickels that had accumulated during the week. But it was the telephone booth that kept him in business.

The only private phone in the area was in the home of Dr. Weitz on Fourth Street between Avenue D and Avenue C. He needed it for his business. And he could afford it, of course, because in the end his patients paid for it. But it was not available to the residents of the neighborhood. I mean a resident of East Fourth Street could not ring the doorbell of the Weitz brownstone and say to George's father, "I'd like to use your phone, please, here's a jit." A jit was a nickel. Derivation: the fare for a ride on what was then the city's main form of public transportation: the jitney bus. Okay, so Dr. Weitz has been ruled out, but the resident of East Fourth Street still wanted to communicate with someone by telephone. What other avenues were available to him? He could go up to Lesser's drugstore, on the corner of Avenue C and Eighth Street. Mr. Lesser had a phone booth. Or he could use the phone booth in Abe Lebenbaum's candy store.

Very few people did either. Making telephone service available to all on East Fourth Street was not unlike dotting filling stations all over the Garden of Eden. Who needed it? Answer: the Zabriskie sisters.

When I first became aware of the Zabriskie sisters, there were four of them. Anyway, that's what people on East Fourth Street said, or believed. But I never saw the Zabriskie sisters in a group. Except as a piece of gossip on the block, therefore, I don't really know of my own knowledge that shortly before I joined Troop 244 one of the Zabriskie sisters married a barge captain who put in regularly with his loads of lumber at the Fourth Street dock, and went to live with him on Staten Island.

The three that remained, Lya, Pauline, and Marie, I saw quite frequently. But I always saw them one at a time. I was never sure which one I was seeing because they all looked alike: short, squat, and solid. Not uncomely, but not fragile. Built close to the ground and, with undergarments of rubberized strength, built up. Bright red hair, obviously dyed, of a crinkly steel-wool type. I can see the Zabriskie sisters now, looking exactly like the wardrobe mistresses in Warner Bros. movies starring Ruby Keeler about backstage life. Sex symbols change, of course, and I was not a very good judge of the time. What kept me awake at night were images of Viola Dana locked in complicated contortions with a senior patrol leader of Troop 244 wearing a uniform that looked, from the merit badges sewed to the sleeve, suspiciously like mine. But the Zabriskie sisters must have had something, because whatever it was they called their mouse trap, the world of the time certainly made a beaten path to their door. It was on the sixth floor of the tenement next to the one in which Abe Lebenbaum lived with his mother.

I would not be surprised, since they were so similar in appearance and I never saw more than one at a time, to be told at this late date that there had been only one Zabriskie sister, a lady who had moved around fast and preferred to be known as three. I wouldn't be surprised, but I wouldn't believe it, either. No one person could have handled the traffic that moved through that sixth-floor tenement flat.

This traffic was controlled by the telephone booth in Abe Lebenbaum's candy store. I'm not saying that during my hours on the job, I didn't sell an occasional Tootsie Roll or once in a while whip up a malted. But most of my time was spent running to the phone booth and taking messages for the Zabriskie sisters. The bell started to ring while Mrs. Lebenbaum was knotting the bandanna more securely under her chin. She lived in constant fear that when she stepped out into the street, some random gust of wind would blow the *sheitl* from her head. Hurrying down the store to the phone booth, I called back across my shoulder to the old lady, "Where's Abe?"

I knew where Abe was, but it was part of the ritual of my job to pretend I didn't.

"He went upstairs a little early," Mrs. Lebenbaum said. "I came down early so he could go up and get a little extra sleep. The poor boy, he's so tired."

He'd be more tired by the time she got upstairs. I grabbed the phone.

"Hello, Pauline?"

True, my voice had not yet changed, but what kind of an idiot was this to mistake me for Pauline?

"No," I said. "This is the candy store downstairs."

"Oh, you the kid takes the messages?"

"That's right."

"Listen, this is Ted Werner."

"Wait a minute. Let me get the pencil." It was tucked into the small notebook Abe Lebenbaum kept in the clip nailed under the shelf below the instrument. I pulled it out and flipped it open. "Okay," I said. "Who'd you say?"

"Ted Werner. I wanna come over tonight."

"Pauline?"

"Yeah."

"Hold it." I checked the reservations Abe Lebenbaum had scribbled during the day. "Not till eleven o'clock," I said.

"Eleven o'clock? It's not even seven-thirty now. What the hellmy gonna do until eleven?"

I refrained from making the obvious suggestion, and turned the page.

"How about Marie?" I said.

"Not again, that broad. Jesus. How about Lya?"

"Hold it," I said.

I did not have to thumb another page. All I had to do was look at the clock. Lya was Abe Lebenbaum's current favorite. I pulled my head back into the booth and made a calculation. Mrs. Lebenbaum had said her son had gone upstairs early. When it was Pauline or Marie, he always went upstairs at six-fifteen. But whatever it was Abe did with Lya did not take as long. With Lya he said I should give him a half hour. Thirty-five minutes to be on the safe side. Abe Lebenbaum was devoted to his mother. He made it a point every night to get out of the Zabriskie flat, scoot across the roof to his own tenement, get down to the flat in which he lived with his mother, and be seated at her kitchen table, eating the evening meal she had set out for him, before she came up from the candy store after I relieved her at seven.

"How soon can you get over?" I said into the phone.

"I'm on Fourteenth Street," Mr. Ted Werner said. "Say a half hour?"

"That's fine," I said. "Werner, you said?"

"Yeah, Ted Werner."

"Okay," I said, writing down his name. "Please be on time. She's very busy." I came out of the booth and said to Mrs. Lebenbaum, "Could you wait a few minutes? I have to deliver a message."

"Could I wait?" the little old lady said. "Of course I could wait. What's more important than business?"

I don't know if she completely understood the nature of the business, but I'm pretty sure she knew the telephone messages helped pay the rent on the store. She had told me many times that she regretted her inability to speak English because when she was alone in the store, she couldn't answer the phone, and she was sure this meant a loss of revenue. Actually, it didn't. Most calls for the Zabriskie sisters came during the evening, when I was on duty, or later, when Abe Lebenbaum came down to relieve me. Between the two of us, Abe and I booked them through the night. Abe himself took all their spare time, for which he did not pay. The girls could not have made a living without his phone booth, and if it had not been for the quarter he charged them for every message we took and logged into the notebook under the shelf in the phone booth, he probably would have had to sell out and go back to the pants shop on Allen Street.

"Be right back," I said to Mrs. Lebenbaum.

"A blazing delight on your golden head," the old lady said. "Don't run or you'll fall."

But I did run. The prosperity of the Zabriskie sisters depended on timing. I was out of breath when one of them opened the door for me. I had given up long ago trying to figure out which was which.

"For Lya," I said. "Half past seven. A guy named Werner."

"Half past seven," the sister in the doorway muttered, fumbling in the pocket of her red and green kimono. "Werner."

She pulled out her small leather purse, snapped it open, fished up a quarter, and gave it to me. Even though I was out of breath, I ran all the way down the six flights of stairs and back to the candy store. I hated to leave Mrs. Lebenbaum alone in the store with the ringing phone. The sound made her nervous. As though the store was a sack of flour and the ringing phone was a hole through which the contents were running out. When I came into the store the phone was ringing, but that was not what made me nervous. What made me nervous was the sight of my mother and father standing at the marble counter. They were talking to Mrs. Lebenbaum across the seltzer taps. Anyway, my mother was talking. My father was swaying away from her, as though he had been nailed to the floor at her side but was trying to dissociate himself from whatever she was cooking up. I stopped in the doorway.

"Benny, answer!" Mrs. Lebenbaum shouted. "Answer!"

I ran down to the store and into the phone booth and answered. I don't know if I answered properly. I had a dim feeling it was a call for Pauline, and the man wanted to spend the night next Tuesday, and I must have written it down properly in the notebook, because I don't recall being bawled out later by Abe Lebenbaum for getting anything wrong. But I handled the transaction automatically, staring all the time out the glass window of the phone booth at the trio up front. I was absolutely certain my mother had not set foot in Abe Lebenbaum's candy store more than once a week on the day she came to collect my salary. I was even more certain my father had never set foot in the store. What were they doing here now?

"Well?"

Not "well," of course. It was actually *Nu?* In a loud accusatory tone. I came out of the phone booth on the double.

"Sorry," I said in Yiddish to Mrs. Lebenbaum. "I had to write down the message."

"Business?" she said.

"Yes," I said.

The little old lady beamed. "Good," she said. "So I'll say good night."

She said it to my mother and my father, then to me, and left the store, one hand on top of her head to keep the *sheitl* from being whipped away by the nonexistent wind.

"You come with me," my mother said.

When I realized she had addressed me, I said, "Now?"

It seemed to me she was repeating the scene we had played the night before when she had appeared in the Hannah H. Lichtenstein gym.

"Yes," my mother said. "Now."

"But I'm working."

I wondered all at once if she had gone crazy. She had certainly acted that way the night before. She had been acting that way today. It occurred to me that maybe that was why she seemed to me to be a stranger.

"Come on," my mother said.

"The store," I said. "I'm all alone in the store."

116

"Never mind the store," she said. "Your father will stay here and take care of the store."

Grasping the insanity of this reply did not stop my mind from clicking into place the answer to why my mother had not allowed my father to go this night to his regular monthly meeting of the First Neustadter Sick and Benevolent Society. She had planned this. She had wanted him available to replace me in Abe Lebenbaum's candy store.

"He can't answer the phone," I said in Yiddish. "He doesn't speak enough English."

"He doesn't have to speak good English to let it ring," my mother said. "Stop wasting time. I'm in a hurry."

6

M Y MOTHER LOOKED STRANGE as she led me around
the corner from the candy store toward our tenement. Her neat little face was set in the tight, turned-
inward look that I had noticed for the first time the night
before when she had led me west from the Hannah H. Lichtenstein House to the meeting with Mr. Imberotti in Meister's
Matzoh Bakery on Lafayette Street. Seeing that look now for
the second time, I saw what Mr. Imberotti's son must have seen
in the kitchen over the matzoh bakery. That look made my
mother look sexy. The notion that my mother was sexy was
irritating. What was she doing looking sexy when I was fighting to retain my sanity by trying to figure out the nature of her
insanity?

All I could see, when we reached the front of our tenement
at the Lewis Street corner, was that she was not heading for
home. My mother took my hand, led me past the entrance to
our house, and across the street to the east side of Lewis.
Where we were heading was obvious. That's what made it
unbelievable.

What made it unbelievable was that night had come down
on East Fourth Street. Not twilight. Not dusk. Not the warm

glow of evening. Night. And it did not descend, or come creeping along on tiny cat feet, or ease its way in like rosy-fingered dawn. Night came to East Fourth Street the way, years later, nuclear fission came to Hiroshima. Boom. End of daylight.

Street lighting provided by the city stopped at the lamppost in the middle of the block between Avenue D and Lewis Street. After that it was every citizen for himself, and if he could see in the dark he had a better chance than most for continuing to be a citizen. At the Lewis Street corner the only available outdoor light came filtering through the dirty windows of Gordon's saloon, and what filtered through was not much more than you could get in the middle of the night from the numbers on the radium dial of an Ingersoll dollar watch. After sundown, at the other side of Lewis Street, just before the dock area began, you either carried your own light, or you did not cross to the other side.

To my knowledge, until that night nobody, at least nobody I knew, had ever crossed to the other side of Lewis Street after dark. Beyond the Lewis Street boundary lay the dock, and the dock was gentile terrain.

This area was divided in half. The left or uptown side belonged to the Forest Box & Lumber Company. The right or downtown side belonged to the Burns Coal Company. Both were supplied by barges that were shoved up and down the river by jaunty little tugs. From my bedroom window I could see them, usually during the day, once in a while at night, easing the barges stacked with lumber or piled with coal into place against the Fourth Street dock moorings, or towing them out empty for the return trip up the river or down. The bargemen were all gentiles. So were the men who worked for the Forest Box & Lumber Company and the Burns Coal Company. This did not stop me and George Weitz and Hot Cakes

119

Rabinowitz and Chink Alberg and the other kids on the block from roaming the dock area. But only during the day. Once night clapped down like a box top on East Fourth Street, the docks and the river became forbidden ground.

I don't know why. Nobody ever told me to stay off the docks at night. Certainly not my mother, who until the night before had never indicated that she knew what I did or where I went when I left the house. My friends and I never discussed it. But they obviously knew what I knew, even though I don't know how I learned it: that once night came crashing down on East Fourth Street, the dock was a dangerous place. We stayed away.

During the past twenty-four hours my mother had done so many things I would never have dreamed her capable of doing that now, when she led me across Lewis Street into the darkness of the dock area, I was not really surprised. I was still confused. I was still convinced that of the two of us, it was she and not I who had gone crazy. But I did not shake my hand loose as she led me toward the river.

It was clearly visible up ahead. The moon, smashing silently in and out of a sky full of cotton-candy clouds, was bright enough to bring little dots of light to the tips of the gently heaving water. When we crossed from the cobblestones that formed the top part of the dock to the timbered section that jutted out into the water, I could see three barges moored in a line on the downtown side. They must have arrived while I was in *cheder,* too late in the afternoon to be unloaded. The piles of coal on the barge decks stood up high against the Brooklyn skyline like great big black ice cream cones turned upside down. Only two barges were tied to the uptown side of the dock. They had apparently come in early that morning, while I was in school, or late the day before. Except for a few scattered boards below the wheelhouse, their stacks of lumber had been unloaded. The third mooring, at the end of the dock, was vacant. My mother led me to the end of the first of the two barges.

"Are you cold?" she said.

This time I was surprised. I'd had the feeling that from the moment we left the candy store she had forgotten my presence.

"No," I said.

"Sit down."

My mother sat down on the broad raised beam that formed the perimeter of the dock. She sat at an angle, so that while her knees pointed toward Brooklyn she faced uptown, looking out across the empty mooring to the place where the river seemed to spread out in all directions, like the splayed end of a lollipop stick that's been chewed too long. I sat down beside her, also at an angle, facing the way she was facing, and all at once I became aware of the silence.

It seemed a curious word, especially in the mind of an adolescent, because as soon as I was off my feet I became aware of all sorts of sounds around me, but they seemed to be knitted together, like the wool of my sweater, to form a protective layer against the noises behind me, the noises that belonged at the other side of Lewis Street, where it was safe to be at night.

I could hear the creaking of the ropes that held the barges to the black iron capstans. And the delicate slap of the water against the piles. Small hissing sounds, like George Weitz spitting out the seeds of an orange he'd chiseled in the schoolyard during lunch hour. And the gentle groaning of the planks under me as the dock fought and held the endless back-and-forth movement of the river. And the choked purr of a tug engine guiding a string of barges somewhere behind me or out of sight up ahead. And the occasional muted boom of a steam whistle. And somewhere far away the tinkle of a bell carrying some message from one part of a barge to another, sounds that had meaning for the mysterious men who worked on the river, but to me were only part of a silence I had never heard before.

Laced through the silence was the sour smell of oil-streaked water. The sharp pleasant stink of rotting piles. The clean cold knife-edge breath of the hosed-down piles of coal. And the gummy odor of the stacked lumber. Over it all, over the smells and the knitted-together silence, the clouds hung low, shoving and poking and wrestling each other as though fighting for the privilege of protecting the moon from wasting too much of its yellow light on me and my mother.

She made a funny little noise, as though she had tried to stifle a cough. I turned to look at her, and I suddenly remembered a picture in my history book. A picture of two Indians on a bluff, staring out across the broad Mississippi, watching LaSalle and his men come down the great big river that until this moment had belonged to them. The breath caught in my throat. My mother had that same look on her face, a look of wonder, as though she was seeing something she had never seen before. Then I heard the low rhythmic chug of a motor. I turned back to the river, and I saw what my mother was seeing.

A motorboat had appeared out of the broad, uptown part of the river, the part that seemed to spread out in all directions like that chewed end of a lollipop stick. The boat was shaped like a small tug, except that there was no smokestack, and it sat very low in the water. I knew most of the river traffic, but I had never before seen a boat like this one. I wondered if that was why my mother was watching it with that strange look on her face, and then I realized that was exactly what this boat was doing. It was cutting across the river at an angle, heading toward us.

I took another look at my mother. The look on her face had changed. Now she seemed pleased. Then the motor cut out and I turned back to the river. The boat was gliding in toward the Fourth Street dock. When it eased past the open mooring, the boat turned gently toward the second barge, almost directly below the place on the raised plank where my mother and I were sitting. The boat slid along the river side of the moored barge. There was a low scraping noise, a slightly louder bump, and then the boat disappeared behind the wheelhouse of the barge.

My mother leaned forward. She was obviously listening. So was I, but all I could hear was the slap of the river against the piles and the creak of the ropes tugging at the capstans.

"Ma," I said.

"Ssshhh!" she said.

It was not exactly a spirited exchange, but the two syllables seemed to unlock something that had been sitting between me and what was happening. All at once I was excited. My mother must have sensed this, because she put her hand on my shoulder as though to soothe me. I think that was the first moment in my fourteen years when it occurred to me that maybe I liked her.

She leaned forward to look down on the barge, and I did the same. Thus I became aware of a new series of sounds from the river side of the barge, at the place where the boat had vanished.

Dull thumps. As though sacks were being dropped on a wooden floor. Several squeaks. Hinges? A stuck window being forced? More squeaks. No, not a window. More like a door. Then a surprising thing happened. The door of the barge

123

wheelhouse, the door facing the dock, came open with an angry snarl of squeaks, exactly like the sounds I had heard from the other side of the wheelhouse. Out the open door came a tall, slender man in a black turtleneck sweater. That's all I could see in the moonlight. A tall silhouette. And a black sweater that came up around his neck. Thin sort of guy. Wiry. He was carrying what looked like a sack, an awkwardly shaped package that seemed familiar. Another thing I noticed. He carried it without effort. The weight didn't bother him.

He dropped the sack on the barge deck and went back into the wheelhouse. A few minutes later he came out again with another package. He dropped it on top of the first and again went back into the wheelhouse. He did this several times, while my mother and I, hidden by the shadows from the wheelhouse, watched. There was something about the way he did it that made pleasant watching. He moved easily, smoothly, and efficiently. Everybody else I had ever seen who carried things did it with resentment. The street cleaners who showed up on our block to empty the garbage cans did it as though they were being forced at the point of a gun to handle something detestable. This man handled these sacks as though he had made them himself and was proud of them. By the time the man came out again and there were six packages on the deck, I knew what it was about them that had looked familiar.

These packages were exactly like the ones I had seen the night before, stacked in the Meister's Matzoh Bakery storeroom through which my mother and I had been led by Mr. Imberotti's son on our way upstairs to the meeting in the kitchen. The same kind of sacking. The same belt of tightly cinched wire around the middle. The same odd, clean, brand-new smell, as though the packages had been put together from freshly woven sacking and wire that had just come out of the factory.

"Call him," my mother said in Yiddish.

"Who?" I said.

"Him."

She nodded down toward the deck of the barge. The tall, wiry man in the black turtleneck sweater was moving back into the wheelhouse. He disappeared.

"What's his name?" I said.

"How should I know?" my mother said. "To call somebody, you have to know his name?"

The man reappeared in the wheelhouse door, lugging the seventh package wrapped in burlap and belted with wire.

"Hey," I said.

In English, of course. Or so I thought. I was too inexperienced to realize that this single syllable is the cornerstone of Esperanto.

"Hey," I said again.

What the man did when he heard my voice told me at once that whatever activity he was engaged in was not one the cops would consider amusing. He dumped the seventh package as though he had suddenly discovered it was red-hot, and he dived back into the wheelhouse.

My mother muttered something savage. In Yiddish, of course. Which is what jolted me. In English it's not so dirty. Before I could figure out if she had addressed me, the heavens, or the man in the turtleneck sweater, she had swung her legs over the side of the dock. And before I could figure out what was happening, my mother had heaved herself down from the dock to the deck of the barge. She gave me no time to worry or think. My mother reached up and dragged me down after her.

"Give your legs a shake," she said.

Shaking her own, she was in the wheelhouse, across the narrow floor, and out the door at the other side before the man in the turtleneck sweater could get his second leg over the edge of the barge. My mother grabbed the first one with both hands and hauled. She tumbled back into my arms. The man in the turtleneck sweater tumbled back into hers.

"Jesus," he said.

Then, for a few moments, nobody said anything. Not counting grunts, that is. Everybody was doing that. All three of us. Then the grunting stopped and we were frozen in a tableau that I think would undoubtedly have been funny to an observer. But there was no observer. Just the three participants. My mother, the tall man in the turtleneck sweater, and me. And we were sitting on the barge deck, in a small circle, the way the teacher used to arrange us in kindergarten class for a game of patty-cake, staring at each other in the moonlight. I was still too confused to be really scared, but whatever fear may have remained with me began to ease away as I stared at the man in the turtleneck sweater.

Looking down on him from the dock, I had noted only his height and the rangy ease with which he moved and jockeyed the wire-belted sacks. Now, sitting on the barge deck, I was looking up into his face. It was like all the rest of him, long and lean, and quite clearly trembling on the edge of some expression to which he didn't seem to be quite sure he wanted to succumb.

Fast, in a matter of seconds, as though my mind were clicking off a series of quick camera shots, I recorded that he was good-looking, his hair was blond as my mother's, he needed a shave, and on the side of his boat, which was tied to the barge rail behind him, appeared a name in large gold letters: *Jefferson Davis II*. Then the man succumbed to the emotion about which he had seemed not to be certain. He started to laugh.

"Jesus," he said. "A broad and a kid."

My mother said to me in Yiddish, "Tell him I want to talk to him."

I told him, and the man said, "Why you talking for her?"

"She's my mother," I said. "She don't speak English."

The laughter eased out of his face. He gave my mother a sharp look, hit me with another one, then said, "Okay, but let's get the hell inside. We don't want an audience."

He stood up, took my mother's hand, and pulled her to her feet. There was something about the way he did it that was not East Fourth Street. Courtliness was still outside my real-life experience.

"This okay?"

The man had led my mother into the wheelhouse and was gesturing toward a bench covered with checked blue-and-white oilcloth.

"What does he want?" my mother said.

"He wants to know if you want to sit there," I said.

My mother gave the man a suspicious look. "What difference does it make where I sit?" she said.

I translated, and the man said, "I want her to be comfortable."

"He wants you to be comfortable," I said to my mother.

She sat down and said, "To be comfortable on a ship a person has to be a fish."

"Okay," the man said. "If you don't mind, now, ma'am, you mind telling me what you're doing here?"

"I want to buy eighteen bottles of whiskey," my mother said.

The man stroked his long blond-fuzzed chin, sent a quick

glance out the wheelhouse window, then said, "From who?"

"From you," my mother said.

"Why do you want to come to me to buy whiskey?" the man said.

He spoke casually, as though he were talking about the weather, and I tried to keep my translations on the same emotional level, but I sensed a tightening in the man's voice. Not in my mother's. She sat up straight on the oilcloth-covered bench, her hands folded in her lap, and spoke quietly but firmly, as though she knew exactly what she was saying because she had given a great deal of thought to her words, and she did not want to be distracted or misunderstood by irrelevant comments.

"Those sacks," she said. She nodded to the pile of sacks the tall man had transferred from his motorboat, carried across the barge through the wheelhouse, and dumped on the dock-side deck. "Grade A milk for Sheffield's store you're not delivering."

After my translation the man took a few steps, four to the door of the wheelhouse, four back, watching his legs as he did so. They were neatly encased in attractive and obviously not inexpensive dark brown boots that laced up to a couple of inches below his knees. Finally he looked up. Gently, through a small smile that did not hide the edge in his voice, the man said, "Ma'am, I think you better tell me who you are."

"There's nothing to tell," my mother said. "I've been working for Imberotti."

"How long?"

"Since Prohibition," my mother said. "Almost eight years."

I was too busy translating to do justice to my own astonishment. Eight years? That meant from the time I was six. How could she have been doing anything for so long without my being aware of it? Answers later, I told myself hurriedly. What had the man just said?

"Ask her how much work she's been doing for Imberotti," he said.

"First only a little," my mother said. "They needed a bottle for the *schul* for Simchas Torah, but this Prohibition it said no, so I found out about Imberotti, and I said if you gave me a bottle I would bring back the money after I sold it to the *schul*."

"Imberotti trusted you?" the man said.

"Why not?" my mother said. "I look like a crook?"

The tall man had been watching her as I translated, but now he seemed to bend down slightly, as though to bring my mother into sharper focus. "No, ma'am," he said finally. "You certainly don't look like a crook, ma'am."

"So why shouldn't Imberotti trust me?" my mother said.

The tall man smiled. It put little nicks into his cheeks just above the corners of his mouth. "Ma'am," he said, "Imberotti would be a fool not to trust you. But now you want to buy from me, so I assume it's you that don't trust him."

"No," my mother said. She shook her head firmly and again said, "No. I trust Imberotti. He is an honest man. But not with me. He is not treating me right."

"In what way?" the tall man said.

"For five years, a bottle for the *schul,* a bottle for a bar mitzvah, two bottles for a wedding, maybe three, all right, for that I'm good enough." An unmistakable touch of bitterness surfaced in my mother's voice. "Don't misunderstand me," she said. "For what I'm good enough to Imberotti, I'm also grateful. It's bitter here on Fourth Street. Very hard. Bread and butter costs. My husband doesn't bring home much to the table. In the slack season he doesn't bring home anything. Everybody has to help. My son, here, he works in Lebenbaum's."

"What's that?" the man said.

"The candy store on Avenue C," my mother said. "Between what my husband makes in the shop, and what the boy makes in the candy store, and what I make from Imberotti, we've been eating. But not a penny to put away if somebody gets sick. You live for a little extra. This Shumansky wedding it could be a little extra."

"What Shumansky wedding?" the man said.

"This dope, he has the chicken store on the Avenue D corner," my mother said. "His daughter in a couple weeks she's marrying a boy from uptown by Lenox Assembly Rooms. I went to see Shumansky and I asked him how many bottles he'll need. Eighteen, he said, but he wasn't sure he could buy from me."

"Why not?" the tall man said.

"A man came to see him, Shumansky said. The man said he shouldn't buy from me because I couldn't deliver such a big order."

"Is that true?" the tall man said.

My mother gave him a look. Don't ask me to describe it. Go read a biography of Queen Elizabeth. Not the one married to the polo player. I mean the virgin. The way she looked at the Spanish ambassador. Or some other jerk she thought was a jerk. That might give you some idea, but only an idea. I am convinced nobody ever looked at anybody the way my mother looked at that tall man in the high-laced boots and the black turtleneck sweater on that moonlit night in the wheelhouse of that barge moored to the Fourth Street dock on the East River.

"What do you think?" she said.

The tall man smiled again. "I think you could deliver anything, ma'am," he said quietly.

Why this reply should have made my mother blush, I don't know, but it did, and in the pause I had a couple of moments to ponder the way the tall man talked. I had noticed it when he first referred to me as the kid. He had not said kid. He had said "kee-yid." Now I noticed when he called my mother ma'am he had pronounced it "may-yim." Just the same it seemed pretty late in this conversation for my mother to blush because of the way the tall man in boots pronounced his words. There was something more to it, I felt. I was dead right, but I didn't know what I was right about. It was my first contact with a southern accent.

"I knew what was happening," my mother said. "A fool I'm not. On eighteen bottles Imberotti wants the profit for himself. I went to see him last night and I told him. I said if I've been good enough for five years for a bottle for the *schul* and a bottle or two for a bar mitzvah, then I'm good enough for the eighteen bottles for the Shumansky wedding." My mother paused. She sat up straighter on the bench. "That's why I came to you."

"How did you know about me?" the tall man said.

My mother nodded toward the wheelhouse window. "We live up there," she said. "The building on the Lewis Street corner. I've been watching you make deliveries for a long time. I don't know for who, but I know what you deliver. If you give me the eighteen bottles for Shumansky's wedding, I'll give you half the profit."

The tall man started pacing again. This time, however, I noticed that he wasn't watching his boots. He was watching me.

"Ma'am," he said finally. "I think this is something you and I better talk over alone."

I translated. My mother blushed again. What was the matter with her? She looked like a pomegranate. Pomegranates were very big on East Fourth Street. Even with people who had never heard of the Song of Solomon. On the Avenue C pushcarts pomegranates were cheaper than oranges. My mother looked down at her hands.

"All right," she said finally. She said it to me. "You go back to the candy store and tell Papa to go home," my mother said. "But don't tell him anything else. You understand?"

"Sure," I said.

"What did she say?" the tall man said.

I told him.

He smiled. "You're a smart boy," he said. "What's your name?"

Sharply, my mother said, "What did he ask?"

I told her.

"Ask his name first," she said.

I did.

For some reason the question made the tall man laugh. "Walter," he said. "Tell her my name is Walter." I told her, and he said, "What's yours, kid?"

"Benny," I said. "Benny Kramer."

"And your mama's name?" he said.

"Mrs. Kramer," I said.

Walter laughed again. "I know that," he said. "I mean her first name."

Nobody had ever asked me that before, but my father called her Chanah, so I said, "Chanah."

"Chanah," Walter said. "That's very nice." He put his hand in his pocket and pulled out a dime. "Here you are, Benny," he said. "You go get yourself some candy and don't come back. I'll see your mama gets home safe after we finish our talk."

I was across Lewis Street, halfway up Fourth toward the Avenue D corner, before it occurred to me to wonder how, with the translator out of the way, they could do any talking.

7

FORTY YEARS LATER, on my way out of the Battenberg Funeral Home, I was still wondering.

Up to this day of her death in the Peretz Memorial Hospital, after living in this country for more than sixty years, my mother had managed to learn just about enough English to get her through the check-out desk of the supermarket around the corner from her apartment house on 78th Avenue in Queens, but no more. On the night in 1927 when Walter Sinclair came into our lives out of the northern reaches of the East River, my mother had not yet learned any English. As for Walter, he may have later learned some Yiddish. But on that first night, when we met on the barge to which he had moored the *Jefferson Davis II,* he did not even know what a *goniff* was.

When Walter found out, it didn't do him much good. It is a word that defies pronunciation by people born south of the Mason-Dixon line. Walter Sinclair had been a Chattanooga boy. Perhaps he still was. Or rather, perhaps he had gone back to being one. On this gloomy Sunday when I was setting out to identify the body of my mother in the Queens County morgue, I had not seen or heard about Walter Sinclair for forty years. Once we left East Fourth Street, my mother never mentioned his name.

Mentioning it now to myself, as I came out into the street, gave me an uneasy feeling. All the memories that were part of those early East Side days had been tucked away for years, at the back of a bottom drawer in my head, a drawer that I never opened. I signaled to a taxi coming my way up Queens Boulevard.

"Where to?" the driver said after I climbed in.

"Queens Memorial Hospital," I said. "Is it far from here?"

"Fifteen minutes," the driver said. "Twenty. Somebody sick?"

"No, somebody dead," I wanted to say.

But I didn't. I suddenly couldn't believe she was dead. Because suddenly I was not seeing the shriveled, broken old body lying in a hospital bed, the scarcely held together scraps of skin and bones to which I had muttered soothing platitudes a few hours before Dr. Sabinson called that morning to tell me "It's all over. She went in her sleep sometime during the night."

Suddenly the taxi and my grim errand seemed to fall away around me, like the shell of a hard-boiled egg. Suddenly it was like being in a movie theater. No, in the movie itself. Suddenly I was seeing a beautiful girl. Gold-yellow hair piled high on her head. Her willowy, restless body encased in one of the black sheaths she sewed for herself. Her high cheekbones, pink with excitement, in her gaunt white face. Her blue eyes bright with anticipation. Suddenly, in the taxi that was taking me to the morgue where I had to identify her body, I was seeing my mother not as I had seen her the day before in the Peretz Memorial Hospital, but as she must have looked in 1927 on the night of the Shumansky wedding.

135

She wasn't dead because she wasn't real. She was better than real. She was Mary Pickford. Made-up, costumed, waiting with every nerve tingling for Mr. Griffith to summon her before the cameras. And talking Yiddish, of course.

"Either eat fast," she said. "Or stop eating. There's a lot to do tonight."

My father and I were sitting at the kitchen table. He had not gone to work that day. His shop had entered the annual slack season, and he was working half-weeks. My mother's remark could have been addressed to either one of us. But I was aware of what had to be done that night, and my father was not, so I knew my mother had addressed him. My father swayed away from his plate, as though my mother had snatched at it.

"I'm finished," he said.

"What's the matter?" my mother said. "All of a sudden my *kreplach* are not good enough for you?"

"They're A Number One," my father said. "The best you ever made. But tonight all of a sudden sopper is so early. So my *moogin* is surprised."

"Carry your *moogin* over to the Erste Neustadter Krank und Interstitzing Verein," my mother said. "That always does you more good than a *krissteer*."

There was some truth in this remark. After his daily dose of Saratoga #2, my father's favorite home remedy was an enema, but the salutary effect of his monthly burial society meeting on his bowels was not to be dismissed.

"The special meeting is tomorrow," my father said.

"You're crazy," my mother said.

She could have said you're wrong, but not in our house. In her conversations with my father, my mother did not shilly-shally. She went for impact.

She said, "The meeting is tonight."

My father looked startled, but that did not stop him from swaying out of my mother's reach as she grabbed his plate.

"It said in the postal tomorrow," my father said.

It had. I'd read the postcard carefully when I brought it up from the mailbox four days before. It was important, my mother had told me, to get my father out of the house on the night of the Shumansky wedding. She had hoped his burial society special meeting would take place on the same night. My mother had relied on hope because she had no way of actually checking the date. Her contempt for my father's one activity that took place without her supervision was so great, and of such long standing, that she had never bothered to note exactly when his meetings took place.

When I gave her the card indicating the special meeting was scheduled for the night after the Shumansky wedding, I thought: Uh-oh, trouble. Not, however, to my mother. She handled the small obstacle in a way that, I see now, was typical.

She put the postcard on the sideboard in the front room, next to the cut-glass bowl full of pomegranates, oranges, and bananas. This was the resting place for all mail that came into our house. When he came home from the shop my father read the card and put it back on the sideboard before he came out into the kitchen for supper. None of us ever carried mail from the sideboard in the front room into other parts of the house. Not even the gas bill. Communications from the outside world were treated like visitors from an upper level of society to which we could not even hope to aspire. Until we found out why they had condescended to call upon us—it was always reasonable, and therefore safest, to assume that strangers had hostile intentions—it was better to do a little bowing and scraping and obsequious tugging at the forelock. So mail, like guests, was handled in the front room.

The following morning, as soon as my father went off to work, my mother tore the card to bits and flushed them down the toilet. Now, three days later, she was telling him he was crazy.

"But, Chanah," my father said. "I read the postal. It said the meeting is tomorrow."

"You're crazy," my mother said. Like many people of much vigor but little imagination, she believed firmly in the persuasive powers of repetition. "Hurry up and get out of here," she said. "Do you want to be late?"

It was like asking Napoleon if he wanted to come straggling in for his coronation. What else did the poor bastard have to live for?

"You want more?" my mother said when my father was out of the house, on his way to a meeting that was scheduled to take place the following night.

"No," I said. "I'm not hungry."

I was also not very fond of my mother's *kreplach*. She made them, as she made everything else she put on our table, grudgingly. As though she felt her time could have been better employed in some more useful pursuit. Years later, when I thought of my mother in the kitchen, I would get a picture in my mind of Madame Curie. Not only because they looked somewhat alike, but because I could imagine how the discoverer of radium might have felt at a moment when she was dragged away from her cauldrons of pitchblende to darn one of Pierre's socks.

"It doesn't matter," my mother said. "There will be a lot of good things to eat at the Shumansky wedding."

"We're not guests," I said.

"We're better than guests," my mother said. "Without us they wouldn't have a wedding. If you're late I'll save you some *kishke*." She looked at the alarm clock on the icebox. "Better get dressed. It's under the mattress."

I went out to the combination storage closet and bedroom at the far end of the flat in which I slept. My freshly laundered scout uniform was laid out neatly under my mattress for its final press. I put it on with a certain amount of uneasiness. I had not worn my uniform since the night my mother dragged me out of the Hannah H. Lichtenstein House gym during the One-Flag Morse contest. When I came back into the kitchen she said, "You look nice."

"Yeah," I said.

"Better go now," my mother said. "There's a lot to do."

Pulling on my sweater, I said, "Walter knows?"

"Of course he knows," my mother said irritably. "What do you think?"

Think? I had forgotten what the word meant. All I did was worry. I had not seen the tall man with the southern accent and the turtleneck sweater since the night on the dock when my mother and I had surprised him unloading sacks of booze from the *Jefferson Davis II*. But I knew my mother had seen him because her whole plan for the Shumansky wedding had been built around Walter's cooperation. My father may not have known what was going on, but I did. Anyway, I thought I did. I had heard my mother tell Walter that first night on the barge that she would split her profits with him. They had obviously agreed, after I left the barge, on how to do it. I decided then, as I have decided many times in subsequent years, that the smartest thing to do was not to think. Worry, yes. What could you do about that? But think? Who needed it?

139

"All right," I said. "I'll see you later."

"Don't talk to anybody," my mother said.

This proved to be surprisingly easy. What was working for me was the time of day. It was a few minutes before six. The starers were indoors. It was the hour when most families on the block were having their evening meal. I got all the way up Fourth, along Avenue D, and into Ninth Street without seeing anybody I knew.

Near the Avenue B corner, as I was approaching J.H.S. 64, I saw my old R.A.1 teacher coming out of the building. It was pretty late for a teacher to be leaving the school, but Miss Hallock had a reputation as a nut who never went home until she had finished correcting every paper the members of her class had turned in that day. I slowed down until she crossed Avenue B and disappeared into Tompkins Square Park on her way to the Astor Place subway station. Then I put on a burst of speed. I made it around the corner and into the Hannah H. Lichtenstein House without anybody seeing me. Anyway, without my seeing anybody who might have been interested in seeing me.

I was swept by a feeling of pride. Since that night on the dock, when she had put her hand on my shoulder and it had occurred to me for the first time that I liked her, I had wanted my mother to think well of me. Crossing the white marble lobby, and trotting down the stairs to the troop meeting room, I couldn't help thinking my mother had put her faith in someone worthy of her.

This opinion changed abruptly the moment I opened the door. Mr. O'Hare was sitting at the table in front of the room. He looked up in surprise from his black looseleaf program book. He had apparently been making notes in it with his gold Eversharp.

"Well, I do declare," the scoutmaster said. "It seems to be our long-lost Benjamin."

It also seemed to be curtains for my mother's plan. My part in what she and Walter Sinclair had cooked up depended on my getting in and out of the Hannah H. Lichtenstein House without being stopped or even noticed. That's why I was wearing my scout uniform. A boy in khaki breeches with a royal-blue bandanna held in place around his gullet by a neckerchief slide woven from gold braid was as conspicuous in the corridors of a settlement house as an onion in a goulash. Except to his scoutmaster, of course, and who would have expected Mr. O'Hare to be in the meeting room on an ordinary weekday evening? Not the senior patrol leader of Troop 244. To my knowledge, the fat man never even set foot in the Hannah H. Lichtenstein House except on Saturday nights.

"Hello," I said. Somehow that didn't seem to be enough, so I added, "It's nice to see you, sir."

"If I may return the compliment," Mr. O'Hare said, "it's nice to see you, too, Benjamin. In fact, you could not have come at a more appropriate moment." He tapped the notebook with the gold Eversharp. "I came down here tonight to complete the plans for our participation in the All-Manhattan rally. As you may have heard, in spite of certain disruptive circumstances, the troop did rather well at the eliminations."

"Yes, sir," I said.

"Oh, then you did hear, did you?" Mr. O'Hare said.

"Yes, sir," I said. "Hot Cakes told me we took three firsts."

"Indeed we did," Mr. O'Hare said. "Knot-tying, flint-and-steel, and bandages with arterial pressure points. Did you say Hot Cakes?"

"Hot Cakes Rabinowitz," I said. "He's in the Raven Patrol."

141

"Oh, yes," Mr. O'Hare said. "I believe he is more appropriately known as Ira, don't you?"

"Yes, sir," I said.

"Ira may also have told you that we took a second in bridge-building, another in basket-weaving, and a perfectly respectable third in camp hygiene, did he not?"

"Yes, sir," I said.

If I have to say it once more, I thought, there could be trouble. My gut was grinding.

"All in all, we did quite well, I think," Mr. O'Hare said. "Of course, we would be in a better position if my expectations in connection with One-Flag Morse had been realized, but then, one can't have everything, can one?"

"No, sir," I said.

That helped a little, but not much. "No, sir" sounds a lot like "Yes, sir." Especially to a jumpy gut.

"I had hoped after what happened on that ill-fated night," Mr. O'Hare said, "I had hoped my senior patrol leader would have had the courtesy of a true scout to come and explain to me the nature of the disruption. The cause, so to speak, of what was surely one of the most startling experiences to which the troop had ever been subjected, won't you agree?"

Not with a "Yes, sir." I couldn't.

"It was my aunt, sir," I said. "She got very sick all of a sudden. In fact, she was dying, and they sent for my mother, but my mother doesn't speak English, so she had to come and get me because she needed someone to do like, you know, to do the translation for her."

I said a lot more, droning on and on without thinking about what I was saying, snatching at remembered bits and pieces I had used on Chink Alberg and George Weitz the day after the disaster, because whatever thinking there was room for in my head was circling around the question: How was I going to get rid of this fatso and do what my mother and Walter Sinclair had sent me here to do?

"I quite understand," Mr. O'Hare said. "And indeed I am most sympathetic, in spite of what your mother's interruption cost the troop on that ill-fated night. But what I cannot understand, and what I find it most difficult to feel sympathetic about, is your subsequent conduct, Benjamin, as I'm sure you can understand, can't you?"

I was not too sure about the word subsequent, but I had a very clear understanding of the word conduct. It appeared every month on my school report card.

I hesitated, caught between "Yes, sir," of which I'd had a bellyful, and "No, sir," which did not seem appropriate. Finally I settled for a hesitant "Well," accompanied by an embarrassed foot shuffle.

"I don't mean to be harsh," Mr. O'Hare said, and he shifted his weight in the chair as though the layers of fat in which he was sitting had suddenly become too much for him. "But eleven—no, twelve—days have passed since the unfortunate incident took place, and I have not heard from you, Benjamin. You did not come to our last meeting, and nobody to whom I spoke, George Weitz and Ira and Morris, none of them seemed to know what your plans were, or if you ever intended to come back to the troop. I mean they didn't know, Benjamin, if I make myself clear?"

I didn't know, either. But the direction the conversation had taken, especially the tone of Mr. O'Hare's voice, seemed to indicate an opening in the gummy mass of dipped-in-chicken-fat syllables the scoutmaster was pouring over me as though I was a blintz on a plate and he was a pitcher of sour cream. I jumped through the opening like Rin-Tin-Tin streak-

143

ing through the crack in the door left open by the careless rustler.

"Oh, no," I said. "I would never leave the troop, Mr. O'Hare. That's why I came here tonight."

Since I didn't know where I was going, I thought I'd better go in his direction. So I matched my voice to his. I mean I tried to copy the throb Mr. O'Hare had got into his last remarks. It wasn't easy. His hot air was coming up out of the barrel of fat in which he lived. All that flabby suet made a marvelous sounding board. But me, I was just a skinny kid with a concave chest and a voice that was trying to make up its mind about changing. All I had to rely on was my talent for invention. I gave it the works. The works worked.

"You mean you came here tonight to explain?" Mr. O'Hare said. "To apologize?"

"Well," I said. Now I shifted from the foot shuffle to the toe stare. I cleared my throat. For a wild moment, in the grip of reckless inspiration, I gave a fevered thought to a tear or two. I was pretty sure I could do it. Crying on order had got me through several jams in school. But here, in the Hannah H. Lichtenstein House, the Scout Law stood in the way. A scout is brave, it said between thrifty and clean. I had a feeling it was the sort of thing Mr. O'Hare would remember. "Yes, sir," I said. "I came to—to—"

My voice broke. Not a crash. Just a sort of crumble. Heartbreaking but manly. It made even me feel sad.

"Benjamin," Mr. O'Hare said. "Benjamin, I don't know how to tell you the extent to which your words have moved me. What you have just said—" He paused. It had apparently occurred to him to give a moment of thought to what I had just said. "But how did you know I would be here?" Mr.

144

O'Hare said. "I did not know myself until an hour ago that I would be coming down tonight. I forgot my program book when I went home after Saturday's meeting. I planned to work on it tonight. When I learned I didn't have my book, I—I—" Mr. O'Hare paused again. "Benjamin," he said, "I am puzzled."

He was also in my way, and time was running out.

"I'm sorry," I said. "I didn't know you'd be here tonight, Mr. O'Hare."

"Then how could you come here to apologize?"

"I didn't come to apologize in words," I said. "I came to— to—I came to do something that would show how I felt about the troop," I said. "I came to borrow the hike wagon."

There is this to be said for a fat face: you can't beat it as a ball park on which to register consternation. It's like dropping a stone into a lake. There is plenty of room for the ripples to spread out. I could understand their spreading out on Mr. O'Hare's face. The hike wagon was a cart the members of Troop 244 had constructed from the scoutmaster's design.

It consisted of a Kirkman's Soap Flakes wooden box mounted on two baby-carriage wheels nailed at one end to an umbrella-shaft axle. At the other end a length of broomstick, running horizontally, had been nailed to form a handle. A top for the box had been fixed on hinges, so that, when the wagon sat flat on the ground, it could be opened for loading and un-loading. In the wagon, when we went on Sunday hikes, we carried the heavy equipment that would not fit into our knap-sacks: the iron grill that went over the campfire; the two big aluminum pots in which we cooked stews and soups; the two baseball bats, the balls, the catcher's mitt, and the pitcher's glove with which we took our whack at the national pastime when we found a level campsite; the folding cot on which Mr. O'Hare took his nap after lunch; the first-aid kit; and the Morse Code flags.

The whole thing was painted a ripe almost golden khaki, and on the cover, in purple and red, appeared a twelve-inch reproduction of the scout badge. Above it, in six-inch type, was lettered: *Troop 244, Manhattan Council, B.S.A.* Below the badge appeared the scout motto: *Be Prepared.*

Because of the way the wagon was constructed, it could be moved easily, like an up-ended baby carriage, along sidewalks leading to the Astor Place subway station, down the subway steps and into trains, onto the Dyckman Street ferry, and when we were across the river, along the hiking paths at the foot of the Palisades. Because of its gaudy coloring, the wagon attracted a lot of attention. There was a good deal of rivalry among the members of the troop for the opportunity to push or lug the wagon in public. Because of its markings, it would never occur to a cop or any other law enforcement officer to suspect that the hike wagon contained anything illegal. Especially if it was being pulled or shoved by a boy in uniform. Anyway, that's what my mother and Walter Sinclair were counting on.

"You came to borrow the hike wagon?" Mr. O'Hare said. "Is that what I understood you to say?"

"Yes, sir," I said.

Again Mr. O'Hare seemed to hunt for breathing space by rearranging the layers of fat that hung on him like saddle-bags.

"How, if I may ask," he said, "how do you think that will help you to apologize for what happened on the night of the eliminations?"

"Maybe not in words," I said, inventing nervously. "I

146

wasn't thinking about words. I was thinking of like, say, a sort of an act? Like putting on a show? Something that would do more for the troop than just words. Something that would make people at the Shumansky wedding realize what a great troop 244 is."

"The Shumansky wedding?" Mr. O'Hare said. "What is that?"

The question was not as stupid as it sounded, although I don't think Mr. O'Hare knew that.

On East Fourth Street, anybody who heard the words "the Shumansky wedding" would know at once that somebody named Shumansky was going to get married. Also, since weddings are identified by the family that foots the bill, a Fourth Streeter would almost certainly conclude that Shumansky was the name of the bride and not the groom. But Mr. O'Hare did not come from East Fourth Street. Mr. O'Hare came from uptown.

This did not necessarily make him a dope. In fact, since he had stated publicly that I was the best One-Flag Morse man he had ever known, I was inclined to think Mr. O'Hare was pretty smart. But people from uptown, I had noticed, were limited in many ways. There seemed to be whole areas of experience with which, when these people came into my life, they never seemed to have made contact.

I did not hesitate. Time was running out. I leaned on the first Scout Law: A scout is trustworthy.

"Mr. Shumansky owns the chicken store on the corner of Avenue D and Fourth Street," I said. "His daughter is getting married tonight in Lenox Assembly Rooms. I thought if I came with the hike wagon, and I did a few things like we do on hikes, knot-tying, maybe, or a few words in one-flag Morse, maybe even a spiral reverse bandage, I thought that would be good for Troop 244. I mean the people at the wedding, they'd see things they never saw before."

Mr. O'Hare stared down at his program book. This did not seem to help. How could it? The only thing that could help this man from uptown was to be shoved back and born again on East Fourth Street. But who had time for that? Mr. O'Hare tried sucking the end of his gold Eversharp. After a while this seemed to produce results. He looked up.

"You know, Benjamin," he said, "I've never been to a Jewish wedding."

Neither had I. But I had a feeling I was ahead of him. So it seemed sensible to say nothing that would cause me to lose my lead.

"Could I borrow the wagon?" I said.

"If you return it safely," Mr. O'Hare said. "Will you be taking it far?"

"Lenox Assembly Rooms is on Avenue C," I said. "Between Second and Third. That's not far."

"By all means, then, help yourself, Benjamin," Mr. O'Hare said.

I went to the closet and pulled out the wagon. It was loaded, of course. I could tell by the weight. But I had expected that.

"Thanks, Mr. O'Hare," I said. I added a little dessert. A man with his shape expected it. I said, "I'm sorry for what happened the night of the eliminations."

"It wasn't your fault," Mr. O'Hare said. "Will you come to next Saturday's meeting?"

"Yes, sir," I said. A lie, of course. How could I go back to the place where George Weitz had earned the top spot on my *verbissen* list? But a scout, in addition to being trustworthy, was kind. Especially to his scoutmaster.

"Good," Mr. O'Hare said. "We missed you at the last

meeting." He smiled. "You look very nice in your freshly laundered uniform."

I was glad to see, as I dragged the wagon up the stairs into the white marble lobby, that I did not look too nice. The upper floors of the Hannah H. Lichtenstein House were cut up into small rooms in which lived Jewish career girls from out of town. They were always wandering around the marble lobby with books and magazines from the library back of the office and vacant looks from wondering why they had ever come to New York in the first place. Very often, when they saw a nice boy scout, they smiled and patted his head. I have dents in my scalp to prove it. On that night, however, I was spared. Nobody paid any attention to me. I got the wagon out into Avenue B and turned downtown, moving a little faster than I would have liked. My next step was to get the stuff out of the wagon.

I had known in advance that I would have to do this, and I had taken into my calculations the time needed to do it. What I had not known was that Mr. O'Hare would be in the meeting room when I got there to borrow the hike wagon. The time it had taken me to get him off my back now began to worry me. It was the first week in May. Without Mr. O'Hare's interruption, I was sure I could get it all done before dark. Now I was not so sure. Old Man Tzoddick lived in a cellar. They said he always had a candle going after dark, but I had never actually seen this.

Old Man Tzoddick was a junk dealer. He didn't do much dealing in our neighborhood because there wasn't much junk to deal in. People on Fourth Street and the surrounding streets used and lived with what they had. Nobody ever threw anything away. Old Man Tzoddick worked further west, toward Second and Third avenues.

He moved up and down the streets, dragging a pushcart, shaking it from side to side at regular intervals. This caused the cowbells hung on a piece of clothesline strung across the top of the cart to clang and attract customers.

Thinking about the contents of Old Man Tzoddick's pushcart could drive a man—well, a boy scout, anyway—crazy.

This boy scout, however, had to remain sane. So I scout-paced it—fifty steps walking, fifty steps trotting—down Avenue B and turned into Eighth Street. As soon as I came around the corner, I knew I was all right. Old Man Tzoddick's pushcart was not standing in the vacant lot.

The Eighth Street vacant lot was used as a dump for old lumber and as a garage for wagons by Burns Coal and other companies that worked from the East River docks and needed more space. On Election Day we used to count on the Eighth Street vacant lot for a good part of the old lumber we used in our Fourth Street Election night fire. I don't know if the Burns Company paid rent to the owner of the Eighth Street vacant lot. It never even occurred to me until years later that there must have been an owner. In those days I assumed that vacant lots were part of the landscape, something provided by nature, like the streams and deserts and mountains I saw in the movies and in the pictures in my geography book. Maybe Old Man Tzoddick felt the same way. I certainly never heard that he paid any rent for parking his pushcart in the lot just outside the stone steps leading down to the cellar in which he lived. If I had felt that in addition to Old Man Tzoddick, I would have to contend with a landlord, I don't think I would have chosen this lot as my first stop after putting my hands on the hike wagon.

The wagon had to be unloaded before I could move ahead with my part of the plan my mother and Walter Sinclair had laid out? Okay. I would unload it. I couldn't throw the stuff away, of course. When I returned the wagon it would have to contain everything that had been in it when I wheeled it out under Mr. O'Hare's nose. My problem was to find a place where the stuff could be stashed for a few hours. What place could be more appropriate than the stone cave halfway down the steps that led to Old Man Tzoddick's cellar?

Ten minutes, maybe less, after I left Mr. O'Hare, I was squatting on Old Man Tzoddick's stone steps. I was shoving into the cave the iron cooking grill, the soup and bean pots, the troop first-aid kit, and the Morse flags, when a voice behind me exploded.

"*Momzer!*" the voice said. "*Goniff!* What are you doing?"

I stopped doing it and turned. It was, of course, Old Man Tzoddick. I had never been this close to him before. I thought fast. It occurs to me, as I survey my youth on East Fourth Street, that there never was time to think slowly. It was always attack and counterattack. I counterattacked.

"Your steamship ticket!" I yelled. "You crazy old bastard, where the hell is your steamship ticket?"

It was around his neck, of course. Old Man Tzoddick did not like this country. He had come to America because he had heard it was a land of easy wealth. He intended to pile up the price of the farm in the Ukraine on which his father had been a serf, then go home and buy the place. To make sure he did not lose sight of his objective, Old Man Tzoddick, then no doubt known as Young Man Tzoddick, with his first American earnings bought a return steamship passage to Europe. He put the ticket into a small leather pouch and hung the pouch around his neck on a leather thong. When the time came to return to the Ukraine, he would be ready.

"My steamship ticket?" Old Man Tzoddick said. His rage

had turned to fear. It always did when his steamship ticket was mentioned. "What did you say about my steamship ticket?"

"It's no good," I said.

He clutched at the filthy pouch on the leather thong around his neck. "What do you mean it's no good?"

"It's worn out," I said, shouting the Yiddish words with mounting shrillness. "The company went out of business. It's bankrupt. The ship doesn't exist any more."

"God in heaven!" the old man wailed. "Oh, my God, my God in heaven!"

He took his head in both hands and banged it against the stone steps, up and down, up and down, as though his forehead was a hammer and he was driving a nail. I was astonished by what I had done. All I had wanted to do was get rid of him so I could unload the contents of the wagon. It occurred to me, as Old Man Tzoddick wailed and screamed and beat his head, that I had. I shoved the stone slab back into place, grabbed the wagon, and dragged it up into the vacant lot.

Here I hesitated. Neither my mother nor Walter Sinclair had specified how I was to perform my part of their plan so long as I completed it before sundown. I had not worked out a sequence for myself. In fact, I had not thought much beyond putting my hands on the hike wagon. All the rest had seemed simple. This feeling of simplicity had been jolted when I realized I had to get rid of the contents of the wagon. Now all I could think of was getting away from the insane sounds Old Man Tzoddick was making on the cellar steps. I looked quickly toward Avenue C. There seemed to be a few people on the corner. I turned and ran west, toward Avenue B, trundling the wagon behind me.

I ran for half a block, then shifted to scout pace. The clock over the Standard Bank at the Fourth Street corner showed twenty minutes to seven. It did not seem possible that I had left my mother and her *kreplach* less than an hour ago. My feeling of guilt about what I had done to old Man Tzoddick disappeared. My spirits zoomed back up to the level where they usually functioned. It looked as though I could still pull off the whole deal. It had seemed difficult when my mother explained it, but simple enough. We had to conceal until the night of the Shumansky wedding eight bottles of Old Southwick Scotch whiskey as Walter Sinclair delivered them to us on the dock two at a time. Two bottles at a time were all he could sneak out of the regular deliveries he made to the dock for the bootleggers who made their pickups in the middle of the night. On the night of the Shumansky wedding, however, he promised to deliver to me in one lump the final ten bottles, adding up to the eighteen my mother had agreed to deliver for the festivities. Walter did not explain how he would manage to put his hands on ten bottles in one lump, and it did not occur to me to ask. I trusted him. I see now what the answer probably was: his bosses trusted him, too.

Ordinarily, concealing two bottles at a time would have been no problem. My mother would have hidden them somewhere around our apartment, probably under the bed where my father kept his case of Saratoga #2 mineral water. But there was something not quite ordinary about this project. It troubled me, and I worried about it, but I could not nail down just what it was that troubled me. I was certain of only one thing: my mother did not want my father to know about her dealings with Walter Sinclair. She had told me so. She had forbidden me to mention to my father what she and I and Walter were doing.

This put me into a conspiracy with my mother against my father. I still wonder why this made me uncomfortable. I had never had very strong feelings about my father. I knew, of course, that he was dominated by my mother. Most East Fourth Street fathers were. So why was she all of a sudden scared of him? I could think of no answer, of course. So I did what my mother told me to do. My mother and Walter Sinclair. For over a week, nine days, in fact, I stashed the eight bottles of whiskey, two at a time, in the various places to which I had access. I didn't doubt that I would be able to complete the assignment to which Walter Sinclair and my mother had committed me. When I reached the front of the *cheder* on Columbia Street, I was sure of it.

The two cones of ashes on top of the garbage cans had been picked flat. The kids from Goereck Street and the Edgie were gone for the day. No trouble ahead. Well, just a touch. I had trouble finding any rocks. I had to dig all the way down through the ashes to the garbage underneath. The two rocks I finally did find should have been ashamed of themselves. They were nothing the Prudential Life Insurance Company would have wanted to photograph for the front of their policies, but they were big enough for my purpose. As rocks went, I didn't need the strength of Gibraltar.

For the climb up the decayed stairs, however, I needed a little more strength than usual. This time I was lugging the wagon behind me. Even empty it weighed something. When I reached the *cheder* door I crouched low and got into position, as always, then eased the door open. The big rat was on the job, nibbling away at the edge of the hole in front of the gold-embroidered purple curtains. I took aim and let go.

Again, no bull's eye, but the rock hit the edge of the hole. The rat squealed and took a dive. I ran into the *cheder*. I set the wagon near the ark that held the Torahs, climbed up to the top of the ark, and pawed around behind the Sheffield Farms milk-bottle crate. My hand found the two burlap-wrapped packages I had hidden there a week before, the day Walter Sinclair made his first delivery to my mother.

I took the wrapped bottles down one at a time, put them into the wagon, and headed for the door. Before I could reach it, something cut at my left ankle like the sting of a red-hot whip. I staggered and turned. Rabbi Goldfarb had just come out of the toilet. He was still buttoning his fly with his free hand. The toilet door was still slowly swinging shut. Rabbi Goldfarb abandoned his fly. When a good shot came into his sights, Rabbi Goldfarb obeyed the instincts of any White Hunter. His toilette could wait. He swung the polished chair rung and caught me on the right ankle. I yelped. It occurred to me that I sounded not unlike the rat I had just sent down the hole. Louder. Rats don't have ankles.

"You bastard," I said.

"What did you say?" Rabbi Goldfarb said.

"Ouch," I said. In English, of course.

"Now say it in Yiddish," Rabbi Goldfarb said.

The polished wood cut me across both Achilles tendons. It served me right. Lesson learned that day in *cheder*: When facing an aroused Jewish White Hunter, don't stand with both feet planted close together.

"You dirty rotten louse," I said. "Go to hell!"

"This is by you Yiddish?" Rabbi Goldfarb said. The chair rung came swishing down. My body went up. Like a scythe swinging across barren ground, the weapon swept harmlessly under my shoes. Rabbi Goldfarb staggered. I came back to the decayed floor with a thump. "You little *momzer*," Rabbi Goldfarb said. He came around in a swinging stagger. This brought the chair rung up and out, pointing at my chest like a sword. "What are you doing in *cheder* at this time?" Rabbi

155

Goldfarb said. "Why weren't you here this afternoon when you should have been?"

"My father is sick and I couldn't come. But I need something," I said, keeping the hike wagon between me and the wooden sword. "I came to get it."

"What did you come to get?" Rabbi Goldfarb said. He had an afterthought. "You big liar," he said.

He was right. I was a liar. I was fairly big, too. That's what made me sore.

"For the troop meeting." I flipped up the tail end of my royal-blue neckerchief as though I were waving an identification card in his face. "The boy scouts," I said. I pointed to the insignia sewed above the breast pocket of my khaki shirt. "I'm the senior patrol leader," I said. "In the Hannah H. Lichtenstein House on Avenue B. The boy scouts."

"Into the earth with you and your boy scouts," Rabbi Goldfarb said. "Let their heads grow underground like onions. What have the *vershimmelte* boy scouts on Avenue B got to do with my *cheder* on Columbia Street?"

The chair rung lunged at my chest. I feinted with the hike wagon. Rabbi Goldfarb's thrust slid harmlessly over my shoulder. Athos would have been proud of me. Porthos and Aramis, too.

"We have a meeting tonight," I said. "After I put on my uniform, I remembered I left something here, so I came to get it."

"What did you leave, what?" Rabbi Goldfarb said.

He had me there. I couldn't think of an answer fast enough. He obviously didn't expect one. He sent a lunging stab to the right with the chair rung. I ducked to the left. Rabbi Goldfarb came back in a low crouch. His free hand caught the hasp on the wagon. He flipped it free and dragged up the wooden box cover. The two burlap-wrapped packages stared up at us.

"So," Rabbi Goldfarb said. He snatched up one of the packages, tore away the burlap, and pulled out the bottle labeled *Old Southwick Scotch Whiskey*. "So," Rabbi Goldfarb said again. He held the bottle up above his head like Moses coming down from the mountain with the tablets. "So this is what you forgot here in *cheder?* This is what you need for the scout boy meeting in the Hannah H. Lichtenstein House on Avenue B?"

A number of answers came crowding into my mind, elbowing each other for precedence. I examined them for a moment, then decided to let them race ahead. To the question Rabbi Goldfarb had asked, none of them could be considered an adequate answer. The high black fedora and the greasy suit, separated by the beard through which words emerged, seemed to share my feeling. Rabbi Goldfarb went on to construct his own answer.

"The boy scouts in the Hannah H. Lichtenstein House on Avenue B," he said. "What are they? A bunch of *shickeerem?* To have a meeting they must have two bottles of *vishnick* to drink?"

"No," I said. "We don't drink whiskey."

"Then why do you need this?" Rabbi Goldfarb said. He waved the bottle under my nose. "What does it say here in gold and red and black, so fancy?"

"Old Southwick," I said. Then inspiration struck. The bastard couldn't read English. "Golden Yellow Malted Milk," I said.

Rabbi Goldfarb's eyes, ordinarily a couple of dirty Fu Manchu slits between his black fedora and his forest of beard, now spread wide into a couple of big fat shiny lemon gumdrops.

"So what I'm holding in my hand it's not *vishnick?*" he said. "It's malted?"

"That's right," I said.

"*Nu*, then," Rabbi Goldfarb said. "You have two bottles, so one for your scout boys it's enough. The second bottle, it'll be for your rabbi a present, no?"

Inspiration, I thought bitterly, for other people, you strike. For me, you erupt.

"Not tonight," I said. "Tonight for the meeting we need two bottles. But I'll get another one for you tomorrow."

"Tomorrow is tomorrow," Rabbi Goldfarb said. "But today is today. A poor man who makes a living teaching boys to be good Jews, when does he need a bottle malted? Today or tomorrow?"

"I'll get you two bottles," I said. "Two bottles tomorrow."

"No," Rabbi Goldfarb said. "Tomorrow you have to get me only one. Because here I already have one of the two." He shoved the bottle of Old Southwick into the huge pocket of his greasy black coat. "And remember," he said. The chair rung swung back and forth under my nose like the punkah in an opium den in an Anna May Wong movie. "Don't come to *cheder* tomorrow without the second bottle," Rabbi Goldfarb said. "Or you won't be able to walk home."

I didn't manage to do more than get up on the balls of my feet. My body never left the ground. The chair rung fanned the air like a machete. Both strokes found their targets. The door slammed shut behind Rabbi Goldfarb. I was left with two throbbing ankles and one bottle of Old Southwick. To describe my state of mind, the language of Shakespeare and Milton is inadequate. I must fall back on the language of my mother. As follows: "*Oy!*"

My job in the plan for the Shumansky wedding had been clearly laid down. Kind as I have always enjoyed being to myself, I could not say at this moment in Rabbi Goldfarb's *cheder* that I was doing my job well.

The first two bottles I had tried to collect had been reduced to one. Even if I now collected all the other bottles I had stashed away, I would arrive at Lenox Assembly Rooms one bottle short.

There was only one solution. In addition to collecting all the bottles I had hidden during the week, I would have to dig up one extra. It meant rearranging my schedule, but there was no other way. Rabbi Goldfarb had fixed that.

The original plan had not involved our own home. As I have said, my mother did not want my father to be aware that she was engaged in the Shumansky wedding enterprise. But I was now short one bottle. I did not want Walter or my mother to know I had been outsmarted by Rabbi Goldfarb. A moment of cunning stabbed at me. A moment of caution came crowding in. Indeed, a moment of warning. But the moment of cunning won. *Why not?* it asked. It is the sort of question for which even in later years, I have never been able to find an answer. The desire to retrieve what has been lost, whether it is time or fortune, is irresistible.

My mother kept the kerosene for the legs of our beds in an old whiskey bottle on the sill of her bedroom window. My father kept his carafe of Passover wine on the bureau in our front room. I could dump the kerosene down the sink, rinse the bottle, and fill it with a mixture of half Passover wine and half sink water. The color might not be the same as the color of Old Southwick, but I could conceal that by wrapping the doctored bottle in the wrappings from the bottle of Old Southwick that Rabbi Goldfarb had not taken from me.

Who would know the difference? Except perhaps the Shumansky guests who found the stuff in their glasses? And would they really know? If I kept that doctored bottle at the bottom of the hike cart? And they started drinking from it after they had put away seventeen bottles of the genuine stuff? I had seen some drinking in my then still short lifetime on East Fourth Street. Mostly by the goyim from the barges who frequented the dock saloons. My observation, completely unscientific, of course, told me that after seventeen bottles of Old Southwick, one bottle of Benny Kramer's Mixture would not attract any special attention.

I carried the hike cart down into the street and started back toward Fourth Street. The clock over the Standard Bank now showed almost seven, so I was still okay on time. Crowded a little, but still okay. I was sure I could swing it even though it would have to be an in-and-out job.

The in part worked fine. I got to our flat, parked the hike wagon in the kitchen, and went into the bedroom. I took the kerosene bottle from the window sill, carried it out to the kitchen, emptied it into the sink, and rinsed the bottle. I then brought the wine carafe from the front room, poured some of the wine into the empty whiskey bottle, and filled the rest with water. All that remained was tidying up. I was all finished, and was about to place the doctored bottle in the wagon, when the door opened. My father came in.

We stared at each other the way years later I learned husbands in passing taxis stare at their wives when they see them coming out of strange apartment houses at unexpected hours of the day.

"What are you doing in your uniform?" my father said.

When he went off to his meeting of the Erste Neustadter Krank und Interstitzings Verein he had left me at the kitchen table wearing my school sweater and knickers and eating *kreplach*. When he went off to the meeting he did not know my mother had lied to him about the date because she wanted to get him out of the house. I decided to start all over again.

"Mr. O'Hare called a special meeting," I said. "He's planning the program for the All-Manhattan rally."

"I hope he's a better planner than your mother."

It was a totally unexpected remark. It had things in it I had never before heard come out of my father's mouth. Not only the tone, which had an edge to it. But also the meaning of the words, which could be interpreted only as a criticism of my mother. I did not want to do any interpreting. The alarm clock on the icebox had shifted from ticking to banging. Each bang said clearly: "Shake it up, kid." Time was beginning to hunch over my handlebars. But my father's unexpected remark made me look at him as though I had never seen him before. In a way I never had. Who looks at the hole in a bagel?

My father was not handsome the way my mother, I had just learned during the past week, was pretty. On the other hand, he was not ugly in the way that the first sight of some people makes you wince and mutter, "Oh, God, will you please go away." My father had a pleasant face. Pleasant the way a clean street of no particular importance or distinction is pleasant. Distinction? No. Importance? No. But my father's face was certainly clean. It looked not unlike a plate from which somebody hungry had just wiped up all the gravy. Leaving nothing but an expanse of crockery. Clean crockery. He was of average height. In fact if Noah Webster had not put the word average into the dictionary, my father might never have been noticed, not even by his own son. His average height was five, six and three-quarters.

He had an average smile: nice, because he had good teeth and his cheeks creased pleasantly—but once he turned the corner, you would probably have trouble remembering you had seen him. He wore average clothes. Gray? Yes, I think gray. But wait. Blue maybe? Could be. How about black? Well, not very black black. I mean not the kind of black you would notice, Fulton Sheen black. In my father's case it was average black. Mixed in with average blue and average gray to form—well, to form my father's color.

His voice? I always thought of it as a grocery store clerk's voice. Men behind the counters of delicatessens have strong voices. They have to. If they didn't, how could you hear their jokes over the noise of the knives slicing pastrami? Butchers are hearty. To lie convincingly about the weight of a chicken, you must sound as though you believe what you're saying. My father never did. He always sounded like the man in the white apron who says apologetically, "I'm sorry, we're all out of the bran flakes, but these things called Nutty Pops, people seem to like them."

Even my father's financial life was average. He never made a living in the strict meaning of the phrase, meaning by strict meaning that he never earned enough to support himself and his family. If he had, my mother would probably not have become a bootlegger, although I'm not sure. She had other things eating her besides the compulsion to pay the rent that her husband was incapable of paying. On the other hand, except for being a bit late for the rent once in a while before my mother started adding to the family income, I don't think my father was ever in debt. How could he be? He never earned enough to attract the attention of the Internal Revenue Service, and what he couldn't afford to buy he did without. That's why his clothes always looked like that. He never bought anything to provide himself with pleasure. He only bought things to last.

During the early years of my life, when I was almost totally unaware of his existence, I think my father fitted squarely in the middle of what I then understood the word schlemiel to mean. Years later, when I got to like him, I realized the turning point had been that night of the Shumansky wedding, and it wasn't only because of what he had said about my mother's talents as a planner. It was because of what happened after I said, "You mean your society had no meeting tonight?" After I said that, the door opened and Mr. Velvelschmidt, our landlord, came in.

"Good evening," he said. "I'm interrupting like maybe sopper, I hope not?"

He wasn't, of course. We'd had our meal an hour ago. There are all sorts of talents, however, and in the area of supper-interrupting Mr. Velvelschmidt could hardly be dismissed as a slouch. If he had been around at the time, I think he could have been counted on to interrupt the Last One.

"Who are you?" my father said.

At first I thought he was joking. Not knowing your landlord on East Fourth Street was like not knowing your warden at Sing Sing. Then I remembered that Mr. Velvelschmidt always appeared between three and three-thirty in the afternoon, when my father was bent over his sewing machine in the pants shop on Allen Street. What was he doing in our house at seven? On a night when all I had left was thirty minutes to round up all the bottles of Old Southwick for the Shumansky wedding?

"Who am I?" Mr. Velvelschmidt said. "Ask your son who I am. Go ahead, ask him."

My father looked at me.

"It's the landlord," I said.

I must have sounded not unlike the way Ham or Shem or Japheth, briefing Noah on the latest developments, might have sounded when they said, "It's the rain, Pa."

163

Landlords on East Fourth Street were something you accepted and made preparations for, but in whose existence when they arrived you didn't quite believe. Mr. Velvelschmidt was more unbelievable than most. Unlike our old landlord, Mr. Koptzin, he was a doctor. And perhaps because he was a doctor, his hours as a landlord were limited. He had, therefore, installed as janitor and guardian of the building his brother-in-law Mr. Noogle. However, Mr. Velvelschmidt could not deny himself the pleasure of collecting his own rents. I don't know, of course, how much Mr. Velvelschmidt saved by doing so, but it must have been enough to compensate him for the loss of pride involved in dropping for a day each month the "doctor" in front of his name for the commonplace "mister." Whatever he lost in this respect, however, was amply repaid by the fun he had. Mr. Velvelschmidt enjoyed being a bastard.

"What a wonderful family this is!" he exclaimed. Not said. Exclaimed. When Mr. Velvelschmidt was not exclaiming, he chirped. "A landlord comes into a house to see one of his tenants, and what does the tenant do? He asks his son who is this man? What a marvelous joke!" To prove it, Mr. Velvelschmidt released a few bars of his barking laughter. "When you think of it," he said after he regained control of himself, "I suppose you could say it's only natural, because I mean we've never met before—no, Mr. Berkowitz?"

"Who is Berkowitz?" my father said.

Again the laughter came pouring up out of Mr. Velvelschmidt like air out of a pinpricked balloon. He was short and fat and very well dressed, but somehow he looked naked. Not the way a human being or most animals look naked. There were no signs of hair on Mr. Velvelschmidt's scalp, face, or hands. He looked naked the way a pig looks naked hanging on a hook in the window of one of those stores on First Avenue with a single word painted on the glass: *PORK*.

"Who is Berkowitz?" he chirped. "What a joker! Who is Berkowitz he asks! You're Berkowitz, Mr. Berkowitz!"

"I'm Kramer," my father said.

Mr. Velvelschmidt turned to me, eyes wide, pink snout tilted toward the gas pipe that hung from the kitchen ceiling. "Your father is not Berkowitz?" he said.

"No," I said.

"Who is he, then?" Mr. Velvelschmidt said.

"He's my father," I said.

"But you're Heshie Berkowitz, no?"

"No," I said.

"Then who are you?" Mr. Velvelschmidt said.

"Benny Kramer," I said.

Mr. Velvelschmidt frowned. He flipped the pages of his receipt book. An idea apparently pushed its way into his mind. He stepped back to our front door and opened it. He looked at the number painted in black on the brown tin sheathing outside. The frown vanished.

"Of course you're not Berkowitz," he said. He closed the door and came back into the kitchen. "Berkowitz is 6-E in the next building next door. You're Kramer."

"I have been for a long time," my father said.

I gave him a quick glance. Where had he picked up this new way of talking? Sort of a little bit like George Weitz, except in Yiddish. I had never before, of course, heard my father utter a word except in the presence of my mother. Even a fool would have guessed that there was some connection between this fact and the way my father sounded now when my mother was absent. I was late for the Shumansky wedding, and getting later, but in spite of George Weitz's insistence to the contrary, I was no fool.

"To tell you the truth," Mr. Velvelschmidt said through his barking laughter, "I'm glad you're Kramer."

"So am I," my father said. "I've been Kramer all my life. I'm too old to change now."

Mr. Velvelschmidt was wearing a snappy sharkskin topcoat with a fly front and a gray velvet collar. If he had worn anything else, I would have been surprised. On East Fourth Street this was the uniform of the rent collector. The uniform now seemed about to burst as Mr. Velvelschmidt's roly-poly figure took a stab at what anybody could have told him was impossible: doubling up. Not with that gut. But apparently there was no other way for him to laugh. He did it the way the contraption at the top of the Mississippi River boats in the movies pumped their paddle wheels: sawing up and down.

"*Oy gevalt!*" Mr. Velvelschmidt gasped. "He's too old to change now! Did you hear that?" he chirped—well, no, he exclaimed—to the gas jet at the end of the ceiling pipe. "He's too old to change now!"

Mr. Velvelschmidt's laughter came to an end the way coal pouring down a chute into a cellar from a Burns Company coal wagon came to an end when the wagon was empty. With an abrupt, total, and unpleasant cessation of sound.

"Where is the missus?" he said.

"I don't know," my father said.

The answer did not strike me as odd. My father rarely knew where my mother was. At the moment, I didn't know, either. All I knew was that she would be waiting for me when I got to Lenox Assembly Rooms with the loaded hike wagon. If I ever did get there.

"You don't know where the missus is?" Mr. Velvelschmidt said.

"No," my father said.

The way he said it must have struck Mr. Velvelschmidt as unusual. Perhaps for the same reason my father's words had struck me as unusual a little while ago. But I'm not sure. All I'm sure about is what Mr. Velvelschmidt, who up to now had been wearing the face of a laughing pig, suddenly seemed to be wearing the face of a pig that was about to bite.

"Why don't you know?" he said.

"What's it your business?" my father said.

I admired his standing up to Mr. Velvelschmidt, but I couldn't understand why he was doing it. Landlords were something you were polite to, and got out of the house as quickly as possible. Arguments, I had learned, did not make anything move faster, especially landlords.

"My business is your rent," Mr. Velvelschmidt said. "Maybe I never saw you before because maybe here in these rooms you're not the one who pays the rent."

He paused, as though waiting for my father to deny this, but my father didn't. My father, I noticed, had recovered from whatever it was that had made him for a brief period seem a stranger to me. My father looked average again.

"My rent it was coming to me last Thursday," Mr. Velvelschmidt said. "Everybody in the building they paid me last Thursday. Everybody except your missus. She said to me she didn't have the rent last Thursday. I should come tonight, she told me. Tonight she'd have the rent for me, she said, your missus. So here I am, it's tonight, and there's not only no rent, there's also no missus."

What my father did next annoyed me. He swayed from Mr.

Velvelschmidt the way he always swayed away from my mother. He did it very quickly, as though it was a skill he had forgotten he possessed, and he wanted Mr. Velvelschmidt to see the talent had not abandoned him.

"I don't know anything about it," my father said.

"So who does know?" Mr. Velvelschmidt said.

"I do," I said.

The landlord turned to me. The look on his face seesawed back and forth, as though he couldn't make up his mind whether he would lose ground if he abandoned the look of a pig that was about to bite and went back to the look of a pig that smiled.

"What is it, then, that you know?" Mr. Velvelschmidt said.

"My mother will get the rent for you tonight," I said.

"You mean I should wait?" the landlord said.

"No," I said. "I mean my mother will get the money tonight. You come back tomorrow. She'll give it to you tomorrow."

Mr. Velvelschmidt turned to my father. "This is true?"

My father swayed away from the now jovial voice and said, "My son is not a liar."

He should have heard me giving it to Rabbi Goldfarb and Mr. O'Hare.

"You better not be," Mr. Velvelschmidt said. "Or you can tell your mother from me, Mr. Benny Kramer, you can tell her what she'll get herself in the letter box is a nice lawyer letter from me."

He slammed out of the house. My father and I looked at each other. The alarm clock on the icebox was banging away louder than ever. I knew what he wanted to ask me. It was what I would have wanted to ask him: How did I know my mother was going to get the rent tonight?

I hoped he wouldn't ask me. I had promised my mother not

168

to say anything to anybody about her business relations with Walter Sinclair. Anybody included my father. If he did ask me, I would have to lie to him. Ordinarily, I would not have minded that. Any more than I had minded lying to Rabbi Goldfarb and Mr. O'Hare. For a few minutes, however, when my father first came into the kitchen and then when he talked back to Mr. Velvelschmidt, it had not been ordinary. It had been something unusual.

The unusual thing had disappeared as soon as the landlord had turned on the screws, but I remembered it. My father apparently didn't. Anyway, he didn't act as though he did. He dropped his glance and swayed away from me as he always swayed away from my mother.

"You better go to your meeting," he said.

I wished I could. Mr. O'Hare and his slabs of fat were a cinch compared with what I still had to face. I dragged the hike wagon downstairs, up Fourth Street, around the corner to Avenue D, and into Abe Lebenbaum's candy store. Abe's mother was behind the fountain. Hiding inside her *sheitl* the way Mr. O'Hare hid inside his fat, the little old lady was performing her daily ritual: emptying the cream from the tops of the Grade A milk bottles into a small pitcher. Sheffield's delivered six bottles of Grade A every morning. When he opened the store in the morning Abe Lebenbaum took these bottles from the doorstep and put them into the ice cream chest. They were not needed during the day because almost nobody came in until eight at night or later to order a malted. On East Fourth Street a malted was, for those who could afford it, a nightcap. In the early evening, after Abe's mother relieved him and waited for me to arrive, she managed to skim off almost a full pint of cream from the six bottles. People who ordered malteds didn't know the difference.

"Benny," Mrs. Lebenbaum said. "You're late."

Like Caesar who, after he crossed the Rubicon, was stuck with *iacte alea est,* Mrs. Lebenbaum was stuck with the only two words she could say in English.

"I told you yesterday I'd be late today. And I'll be even a little later," I said. "I have to pick up something and make a delivery. Only a few minutes, Mrs. Lebenbaum."

"It's business?" she said in Yiddish.

"What else?" I said.

"Where are you going?" she said.

"In the back," I said.

"Be quiet," she said. "Mr. Heizerick is by the slot machine."

Jesus, I thought. But Jesus I did not say. Not while wearing my scout uniform. "How long has he been out there?" I said.

"From not even a minute after Abe went upstairs for supper," Mrs. Lebenbaum said. "You wouldn't believe it. Like almost a miracle. I came in the store. Go upstairs, I said. Eat and sleep, I said. Abe went upstairs. The door it closed behind me like to you I'm talking now, Benny, and it opened again. Mr. Heizerick came in, and he gave me ten dollars. I'm lucky I had enough nickels."

Luck, of course, had nothing to do with it. Mr. Heizerick's appearance in the candy store at least twice and sometimes three times a week was as expected as Mr. Velvelschmidt's monthly appearance in our flat. In preparation for these visits Abe Lebenbaum went regularly to the Standard Bank and laid in a supply of rolls of nickels the way the owner of an opium den might regularly lay in a supply of poppy fruit for his favorite addict. Froyim Heizerick was as hung on the slot machine in the back room of Abe Lebenbaum's candy store as Edwin Drood was hung on the juice of *papaver somniferum.*

I hurried into the back room to pick up the four bottles of

Old Southwick I had hidden there two at a time three nights ago and the night before.

They were sitting behind the crates of Sheffield empties. I had made a small nest between the crates, which were reasonably stable because Sheffield picked up its empties only twice a month, and the door to the toilet, which was never closed because both hinges had rusted over the years into solid blocks of crumbling red metal. The slot machine stood against the wall at the other side of the room. Mr. Heizerick, feeding nickels into the slot and pulling down the lever, had his back to me. I eased the wagon past him and maneuvered the carriage wheels into the open space in front of the toilet. The click of the nickels going home, and the clunk of the lever going nowhere, continued steadily behind me as I eased the four burlap-wrapped bottles out from behind the Sheffield crates, put them into the wagon, and fastened the hasp. When I stood up and turned, I found myself facing Mr. Heizerick.

"Whatcha got innair?"

I can't remember what surprised me more: the fact that I had heard words coming out of Mr. Heizerick's frozen face, or the fact that they had been spoken in English. The only two places in which I ever heard English spoken were J.H.S. 64 and the Hannah H. Lichtenstein House.

"I didn't mean to disturb you," I said. "Just getting some stuff out."

I tried to pull the wagon around Mr. Heizerick in an arc.

"What kinda stuff?" he said.

"Troop meeting," I said. Very crisp. Very busy. Very gotta-get-on-with-it-mister-so-get-out-of-the-way-please. "Boy scouts," I said. "Hannah H. Lichtenstein House. Over on Avenue B. I'm the senior patrol leader."

"Let's see what's inna box."

"Just some signal flags," I said, keeping up the rapid flow of camouflage schmaltz. "We got the All-Manhattan rally coming up. We did pretty good in the eliminations. Three firsts, two seconds, and a third. Mr. O'Hare feels we got a pretty good chance in the finals. This meeting tonight, he's got to lay out the program for—"

"Opena box," Mr. Heizerick said.

I thought fast. This was turning out to be some night. Nobody was giving me a chance to think slow. Thinking fast, I wondered what I could lose by showing this zombie what was in the wagon. Maybe if they'd given me a chance to think slow, I might have wondered something else and the whole game might have come out another way. I don't know. Forty years later, in the taxi that was carrying me across the Borough of Queens to identify my mother's body in the morgue, the thing Mr. Heizerick did next still seemed to me as inevitable as it had that night in the back room behind Abe Lebenbaum's candy store. The man in the gray fedora swung his leg in a curiously graceful arc. His foot caught the hasp on the side of the wagon, flipped it up, and with a slight jogging movement, as though changing the direction of a bullet, his toe kicked open the lid of the box. Mr. Heizerick dipped down, took up one of the burlap-wrapped bottles, and sniffed it.

"Some signal flags," he said. "How much?"

"What?" I said.

On my word of honor. That's exactly what I said. Nothing else came to mind.

"Wuddeyeh get for this stuff?" Mr. Heizerick said.

I could have repeated my previous remark, but I sensed that it would put me in a bad light. When you are caught with your pants down, I had already learned, it is pointless to ask the man in the doorway if you are headed in the right direction for the turn-off to Prospect Park.

"I'm not supposed to sell it," I said.

"You're selling it now," Mr. Heizerick said. He tore open the top of the burlap, pulled out the bottle of Old Southwick, and sniffed at the cork.

"Boy, this stuff muss be right off diboat," he said. "How much?"

The way he held the bottle told me something that the tone of his voice, and his curious manner of running his words together, had caused me to suspect. This strange, doomed man who appeared in our midst out of nowhere to act out his own special dance of death, this poor dopey crazo was just an old-fashioned, common, garden variety *shikker*.

"How much?" Mr. Heizerick repeated.

Thinking fast, my reasoning went like this. As of now I was supposed to have in the hike wagon six bottles of Old Southwick. I had only five because Rabbi Goldfarb had copped one. And because of that bastard landlord, I had left the fixed bottle behind me. If I allowed Mr. Heizerick to take another, I would be two behind. I was headed toward the place where, I'd felt since I left Rabbi Goldfarb, I could promote a bottle. Why not, I thought, since I was thinking fast, why not promote two? All I needed was the money, and this strange drunk who thought nothing of shooting the bottom out of fifty bucks' worth of nickels several times a week certainly seemed to have plenty of money.

"I don't know how much," I said. "I don't sell it. I just collect it for my boss. If he finds out I gave away a bottle, he'll be sore at me." This seemed inadequate. Not the words. The way I was rattling them out. There was no heart-throb. No tremor

173

of terror. I thought of Oliver Twist asking for more. He didn't get it, of course, but the way he asked for it captured the hearts of the English-speaking world. It had made an impression on me. I dipped down at the knees in what I felt was a quite respectable cringe. I crinkled my eyes as though to hold back tears. And I revved up a respectable whine. "He'll kill me," I said. "My boss is a gangster. He'll shoot me dead. You can have the bottle, but please, I don't want to die, please give me enough to pay him."

Mr. Heizerick surveyed me with the contempt I am sure I deserved. Then he put his hand in his pocket, pulled out a folded wad of money, and peeled off a bill. "This okay?" he said.

I took the bill. A ten-spot. He'd handed me ten-spots many times, whenever he needed nickels for the slot machine. But this was a whole new ball game. I wasn't making change for a compulsive gambler. I was doing business on my own. There was no point in trying to think slow. This insane night had conditioned me to thinking fast. I went right on doing it. Like this. I did not know how much my mother was going to charge the Shumanskys for the bottles of Old Southwick. But I had to get enough out of Mr. Heizerick to buy two bottles before I got to Lenox Assembly Rooms. I had no idea what I would have to pay for them, but the more cash I had the better my chances would be to get them. If this drunk in the pearl gray fedora was willing to throw me a ten, why shouldn't he throw me two tens?

"My boss will kill me," I said. I listened to a replay of my voice. Not quite up to Oliver. I sank a little lower. Almost to my knees, but not exactly to my knees. I didn't want to soil my freshly washed khaki breeches. "He'll murder me," I whimpered. "He's a gangster. He carries two guns. He shoots people for nothing. If I don't come back with the bottles, or with the money to pay for them—"

My voice petered out. Too much Oliver. The whine was making me sick. It seemed to have the same effect on Mr. Heizerick. He tore another ten-spot from his wad, crumpled the bill, and threw it at me. Not inappropriately, it hit me in the mouth. Words failed me.

"Hee-yuh, hee-yuh," Mr. Heizerick said. "Now git the hell odda hee-yuh, yuh liddle bastid."

I still think that "bastid" was uncalled for, but I obeyed instructions. I lugged the hike wagon out into the store and loped on the double toward the front door.

"I'll be right back!" I yelled to old Mrs. Lebenbaum in Yiddish. "Don't go away! I'll be back in just a few minutes!"

"Benny!" she called after me. "Benny, are you crazy?"

For forty years, whenever this scene invades my mind, I have found it helpful to assure myself that Mrs. Lebenbaum's question was rhetorical. After all, Mrs. Lebenbaum was not really interested in my answer. Suppose I had called back across my shoulder, "You bet I am! Nutty as a fruit cake!"

For one thing, I would not have known how to say that in Yiddish. And what other language did Mrs. Lebenbaum understand? For another, what would have been accomplished if she had understood? Benny is crazy? My poor son Abe, he pays a boy five dollars a week because Abe has a good heart, and the boy turns out to be crazy! And finally, I didn't quite understand the situation myself. My emotions were not exactly orthodox.

I was tense and nervous about whether I would have enough time to carry out my part of the plan Walter Sinclair and my mother had cooked up. But I was also excited. I'd had a one-bottle setback from Rabbi Goldfarb, true. But I'd made it with ease past the hill of that louse Mr. Velvelschmidt. And while I'd slipped back another bottle at the hands of Mr. Heizerick, the stone-faced drunk had handed over two ten-spots. Never in my life had I held such a sum in my hands.

Any man, and that's how I thought of myself at the time, any man who had twenty dollars to work with, and couldn't fashion the course of history, didn't deserve to be trusted by people like my mother and Walter Sinclair. Racing up Avenue D, dragging the wagon behind me, I realized for the first time how much I wanted their approval. Approval? What was I talking about? I wanted their admiration. And I knew how to earn it, too.

If it is possible, while dragging a wagon that contains four quarts of Old Southwick, to race up six flights of tenement stairs, then I raced up to the top-floor door behind which the Zabriskie sisters lived and plied their trade. Here, with my hand raised to knock, I didn't. I was suddenly assailed by my lack of knowledge of the terrain I was invading.

I knew Abe Lebenbaum was behind that door, being entertained by Lya. But who else was there? I stood motionless in the smelly hall, closed my eyes, and forced myself to summon into my mind the appointment book clipped under the shelf in the candy store telephone booth. Who was booked for tonight? More accurately, who had been booked for six-thirty?

The Zabriskie sisters usually worked half-hour shifts. It was now shortly after seven. Whoever was in that flat getting his ashes hauled had started the treatment at six-thirty. But who was he? He? Christ, it could be they. There were three Zabriskie sisters. It was rumored that some elements of their treatment were so unique that some of the biggest spenders uptown had never heard of them. And they were reputed to have customers who paid handsomely for treatments so unique that they could not be described. Except, perhaps, by George Weitz, and he was notoriously unreliable because, while he claimed he got his information from his father's medical library, I suspected he made it all up, like his jokes. Once, when he was telling me there was a form of hauling ashes that involved three women and one man, and I refused to believe him, George drew me some diagrams to prove it. I was not exactly convinced. There is something about a diagram, especially of a woman, that lacks verisimilitude. Especially when you're fourteen.

I concentrated on the appointment book inside my head. I had made no entries in the book tonight, of course. Tonight I had not yet taken up my post in the candy store. But the night before had been peppy. I recalled that the phone had not stopped ringing from the moment I came on duty. I retraced in my head the entries I had made in the book. Two or three had been the usual replacements for dates scheduled for the night before. That happened all the time. Men got excited, picked up the phone, made a date, then found out when they got home that the little woman had also made a date. Aunt Tillie was coming from Bensonhurst. Aunt Tillie and the Zabriskie sisters were mutually exclusive. Result: another phone call. Most of those I had taken had been, as always, for the weekend. Those weekends. God. I still wonder how those three poor girls ever got through their Saturdays and Sundays. Group therapy, no doubt.

Then the electric light bulb inside my head went *boing!* The guy who had called the day my mother had mysteriously appeared in Rabbi Goldfarb's *cheder* to make sure I got home for supper on time. The night my mother had refused to let my father go to his Erste Neustadter Krank und Interstitzing Verein meeting. The night she had led me to the dock to meet

Walter Sinclair. The night this slob had called from a phone booth on Fourteenth Street for a date with Pauline, refused Marie, and settled for Lya. The slob named Ted Werner. He had apparently been satisfied with Lya's treatment. He had called back the night before, to make another date for tonight. At six-thirty. How Lya was handling both Abe Lebenbaum and Ted Werner was none of my business. George Weitz and his diagrams might have brought it closer to my business, but now there was no time for that. I had to get to the Shumansky wedding, and I had two more stops to make before I even pointed myself in the direction of Lenox Assembly Rooms. Knocking on the door of the Zabriskie sisters' flat would be a mistake. There were at least two men in there. I didn't want company or witnesses. I wanted my two bottles of Old Southwick.

I turned and ran toward the skylight steps. Then my brain started functioning and I turned again, ran back, and grabbed the hike wagon. I couldn't leave that outside the door of the Zabriskie sisters' flat.

I dragged the wagon up the skylight steps and pushed my way through the iron door to the roof. The fact that there was still plenty of daylight was refreshing. It was as though I had been given the present of having the clocks turned back to assure me I would accomplish every step of my assignment and not be late for the meeting with my mother.

I dragged the wagon across the buckling tar-paper roof to the fire-escape ladder on the side of the tenement where the Zabriskie sisters lived. Luckily, their flat faced the courtyard. Nobody would see me from the street. As I eased the wagon over the edge of the roof, I paused for a quick look around. To the east I could see the back of our tenement on the Lewis

Street corner. Beyond it, I could see the Fourth Street dock jutting out into the river. To the west and north I could see the two bulging spires of Lenox Assembly rooms, like great big fat onions stuck on the tops of flagpoles. I climbed over the edge, got a good grip on the wooden crossbar of the wagon, and started down the black iron ladder. It wasn't much of a climb, but I had to do it holding the wagon away from the ladder with one hand so the banging of the box against the metal would not announce my arrival. I got down to the fire escape outside the Zabriskie flat without a single bang. I leaned the wagon gently against the dirty brick wall, knelt down on the iron slats of the fire escape, and peered into the window.

To begin with, I had never before in my life seen a completely naked woman. Parts of naked women, yes. But a whole naked woman, no. Mr. O'Hare had twice taken the troop to Coney Island on hot August Sundays when a hike to the Palisades had seemed too difficult and potentially unpleasant. These trips to Coney Island proved to be eyeopeners.

In the men's locker room of the Birnbaum Baths on Surf Avenue, where I changed into my bathing suit with the entire Raven Patrol, George Weitz and I had discovered a couple of knotholes in the cheesily hammered together wooden wall that separated us from what proved to be the women's locker room. In those days, of course, my life was run more or less by the elevated standards of the Scout Law. Just the same, when I found a knothole I forgot all this nonsense about a scout is courteous, and share and share alike. When I found a knothole I hung onto it.

As a result, by the time I found myself on the fire escape outside the Zabriskie sisters' bedroom, I had seen my share of female blubber. Maybe more than my share. Who could possibly have parceled out equitably the women who in my youth changed bathing suits in the locker room of the Birnbaum Baths at Coney Island?

Only Rubens could have done them justice. I refer, of course, to Itzick Rubens, the house painter on Avenue C, who used brushes ten inches wide. Or maybe the ministers of Catherine the Great, who were accustomed to partitioning things like Poland. What I am getting at is that until that night on the fire escape, outside the Zabriskie sisters' bedroom, the naked women of whom I had seen parts had not been small.

What I saw now turned my knees to Jell-O. What it did to my mind I still don't know. All I remember is a wild sort of churning. As though I were being given the third degree. Questions hurled at me from all directions. Answers flung back at me in the form of flashed snapshots. Like arrows whamming into the huddled nest of covered wagons behind which the ambushed forty-niners were trying to hold off the encircling Indians.

First question. What were three naked women doing in that bedroom? Up like a lantern slide, first fragmentary but graphic reply. Oh, no! Another shot. Oh, yes! Jesus Christ, it's not possible. Take another look, Benny. I did. Not easy to do because there was a lot of movement, but I managed. Jesus Christ again. That's what they were doing, all right. But to whom? Keep watching, kid. What was that? A naked man? No, only part of him. What part? Hard to tell. More movement. A face appeared somewhere in the middle of the three Zabriskie sisters. Could it be? Of course it was. But what about the rest of Abe Lebenbaum? I'd never seen my boss except in his blue denim shirt and his sharkskin pants. The rest of Abe now came into view. Incredible. That's all those pants concealed? Abe, what have you done to yourself? Wait, there were two of them.

Two men, I mean. This one seemed to emerge from under the bed. He moved to the closet near the door. When he turned, and I saw what he had in his hand, my mind came clear. The dirty rotten bastard was holding one of the two bottles of Old Southwick I had paid Pauline Zabriskie a quarter to hide for me.

"Put that down!" I screamed.

The scream was inside my head. I couldn't let those wrestlers know I was there. I also had to stop them from drinking my Old Southwick. How? The scout motto came to my assistance: *Be Prepared!* I was sorry Mr. O'Hare couldn't see me as I crawled to the wagon and worked the hasp loose. I had removed and placed in the stone cave on the steps down to Old Man Tzoddick's cellar the Morse signal flags, the iron cooking grill, the two big soup and bean pots, and the troop first-aid kit. I had not bothered with the smaller items.

Now I rummaged around under the bottles of Old Southwick I had picked up thus far. I found the piece of flint. I rummaged faster and came up with the envelope full of charred gauze. The one thing I could not find was the six-inch length of steel file. It must have dropped out while I was emptying the wagon on Old Man Tzoddick's cellar steps.

"Jesus," I muttered.

You can't make fire with flint and charred gauze. You've got to have a piece of steel. I took a fast look through the window. Lya was coming into the bedroom carrying glasses. Or maybe she was Pauline? Or Marie? I had never been able to tell them apart on the street, or when they answered the door in their flowered kimonas. How was I going to tell them apart now? I dismissed the question from my mind. Telling the Zabriskie sisters apart was not my problem. My problem was to stop them and Abe Lebenbaum and the other man from drinking the Old Southwick I had promised my mother and Walter Sinclair I would deliver to the Shumansky wedding.

How? Come on, Benny, think. How? The metal slats of the fire escape seemed to say: What about us, you dope? I pulled a wad of charred gauze from the envelope, cupped it in my palm under one of the slats, and hacked at the iron slat with the piece of flint. Sparks flew. Unfortunately, they flew in the wrong direction. I came in closer, shifted the lump of flint to get a vertical stroke, and hacked again. The shower of sparks hit the wad of charred gauze.

I dropped the flint, cupped the gauze in both hands, raised it to my lips, and blew. I did it the way Mr. O'Hare had taught me. As though I were cooling a spoonful of soup. The tiny glow in the middle of the gauze caught and spread. I looked around desperately. I had no paper. Yes, I had. I had the envelope in which the gauze had been packed. With my teeth I tore the envelope sideways and dipped the ragged edge into the glow in the middle of the gauze. It caught. The flame started to creep up. Now I needed something that would really burn. I looked around fast. Like everybody else on East Fourth Street the Zabriskie sisters used their fire escape as an auxiliary refrigerator.

The window sill had strung out on it half a bottle of milk, two paper bags, and four tomatoes. I tore open the paper bags. One contained potatoes. The other was wrapped around a Moxie bottle with a cork in it. I sniffed. It did not contain Moxie now. It smelled like the stuff my mother poured into the empty Heinz pickle jars. It occurred to me that girls who made their livings in bed could not afford to turn their backs, or indeed anything else, on this problem.

I pulled the cork with my teeth, poured some of the benzine on the paper bag, and touched the burning gauze to the paper.

The *poof* of flame that went up almost cost me my eyebrows. I took the Moxie bottle in one hand and banged it against the bedroom window. The glass shattered into the room. I shoved the blazing paper bag through the hole. The curtains caught.

"Fire!" I yelled through the hole. "Fire! Fire!"

I was unable to make out exactly what the five people in the bedroom did next. None of it, of course, bore any resemblance to what they had been doing when I caught my first glimpse of them. Now I caught a new glimpse of different parts of the Zabriskie sisters. Or so I thought, anyway. It is possible that what I saw were several parts of only one Zabriskie sister. Anyway, the parts were heaving around like a newsreel shot of lava bubbling away in the crater of a volcano. The same was true of the other man, or, as I had logged him into the date book down in the candy store, Ted Werner. About Abe Lebenbaum all I can honestly report is that I saw his face for a moment. The smoke had started to grow and billow like foaming soapsuds. Then Abe dove headfirst into the suds, moving in the general direction of the door that led to the kitchen. From then on all I remember about the Zabriskie sisters and their two customers was one great big confused screaming contest. I guess it was all that undraped flesh coming into contact with the mushrooming fire. I let them scream. I had work to do.

I started by banging the rest of the window out of the frame with the Moxie bottle. This made it possible for me not only to climb into the bedroom. It also spread the rest of the benzine across the bed in great wide squirting sprays. As a result, what happened to the room was probably not unlike what happened to Chicago when Mrs. O'Leary's cow kicked over the lantern. It was clear that I didn't have much time.

I went through the window, circled the flaming bed, and reached the closet. On the floor, just inside the door, my foot

kicked the bottle of Old Southwick that Lya—Pauline? Marie?
—had been about to open when the scout motto came to my
rescue. I scooped it up. The burlap wrapper was beginning to
smoke but the cork had not been touched. I slapped the smoke
out of the burlap by banging the bottle against my khaki
breeches, and dove into the closet. My second bottle was
exactly where Pauline—Marie? Lya?—had stashed it three
days ago. I grabbed it, turned, and tripped. The closet door,
swinging shut behind me, had caught my shoulder.

I kicked the door back and caught my foot in one of the
pink wrappers the girls wore when they were not working. As
I sagged, the wrapper tore with my weight. When I hit the
closet wall and pushed myself up straight on my feet, I saw
what was behind the wrapper: a shelf with what looked like a
dozen bottles of Old Southwick.

They were not wrapped in burlap. They were just standing
there, neat and naked. I looked at them, blinked, coughed
away some smoke, and tried to think of the appropriate Scout
Law. I couldn't. The men who had decided that a scout was
trustworthy, loyal, helpful, and so on, had clearly never con-
templated the dilemma of a scout who had to meet his mother
at the Lenox Assembly Rooms with a specified number of bottles of Old Southwick and was two bottles short.

I didn't have time to think it through. I grabbed two of those
bottles. I belted my way out of the closet, across the bedroom,
through the broken window, and out onto the fire escape. I
shoved the four bottles of Old Southwick into the wagon, fastened the hasp, and started down the fire escape, dragging the
wagon behind me. I made it to the yard before I heard the fire
engines. Hearing them settled one thing. Back out into Avenue
D meant back out into the hands of the cops. Not for Benny.

I turned and cut across the yard, through the open back door of the tenement facing Third Street. I scuttled across the ground-floor hall and made it to the sidewalk. I was halfway down Third Street, heading for Lewis, when I was struck by an assessment of my position.

I had caught up on the number of bottles of Old Southwick my mother was expecting. I had done it without using the two ten-spots Mr. Heizerick had given me in the back of the candy store. Nobody except Mr. Heizerick and I knew about those two ten-spots. Mr. Heizerick, feeding nickels into the slot machine in the back of the candy store, was undoubtedly too drunk to remember he had given me the money. Conclusion: I was not only in my mother's good graces. I was also in possession of twenty bucks that nobody knew anything about.

Next question: Was it necessary for anybody to know about it? The answer was obvious, of course, but as I hustled around the Third Street corner, dragging the wagon into Lewis Street, it seemed only right to subject the question to the rigorous scrutiny of the Scout Law.

A scout is trustworthy? Of course. Loyal? Why not? Helpful? Certainly. Friendly? What else? Courteous? By the time I got to a scout is reverent I had also reached the Fourth Street corner. Dusk was closing in. Moral issues would have to wait. I forgot the two ten-spots in my pocket and dragged the wagon down Fourth Street into the dock area.

As usual, when night was about to come down on East Fourth Street, the dock was deserted. I moved down toward the uptown side. It was lined with barges. They had obviously arrived during the day. All were piled high with coal.

The motorboat was moored to the far side of the middle barge. No lights were showing. I eased the wagon against the edge of the dock and looked around. Nobody was in sight. I leaned down toward the barge.

"Chanah's boy," I called softly.

It was the password on which my mother and Walter had agreed.

"Chanah's boy," I called again.

The ropes creaked. The capstans groaned quietly. The river slapped against the piles. The beams moved uneasily under my feet. Not much. Maybe not at all. But the illusion of movement was very real. It made the whole night seem very unreal. As though everything I had done from the moment I left home to pick up the hike wagon in the Hannah H. Lichtenstein House was part of a dream. It had been easy enough to believe in the dream while I was racing from the Hannah H. Lichtenstein House to Old Man Tzoddick's cellar steps, and Rabbi Goldfarb's *cheder,* and back to our house, and down to Abe Lebenbaum's candy store, and up to the apartment of the Zabriskie sisters, collecting the bottles of Old Southwick. But now the racing was over. It was quiet on the dock. The dream was finished. I felt awake. Awake and scared.

"Chanah's boy!"

"Not so loud, kee-yid."

The tall, thin figure in the black turtleneck sweater came easing gently out of the wheelhouse door on the barge directly below me.

"Sorry," I said. "I thought nobody was here."

Walter laughed. This was only the third time I had met him, but I realized at once that what I had remembered most clearly about him was his laugh. This puzzled me. It wasn't exactly as though this tall young rumrunner had just done something important. All he'd done was laugh. You don't get to be fourteen without having heard a certain amount of laughter. There was a great deal of laughter on East Fourth Street. I never thought of it until I met Walter Sinclair because until I met Walter, I see now, I'd had the wrong idea about laughter.

All my life laughter was a noise you and other people made to protect yourself. A bastard like Mr. Velvelschmidt showed up with his pig eyes and his receipt book to collect the rent, and you didn't have it, as my mother often didn't, so you laughed the bastard off, screaming at his remarks as though he was Ben Turpin, and if you laughed loud enough, he stopped threatening with the lawyer letters and went away, thinking maybe you were not just a stupid deadbeat trying to *goniff* him out of his twenty-three bucks, because a person who laughs at your jokes can't be all bad, and maybe you were telling the truth about having the rent for him next week.

Walter Sinclair, however, he didn't laugh that way. He wasn't baring his teeth like a dog to keep you at bay so you wouldn't take a bite out of his tail. When Walter Sinclair laughed he made a sound I'd never heard before. Certainly not on East Fourth Street. It made me feel good.

"You're a smart boy," Walter said. "If nobody was here, how'd the Old Jeff get herself tied up to this here baby?"

I took a stab at the kind of laughing Walter did. It didn't come out exactly right. After all, it was my first try. But even so, I could feel the improvement.

"What I meant," I said, "I meant I've got only about ten minutes, and I don't want to lose any time."

"You won't," he said. "Not while Walter Sinclair is around. You got your bottles?"

"All eight," I said.

"Good boy," Walter said. "Now here comes the rest."

187

He stepped back into the pilot house, came out with a big burlap-wrapped sack, and handed it up to me. "Too heavy?" he said.

"No," I said. "I got it."

"Lay it in nice and easy," Walter said. "They're packed good, but it's five bottles."

I put the sack into the wagon at the bottom of the box. By the time I came back to the edge of the dock Walter was holding up a second package.

"That's ten, now," he said. "Ten, plus the eight you collected, that's the eighteen bottles your mama said she needs for tonight. I could get hung for these ten. I had to steal them from two deliveries. But I promised your mama I'd get them, didn't I?"

"That's right," I said.

I put the second one on top of the first, then wedged them both with the eight loose bottles. It made a tight fit, but when I got the hasp down and clicked it into place I knew there would be no rattling on the trip west.

"You all set, now?"

Walter was standing below me on the barge deck, his hands resting on the edge of the dock, looking up at me with a smile that kept rising and falling gently as the barge rose and fell on the movement of the river.

"Ready to go," I said.

"You take care of your mama, now," Walter said. "You hear?"

I must have looked puzzled. I certainly felt puzzled. Being told to take care of my mother was like being urged to make sure the sun rose the next morning. Who had to take care of a force of nature?

"Yes, sir," I said.

188

Walter laughed again. "You calling me sir," he said. "Like I was your teacher or something."

"I didn't mean that," I said. "I mean—"

My voice trailed away. I didn't know how to say what I meant. I was suddenly confused by an astonishing thought. I had never really liked anybody. There were people I preferred to others. Chink Alberg, for instance, gave me less of a pain than Hot Cakes Rabinowitz. But neither was a big deal in my book. My father was someone to whom I was loyal because that was expected of me. But I was well aware that he was generally considered to be a fool, and I didn't really like fools. My mother was the cop who ran my life, and the rule with cops was simple: smile when you pass them. Mr. O'Hare was a dope from uptown whose approval I valued because it made me a big shot in the troop. My teachers were custodians of the world I had discovered when I left the three rooms where for the first five years of my life I had never spoken anything but Yiddish and Hungarian, and who warms up to custodians?

What I'm getting at is that up to this moment on the Fourth Street dock the people with whom I had spent my life had been people with whom I had to get along in order to survive, and I was the boy who knew how to work that little trick. This tall, slender, curly-headed man in the turtleneck sweater with the smile that was as warming as our kitchen stove in January was the first person I had ever met from whom I didn't want anything. Well, no. That wasn't quite true. There was something I wanted from him. All of a sudden I wanted Walter Sinclair to like me.

"Well, you go along, now," he said. "You be a good boy and you take care of your mama. She's a real fine lady. Not many boys got mamas as fine as you got. Okay?"

"Okay," I said, but I didn't exactly know what I was saying

189

okay to. How could I take care of my mother? It was the other way around, wasn't it? She was always taking care of me. But this man obviously thought highly of her, and I liked him, and he wanted me to take care of her, even if I had to invent ways to do it. "Okay," I said again. "You don't worry."

Walter laughed, reached up over the edge of the dock, and punched my shoulder lightly. "Worry?" he said. "Me? Not while I've got me a smart boy like you in my corner."

It occurred to me I'd better get out of his corner fast, and over to the Lenox Assembly Rooms, or my mother would take me into a corner of her own and give me a piece of her mind. It was, I see now, a pretty good one, but the pieces she gave me had sharp edges. I still bear some of the scars. On that night in 1927, dragging the Troop 244 hike wagon toward the Shumansky wedding, I did not want to add to my collection. As soon as I turned into Avenue D, I switched to scout pace.

This brought me past the clock over the Standard Bank at twenty-five minutes past seven. I had two blocks to go, and five minutes in which to cover them. Everything had worked out. It didn't seem possible, but everything had worked out. I would be at Lenox Assembly Rooms on time.

I had been inside the place only once in my life, years before, when I was a little kid. It was during an election campaign, and a man named Eugene Debs was running for President on the Socialist ticket. Eugene Victor Debs. Word spread on East Fourth Street that this man was actually a prisoner in jail. How could a prisoner run for President? Nobody on Fourth Street seemed to know, but everybody on the block enjoyed talking about it, including my father.

One night he came home with the news that this man named Debs was coming to Lenox Assembly Rooms on Saturday night to make a speech. My mother told my father to stop talking like a fool and eat his *kalbfleish*. My father ate his *kalbfleish,* and when my mother went to the stove, he told me in a way that must, I suppose, be described as out of the corner of his mouth—although my father was not a corner-of-the-mouth type—that it was true, Mr. Debs would appear at Lenox Assembly Rooms on Saturday night. My mother came back from the stove and told my father—in a manner that could not possibly be described as out of the corner of her mouth—to stop being crazy. I don't recall how he was able to convince her he was complying with this request, but my father must have swung it, because my mother dropped the subject.

On Saturday, at supper, he asked her if he could go to the meeting. My mother said she didn't care what he did. What my father did was take me along.

Years later, when I discussed this with my mother, she said the only reason she allowed me to accompany my father was that she did not know what a meeting was. Neither did I. After all these years I'm still not sure that what I saw was a meeting.

This is what I saw.

The sidewalk in front of Lenox Assembly Rooms. Exactly like every other sidewalk I had ever seen except that this one ended not against the front stoops of tenements, but against a set of wide sandstone steps that rose elegantly inside a set of curling stone banisters. On both banisters were set fat black iron posts surmounted by round yellow carbon arc lamps as big as basketballs. They hissed. A lot of people were waiting on the sidewalk in front of the sandstone steps. I recognized some of them, but many were strangers. There was a great deal of back-and-forth movement, as though the waiting people couldn't decide from which direction Mr. Debs would arrive. What interested me most were those great big round yellow lamps. I liked the way they hissed.

Suddenly, from out of Third Street, a wagon emerged. A hay wagon. It was drawn by two enormous horses. The driver sat up high, flailing away at the air with a whip, hitting nothing and laughing his head off. He guided the wagon around in a swinging arc and pulled up in front of the sandstone steps under the hissing lamps. A cheer exploded from the people on the sidewalk. I couldn't see why. All I could see was the flat bed of the wagon, which was piled high with hay. The smell was pleasant, but that's all.

Then the hay began to move, and out of the middle, sliding down on his rear end toward the tailgate of the wagon, came a baldheaded man who seemed to be all angles. As soon as I saw his face I understood why the driver had been laughing. The man sliding out of the wagon was laughing in the same way. It was the way Walter Sinclair laughed years later. The people on the sidewalk moved forward. The cheering grew louder. I was astonished to notice that my father was cheering, too. The people nearest the tail gate grabbed the baldheaded man, lifted him to their shoulders, and carried him up the stone steps. My father pulled me along.

At the top of the steps two wide doors opened into a high hall from the ceiling of which hung a crystal chandelier. The crowd moved across this hall, making a lot of enthusiastic noises many of which were shouted words I did not understand. I understood clearly, however, that the words were enthusiastic. Suddenly, pulled along by my father as though I were on a leash, we erupted into an auditorium lined with benches.

The people carrying the man from the hay wagon moved on forward to a platform up front. They climbed the steps while the people down on the floor scrambled for seats. My father, who always moved so unobtrusively at home, astonished me by the speed and skill with which he darted around, never dropping my hand, and managed to find a couple of clear places on a bench about halfway down toward the platform. He shoved me onto the bench and then sat down beside me. The men on the platform set the baldheaded man down on his feet. He raised his hands high in the air. The crowd exploded. My father beat his palms and shouted. I remember thinking he was acting funny, and that's all I do remember.

More accurately, when next I became aware of my surroundings, I was in bed at home, and it was morning. I never heard a word of what Eugene Victor Debs said the night before about why his listeners should vote for him for President. But I saw him. It was quite a sight. I never saw anything like it again. Not even in the Lenox Assembly Rooms on the night of the Shumansky wedding.

The first thing I saw when I pulled up with the hike wagon in front of the sandstone steps caused me to think all at once that maybe my mother was not as smart as Walter Sinclair had said she was. She had told me to meet her in front of the Lenox Assembly Rooms at seven-thirty. It was now seven-thirty, and I had made it to the front of the Lenox Assembly Rooms, but my mother had obviously not. Instead of my mother, what was waiting for me was another familiar figure: the young man in the Rogers Peet suit who had opened the door of Meister's Matzoh Bakery on Lafayette Street for me and my mother the night of the All-Manhattan eliminations. He was leaning against one of the curling stone banisters, directly under the lowest of the big fat round hissing carbon arc lamps.

"Hi, kid," he said. "Don't you ever take off that uniform?"

I was so confused by my mother's absence and his presence

193

that I did not grasp at once what he meant. Then I remembered I had been wearing my uniform that Saturday night and I was wearing it now.

"Troop meeting," I said. "I'm going to a troop meeting."

"Here in Lenox Assembly Rooms?" the young man said.

"What?" I said.

I didn't really mean "What?" I meant "Jesus Christ, what's going to happen now?" But who could I ask?

"When you and your mother came over to see my father, you said your scout troop they have their meetings in the Hannah H. Lichtenstein. Remember?"

Actually, I didn't. To compensate for this deficiency, however, my mind came up with the recollection that Mr. Imberotti, the young man's father, had addressed this little bastard as Mario.

"That's where I'm going," I said, and then I said something stupid. "I just stopped off here a minute to see my mother."

To see my mother? What was the matter with me? Didn't I remember what had happened to Little Red Riding Hood when she had been dumb enough to tip her mitt in exactly the same way to the wolf?

"What for?" Mario Imberotti said. "Give her a kiss, maybe?" His sardonic voice and his puzzling words did nothing to clear up my confusion. He must have grasped that the only thing racing around in my mind was the not very productive question: What the hell is this guy talking about? Mario said, "You give your mother a kiss every time you go to a meeting?"

There was only one reply any red-blooded East Fourth Street boy could make to that remark. Even a red-blooded East Fourth Street boy who was also chicken-livered. Scout uniform or no scout uniform, I made it, then I swung the

194

wagon around in a wide arc and started up the stone steps. I had no idea where I was going. Into Lenox Assembly Rooms, sure. But what part of Lenox Assembly Rooms? It was a four-story building, with meeting halls all over the place. How did I know in what part of the building the Shumansky wedding was taking place? I didn't. But I did know my mother had contracted to supply the booze for the occasion, and I knew I had just broken my back for an hour and a half collecting the stuff, and I knew I had the giggle water tucked away neatly in the troop hike wagon. I also knew that if I wanted to get the tail I had just broken back into one piece, I had better get the stuff to my mother, and I knew there was some connection between my mother not being out on the sidewalk to meet me, as she had promised, and the presence of this bastard in the uptown suit standing in the place where my mother had said she would meet me.

She had laid it on the line to Mr. Imberotti in the kitchen over the matzoh bakery. I had heard her say it. I had also heard Mr. Imberotti's answer. Even huddled in a towel and breathing steam out of a kettle, I could tell from Mr. Imberotti's voice when he told little Mario that he felt in my mother they had got themselves a bad one, I could tell the old man was not just making a rueful remark for the record. I suddenly remembered what Walter Sinclair had said. "Take care of your mother." The words didn't seem so silly now. All of a sudden I was scared.

The moment the feeling of fear hit me, something hit my ankle. I fell sprawling—what the sportswriters call supine when they mean prone—spread-eagled on my kisser against the stone steps. I could hear the wagon bumping back down behind me, step by step, to the sidewalk. I swung around on my back and desperately shoved myself up on my feet.

"You rotten bastard," I screamed at the bastard who had tripped me, and I lunged for the handle of the wagon. I missed. The wagon's carriage wheels hit the bottom step. The wagon went up in the air. I cringed back against the sandstone steps, waiting for the crash. It never came. At the bottom of the steps, standing on the sidewalk, were Mr. O'Hare and Mr. Norton Krakowitz. The scoutmaster's fat body moved faster than I would have thought he could make it go. He caught the handle of the wagon about a foot from the ground. Mr. Krakowitz, who always moved fast, especially when he was asked to sing "Me and My Shadow," shot out a helping hand. They managed to get the wagon to the sidewalk without a crash. Just a slight bump.

"Look here, my good man," my scoutmaster said to Mario Imberotti. "May I inquire just what it is you think you are doing?"

My good man? To this junior gangster? *Oy!* I could see the whole Boy Scouts of America empire tottering.

"And you do some looking here, too, you fat slob," said Mario. "What the hell do you think *you're* doing?"

"Protecting the property of Troop 244," said Mr. O'Hare. "Of which I happen to be the scoutmaster. This hike wagon belongs to my troop. We saw you trip this young man, did we not, Norton?"

"Most emphatically yes," said Mr. Norton Krakowitz. "We saw you extrude your leg, or perhaps I should say foot, and thus cause the toppling of Senior Patrol Leader Kramer to the stone steps of this edifice."

When he wasn't singing "Me and My Shadow," Mr. Krakowitz was talking like an educated Arab.

"And who the hell are you?" said Mario Imberotti. "My good man?"

This was a mistake. Norton Krakowitz was not a real man, good or bad. He was a public image to which Mr. Krakowitz spent his life adding brush strokes intended to create the illusion of reality.

"I am Norton Krakowitz," he said. "Owner and president of Krakowitz's Men's and Boys' Clothes, Inc., located at 47 Avenue B. I am also the district leader of the Boy Scouts of America for the Southern Manhattan area," said Mr. Norton Krakowitz to the skinny body encased in the little gangster's Rogers Peet suit. "My business status in this community, as well as my official position as the executive in charge of the welfare of the youth in our area, have provided me with a number of significant and important friends in the police department. I refer specifically to the hierarchy of the Seventh Precinct, with which I am sure you are familiar."

Mr. Norton Krakowitz paused to make two sweeping adjustments to his sideburns. He used his palms. A couple of garden rakes would have been inadequate. Mr. Norton Krakowitz had gray-white hair that was made of tightly kinked rolls of steel wire. Nothing he did to it with his hands could possibly affect the way the growth hugged his scalp and the side of his head. Like shining barnacles on the hull of a ship. But the gesture had an astonishing effect. As though with the two backward brushing motions of his palms Mr. Norton Krakowitz had set a frame around his head. It made him look like those pictures of senators and emperors on Roman coins.

"In short and in summary and in conclusion, Mr. Mario Imberotti," he said, "and I trust you will make note of the to you perhaps surprising fact that I know your name, and I also happen to know the activities in which you and the members of your family are engaged, if you don't answer Mr.

O'Hare's question at once, young Mr. Imberotti, I can promise you that before this night is over, you and the other members of your family will find yourselves in very big trouble. In short and in summary and in conclusion, young man, don't you fool around with Norton Krakowitz." The Jewish Roman Emperor of Avenue B turned to Mr. O'Hare. "You may ask your question again," he said. "Speak freely, Mr. O'Hare. You will be answered."

"It isn't really a question," said the scoutmaster of Troop 244. "I merely stated what you, too, saw, Norton, namely and to be specific, as we approached these steps we saw this young man reach out his foot and trip my senior patrol leader, Scout Kramer, thus endangering the property of Troop 244, namely and to be specific, this hike wagon. I would like to know why Mr.—What did you say his name is?"

"Imberotti," Mr. Norton Krakowitz said. "Mario Imberotti."

"Thank you," Mr. O'Hare said. "I would like to know why Mr. Imberotti would do such a thing. Will you tell me, please, Mr. Imberotti?"

I now saw, or rather sensed, that there was more to Mario Imberotti than his suit. He looked at Mr. O'Hare and Mr. Krakowitz with what they apparently thought was great respect. I did not share this thought, and I was at least thirty years younger than either of these two jokers. How come I was smarter than my scoutmaster and the president of Krakowitz's Men's and Boys' Clothing, Inc.? Very simple. The look in Mario Imberotti's eyes reminded me of the way I had looked at Mr. O'Hare when he got in my way at the Hannah H. Lichtenstein House and I had to shoot him a load of bull to get my mitts on the hike wagon right under his nose.

198

"It's like this," Mario Imberotti said. "My father he's a good friend of Yonkel Shumansky."

"Who is he?" Mr. O'Hare said.

"The father of the bride," Mario Imberotti said. "This wedding that's going on here tonight." The young gangster gestured up the sandstone steps toward the Lenox Assembly Rooms. "It's Mr. Shumansky's daughter. He's very proud she's getting married, and my father wants everything should go okay, because he and Mr. Shumansky they're good friends, so my father sent me over to make sure nothing goes wrong."

Mr. O'Hare's acres of face began to look a little the way all that skin had looked the Saturday night my mother had appeared on the floor of the Hannah H. Lichtenstein House gym while George Weitz was wigwagging to me Matthew, XXV, 29.

"What on earth could go wrong?" he said.

"On earth, who knows?" Mario Imberotti said. "On the second floor of the Lenox Assembly Rooms, the guests could go blind."

"Blind?" Mr. O'Hare said.

It occurred to me that when David picked those stones from the brook and wound up his slingshot and let Goliath have it, Mr. O'Hare had the perfect voice for the boy on the Philistine side who said, "In the forehead?"

"Sure," Mario Imberotti said. "People go blind all the time from drinking the wrong kind of stuff."

"From drinking what?" Mr. O'Hare said.

Mr. Norton Krakowitz was no Philistine. Or maybe a man who sold men's and boys' suits had to have an instinct for picking the winning side. He took a couple of swift swipes at his steel-wire sideburns and stepped forward.

"Mario," he said. "If your father is supplying the liquid

refreshment for this wedding, I am certain nobody is going to go blind."

"My father is not involved in this wedding except as a close friend of Yonkel Shumansky," Mario Imberotti said. "That's why I tripped this young snotnose."

"You will please be good enough to watch your language," Mr. O'Hare said. "The eleventh Scout Law says a scout is clean, and Scout Kramer has never to my knowledge violated any of the ten preceding it or the twelfth that follows it. Am I correct, Scout Kramer?"

Well, I was not a snotnose. "No, sir," I said.

"You admit, then, that you tripped Scout Kramer on these steps?" Mr. Norton Krakowitz said.

"I had to," Mario Imberotti said.

"You had to?" Mr. O'Hare said.

Come to think of it, I don't believe the Philistines could have stood this bastard.

"What else could I do?" Mario Imberotti said. "I had to see what's in that wagon."

He walked toward it. He reached down to take the hasp. I thought of Walter Sinclair. "Take care of your mother." The words gave me strength. They even did something for my aim. The toe of my shoe caught Mario Imberotti in one of the world's great targets.

The little gangster screamed and did a Four Wings and Scram. When the law of gravity brought him back to the side-walk, he toppled to the left. Mr. Norton Krakowitz caught him.

"Who the hell did that?" Mario Imberotti yelled. "Who's the son of a bitch did that?"

Mr. O'Hare stepped forward. "I did," he said.

I was pleased but not surprised by this intervention. I had

suspected for a long time that Mr. O'Hare was crazy. Mr. Norton Krakowitz, staring at the scoutmaster, clearly thought so, too.

"What the helldjewanna do a thing like that for?" Mario Imberotti said, rubbing the area where I had connected.

"Because I know what is in that hike wagon," Mr. O'Hare said. "It is, as I've told you, the property of Troop 244. Only members of the troop are allowed to handle our hike wagon. We do not allow strangers to paw about among our possessions. You are a stranger, Mr. Imberotti."

"All right, I'm a stranger," Mario Imberotti said. "I'm just trying to see what's in there, that's all."

"What's in there," Mr. O'Hare said, "is the equipment with which Scout Kramer will give his demonstration here tonight."

"His what?" Mario Imberotti said.

Maybe if the Philistines got fed up with Mr. O'Hare, they would look with favor on this young bastard? Rogers Peet suits were very adaptable.

"His demonstration," the scoutmaster said. "Come along, Scout Kramer." He grabbed the hike wagon with one hand and my arm with his other. "Norton?" he said.

"Coming," said Mr. Norton Krakowitz. He stepped up beside me and took my other arm. He turned to the little gangster and said, "You can go home now, Mario. Tell your father he has nothing to worry about so far as his friend is concerned. Mr. Shumansky's daughter's wedding is in good hands."

I wondered whose hands the dope meant. As they marched me up the steps of the Lenox Assembly Rooms, with the hike wagon dragging behind us, it seemed to me I was in worse trouble than I had been in when Mario Imberotti had tripped me on the stone steps. These two boobs clearly believed what I had told Mr. O'Hare in the troop meeting room at the Hannah H. Lichtenstein House earlier in the evening, namely, that I was going to the Shumansky wedding to entertain the guests by putting on a demonstration of boy scout skills. The wagon we were all lugging up the sandstone steps contained, they believed even more clearly, the troop equipment I had actually shoved into the stone cave on Old Man Tzoddick's cellar steps. When Mr. O'Hare and Mr. Krakowitz and I reached the top of the Lenox Assembly Rooms steps, and they led me through the big front doors, and we came out into the lobby through which I had once seen Eugene Victor Debs carried on the shoulders of men who had helped him out of a hay wagon, my temporarily stalled memory machine started to turn over again. On the sidewalk Mario Imberotti had said to Mr. O'Hare, "On the second floor of the Lenox Assembly Rooms, the guests could go blind." So I had one piece of information that I had not had when I arrived and discovered my mother was not there to meet me.

"Mr. O'Hare, sir," I said.

The scoutmaster turned. "Yes, Scout Kramer?"

"Thanks very much for your help," I said. "You, too, Mr. Krakowitz. But now I'd better get upstairs to meet my mother."

"Your mother?" Mr. O'Hare said.

He sounded as though I had announced my intention to keep an appointment with Typhoid Mary.

"She told me to meet her here," I said. I could see the what-on-earth-for bit beginning to shape up inside his brain pan. I did not feel this would help. I headed him off at the pass. "My mother was the one arranged with Mrs. Shumansky

I should give this demonstration at the wedding," I said. "I mean, Mr. O'Hare, it was my mother's idea."

And so was Eli Whitney's cotton gin.

"How splendid," said Mr. O'Hare. He turned to Mr. Norton Krakowitz. "One never knows where one's strongest advocates come from, Norton, does one?"

"Never," said Mr. Norton Krakowitz. "You must remind me some day to tell you the story of the coalition we were able to put together to elect Mayor Hylan. We put all of Avenue B behind him. From Krakowitz's Men's and Boys' Clothes all the way up to Fourteenth Street. People who had never seen a ballot before. Immigrants, most of them. Immigrants like Scout Kramer's mother, and yet as politically aware as any Tammany chief."

"Where do you intend to meet your mother?" Mr. O'Hare said.

"On the second floor," I said. "That's where the Shumansky wedding is being held."

Uptown, I learned years later, weddings took place. On East Fourth Street they were held.

"Well, then," Mr. O'Hare said. "We'd better get cracking."

That's exactly what my mother would do if I showed up with these two schlemiels. And what she would start cracking was my skull.

"You don't have to bother," I said. "Thank you very much. I know where the second floor is."

"Good," Mr. O'Hare said. "Then you may lead us to it."

Jesus, I thought. Screwed again.

"It's nothing special," I said. "Just a second floor."

"But a second floor on which a Jewish wedding is about to take place," Mr. Norton Krakowitz said. "The reason Mr. O'Hare asked me to accompany him here tonight, Scout

Kramer, is that your scoutmaster has never seen a Jewish wedding. I assured him it was a spectacle that he would enjoy very much. We will all go up together."

What was the alternative? Going up separately? We went up together. The stairs circled like a bridge across the ground-floor hall in which years ago I had fallen asleep before Eugene Victor Debs could begin to speak. It was very quiet on the stairs. Then, when we came out on the second floor, we were met by an explosion of noise. From a door down the hall on the right came the sounds of a band playing "Yes, We Have No Bananas." On the left there were four doors, spaced perhaps ten feet apart. From one or more of them came the sounds of voices raised in argument. I couldn't make out any words, or decide from behind which doors the voices were hammering at each other.

"Scout Kramer," Mr. O'Hare said. "Wait here."

He dropped the handle of the hike wagon and made a gesture to Mr. Krakowitz. The two men went down the corridor and stopped at the door on the right through which the music was blasting out into the hall. Whatever they saw must have interested them, because after a couple of moments the two men stepped through the door and disappeared. Okay. With them out of the way, I thought, all I had to do now was find my mother, and that was as far as my thinking went, because at that moment she came out into the corridor through the door nearest me on the left.

"Hey, Ma!"

She gave me a sharp look, shot another one down the hall, then ran toward me. She grabbed my arm and the handle of the wagon.

"Ma," I said. "I was looking for—"

"Hold the tongue!" she said.

She dragged me and the wagon through the door out of which she had just come, and pulled it shut. I didn't have much chance to look around, but I got the impression that I was in some sort of dressing room. There was a beat-up old leather couch against one wall, and against another wall, a table with a mirror over it. On the table I saw a pincushion, an ashtray, a pair or scissors, and what looked like scraps of pink ribbon.

"Where have you been?" my mother said.

She was bent over the wagon, struggling with the hasp.

"Downstairs," I said. I dropped to one knee and gave her a hand. The hasp came free. "Out in front," I said. "Where you told me to wait. Where you said you'd meet me."

My mother tapped the bottles, muttering to herself as she counted.

"In the big ones," she said, pointing to the large sacks Walter Sinclair had turned over to me on the dock. "How many?"

"Five each," I said. "Eighteen bottles all together. Where were you?"

"I was here, upstairs," my mother said. "I was watching for you from the window. When I saw you coming on Avenue D, I ran down. Then I saw him, the *momzer,* waiting on the sidewalk, so I ran back up here."

"The gangster?" I said. "Imberotti's son?"

My mother was ramming the hasp back into place. She looked up. "How did you know?"

"He was waiting down there when I got to the front," I said. "He tried to stop me coming in the building."

My mother stood up. "He saw what was in the wagon?"

The mixture of anger and fear in her voice gave me a chance I could not resist. "What do you think I am?" I said. "A dope? I told him to beat it."

My mother looked at me with a frown. I could tell I had overdone it. She went quickly to the window, peered out, and turned back to me. "He's still there," she said.

Okay, boy, get yourself out of this one. "I can't chase him away," I said. "All I could do is tell him."

"What are you talking about?" my mother said.

I nodded down toward Mario Imberotti. He was leaning against the stone balustrade, staring idly up Avenue D. "The gangster," I said to my mother. "I told him to beat it. I didn't mean he should go away. I meant he wasn't going to look in my wagon, and let me tell you something, he didn't. I came upstairs and I was looking around for where to go find you, when you came out of here and pulled me in."

My mother gave me another of those long looks. She must have known I was full of malarkey. What her glance was saying was: How full?

"All right," my mother said at last. "You wait here."

She dragged the wagon out of the room and pulled the door shut behind her with one of those bangs that say more than I am closing a door, kid. I didn't worry too much about what that more was. My first feeling was a sense of relief. I had been ordered to collect the eighteen bottles of Old Southwick and deliver them to my mother in front of the Lenox Assembly Rooms at seven-thirty. I had done the job. If she would not remember to be proud of me, I was sure Walter Sinclair would.

My next feeling was a little more confused. I had lied to my mother about how I had managed to get past Mario Imberotti with the hike wagon. There was no reason why this should have made me uneasy. I had been lying to her for years. I did it as easily as I ate her honey cake. Just the same, this time I didn't feel relaxed about it. On the contrary. I felt I had left something out. What had I forgotten? A moment later I knew what was wrong. I should have told my mother Mr. O'Hare and Mr. Norton Krakowitz were loose in the building. A moment after that the door opened and two women came in. They came in the way my mother came into our kitchen. As though nobody was going to be dopey enough to question her right to enter. These women were wearing beaded dresses, and their hair was combed in a complicated way, and they had roses pinned to their shoulders. What they had pinned to their faces were those sweaty fat smiles of women up to their ears in the arrangements for a Jewish affair. The smiles took a sock in the *kishke* when they saw me. They gave me the hairy eyeball, then turned the X-ray looks on each other.

"It's a uniform," one woman said. "He's wearing a uniform."

The second woman turned back to me and said, "You're the pageboy?"

I was a very confused boy scout.

"My mother told me to wait here," I said.

The two women looked at each other again. Then they shared a shrug and hurried across the room to the leather couch. From behind it they pulled a large white cardboard box. From the box they drew a blue velvet cape with gold embroidery at the edges. It could have been one of the curtains behind which Rabbi Goldfarb kept the Torahs. The women brought the cape across the room. I stood there like a dope while they hung it around my shoulders and fastened it at my throat with a brass clasp. I had a moment of desperation. What was going on? How did this fit in with my mother's plans? Should I shove my way out of the room and run? They stepped back and cocked their heads to one side. Then they tipped their heads the other way, and they shared another shrug.

"Not bad," the first woman said finally in Yiddish.

"Anyway, it hides the uniform," the second woman said. She hurried back to the white cardboard box, pulled out a mass of tissue paper, and picked the paper apart as she approached me. Out of the tissue paper came a king's crown made of golden cardboard. That's right. A king's crown. Like in the pictures of Arthur pulling the sword from the stone. This fatso set the crown on my head, rammed it down as though she were fixing a hoop around a barrel, and said, "It hurts?"

"A little," I said.

"You won't have to wear it long," the first woman said. I reached up to ease the damn thing. She slapped my hand. "Don't touch!"

"God in heaven," the second woman said. "The music!"

She grabbed another bundle of tissue paper from the white cardboard box, and while her partner helped by pushing me from behind, dragged me out into the hall. As they hurried me across to the large door through which I had earlier heard the sounds of music, I understood what the second woman's last remark had meant. The music had changed. When I had emerged on the second floor between Mr. O'Hare and Mr. Krakowitz, the unseen band had been playing "Yes, We Have No Bananas." Now it was playing something insanely familiar.

"Ssshh!" the first woman *ssshhed* in my ear. "Only a minute we'll have to wait."

I filled the time by examining the large room. It contained what seemed to me a couple of hundred people, although there were probably fewer than that. All the women wore beaded dresses, with roses pinned to their shoulders and those fat sweaty smiles pinned to their faces, and all the men wore

208

tuxedos. They were arranged in two long rows that stretched all the way down the big room. The rows of guests formed an aisle that looked as though it had not been properly swept. A moment later I realized this was deliberate. The aisle was strewn with rose petals. At the far end of the aisle, under a blue velvet canopy, stood Rivke Shumansky and a skinny young man in a tuxedo. They were facing each other in front of a man with a beard and a black fedora who could have been Rabbi Goldfarb but wasn't. At the other end of the aisle, near the door in which I stood with the two women who had put the cape and the crown on me, a four-piece band was pounding away on a small raised platform. What they were playing sounded insanely familiar because, at the foot of the platform, Mr. Norton Krakowitz was singing "Me and My Shadow."

When he hit the chorus, the two women behind me started picking apart the bundle of tissue paper they had brought from the dressing room. They worked at it as though they were plucking the leaves of an artichoke. They freed a white satin pillow with golden tassels hanging from the corners. The first woman pulled my hands out, and when the second woman set the pillow on my upturned palms as though she were handing me a tray, I saw that a wedding ring was basted lightly to the satin with white thread.

"Go slow," the first woman whispered in my ear. "Try to keep time to the music."

Not until I felt her gentle but firm shove did I realize she had led me to the top of the two rows of guests and set me in motion down the aisle toward the bride and groom under the canopy. I am not much of an authority on music but I feel reasonably certain "Me and My Shadow" was not written as a marching song. Trying to keep in step with Mr. Krakowitz's rendition caused me to move down the aisle in a series of shuffling stumbles. My awkwardness seemed to impress the audience as enchanting. I never heard such audible *kvelling*. To me, concentrating on keeping the satin pillow on an even keel, the oohing and ahing on both sides was deafening. This may be why I was apparently not aware that I had reached the canopy, or the proper place under it, until the rabbi reached down and put his open hand sharply against my chest.

"Oof!" I said.

Involuntarily, of course.

"Take the ring," he said.

I was about to obey when I saw the groom reaching for it, and realized the rabbi's order had not been addressed to me. The groom tore the ring away from the threads that held it lightly to the white satin, and turned toward Rivke Shumansky. The rabbi tipped his head up to the blue velvet canopy and rolled into a chant that sounded like some of the *Chimish* we sang for Rabbi Goldfarb every day. It had the same effect on the bride and groom. The sounds made them look solemn. The chant ended in a few spoken words, to which the groom responded by slipping the ring onto Rivke's finger. Then the rabbi took an electric light bulb from his pocket and set it on the floor.

"Stamp on it hard," he said to the groom in Yiddish. "You have to break it good."

It seemed to me Rivke's groom stamped on it better than good. The skinny little guy tried to drive the damn thing through the floor. I had heard electric light bulbs smash before. In fact, I had smashed a few myself. We stole them from Old Man Tzoddick's junk wagon and exploded them like grenades on the sidewalk. But I never heard one make the sound this one made when the shoe of Rivke Shumansky's groom hit it.

What emerged was not one sound but a series of sounds. It was as though a string of firecrackers had been set off.

Then I heard the screaming all around me, and I was shoved against one of the poles that held up the blue velvet canopy, and the golden crown fell off my head. The last thing I saw was the way the red spots were slowly spreading wider and wider on Rivke Shumansky's groom's boiled-shirt front, as though some bastard had splashed him with horseradish sauce. I remember wondering stupidly what he was doing on the ground, writhing around like that, when the blue velvet canopy hit me and knocked me down beside him.

8

FORTY YEARS LATER I still had an uneasy feeling about
the color red. It glared down at me from the sign over
the Queens County General Hospital's black iron gate-
posts. It read: *Morgue.*

Read in red electric lights. Small bulbs, each one looking
like one of those stains on the shirt front of Rivke Shumansky's
brand-new husband of about thirty seconds. The poor guy had
certainly hung up a record for the shortest unconsummated
marriage in the books.

"This is where you want to go?" The taxi driver jerked his
thumb up toward the blood-red sign. "Here?"

"That's right," I said.

The driver turned to give me a look. Troubled? Puzzled?
Annoyed? I couldn't decide. It seemed unbelievable, and yet
I was willing to bet it was true: this New York taxi driver had
never before been asked to take a fare to a morgue.

"Hodde we do this?" he said.

"I don't know," I said. "It's my first time. Why don't we ask
that guy in the booth."

The booth was just inside the iron gates. It looked somewhat
like one of those sentry boxes in front of Buckingham Palace.

A bit wider, perhaps. With a window, and a ledge, and a complicated little IBM machine with a clock and a stamping device to log visitors in and out. Also, a guard in a shapeless dark blue uniform to do the logging. He looked at me suspiciously when the taxi pulled up at the window ledge and I leaned out.

"I've been sent up here to identify a body," I said. "Could you tell me where to go?"

His face cleared at once. A man trying to sneak through for the purpose of stealing an X-ray machine or raping a nurse's aide wouldn't fix his feet with Lady Luck by using the terrifying reality of death as a cover story.

"Straight up the drive to that there circle," the guard said. He leaned out of the booth, into the gray, now faintly drizzly nastiness of the day before Christmas, and pointed. "With the sort of like gravel around the sign? You see the place?"

"Yes," I said.

The guard looked relieved. He was obviously trying to get rid of me. Who could blame him? If our positions had been reversed, I would certainly be trying to get rid of him. Not an easy thing to do if you're dealing with a visitor so dumb that he can't see a gravel traffic circle when it is pointed out to him.

"Well, you just go on up there and turn left," the guard said. "The drive leads right up to the door. A sort of red brick building, the bricks, I mean, with gray stone around the doors. You can't miss it."

"Thanks," I said.

"Tzokay," the guard said, and then he took me by surprise. "Merry Christmas," he said.

"Schmuck," the taxi driver said as he sent the cab up toward the gravel circle. "A guy comes to the morgue to identify a body, so this putz says Merry Christmas."

"What else could he say?" I said.

"He could shut up," the driver said.

A thought for today.

"Here we are," I said.

A thought for any day.

"You want me to wait?" the driver said.

I was climbing out of the cab. I paused, one foot on the ground, the other still in the taxi. How long did it take to identify a body in a morgue? Was it something you could do while a taxi meter was ticking away outside?

"I don't know," I said to the driver. I tried to bring to mind the area through which we had just driven. Unfortunately, I had not been paying much attention. All I had was a general impression of desolate streets. "Is it tough to get a cab out here?" I said.

"The other side of the hospital, probably not," the driver said. "I mean, you know, it's sick people, there's visitors coming and going all the time. But this side, I mean here—" He paused and looked out at the entrance to the morgue. "I don't know," he said. "This is my first visit."

I pulled my foot out of the cab.

"Mine, too," I said. "If you don't mind waiting, I'd appreciate it. I'll take care of you."

"That's all right," the driver said. "You just pay what's on the clock."

"No, I'll take care of you," I said. The man who had brought me from my home in Manhattan to the Peretz Memorial Hospital where my mother had died had benefited from my sense of guilt to the extent of a six-dollar tip. Was this man entitled to less? Who could I ask? Certainly not him. "I'll make this as fast as I can," I said.

"Take your time," the driver said. "There's no rush."

Maybe not at his age. But I had come around the pylon into

my fifties. More than half the race was run. And the best part, at that. If I didn't get my mother off my back soon, I probably never would. According to the *Reader's Digest,* I was now living squarely in the middle of the coronary belt. If I died before I learned what my mother had been all about, I would never forgive myself.

"Yes, sir? Can I help you, sir?"

Where had the words come from? I looked around. I was in a sort of square hall. Why sort of? Because the chamber had several offshoots from an essentially though not conclusively square center. As though somebody had decided to design it as a wheel, and only when the spokes were built, did it occur to the designer that the center of a wheel is round. Whatever the shape, even with my eyes closed I would have known I was in a municipal institution. The place smelled exactly the way P.S. 188 and J.H.S. 64 used to smell. Which is the way subway toilets still smell, reform administration in residence at Gracie Mansion notwithstanding. Then I became aware that there seemed to be some point to the offshoots. One, I noticed, was lined with fumed-oak benches. Nobody was on them, but this was a really mean day, and it was also the day before Christmas. On better days I suspected this offshoot and its benches served as a waiting room. But in a morgue, what were better days? And what did people wait for in a place so inescapably terminal? The happy face appearing at the door? The uplifted voice? "Hey, sorry! It's not your mother at all! It's just some old lady we picked up in a gutter who looks like her!"

"Can I help you, sir?"

I turned toward the repeated words. Repeated this time with a rising inflection. And in another offshoot above a marble ledge I saw a small information-inquiry-"Who are you looking for, mister?" type window. Framed in the window was the man

who had directed me from the sentry box at the iron gates outside. I know this sounds silly, but it had to be the same man.
There couldn't be two of them. Not even twins could manage
to look so alike. And yet, how did he get here? He had certainly not leaped out of the sentry post and sprinted past the
taxi as we drove up the path. Or had he? A mental picture took
shape in my head. I could see the whole thing clearly. The man
in the shapeless blue uniform leaving the sentry box as the
taxi pulled away. Racing like crazy all the way around to the
front entrance of the hospital. Belting through a labyrinth of
corridors. Bowling over with his pumping elbows doctors and
nurses and patients and visitors and orderlies carrying trays
loaded with hot meals. Emerging breathlessly from the back
of the building into the hall of the morgue a moment before I
came in from the front, just in time to appear at the window
above the marble ledge and say, "Can I help you, sir?"

Except that he didn't sound breathless. And examining his
face, I knew that no matter when he reached his appointed
place on the old slab, this man would never look deader than
he looked now.

"I've come to identify a body," I said.

"Of course," he said.

The response annoyed me. I don't know why. After all, he
couldn't really have been expected to say oh, I thought you'd
popped in to have yourself measured for a new set of dental
plates.

"What's the name, please?"

I told him. He examined a sheet of paper attached to a clipboard. It seemed to me he took a long time doing it.

"You sure?" he said finally.

"About what?" I said.

"The name," he said.

216

Always, I thought, there are jokers. In the most unexpected places, out of the most improbable faces, at the most inappropriate moments, the voice of the smart-ass rises in the land.

"It was her name for more than eighty years," I said. "It's been mine for over fifty. I ought to be sure."

"You mind spelling it?" he said.

I forced back my irritation. After all, he could have asked me to wigwag it in Morse. I spelled it. He listened attentively.

"Hmmm," he said. I sensed a note of suspicion in the single syllable. Considering my record as a speller in P.S. 188, this boy was flirting with a caustic riposte. He stared at me for several moments, then said, "You mind waiting a minute?"

What I minded most was the way he began every sentence with "You mind." I began to have a feeling that my reactions were all wrong. I felt as though I were watching a movie and the sound track was out of synch.

"I've got a taxi waiting," I said.

But he was gone. I dipped down to peer through the information window. I wanted to see how he had done it. My examination indicated that he had obviously sunk through the floor. In the room behind the information window there were no doors. Only a picture of John V. Lindsay smiling down with self-confident sincerity from the facing wall.

"This way, please."

I turned. The man who had directed me at the sentry box, the man who had asked if I minded waiting a minute at the window, that man was now beckoning me into one of the offshoots from the square center of the hall. This boy was obviously better than Charlie Paddock, who when I was a boy had been known as the world's fastest human. And Charlie had been forced to wear running pants to prove it. I moved toward New York City's fastest civil servant. He moved down the offshoot, beckoning me to follow. Near the bottom of the corridor he stepped in front of a gray metal door and waited for me.

"Mr. Bieber will see you," he said.

"You mind spelling it?" I said.

Inexplicably, I suddenly felt mean. It embarrassed me, but it didn't stop me from sounding the way I sounded.

"What?" the man said.

"The name," I said. "How do you spell it?"

"Oh." He scowled. "Why do you want me to spell it?"

Because you wanted me to spell mine.

"It could be B, e, e, b, e, r," I said. "Or it could be B, i, e, b, e, r. I'd like to get it straight."

"Oh," the man said again. He gave the matter some thought. So did I. Always, I thought again, always there are the voices of jokers. And with all too increasing frequency, I reflected grimly, the voice is proving to be yours. The man's face cleared. He pointed to the gray metal door. On it in black was lettered: Mr. Beybere. The man said, "Those other two, no. It's B, e, y, b, e, r, e."

"Thanks," I said.

He opened the door, waited until I passed him, then closed the door behind me. I looked around. This room looked like the others I had seen in the morgue. A gray metal desk. Two gray metal chairs. A window that looked out on the gray sky, the dismal gray drizzle, and the gray rear bumper of the taxi that had brought me here. On one wall another print of the same picture of John V. Lindsay smiling down with self-confident sincerity. And behind the desk the same man who had directed me at the sentry box, questioned me at the information window, and led me down the corridor to this room. I hoped John Lindsay was smiling because he was looking down on a civil servant of such peripatetic dedication that he managed to fill all those posts without the help of Charlie Paddock's running pants.

"Mr. Beybere?" I said.

"No, Beyber," he said. "A lot of people think it's French on account of the way it's spelled, but we, the family, we always pronounced it Beyber."

"I'm sorry," I said.

Was I?

"That's all right," Mr. Beybere said. "Please sit down."

I sat down. He studied a sheet of paper on the desk in front of him. It was, of course, fastened to a clipboard.

"You all right?" Mr. Beybere said.

I came up out of my thoughts. "How do you mean?" I said.

"You look a little sort of like, I don't know, feverish?"

My thoughts stopped. It occurred to me that since Dr. Herman Sabinson had called me in the morning, they had not been very good thoughts. Maybe I *was* a little feverish. I put my hand to my forehead. Damp? Yes. Undeniably damp. But not hot. Definitely not hot. On the contrary. Cool as the big brass balls on my bed against which I used to put my bare feet on hot summer days in the years when my mother was running booze for the bar mitzvahs of East Fourth Street.

"No, I'm fine," I said. "Or nearly fine. This sort of thing is probably more upsetting than I thought."

"You're not kidding," Mr. Beybere said. "People they come here, they think it's a simple thing. Why shouldn't they? Identifying a body? A person they've probably known all their lives? I mean seen every day for years, probably. What's so hard about that? And yet you know something?"

There were times, and this was suddenly one of them, when I was assailed by the terrifying feeling that I knew nothing. That more than half a century of complicated living had been nothing but a workout in the gym. The bout had never really taken place. No decision had been handed down.

"What?" I said.

"A lot of those people, husbands they've come to identify wives, wives husbands, children their fathers and mothers, they can't do it."

"They can't do what?" I said.

"Identify the dear one," Mr. Beybere said. "They're in a state of shock."

The phrase hung in the air between us like an accusation. The muscles concealed under Mr. Beybere's dead white face, as shapeless as his uniform, pulled enough of its spongy bits and pieces together to convey a recognizable facsimile of a truculent scowl. He was waiting. Daring me.

"I'm sure I can do it," I said.

"Of course you can," Mr. Beybere said. Out of the past came the voice of my French teacher in J.H.S. 64, saying: *A boy like you? With your marks? Afraid of the subjunctive? For heaven's sake, Benny, don't make a person laugh!* Mr. Beybere laughed. Not hysterically. Not a fun laugh. Little fragments of reassuring sound. I tried to move my thoughts into happier terrain. I wanted to think something nice. Or at least friendly.

"What?" I managed to say with a degree of restraint that surprised and pleased me. There was hope for Benny Kramer yet.

Flashing through my mind, the way I've seen these things happen to drowning people in the movies, came the moments I could remember out of my shapeless life when I had been in a state of shock. Item: the night my mother appeared on the floor of the Hannah H. Lichtenstein gym while George Weitz was wigwagging to me a fragment of Matthew XXV:29.

Item: the next day when George, to whom I was making a peace offering of two pieces of fruit, both unspotted, gave me a shot in the mouth. Item: the night on the dock a week later when Walter Sinclair asked me to leave him alone with my mother so they could have a talk and I realized as I walked up Fourth Street that they couldn't talk without me to act as interpreter. Item: the moment under the blue velvet canopy at the Shumansky wedding when I saw the red stains begin to appear and spread on the boiled shirt of the young man who had just been married to Rivke Shumansky.

I ran the cards of these moments through the machine of my mind, fished the result out of the slot, and checked it against the way I felt now in this room at the Queens County morgue. It was not the same.

"I guess I'm probably a little upset," I said to Mr. Beybere. "But I'm not in a state of shock. Not yet, anyway. I might get into a state of shock if this takes too long. That taxi out there is waiting for me. The driver's got the meter running. Could we get going, Mr. Beybere?"

I got instead another dose of the disapproving scowl. What was I doing wrong? The situation didn't exactly have in it the ingredients for Hamlet's beef about posting with such dexterity to incestuous sheets. It was all very simple. There was no reason for me to make a production out of it. My mother was dead. And I had been ordered, I didn't know why, to show up in this dismal set for an Off-Off-Broadway play to identify the body. Was it disrespectful to the departed, did it show a lack of love for the deceased to want to dispose of this unpleasant chore as quickly as possible? How the hell did Mr. Beybere know how much I had loved my mother? Suppose I hadn't loved her at all? What business was it of his? He was paid to be here. I wasn't. The smiling face of John V. Lindsay indicated that he approved of the way Mr. Beybere handled his job. Why, in God's name, didn't the old fool get on with it?

"I understand your feelings," he said. "But there are a few questions I have to ask. I mean it's my duty. I'll try to make them as brief as possible. I hope you don't mind?"

Why did I have to worry about his hopes? Who cared if he minded or didn't mind? I had always thought death was a private affair.

"Of course not," I said. "You ask. I'll answer."

"Thank you," Mr. Beybere said. He consulted the sheet of paper on his clipboard. "Your mother died in an accident, is that correct?"

The answer was, of course, yes. She had not thought up the Eighteenth Amendment. She had never heard of the Volstead Act. But they had come hurtling into her life and changed it as surely and as violently as it would have been changed if she had been hit by a truck.

"No," I said. My private feelings about my mother were my private business. This protégé of John V. Lindsay wanted the facts. He was entitled to them. I let him have them. "My mother fell down in her apartment and broke her hip late in November," I said. "She was taken to the Peretz Memorial Hospital on Main Street. She was operated on, they put in a silver splint or a pin, whatever it's called, and for a while it looked as though she'd be all right. I mean, she's broken her hip twice before during the last ten years, and she recovered both times without too much trouble. But this last break was apparently more than she could handle. She was, after all, a very old lady. Anyway, she was in the hospital for thirty-two days. The last two weeks, almost three, the doctors have made it pretty clear they didn't think she'd ever get out of the hospital. She just sort of ran down, you might say. I saw her last night. She looked pretty weak but she wasn't in any pain. After she fell asleep, I left the hospital. This morning her doctor called me and said she'd died quietly during the night. He wanted to perform an autopsy, and he said I had to sign some papers to give him permission. So I went out to the hospital, signed the papers, and went over to the funeral parlor. I made all the arrangements there, and then they hit me with this surprise."

Mr. Beybere nodded. "They said you had to come out here to identify the body," he said.

"They sure did," I said. "And I don't mind telling you I'm pretty confused. The man at the funeral parlor didn't know why I had to do this. He said all he knows is that the hospital called and told him to give me the message when I showed up. I don't understand it. My mother died in the Peretz Memorial Hospital on Main Street just a few hours ago. What is her body doing here in the morgue?"

The look that gathered slowly on Mr. Beybere's face seemed to me to be building clearly as an accompaniment to the words "I don't know." What gathered slowly inside me as I watched was the certainty that if that's what this fool actually said to me, my reply was going to be, in a voice as cold and hard and unpleasant as the weather outside the window, "Why the hell don't you know?" Mr. Beybere, like his counterpart at the sentry box, took me by surprise.

"You paid her hospital bills?" he said.

"Who?" I said. I was, as I said, surprised.

"Your mother," Mr. Beybere said.

All of a sudden I didn't want to tell him the truth. I wanted to tell him my mother's illness had been a severe financial blow to me. A long, slow, draining disaster that had driven me to the edge of bankruptcy but not even remotely to the edge of hesi-

223

tation. Without flinching, without a murmur of complaint, I had been for months writing checks like mad. Borrowing heavily from the banks. Mortgaging my home, my future, the future of my wife and children, and my career. Flying in doctors from Switzerland, or wherever the most expensive doctors fly from. Hiring extra nurses, nurses that were not even needed but looked good standing there in phalanxes around my mother's bed. Stuffing her hospital room with color TV sets. Baskets of fruit from Madison Avenue shops in which a single candied prune went for eighty cents. Bed jackets from Bergdorf. And even making a special deal with Muzak to pipe Yiddish melodies from Tel Aviv direct to her bedside.

I felt this was the sort of thing Mr. Beybere wanted to hear. I sensed this was the language that would convince him I had loved my mother. With me and my mother, I wanted him to believe, it had been like with Daddy Browning and Peaches Heenan. I wanted him to believe that when it came to being shattered by her death, Abélard had nothing on me. I wanted this idiot to think well of me.

I was clearly going off my rocker.

"I have contributed to my mother's support ever since I was a boy," I said. I had the feeling, from listening to my own voice, that I was dictating an affidavit intended to clear a slur on my character. "Luckily, in the case of her last illness, Medicare and Medicaid took care of all the hospital and doctor's bills. Not the extras, you understand. The specialists. The private nurses. The things like that. I paid all that out of my own pocket. But the basic bills," I said, "Medicare and Medicaid took care of all that."

"They did?" Mr. Beybere sounded pleased as well as astonished.

"They did," I said.

224

"How does it work?" Mr. Beybere said.

I looked at him sharply. "Are you serious?" I said.

Mr. Beybere obviously sensed the skepticism in my voice. He looked hurt. "I really am," he said.

"Why?" I asked.

"My mother-in-law lives with us," Mr. Beybere said. "She's a very old lady and she's not well and she's getting sicker and sicker all the time. My wife and I have been able to take care of her up to now, at home, I mean, but if she gets worse, and she has to go to the hospital, my wife and I, I don't know, we're going to be in the soup. It's a problem that's hanging over us, and we're, you know, we're scared."

He certainly looked scared. His fear made me feel better. My emotional state at the moment was clearly such that only to people being sucked into a whirlpool and calling desperately for me to fling them a life preserver could I feel superior. I took full advantage of this. I immediately felt sorry I had thought of Mr. Beybere as an idiot. Not that I felt he was not. In many years of contact with the type that attracts this designation, I had never met anyone who—pending investigation that might lead to a subsequent change of opinion—more clearly deserved to be called an idiot. Just the same, I was sorry. I had to be, to save myself. My voice began to drip with that most inexpensive and readily accessible of all human lubricants: the milk of human kindness.

"It's really quite simple," I said.

I explained. In detail. With footnotes. And quiet, brotherly gestures. I made this idiot—sorry—I made this unfortunate man take notes as I spoke. I don't think I have ever more greatly enjoyed one of my own conversations.

"Got all that?" I said finally.

"Oh, yes," said Mr. Beybere.

"Any questions?"

He asked a few. I answered them. He added my answers to his notes.

"Okay?" I said finally.

Enough is enough.

"Yes, perfect," Mr. Beybere said. "My wife and I are most grateful to you."

"Not at all," I said.

"I wish there was something I could do to repay you," said Mr. Beybere.

"There is," I said.

"What?" he said.

"Lead me to wherever it is I have to go to identify my mother's body," I said. "I'd like to get out of here."

Mr. Beybere's shapeless face fell apart. "I can't do that," he said.

"Why not?" I said.

"I have no idea where your mother's body is," Mr. Beybere said. "It's not here in the morgue."

9

BY A CURIOUS COINCIDENCE—in reverse, of course—
my father was using almost exactly the same words
when I came home from *cheder* shortly after six
o'clock on that day in 1927 following the Shumansky wedding.

"She's not here in the house" was what my father actually
said.

Since he said it in Yiddish, the words made no particular
impression on me. At home he always talked Yiddish. More
accurately, on this occasion I assumed he was talking to a
neighbor. Or maybe to some friend from the Erste Neustadter
Krank und Unterstitzing Verein. Since our family was clearly
in some kind of trouble, a visit from a neighbor or a member
of the Verein seemed almost inevitable. The central figure in
the social life of our block, as I had observed it, was the busybody, and we had certainly earned ourselves the right to be
the target of the local busybodies. Boy, had we earned it!

Consider. My mother had not been in the house when I got
home the night before from Lenox Assembly Rooms. My
mother had not been in the house when I came home from
school to leave my books and knock back my glass of milk and

slab of honey cake. And my mother had not been in the house when I set out for Rabbi Goldfarb's *cheder*.

What I'm getting at is that with these facts already on the record, why should my father be saying "She's not here in the house" unless he was being patiently polite to a well-intentioned busybody?

"This is my son," my father said.

"This is Mr. Kramer's son," another voice said.

Turning to the other voice, I grasped two points: it was my Aunt Sarah from New Haven who had translated my father's Yiddish statement for the stranger in our kitchen, and our family was in worse trouble than I had suspected. My Aunt Sarah from New Haven came down to East Fourth Street only for catastrophic events: the birth of my kid brother that had almost killed my mother, and the pneumonia that had almost killed my father the winter before the Shumansky wedding. All at once the smell of death was in the room. It cleared the air.

The strange creature in the kitchen facing my father and my Aunt Sarah from New Haven was a goy version of Mr. Seaman, the Avenue C undertaker.

"I'm very glad to meet you, Mr. Kramer," this man said. It was not until he shoved his hand at my bellybutton that I realized the man had meant me. Mr. Kramer? I took the hand and shook it. Not exactly a bracing experience. This guy had a hand that felt like a slab of cold matzoh *brei*. "I'm Jim Kelly," he said. "Special Investigation."

"Mr. Kelly wants to ask you a few questions," my Aunt Sarah said in Yiddish. Since I knew she spoke English, I also knew she was trying to tell me something over Mr. Kelly's head. "He's from the government," my Aunt Sarah said. "He's been here already an hour. The questions he asks, a person

could *plotz,* but you do just like your father and I have been
doing. You give him the answers you think he wants to hear,
and there will be no trouble." My Aunt Sarah turned to the
man and said in English, "He's a very delicate boy. With
Benny it's books, books, books all the time. Like you could
say, a saint. The real world outside, in the street, Benny doesn't
even know it exists. He's studying to be a rabbi. That's where
he just came from. I mean this minute. Now. From *cheder.*
You know what a *cheder* is, Mr. Kelly? It's a school. A holy
school. Where only the boys who want to serve God are allowed to study. It's like by your people, Mr. Kelly, a school
where they allow to study only those boys who some day they
want to be the Pope. To want to be the Pope, this is bad? Of
course not. It's like wanting to be God. That's Benny. So please
be careful. This boy will tell you the truth. Benny doesn't even
know what the word lie means. But when you talk to him, it's
got to be like you're walking on eggs, or he'll break into tiny
little pieces. Benny is very delicate. All right, Mr. Kelly?"

"Of course," said the man from the Special Investigation.
"I'm very grateful to you for your help," he said. "I will do my
best to be gentle."

"Thank you," my Aunt Sarah said. She turned to stroke my
hair as though it were a bundle of rare spun glass not a splinter
of which did she dare to snip off under penalty of some un-
speakable tribal rite. "Sit here," my Aunt Sarah said. She
pointed to one of the chairs at our kitchen table, using both
hands in a gesture of reverence, as though, after a long ordeal
by fire—who knows? maybe water, too—during which I had
not flinched by so much as a quivered lip, I as the young prince
had earned the right to ascend to the throne. I sat down in
front of a large glass of milk and a slab of warm *lekach* as
thick as my school textbook on the Basic Principles of Ele-

mentary Biology. It was clear that my Aunt Sarah had not just arrived. She had been in the house long enough to bake a honey cake. "You mind if he takes a little bite on something while you talk to him?" my Aunt Sarah said to Mr. Kelly. "The poor child, he hasn't had anything in his mouth all day."

Except my heart, of course. But how much nourishment did that provide?

"No, no, of course not," said Mr. Kelly. "It's quite all right. I want him to be completely relaxed."

So did I, but everything inside me that could be stretched tight was in perfect condition for being strung on a ukulele.

"Joe," my Aunt Sarah said to my father. "You sit here."

I watched him take the chair facing me at the other side of the kitchen table. Except for those few totally unexpected moments the night before, when he had surprised me by the way he talked to Mr. Velvelschmidt, my father's movements had never held my attention for very long. They didn't exactly absorb me now, either. But I remember thinking: Watch it; whatever you say to that man will also be heard by the old man.

"Now, then, Benny," Mr. Kelly said.

"You want a bite?" I said.

"What?" Mr. Kelly said.

"In *cheder*," my Aunt Sarah said. "In these religious schools, Mr. Kelly, the children are taught to share and share alike."

"What?" Mr. Kelly said again.

"They don't really belong to the real world," my Aunt Sarah said. "It's like you could say the Kingdom of God, Mr. Kelly. A boy has a piece of honey cake? The minute he sees someone who doesn't have any honey cake, the boy says here, take mine. Most people they understand the emotion this comes from.

When a boy says here, take mine, they know it's polite and decent to take only a *piece* of mine. I mean of his. The boy's. Because if you interpreted what he said to mean here, take all of mine, what would be left for this poor religious boy? So take a bite, Mr. Kelly, not the whole thing. Go ahead. Don't be bashful. You don't even have to be scared. Sick it will never make you. I baked it myself. Honest."

Mr. Kelly reached out and, gingerly, took my piece of still-warm *lekach*. He chomped off a couple of square inches, and returned the base to me. "Thank you very much, Benny," he said. "This is delicious. I mean it's not only delicious, it's also very tasty."

"The butter," my Aunt Sarah said.

"Pardon?" Mr. Kelly said.

"The butter," my Aunt Sarah said. "Most people, they're baking, when it comes to the butter they become cheapskates. A very bad mistake. The whole secret of baking is the butter. You got to use butter until it's coming out of your ears. Remember that, Mr. Kelly."

"Thanks," Mr. Kelly said. "I will."

"Another piece?" my Aunt Sarah said. "I have it here on the stove."

"No, thanks," Mr. Kelly said. "This is superb, really it is."

"It's what?" my Aunt Sarah said.

"He likes it," I said.

"I do indeed," Mr. Kelly said.

"Well, if you change your mind," my Aunt Sarah said, "how much work is there to cutting off another piece? A chop with the wrist, that's all. I'm already holding the knife."

"You're very kind," Mr. Kelly said.

"Say only I'm a good *lekach* baker," my Aunt Sarah said. "You ready, Benny?"

231

"Could I have a little more milk?"

My Aunt Sarah went to the icebox and came back with the bottle. "A boy who likes milk," she said as she refilled my glass. "This is a kind of boy you don't find any more. You should pay attention, Mr. Kelly. Keep your eyes open in this world for boys who like milk."

"I will," said Mr. Kelly.

"Enough?" my Aunt Sarah said.

"Yes, thanks," I said.

What else could I have said? The stuff was slopping over the edge of my glass.

"So drink already," my Aunt Sarah said. "Milk costs money. You want me to waste it?"

"May I start?" Mr. Kelly said.

"I'm stopping you?" my Aunt Sarah said.

"Well, now, Benny," Mr. Kelly said. "You are aware, of course, of what happened last night?"

"Last night?" I said.

If you are ever grilled by the cops, try to arrange to have it done while your mouth is full of *lekach* and milk. Very confusing to an interrogator. It's even better if you can arrange to be young. Cops are scared of children.

"I must say I can't blame you for being a bit confused," Mr. Kelly said. "But surely you are aware that last night, in the Lenox Assembly Rooms on Avenue D, a young man named Aaron Greenspan, who was marrying the daughter of a neighbor of yours, a chicken merchant named Yonkle Shumansky, this young man was shot and killed under the canopy where only a moment earlier he had been married? You are aware of these basic facts, are you not, Benny?"

"Could I have some more?" I said.

"Which?" my Aunt Sarah said. "The *lekach* or the milk?"

232

"Both," I said.

Mr. Kelly looked annoyed. To go to the stove, cut a slab of *lekach,* then go to the icebox and get the milk bottle, these are not complicated activities. But they do blunt the edge of an interrogation. Especially when these acts are being performed by my Aunt Sarah in the grip of a conviction that she was imbedded in the Song of Solomon and was doing a bit of comforting with apples.

"Drink slow," my Aunt Sarah said. "From hiccups a person could die."

I slowly drank, while Mr. Kelly slowly burned.

"You finished?" Mr. Kelly said.

"Yes, sir," I said.

"Well, now, look, sonny," said Mr. Kelly, and I knew I was in trouble. It was that word "sonny."

"Yes, sir," I said again. It seemed the safest comment.

"When that young man was shot to death last night," Mr. Kelly said, "you were right next to him. Is that correct?"

"Well, uh," I said.

"Let me refresh your recollection," said Mr. Kelly. He pulled a small notebook from his breast pocket, flipped a few pages, and read aloud. "Party involved named Benjamin Kramer was standing under the blue velvet canopy approximately twenty-four inches from deceased Aaron Greenspan when bullets entered thoracic cavity and caused instant death." Mr. Kelly looked up from the notebook. "You were there, sonny, were you not?"

I nodded.

"What did you say?" said Mr. Kelly.

"He didn't say anything," my Aunt Sarah said. "He shook his head like this."

She bobbed her head up and down. The imitation was impressive. Like bringing in Niagara Falls to impersonate a leaking faucet.

"What does that mean?" said Mr. Kelly.

"It means he was saying to you yes," my Aunt Sarah said.

"Would it be possible for him to say it himself?" said Mr. Kelly.

My Aunt Sarah turned to me. "Say it," she said.

Unfortunately, I had a mouthful of *lekach* beautifully sogged up and crumbled with milk.

"Yes, sir," I said.

My Aunt Sarah leaped from her chair. She brought the dishrag from the nail over the kitchen sink and dumped it in my lap.

"I'll just brush it off," she said to Mr. Kelly. "It'll all come out, believe me," she said. "You use only Grade A milk, and you don't be a cheapskate with the butter when you make a *lekach,* you'll never have a stain on your pants."

While Aunt Sarah worked on my pants, I worked on my defense. Up to now I had been rattled. I had been stalling for time. Aunt Sarah had given it to me. Now I knew what to say.

"May I proceed?" said Mr. Kelly.

"If the boy is dry enough," said my Aunt Sarah. She tested. "He's dry enough," she said.

Mr. Kelly turned back to me. "Last night, when Aaron Greenspan was shot to death under the wedding canopy in Lenox Assembly Rooms," he said, "you were standing in front of him, Benny, and what I want to know, what the government wants to know, what we all want to know, Benny, is what killed him?"

"The bullets, sir," I said.

"We know that," Mr. Kelly said not without asperity. "What the government wants to know is what led up to the bullets."

"Well," I said, "first there was the noise. Then the red spots on his shirt. Like paint but spreading out. Where the bullets hit him. That's what killed him, sir."

Mr. Kelly bowed his head over his notebook. It gave me a chance for a quick look at my father. He looked frozen. His eyes were like ice. My heart jumped. I had never before thought of my father as a man who distrusted me.

"Yes, Benny," Mr. Kelly said finally. "You're quite right. What killed Aaron Greenspan was those bullets. What we, what the government, what all of us want to know, Benny, we want to know where the bullets came from. Can you tell us that, Benny? Where did those bullets come from?"

My Aunt Sarah reached out as though to stroke my hair back into place, but actually what she did was give my cheek a "knip." A knip is a pinch of approval performed by taking between the middle knuckles of the forefinger and middle finger a lump of flesh, usually from a cheek, although a fore-arm or thigh will do. Buttocks will also serve, but if buttocks are employed, it is wise to make sure the recipient of the acco-lade is below the age of puberty or above the age of consent. Knips have been known to be misinterpreted. I did not mis-interpret my Aunt Sarah's knip on that day after the Shuman-sky wedding. She was saying, "Keep punching, Benny, we're in this together, I'm on your side." It sounded different in Yiddish, of course. Especially unspoken Yiddish.

"Madam," said Mr. Kelly. "This boy was an eyewitness to a murder. We have reason to believe he knows a good deal about it." He whirled on me. "Benny," he rapped out. "What were you doing under that wedding canopy?"

I had a moment of panic. The simple question suddenly seemed terrifyingly complicated. What *had* I been doing under that canopy? My Aunt Sarah sensed I had fallen off the sled, so to speak. She reached over and gave me another knip. I came to.

"I was the pageboy," I said.

"You were the what?"

"Tell him," my Aunt Sarah said.

She sounded as though we had been approached by a very sick man and I was in a position by my kindness to cure his ailment.

"The pageboy carries the ring," I said. "The wedding ring. He carries it down to the rabbi, and at the right moment, when the rabbi says okay, the man takes the ring from the pillow."

"How many pageboys does a wedding usually have?"

I looked at my Aunt Sarah.

"What do you mean?" she said sharply.

"I had a talk this morning with the mother of the bride," said Mr. Kelly. "She said she was a very surprised woman last night. She still is. The pageboy who was scheduled to come down the aisle with that satin cushion was her nephew. When another boy came down, she was astonished. Before she could do anything about her astonishment, other things happened, as you know. So it was not until this morning that she learned the reason her nephew had not been the pageboy the night before was that her nephew was in the bathroom with an upset stomach. Vomiting."

My Aunt Sarah spoke quickly. "That's why they grabbed Benny," she said. "That's why they stuck him in. Isn't that right, Benny?"

I nodded. It seemed safer than uttering sounds.

"I see," Mr. Kelly said. He flipped another page of his notebook. "Benny," he said. "Do you know a Mr. O'Hare?"

"He's my scoutmaster," I said.

Mr. Kelly nodded. "So Mr. O'Hare told me earlier today,"

he said. "Benny, do you also know a Mr. Krakowitz? Mr. Norton Krakowitz?"

"Yes, sir," I said.

"Well, now, Benny," Mr. Kelly said. "I also had a talk earlier today with Mr. O'Hare, and I had another talk with Mr. Krakowitz. They both spoke very highly of you."

"How can you question it?" said my Aunt Sarah. "Just look at the boy, Mr. Kelly. Did you ever see such a boy?"

"Several times," said Mr. Kelly.

"Where?" said my Aunt Sarah.

"In reform schools," said Mr. Kelly.

"Oh, my God," my Aunt Sarah said.

My father spoke. "Shut up, Sarah," he said.

Even though I was frightened, and I knew my Aunt Sarah was trying to conceal her fright, I was shocked by my father's interference.

Mr. Kelly turned. "Thank you, Mr. Kramer," Mr. Kelly said.

"You go ahead and ask anything you want," my father said quietly. "My son will answer."

"Thank you, Mr. Kramer," Mr. Kelly said again. Mr. Kelly turned to me. "It's like this, Benny," he said. "Mr. O'Hare told me earlier today that you came to Lenox Assembly Rooms last night with a thing called a hike wagon. He said you came there to entertain at the Shumansky wedding. You were going to give a demonstration of boy scout skills with the Morse Code flags and other equipment from the hike wagon. That is why, Mr. O'Hare told me, that is why he allowed you to depart with the wagon from the troop meeting room in the Hannah H. Lichtenstein House last night. It is also why, he told me, why he called Mr. Krakowitz and asked him to come along with him to the Shumansky wedding." The pages of the notebook flipped. "Mr. O'Hare reports," said Mr. Kelly, "that when he and Mr. Krakowitz arrived last night at the Lenox Assembly Rooms, you were involved in an altercation with one Mario Imberotti. You know him, of course?"

I took a chance. "No, sir," I said. "I mean, not exactly."

"Well, now, that is extremely interesting," said Mr. Kelly. The pages of his notebook flipped. "We have been informed that you and your mother recently visited Mr. Imberotti and his father in their quarters above Meister's Matzoh Bakery. On Lafayette Street? Is that correct, Benny?"

My Aunt Sarah stroked my hair gently, as though to relieve the congestion inside my head.

"Leave him alone," my father said sharply.

I had never heard him say anything sharply.

"Joe," my Aunt Sarah said. "The boy is only a boy."

"He's old enough to answer a question," my father said.

"And old enough to tell the truth," said Mr. Kelly. "Tell us, Benny. Tell us truthfully, didn't you and your mother visit Mario Imberotti in Meister's Matzoh Bakery?"

I knew I was caught, but I made a last try. "No, sir," I said. "We visited his father."

It was not a very good try.

"I see," said Mr. Kelly, and I had an uneasy feeling that he did see. But I had an even stronger feeling that what he was seeing and what I was seeing were entirely different things. "What you want me to believe then, Benny, is that the young man who accosted you last night on the steps of the Lenox Assembly Rooms was a total stranger. Is that what you want me to believe?"

"What's accosted?" my Aunt Sarah said.

"Interrupted," Mr. Kelly said. "Stopped."

"Benny," my Aunt Sarah said. "This happened to you?"

238

"Well, when I was going up the steps with the hike wagon," I said, "somebody tripped me."

"God in heaven!" my Aunt Sarah said.

"According to Mr. O'Hare and Mr. Krakowitz," said Mr. Kelly, "nothing happened."

"What have they got to do with it?" my Aunt Sarah said. "How do they know how it hurts a boy when he falls on stone steps?"

"They were there," Mr. Kelly said. "They saw Benny get tripped. They helped Benny back to his feet. They helped Benny drag his wagon into the Lenox Assembly Rooms."

"And they did nothing to this rotten *momzer* who tripped Benny?"

"Very few people do anything when they are confronted by gangsters," said Mr. Kelly. "That is what makes our work so difficult."

"Gangsters?"

Aunt Sarah's reading of the single word astonished me. I had expected a scream. But no. She uttered the two syllables with one hand on her bosom, and the other outstretched as though warding off a visible evil. In a scarcely audible whisper that rang through the kitchen like the clash of cymbals.

"Yes, gangsters," Mr. Kelly said. "Let me give you the picture." He flipped the pages of his notebook. "There is a law on the statute books of this country. It is called the Eighteenth Amendment to the Constitution of these United States. It forbids the manufacture and sale of alcoholic beverages."

"What's that?" my Aunt Sarah said.

"*Schnapps,*" Mr. Kelly said.

"What?" we all said.

I mean all. And I mean we. My Aunt Sarah. Your correspondent. And my father.

239

"*Schnapps,*" Mr. Kelly said. "Anything else you don't understand? Just ask me. I speak Yiddish."

I looked down at my hands. I knew we were trapped.

"Now, you all better listen," he said. "Even though it's against the law," Mr. Kelly said, "I think you ought to know that there are people who are manufacturing and selling *schnapps.* Among them is a family named Imberotti. And among those who have been acting as their salesmen, or maybe I should say salesladies, Benny, is your mother."

"Oh, my God!" said my Aunt Sarah.

"Sarah," my father said. It came out *Sooreh.* "Hold your big mouth."

"What Mr. Kramer said is good advice," Mr. Kelly said. "Madam, please shut up. Benny's mother, here, the maternal parent of this prize boy scout, is a bootlegger who has been carrying alcoholic beverages or *schnapps* from the Imberotti warehouse on Lafayette Street to the people of this neighborhood for at least a year, maybe longer. For the Shumansky wedding last night at Lenox Assembly Rooms, the Imberotti family decided to deliver the *schnapps* themselves. They felt it was too large an order for your mother to handle. Your mother, Benny, disagreed. She obtained the *schnapps* from another source, eighteen bottles according to our information, and arranged for you to deliver those bottles to Lenox Assembly Rooms last night. This annoyed the Imberotti family. That is why son Mario was waiting for you in front of the Lenox Assembly Rooms last night. This is why son Mario tripped you on the steps. Because your hike wagon, Benny, was not full of signal flags and other materials with which you were going to give a demonstration of boy scout skills. Mario Imberotti tripped you on the steps, Benny, because your hike wagon contained eighteen bottles of *schnapps* which your mother had obtained from another supplier, a rival of the Imberotti family. Is that correct, Benny?"

I did not answer.

"I think you had better understand some of the consequences of interfering with the functioning of the law," said Mr. Kelly.

"We respect the law," my Aunt Sarah said. "This is a respectable Jewish house."

"Is it?" Mr. Kelly said. "Your nephew, this boy scout with his merit badges, you know what he was doing last night?"

"He was a pageboy," my Aunt Sarah said. "With a golden wedding ring on a satin cushion. You heard him yourself."

"And you heard me," Mr. Kelly said. "Your so-called pageboy nephew was dealing with criminals."

"Criminals?" my Aunt Sarah said. This time she turned her back on the whisper and embraced the scream.

"Yes, criminals," Mr. Kelly said. "Your sister used her son, this boy scout, to collect the bottles of booze she had promised to deliver to the Shumansky wedding. This bright, sunny-faced, smiling young chap spent a very interesting time yesterday. Let me see." Mr. Kelly consulted his notebook. "Yes," he said. "As follows. This shining boy scout, what did he do? He came home from school. And the next thing we know a young man named Aaron Greenspan was gunned to death in a bootlegger's war started by your sister."

"No, please," my Aunt Sarah said. She put her hand on my head. "This is a good boy. This boy not only can signal with a Morse Code flag better than any boy Mr. O'Hare ever saw, but this boy also loves his mother."

"Where is she?" Mr. Kelly said.

"What?" my Aunt Sarah said.

"Your ears seem to be peculiar," Mr. Kelly said. "Things

241

you want to hear, you pick up with the greatest of ease. Things you don't want to hear, elicit from you only the word what. The bootlegger who is this boy's mother. Where is she?"

My Aunt Sarah wheeled around like a carrousel grunting into action. "Joe," she said to my father. "Where is Chanah?"

All at once my father's face looked as though it had been frozen. "I'm waiting for you to tell me," he said.

They stared at each other for a few moments. Then my Aunt Sarah turned back to Mr. Kelly. "My sister Chanah has gone away for a rest," she said.

"With whom?" said Mr. Kelly.

No one spoke. My mother was not there, of course. As I have already indicated, she had disappeared out of our lives the night before, when the red spots started to spread out on the shirt front of Aaron Greenspan. But suddenly, in that tiny kitchen, I could feel her presence.

"My sister has gone away to take a rest," my Aunt Sarah repeated.

"With whom?" said Mr. Kelly again.

"*Huh?*" said my Aunt Sarah.

In Yiddish, of course. It loses in the translation.

"With whom?"

I almost jumped. The two words had been uttered by my father.

"I don't know," Aunt Sarah said.

"Perhaps I can refresh your recollection," said Mr. Kelly.

He moved around the kitchen table, into the hall that led like a tunnel to the front door. He pointed to a section of the green-painted wall. Like every other kid on the block, I used the hall leading to the kitchen of our apartment as a blackboard. As high as I could reach with a pencil, anyway. Here I worked out my arithmetic problems, parsed the sentences

I had been assigned as homework, jotted down reminders of things I had to do for the scout troop, and even took a stab now and then at verse. Once in a while I tried a bit of sketching. I had no talent as an artist, but I enjoyed making pictures. My mother had never objected. Probably, I suppose, because she could not read what I wrote. Perhaps because she thought the scrawls and jingles and sketches were decorative. I do not think they would have caused the young Tintoretto to go green with envy, but I think the stuff was more decorative than what the landlord had provided. Following Mr. Kelly's finger, I saw he was pointing to a poem George Weitz had made up a few months ago. It had taken my fancy, and when I came home from school, I had lettered it neatly on the wall:

> *So roses are red,*
> *So violets are blue,*
> *So sugar is sweet,*
> *And so-so-so are you.*

Then I saw that Mr. Kelly was not pointing to the poem. He was pointing to the sketch of a man's head. A head with closely cropped hair. The head of a man wearing a black turtleneck sweater. A man with a smiling face. Young. Attractive.

"Okay, boy scout," said Mr. Kelly. He put his pointing finger on the upturned nose of Walter Sinclair. "Tell me, sonny," Mr. Kelly said. "Who is this man?"

10

THE OBVIOUS ANSWER WAS: "You're the Feds. You're
supposed to know all about this kind of thing."

But even if I didn't know anything else, I knew it was
neither the time nor the place for obvious answers. On East
Fourth Street, when there was trouble in the family, you
didn't go running to the police station.

"I'm not sure," I said to Mr. Kelly.

"Now, I find that most interesting," said Mr. Kelly. "You
go ahead and you draw the picture of a man on the wall of
your family's kitchen," he said. "And then you say you're not
sure who he is?"

My Aunt Sarah entered the battle. Without much conviction, I'm afraid. "It could be somebody he saw on the street,"
she said. "Somebody whose face he remembered, so he made
a picture on the wall. The boy draws all kinds of things on the
wall. Look."

"Is that what happened?" Mr. Kelly said to me.

I thought of Walter Sinclair. I couldn't believe he would
have wanted me to lie. "No," I said.

"Oh, my God!" my Aunt Sarah said.

"Shut up, Sooreh," my father said.

"What did happen?" Mr. Kelly said.

I hesitated. Not because I didn't know how to tell a plausible lie. I hesitated because I didn't know how to tell this particular truth. "He's a man I met on the dock," I said finally. "He gave me a dime to buy candy."

"That's all you know?" Mr. Kelly said.

I gave the question some thought. Again, not because I was unequal to the task of inventing a lie that would work. I took some time with the question because I wondered if I did know any more. I thought about my mother on the barge, the night we had met Walter. I thought of her face. I decided to stop thinking.

"That's all I know," I said.

"Well, then, maybe I can help you," Mr. Kelly said. "It might interest you to know that the man whose picture you drew on the wall is a man the government has been looking for."

"Oh, my God," my Aunt Sarah said.

"Because he is a gangster," Mr. Kelly said. "And what seems to be starting here in this neighborhood is a full-fledged gang war. That Greenspan kid last night could be only the beginning. Whatever is about to happen, it's our job to stop it."

"Everybody in this house," my Aunt Sarah said, "believe me, we wish you success with your job."

"Is that why you are here in New York, ma'am?" Mr. Kelly said. "To help me and the government achieve this success?"

"Why am I here?" she said. "I am here because I am a human being. Because I have a sister named Chanah. And this morning, in my own home in New Haven, Connecticut, I received a call on the telephone from this—this—"

My Aunt Sarah's right arm, which could easily have accounted for at least twenty of her two hundred or more pounds, hurled itself out toward my father.

"This Mr. Kramer?" Mr. Kelly said.

"My brother-in-law," said my Aunt Sarah. "My brother-in-law said on the telephone Chanah has disappeared," my Aunt Sarah said. "Come quick."

"And that is all you have to tell me?" said Mr. Kelly.

"What more can I tell?" my Aunt Sarah said. "The price of the railroad ticket how much it costs from New Haven? That the President is we have a man named Coolidge? The handles on the clock on Grand Central how they stood when I reached New York? A family is a family. You get a call from your brother-in-law on the telephone. He says your sister she's disappeared. You say I'll be there by the first train. Here I am. You'll try a piece of this *lekach,* maybe? I just baked it fresh. It's nice and cool now."

"Some other time, perhaps," Mr. Kelly said. "Right now I think my time would be better employed if I set you and your brother-in-law and your senior patrol leader nephew straight about what your situation is. The government feels your sister is connected with the death of that Greenspan boy."

"You are calling my sister a murderer?" said my Aunt Sarah.

No whisper this time. No scream. This time ice.

"I am calling her a person who has information about what happened last night," Mr. Kelly said. "Information that we want, and will continue to want, from your sister. Where is she?"

"I told you from the minute you came in here in the house," my Aunt Sarah said. "I don't know. My brother-in-law doesn't know. That's why he called me on the telephone in New Haven."

"How about you?" Mr. Kelly said to me. "Where is your mother?"

I had no trouble with this answer. "I don't know," I said.

Mr. Kelly clapped his notebook shut. "Very well, members of the Kramer family," he said. "I suggest you find out where she is, because if you don't, the government will, and then you will all learn for yourselves a very revealing lesson in how the government of the United States treats people who break its laws."

He picked up his hat, set it on his head as though he were recapping a fountain pen, and disappeared into the long green corridor. When the door slammed shut behind Mr. Kelly, something happened that I still find it difficult to believe I actually witnessed. My father stood up, came around the kitchen table, and stopped in front of me.

"You little liar," he said.

If he had said *How sharper than a serpent's tooth it is to have a thankless child,* I could not have been more astonished. After all, I knew a little something about Shakespeare, even if I had learned this particular fragment from Mr. Norton Krakowitz, but what did I know about my father? I now found out.

"Joe!" my Aunt Sarah said.

Too late. It was like the day after the All-Manhattan rally eliminations when I tried to placate George Weitz in the schoolyard during lunch hour by holding out my two pieces of fruit and he gave me a shot in the mouth. I could see my father's arm go up and his outspread palm start down, but it never even occurred to me to duck because I didn't believe what I was seeing. Even when my father's slap caught me across the face and I fell into the baking tin on the kitchen table, I still didn't believe it.

"Look what you've done to my *lekach*," my Aunt Sarah said.

I said nothing. Not out loud, anyway. Inside my head, however, what I said seemed to me perfectly reasonable. "Pa," I said in the stunned silence of my mind, "you never hit me before."

11

H E NEVER DID IT AGAIN. Not once during all the re-
mainder of his eighty-two years. But how was I to
know that? I mean in 1927 on the evening following
the day of the Shumansky wedding? I didn't know it. So I
turned and ran. Up the green corridor, through the front door,
and down the steps. On the stoop I slowed down. It occurred to
me that everybody on the block knew what had happened the
night before at the Shumansky wedding. East Fourth Street in
those days was a place that did not surprise easily. But murder
gets around. That much I'd learned during the earlier part of
the day. What I had not learned was whether the people on the
block were aware of my mother's connection with the death
of Aaron Greenspan.

It was a connection that could be described as accidental.
I would have felt easier in my mind if I had been able to
describe it that way, if only to myself. But I couldn't. The
mechanics of what had happened were sharp and clear. Any
kid on East Fourth Street would have understood it.

Mr. Imberotti and his family were the leaders of an apparatus they had fashioned to produce revenue for themselves.
They had recruited my mother and she had become a part of

that apparatus. The Imberottis had been pleased with her role. But she had refused to remain in her role. Ambition had seized her. My mother had demanded a larger part in the play. The Imberottis could not tolerate such demands. Larger parts were reserved for the family actors, and my mother was not a member of the Imberotti family. This had not stopped her. In fact, I think it inflamed her. She tended to suppress her pride because in this New World she did not know the retaliations waiting to destroy people who were guilty of the sin of pride. But pride runs on its own motor. In my mother's case it escaped her normally cautious controls. It seeped out under pressure in unexpected corners of her life. I suspect the corners took her by surprise.

She should have accepted the rules Mr. Imberotti laid down. Given a normal situation, a normal period in which to think, I believe she would have accepted it. The guiding principle of her life was survival. But the situation created by the Shumansky wedding was not normal. It stirred something beyond my mother's normal instincts for caution: greed.

It has been my experience that when you are hungry you will eat whatever crumbs drop your way. Once the crumbs have eased the cutting edge of desperation, however, watch out. The loaf from which the crumbs have fallen suddenly begins to look within reach. Why not? If somebody else owned a loaf, somebody no more spectacularly endowed with brains or talent than you, why can't you own a loaf? I think that's what happened to my mother.

She had earned small sums through the Imberottis. In doing so, she had earned larger sums for them. Instead of being grateful, they proved to be hateful. A phrase that seems to have slipped out of the language describes, I think, my mother's reaction. She saw red. It is not a good color. Whom the gods destroy they first make mad, I was taught in high school. If my mother had not gone mad, Aaron Greenspan would probably not have been killed under the blue velvet canopy at his own wedding in the Lenox Assembly Rooms.

On the other hand, I might have been the one who was killed. Because I knew in my bones that the Imberotti family trigger man who had killed Aaron Greenspan had been drawing a bead on somebody else. Somebody whose death would scare off this ambitious woman who had forgotten her place and was threatening the apparatus. Her son. Me.

I was grateful, of course, that the bullet had missed its mark. I was aware, however, that an apparatus that would attempt to eliminate an irritation by killing a pageboy under a wedding canopy would not abandon the effort merely because a first try did not work. In short, I was still the target.

Going up East Fourth Street, I moved uneasily. I had no idea who was watching me. I had no idea if the people on the block knew that my mother had been missing since the night before. It seemed sensible not to be seen running. In those days people who ran collected stares, or cheers, or jeers, or bullets. If the Imberotti trigger man had me in his sights, I could not escape by running. I hit the street at a walk and started up the block toward Avenue D.

Why? Because night was coming in fast across the river from Brooklyn, and that meant I was due in Abe Lebenbaum's candy store to relieve his mother behind the counter. Moving along in the gathering darkness through the deeply rutted grooves of habit, I began to think more clearly about Mr. Kelly.

The government man had indicated in our kitchen that he knew all about what had taken place the night before. It seemed reasonable to assume, therefore, he knew that I

251

worked for Abe Lebenbaum in the candy store. Mr. Kelly had made it perfectly clear that he knew about my dealings with Mr. Heizerick. And he knew about the fire in the Zabriskie sisters' bedroom.

The fire had not until this moment seemed any more important than any of the other events of the night before. Now I began to understand that while I may have forgotten about the fire, the Fire Department had not. I could suddenly hear again the bells of those fire engines as I raced down the fire escape with the hike wagon. I could hear those bells, and I could hear something else. The excited voices of Lya and Pauline and Marie—shivering a little maybe; after all there had been no time to put on any clothes—as they explained to the authorities that they had been minding their own business—who else could they get to mind a business like theirs? —when suddenly they were enveloped by flames.

The key word, I suddenly grasped, was authorities. Whoever they were, meaning cops, the odds were good that they would learn as much as Mr. Kelly had learned. Which meant the cops could very well be waiting for me in Abe Lebenbaum's candy store. It seemed sensible to let them wait.

At the Avenue D corner I did not turn left toward the candy store. I kept right on going, across Avenue D, toward Avenue C. Halfway up the block my brain started to come to life. I could suddenly see the mess I was in as a two-parter. Part one, what had happened the night before. Part two, what was going to happen as a result of those events.

I knew a good deal about the first. I had no idea about the second. All at once the part I understood, the events in which I had been involved, became more important than they had seemed when I was racing through them. Holes, I saw, had to be plugged. The most obvious one hit me like my father's slap.

I turned and doubled back toward Avenue D. When I arrived in front of Lenox Assembly Rooms, night had settled in. The great big globes on the black iron poles set in the sandstone balustrades were not lighted. The steps were deserted. Either no bar mitzvahs or weddings were scheduled for that night, or Mr. Kelly had anticipated my move and set a trap for me.

My first instinct, naturally, was to turn and run. I did not turn and run because I could manage only one half of the operation. I turned, and stopped dead. Coming up the street toward me was Mr. Norton Krakowitz and a cop.

The cop was so absorbed in whatever it was Mr. Krakowitz was saying, and Mr. Krakowitz was so absorbed in the sounds he was making, that neither saw me. I turned back and ran up the sandstone steps.

How to describe my feelings when I reached the top and pressed against the front doors and they opened inward? Very simple. I suddenly believed in God. I am convinced He was responsible for getting me from those front doors up the marble stairs to the second floor, down the shadowy corridor, and into the small dressing room, where the night before the velvet cape of the pageboy had been wrapped around my shoulders, and the golden cardboard crown had been pressed on my head.

I thought for the first time about the kid who had actually been scheduled to be the pageboy at the Shumansky wedding. Suppose that boy had not been delayed? Suppose he had arrived under the canopy on time? Would the trigger man have looked elsewhere for the son of the woman who had enraged the Imberottis? Would he have waited to get the woman herself in his sights? My mother? Would Arnold Greenspan now be alive?

253

The only light in the dressing room when I slipped through the door came from a lamppost out on the street just below the single window. It was enough to show that the Troop 244 hike wagon was sitting exactly where I had left it the night before.

I flipped open the lid. The wagon was empty. I grabbed the handle, dragged the wagon out of the room, and started back up the corridor. At the top of the divided stairs I stopped. Mr. Krakowitz and the cop were coming up the left wing. They were moving slowly, placing their steps carefully one at a time into the small splash of yellow from the cop's flashlight. They reminded me of a couple of kids tiptoeing through a string of puddles after a rainstorm. I ducked below the level of the marble rail and pulled the wagon toward the right wing of the stairs. When the yellow splash of light reached the top on the left, I crouched low and started down on the right.

Mr. Krakowitz and the cop were still moving along the corridor toward the dressing room when I reached the lobby. I was through those front doors, down the sandstone steps, and on my way back up Avenue D before the two men could possibly have reached the dressing room in which the night before I had turned over to my mother all those bottles of Old Southwick.

Now that it was dark my problem was simpler. I reached Eighth Street without being stopped or recognized. My confidence went up. When I reached the steps leading down to Old Man Tzoddick's cellar, the feeling that I was on top of it, the feeling that I had the ball game sewed up, all that vanished abruptly. Old Man Tzoddick's pushcart was parked in the vacant lot next to the steps.

Only someone who understood the role the pushcart played in Old Man Tzoddick's life would have known this meant he was at home. Except for the lampposts at the Avenue C and Avenue B corners, Eighth Street was dark. Not a hint of light was visible from the cellar, and there were plenty of places through which light would have leaked. If a candle stump had been burning inside that cellar, everybody on Eighth Street would have been aware of it. Nothing was burning. The conclusion of Senior Patrol Leader Kramer was that Old Man Tzoddick may have been in residence but he was zonked out.

I tiptoed down the stone cellar steps. As I did so, I reflected on how much of my life was being spent these days on the tips of my toes. Before my mother exploded into the Hannah H. Lichtenstein House gym on the night of the All-Manhattan Rally eliminations, I had walked like everybody else. Anyway, like most people. Clumping along, heel and toe. Making the normal amount of noise. Now, since Walter Sinclair and the Federal government had entered my life, it was all on tiptoe.

It was not the sort of reflection that would help me retrieve the stuff from the wagon that I had stuffed into the cave behind the loose stone the night before. I got off my toes, squatted down, pulled out the stone, and started unstuffing it. I had the two cooking pots, the iron grill, and the signal flags safely transferred from the cave to the wagon, and I was reaching for the tied bundle of six-inch pieces of file from the flint-and-steel sets, when there was an explosion behind me.

"You little *momzer!*" Old Man Tzoddick screamed. "You big crook!"

As always, even when flat on my back at the bottom of a set of cellar steps, my first thought was irrelevant: Why don't you make up your mind? How could a senior patrol leader, sixty-two pounds on the Hannah H. Lichtenstein gym scale, be both a little *momzer* and a big crook?

"You dirty *goniff!*" Old Man Tzoddick screamed.

This was hardly an answer. But it cleared my head. Just in time, too. The filthy old ragpicker was swinging what looked like a stubby length of metal pipe. I rolled over fast, caught the blow on my arm, snatched the pipe from his hand, and shoved him away. He fell back through the cellar door. I grabbed the wagon, dragged it up the stone steps, and set off for Avenue B at a gallop. The length of metal pipe, I discovered, was the long flashlight we kept in the hike wagon for signaling Morse at night.

By the time I got around the corner, I was pretty sure Old Man Tzoddick was not following me. By the time I got down into the basement of the Hannah H. Lichtenstein House, I had recovered the feeling that I was doing the right thing. The troop meeting room was dark.

I flipped on the light and dragged the wagon to the closet. Before shoving it into the space from which Mr. O'Hare had given me permission to take it the night before, I checked the contents. Everything was back in the wagon except the flashlight and the envelope of charred gauze I had used the night before. Nobody would miss that. I decided to hold onto the flashlight. Walter Sinclair was a Morse man. He had told me, if things went wrong, I was to head for the Fourth Street dock and he would communicate with me somehow. Things had sure gone wrong. I closed the wagon, pushed it into the closet, shut the closet door, and flipped off the light. I climbed up the stairs and headed for the dock.

When I got there I wondered how a communication from Walter would solve anything. Sooner or later I would have to go home. In fact, the later I got home the worse the mess would be. My father and my Aunt Sarah would be sure to be waiting up for me. And yet, just being on the dock made me feel better.

256

For the first time since I'd seen the red stains start to spread across Aaron Greenspan's shirt the night before, I didn't feel the compulsion to think. I just sat there on the edge of the dock, dangling my feet over the hill of coal on the barge lashed below me. Smelling the oil-dirty yet curiously clean smell of the river. Hearing the creak of the mooring ropes. Catching, without actually listening, the muted whistles and bells from the barges moving across the Brooklyn skyline like flies across a pile of spotted peaches on an Avenue C pushcart. Watching the lights on the tugs in the distance winking on and off like Morse dots and dashes.

I came awake. I had not realized that I must have dozed off. Half asleep, my mind had been counting those lights winking on and off aimlessly at the other side of the river. Counting them, and timing their length, without knowing I was doing it. Now I realized there had been a pattern to some of them. Long lights were dashes. Short lights were dots. The best Morse man Mr. O'Hare had ever known had recorded those dots and dashes even while half asleep. And the recording had formed the pattern. Dash, dot, dot, dot. B. Dot. E. Dash, dot. N. Dash, dot. N. Dash, dot, dash, dash. Y. B–E–N–N–Y. Benny. Benny? That was me! Benny Kramer!

I leaned forward on the edge of the dock and concentrated. I knew who was trying to communicate with me. He had said he would. He was a Morse man. The lights that were forming the pattern were coming from a dark lump lying low in the water all the way across the river. It was surrounded by larger lumps, tugs and barges, but these larger lumps were moving. This smaller lump was motionless. I grasped that this was why the lights had been making a pattern. The other lights also winked on and off but they had no meaning because they hurried away from themselves, like scattered confetti. But these lights from the smaller lump lying low in the river at the far side of—

— • • •

•

— •

— •

— • — —

BENNY.

— • • •

•

— •

— •

— • — —

BENNY.

I was suddenly pleased with myself. I had been smart to hold onto the long flashlight when I repacked the wagon. I was pleased because I saw that Walter Sinclair had expected me to be smart. Sometimes, at fourteen, you have to make your own medals.

I stood on the dock edge, hesitated, then jumped down to the barge. I hit the coal, felt my knickers tear over the right knee, then started up the pile. When I got to the top, I was eight or ten feet higher than the edge of the dock. I got myself set in the coal and started to flip the switch of the flashlight on and off.

—

• • • •

• •

• • •

THIS

● ●
● ● ●

IS

— ● ● ●
●
— ●
— ●
— ● — —

BENNY.

I signaled it again. And again. And again. Praying that the batteries would hold.

THIS IS BENNY.

THIS IS BENNY.

THIS IS BENNY.

In the middle of my seventh signal the pattern of lights from the other side of the river took on a new shape. I stopped signaling and started to read the new arrangement of dots and dashes. I caught the letters without any trouble. But they made no sense. I wished desperately that Chink Alberg or Hot Cakes Rabinowitz was crouching at my knees with a pad and a pencil. What I wanted was to call the letters as I read them without having to try to make words out of them. But what you want and what you have are not always the same. Life.

So I kept reading the letters over and over again. The same letters:

259

```
·  ·
·  —  ·
·
·  —
—  ·  ·
—  ·  —  —
—  —  —
·  ·  —  ·
```

I READ YOU.

My mind recorded the dots and dashes about eight times. Maybe more. Then the signaler obviously assumed I had it. Anyway, the signal changed. I had no trouble with the new words. They were very simple. I didn't need Chink Alberg or Hot Cakes Rabinowitz to translate for me the message that came in across the river in winking lights.

YOUR MAMA SAFE DO NOT WORRY JUST KEEP YOUR MOUTH SHUT AND YOUR EYES OPEN FOR FURTHER MESSAGES YOU ARE A GOOD KID.

Using the troop flashlight, I signaled to the *Jefferson Davis II* at the other side of the river the words that were now perfectly comprehensible and, for almost half a century, always would be. They still are.

I READ YOU.

12

THERE ARE PHRASES that invade the mind like infectious diseases. Or love. Which may not be dissimilar.

I READ YOU.

Strictly speaking, not even a phrase. A combination of syllables invented by a creature from another world. A hero who came out of the East River mists to capture the heart of a young boy. Not to mention the heart of the boy's mother.

Physiologically, I know this is not quite accurate. But emotionally, as I look back on many years of perhaps needlessly crowded living, the word does the job. I don't know how to explain or even discuss physical attraction. But I know all about the heart. I was jettisoned into a cram course before I even knew the name of the subject. It happened to me at fourteen and I saw it happen to a beautiful woman well past her youth. My mother. It changed my life. As follows:

When I came home that night on the day after the Shumansky wedding, my Aunt Sarah was sitting at the kitchen table reading the *Jewish Daily Forward*.

"Papa has gone to bed," she said.

The simple statement took me by surprise. I had expected her to ask where I'd been. I think I had also expected my father to be waiting up for me. I say I think because I really was not sure. My father always went to bed early. Not only because he was an early riser, but also because he believed plenty of rest was good for him. On Saturday nights, when I came home from my weekly scout meetings sometime between eleven and midnight, he was always asleep. On other nights, when I came home from my job in Abe Lebenbaum's candy store, I could hear my father's snores before I was halfway down the green hall from the front door to the kitchen.

My father in the sitting-up position was a picture that existed only at the kitchen table. The picture included, of course, the consumption of food. From the moment that night when he walloped me after Mr. Kelly left our kitchen, all the pictures changed. It was as though my life, up till then a neatly stacked deck of cards, had suddenly been tossed up in the air, and I had not yet had a chance to see the cards flutter to the ground and settle. That's what took me by surprise about my Aunt Sarah's statement. It was normal to the point of abnormality.

"Papa has gone to bed."

Where else did Papa go every night after supper? I couldn't say, of course, about the night when our family was accused of being involved in a murder. The night my mother disappeared into the mists of the East River. And the night my father exploded in a fit of astonishing rage that caused him to beat my head against the *lekach* baking pan.

"Do you know where she is?" my Aunt Sarah said.

"No," I said.

"No what?" my Aunt Sarah said.

"No, I don't know where she is," I said.

My Aunt Sarah stared for a few silent moments at the newspaper. "You don't know where your mother is," she said. "This is what you are telling me?"

It was a relief to be able to tell the truth. "Yes," I said. "I don't know where she is."

"When you say you don't know where your mother is," my Aunt Sarah said, "do you mean you have no idea absolutely and positively where she is? Or do you mean you know like maybe where she might be but you don't know exactly like how to put your finger on the street number, let's say, and the house maybe?"

I have in my day, like most people, answered some difficult questions. None was more difficult than this one. "Aunt Sarah," I said, "please don't ask me any more."

She raised her eyes from the *Daily Forward*. I think, as the scene comes back into my head, that it was because of the way she looked at me on that terrible night that I have loved her for all these years. Faith cannot be counterfeited.

"All right," my Aunt Sarah said. "She's your mother. But remember this. She's also my sister. I have a right to ask. But I won't. Because I trust you. So even though I won't ask any more questions, there is something I can tell you. All right?"

"All right," I said.

"What your father did," my Aunt Sarah said. "The hit?"

My gut tightened. I didn't want to hear about that. "Yeah?" I said.

"He wasn't hitting you," my Aunt Sarah said. "He was hitting something that's not a person. He was trying to understand what no man ever understands. For this I want you to do me a favor. For me, not for him. For me I want you to do it. You understand me?"

I didn't, but I knew the answer she wanted, so I said, "Yes."

"Don't hate him," my Aunt Sarah said. "Forget that he hit you."

"Okay," I said. And then I uttered the first declaration of

263

love that ever came into my conscious mind. I said, "For you I'll do it."

I went to bed with a sense of pleasure and well-being that was totally new to me. The cop around whom I had always had to work for every breath, my mother, was out of the house. The woman with whom I realized I was in love was sleeping on the couch in the front room. Life, which I had always found interesting, was suddenly wonderful. I couldn't wait to wake up.

When I did, my father had carried his *moogin* off to the shop, and my Aunt Sarah was doing something my mother had never done. She was cooking breakfast.

"Farina," she said.

I stared in amazement. With my mother, breakfast was always a roll and a glass of milk.

"Be careful," my Aunt Sarah said. She set before me a soup plate from which arose a delicious steaming smell. Into the center of the plate she dropped a lump of butter as big as a walnut. "Eat slow," my Aunt Sarah said. "It's hot."

It was hot. And I ate slow. And it made me feel like Romeo telling the whole story to that foolish friar. I had given my heart to the right girl.

"More?" my Aunt Sarah said.

I nodded. She refilled my plate. When it was empty she carried the plate to the sink, came back to the table, and sat down facing me.

"It's different from yesterday," she said. "You know that, don't you?"

I did, but I wasn't quite sure. "Why?" I said.

"Yesterday, when you went to school, when you went to *cheder,* it was before that Mr. Kelly," my Aunt Sarah said. "Now, today, everything you do, every place you go, he'll be watching."

The thought had occurred to me. But I had not explored it. I could tell my Aunt Sarah had. So I waited.

"I said last night I won't ask any questions," she said. "But I didn't say I won't do something to help a little. Till she comes back, your mother, my sister, we have to do something. Are you listening?"

"Sure," I said.

"So why do you sit there without talking?" my Aunt Sarah said.

"Tell me what you want me to do," I said.

"Be sick," my Aunt Sarah said.

"Be what?" I said.

"Be smart," my Aunt Sarah said. "Don't go where that Mr. Kelly he can follow you. I'll go to school and tell the teacher you won't be there today because you're sick. Me he can follow, and what good will it do him? Then I'll go to Mr. Lebenbaum and tell him you won't come to the candy store tonight. If you're sick you can't come. And Mr. Kelly he can follow me there, too. Then I'll go to Rabbi Goldfarb and tell him you won't be in *cheder* today because you're sick—and Mr. Kelly can *plotz*."

I thought that over. My thinking seemed to annoy my Aunt Sarah.

"Now you can talk," she said. "There's nothing more to listen to."

I had a feeling she'd left something out. But I couldn't put my finger on what it was.

"You don't have to go to all those places," I said. "A lot of kids don't come to school every day. The teachers don't do anything about it until a kid doesn't show up for three or four days. Then they report it to the principal. Abe Lebenbaum, too, he won't worry too much. His mother will be there until he comes down from his sleep. Besides, he probably doesn't want any trouble with the Zabriskie sisters."

"The who?" my Aunt Sarah said.

"They work sort of like customers for Abe Lebenbaum," I said. "The night this terrible thing happened at the Shumansky wedding, these girls, the Zabriskie sisters, they had a fire. I think Mr. Lebenbaum wouldn't want anybody asking about that."

"Why not?" my Aunt Sarah said.

"Mr. Lebenbaum doesn't like trouble with cops," I said. "He has a slot machine out in back."

My Aunt Sarah nodded. The relationship of the slot machine to police authorities had apparently penetrated to the immigrant culture of New Haven.

"So he won't say nothing?" my Aunt Sarah said.

I thought of Abe Lebenbaum up there in the apartment of the Zabriskie sisters. I mean I thought of the view from the fire escape. It seemed to me Abe's mind would not be on conversation.

"I'm pretty sure he won't," I said.

"But if you don't come to work in the store tonight?" my Aunt Sarah said.

I thought some more. The nighttime was now my time. My only time. The *Jefferson Davis II* would not risk making contact during the day.

"I think maybe it would be good to tell Mr. Lebenbaum I'm sick," I said.

My Aunt Sarah nodded. "I will keep him from coming over."

She did. And she kept everybody else from coming over, so that by the time my father got home from the shop that night, we had put the buffer of a quiet day between us and the visit of

Mr. Kelly. I spent most of that day in the front room, pretending to do my school homework. Actually, I kept looking out at the dock, wondering what my next move was going to be. I knew it would be dictated by Walter Sinclair, and I knew the dictation would come from the river. I kept so close to the window that I did not hear what was going on in the kitchen. All I knew was that my Aunt Sarah was cooking. The smells told me that. A person would have to be nailed down by the world's champion head cold of all time not to be aware that a Hungarian goulash, Berezna style, was being put together on the premises. But the opening and closing of doors escaped me.

So that when the angry voices erupted in the kitchen, I was not quite sure to whom they belonged. I soon found out.

"Benny!"

I ran to the door that led into the kitchen and opened it. At once I understood something my teachers in P.S. 188 and J.H.S. 64 had been mumbling about for years: Pandora's box. They were right. Some things are better left unopened. Mainly because you can't close them. I certainly couldn't close that door between our front room and kitchen. My Aunt Sarah was leaning against it. All two hundred pounds of her.

"Benny," she said. "You know this man?"

"Mr. Velvelschmidt is our landlord," I said.

Mr. Velvelschmidt seemed to expand inside his fly-front topcoat with the gray velvet collar as though he were a balloon into which an extra blast of air had been pumped.

"And a landlord is entitled to his rent," he said. "Where is it?"

On this last question Mr. Velvelschmidt turned, and I saw my father sitting at the kitchen table. He was staring down into a plate of goulash.

"It's in the shop where my brother-in-law works," my Aunt

267

Sarah said. "Now is the slack season. When things get busy he'll start earning again. He'll bring home money from the shop, and you'll get your rent."

"And in the meantime?" Mr. Velvelschmidt said. "Me and Mrs. Velvelschmidt and my children, God bless them? What are we supposed to live on?"

"What you live on now," my Aunt Sarah said. "Bloodsucking."

Mr. Velvelschmidt's face, ordinarily the color of General Robert E. Lee's uniform, now took on abruptly the color of General Grant's. He turned to my father. "Where's the missus?" he said.

My father's absorption in the plate of goulash, which had been deep, now became total.

"What's the missus got to do with it?" my Aunt Sarah said.

"What have you got to do with it?" Mr. Velvelschmidt said.

"I'm her sister," my Aunt Sarah said.

"So why aren't you with your family?" the landlord said. "Wherever they are, why aren't you with them? What are you doing here?"

"Cooking for my brother-in-law and my nephew. This is a crime?"

"It could be," Mr. Velvelschmidt said.

"To cook for a brother-in-law and a nephew?" my Aunt Sarah said. "This is a crime?"

"Yes, if you're cooking for them because the missus who should be doing the cooking she's hiding from the police," Mr. Velvelschmidt said.

"This you're saying about my sister?" my Aunt Sarah said.

"I'm saying where is she?" Mr. Velvelschmidt said. "Everybody knows the Greenspan boy, two nights ago, Aaron his name was, the poor boy, less than a minute after the rabbi said he was married to Rivke Shumansky he was killed under the *chuppe* in Lenox Assembly Rooms. Everybody knows who brought the *schnapps* to the wedding. Everybody knows everything except where is Mrs. Kramer?"

"So because Mrs. Kramer is not here in the house," my Aunt Sarah said, "this by you means she's hiding from the police?"

"If she's not," Mr. Velvelschmidt said, "where is she?"

"She's where it's none of your business," my Aunt Sarah said. Mr. Velvelschmidt staggered back with a small, chirping scream of astonishment as she shoved him toward the hall. "What kind of a world is this?" my Aunt Sarah demanded. "Where a person can't get sick and go away to the country to rest for a few days without dirty rotten bloodsuckers breaking down the doors to call her names?"

"Who is breaking down doors?" Mr. Velvelschmidt almost whimpered. "I knocked like a gentleman, and you let me in."

"This is a mistake I will never make again," my Aunt Sarah said. "Get out of here," she said. She gave him another shove. "And don't ever push your fat *lottke* face into this house again."

Stumbling backward down the long green hall covered with my pencil scrawls, Mr. Velvelschmidt screamed nineteen terrifying words.

"I won't have to come back! What's going to come back here to this house is a *moof tzettle!*"

It was, on East Fourth Street, the ultimate threat.

Mr. Shumansky might become a bit nasty about the fact that you had not paid for your last Sabbath chicken. Mr. Deutsch could threaten to cut off your credit unless you made at least a token payment on your grocery bill. The Burns Coal Company on the Fourth Street dock would coldly refuse to deliver the two tons of anthracite you needed to take you through the winter unless you put your cash on the bookkeeper's counter. Life on East Fourth Street in those days was, in fact, an endless series of threats evaded, thrusts parried, and warnings disregarded. Nobody, however, evaded or parried or disregarded a *moof tzettle*.

First, because it was not a verbal statement but a typewritten document, and the typewriter was to East Fourth Street what the Lilliputians were to Gulliver. Second, because it was typed not in Yiddish but in English, and English was to East Fourth Street what the knife is to a throat. And third, because the *moof tzettle* was always delivered in person by a member of the *politzei,* a word that meant to the immigrants of East Fourth Street any two-legged creature from a Russian officer with drawn sword leading a cavalry charge in the Ukraine against a huddled mass of unarmed Jewish peasants, to a corpulent Irish minion of the New York City Municipal Court performing his civil function of advising tenants in arrears that by failing to pay their rent they had violated the law, and unless they removed themselves and their possessions from the splinter of private property they were now illegally occupying, the police would arrive and do it for them.

The core of the terror in this threat taught me something at a time when I was totally unaware of the learning process. I was picking things up the way the collar of a blue serge suit picks up dandruff. The truth of what I picked up from the *moof tzettle* was for many years unacceptable: shelter is more important than food.

For years I knew, but did not want to believe, that if you have a roof over your head, you can listen with reasonable equanimity to the grinding of the rapacious digestive juices prowling through your stomach for their raw material. But if rain is banging down on your forehead, the noises in your empty stomach are louder and they hurt more. Our family had never been hit with a *moof tzettle*. But we had been many times elbow to elbow with families that had. So, apparently, had my Aunt Sarah up in New Haven. I could see the smear of fear wash across those extraordinary blue eyes like a painter's brush slashing across a virgin canvas.

"Don't worry," I said as the door at the end of the green corridor slammed behind Mr. Velvelschmidt. "The rent, it'll be paid before he sends the *moof tzettle*."

"How?" my Aunt Sarah said.

I could have told her. I had in the pocket of my knickers the two ten-spots Mr. Heizerick had given me two nights ago in Abe Lebenbaum's back room for the bottle of Old Southwick. They were not enough. But I had other resources. My faith. My faith in a stranger named Walter Sinclair was not unlike the faith of Miles Standish in John Alden. But my father was in the room. He was no longer staring into his plate of goulash, Berezna style. My father was staring at me.

"I'll tell you later," I said to my Aunt Sarah. And I started down the long green corridor.

My Aunt Sarah called after me. "But I'm making *lekach!*"

"I'll eat it later," I called back.

She was calling something else after me as I ran through the front door and down the gray stone steps to the street, but I did not catch the words and I did not pause to ask her to repeat. It was the bottom of the ninth. The Kramer family was behind. And the sun was going down so fast, the game might have to be called on account of darkness. This was no time to waste precious minutes on reading signals from the dugout. I had to swing at the next pitch. To my surprise, it was delivered by Abe Lebenbaum.

I say surprise because I had assumed, as I ran up the street

271

to Avenue D, that when I came into the candy store I would be greeted, as I was every night when I arrived on the job, by Abe's mother with the only two words she was able to speak in English: "You're late." Instead, I was greeted by Abe. He was standing behind the fountain, cleaning away with his pocket-knife the black sugary encrustations around the spout of the Moxie syrup pump. And his greeting consisted of four words: "What do you want?"

The answer was simple enough. But I had not intended to make it to Abe Lebenbaum directly. In fact, I had not antici-pated the question. I had worked out in my mind very clearly, when I left my father and my Aunt Sarah in our kitchen, how I would tackle the next problem in what was beginning to im-press me somewhat nervously as an extremely complicated life for a member of the Manhattan Council. I was struck by some-thing that I still feel I was too young to be struck by: the unfair-ness of the problems that are pitched to the young, most of whom don't even have the muscles to bring a regulation-size bat up to their shoulders.

Abe cringed back against the mirrored wall behind him. "Stay away from me with your German measles!"

I had just about decided he had gone crazy, when I remem-bered what I had told my Aunt Sarah at the breakfast table she should tell Abe about why I would not be coming to work: I was sick, with the most popular ailment of the day: German measles.

"It's all gone," I said. "I'm cured. Mr. Lebenbaum, where's your mother?"

"Upstairs cooking sopper," Abe Lebenbaum said. "Stay away from the counter! German measles nobody cures so quick. Where do you expect her to be?"

The fact that I had expected his mother to be behind the

fountain now seemed irrelevant. I looked at the Seth Thomas under the Moxie sign on the mirrored wall. To my astonishment the clock showed a few minutes after six. The fight with Mr. Velvelschmidt in our kitchen had seemed to me interminable. I saw now that it could have taken no more than a few minutes. I was an hour and a half early for work.

"I thought it was time to come to work," I said.

Bright? No, not very. But at least honest. I had not realized my life had fallen an hour and a half behind the rest of the world.

"Your thinking, from now on," Abe Lebenbaum said, "you can carry out to the garbage pail. Here, in this store, we don't need it."

I was pretty smart for my years. Anyway, my mother kept telling me I was. I could read the handwriting on the wall even when the wall was Abe's invisible larynx and the face he presented—who, after all, would have paid to see it?—to the world. A lump of soaring time had come down to earth with a sickening splash. An era had ended.

"I can explain," I said.

"You little bestitt!" Abe Lebenbaum said, and I was glad the stained marble fountain top was between us. The blade of his pocketknife swept angrily through the air. Not threateningly. Probably for nothing more than emphasis. But this was a man who had hacked off his thumb to avoid the draft. With only four fingers he probably did not have complete control over that swinging knife. A gummy pellet of Moxie syrup hit me on the head. Abe Lebenbaum said, "You rotten little traitor."

Abe was, of course, an immigrant like his mother. He, and later she, had come to America when he was a grown but still young man from those same Carpathian mountain slopes that were my mother's native land. Abe spoke English adequately, but with a marked accent. The word "bestitt," when he hurled it at me, was not a surprising rendition of the word bastard. But where had Abe Lebenbaum come up with the word traitor? Pronounced impeccably in English.

"Who, me?" I said.

I was a pretty scared senior patrol leader at the moment, and my mind was fixed on what I had come to get, but I could not help feeling a jolt of surprise. It was the snarl in his voice. I had always thought of Abe Lebenbaum as a gentle person. He was a tall, thin man who always seemed to be on the verge of dipping down to pick up a dropped coin: his right arm was longer than his left, and at the end of it, his surprisingly large right hand hung like a ham that kept him doubled over, swinging out of control somewhere around his knee and keeping him off balance. It was probably an accurate representation of his physical state. Abe couldn't have been very far from exhaustion when he came tottering into the candy store every evening from his daily session with the Zabriskie sisters. But it was Abe Lebenbaum's face that made you want to drop what you were doing and hurry over to help him find that coin he was groping for. It was the sort of face I found years later carved into the statues of saints in European cathedrals. Out of those sad features, arranged in that look of suffering supplication directed toward God—the eyeballs always turned upward—should come a growl that would have been appropriate to a lion in the zoo? It didn't seem right.

"Listen, Mr. Lebenbaum," I said.

"I should listen?" Abe said. "You do the listening, you and your whole rotten family, you hear? I don't want you should ever come in this store again, you hear? You're troublemakers, all of you, and I want to turn around and look the other way like I never saw you before, any of you, you hear?"

Considering the decibels of sound Abe was uttering, it seemed to me Walter Sinclair, somewhere out there on the river in the *Jefferson Davis II,* could also hear him. Somehow I found this reassuring. I was not alone. My spirits, which had been dragging, now went up. Unfortunately, they went up too far. I should have asked Abe Lebenbaum to give me what I had come for. Instead, I succumbed all at once to an instinct I had never felt before: the compulsion to defend my family.

"Who wants to come in here?" I said. "Crazy people, maybe. Not my father or my mother. Not me even. This is a rotten place. I don't want to come back. My mother doesn't want me to come back. Just give me my money and I'll get out of here for good."

"What money?" Abe Lebenbaum said.

"What money?" I said. Not a question. A scream. I imagine that's how most revolutionaries get started. Not with a whine but an explosion. "The money for my work," I screamed. "The last time you paid me was last Monday. I worked here a whole week since then. I want my money."

I was right up there. I'd never seen or heard of a barricade. But the noise I was making would have held its own with the best that was produced at the fall of the Bastille. It was my first experience with the joy of irrelevant noisemaking. It had an astonishing effect. It brought from the back of the candy store the snappily tailored figure of Mr. Heizerick.

"What the helliz gawn nahn out here?" he said.

Abe Lebenbaum snapped shut the blade of his pocketknife. "Gangsters," he said. He didn't say it in a way that could be described as friendly. Snarls seldom are. But on a barricade

275

Abe Lebenbaum would not have stood out. "You hire a boy to help you in the store," he snarled. "You trust him." There was no savagery in Abe's snarl. Just a kind of irritated wail. He didn't want to kill anybody. He merely wanted the world to know he had been betrayed. "Why shouldn't you trust him?" Abe said. "He's a scout boy. He wears a uniform covered with medals. He's got a mother she comes in regular to see he's doing his job right. So what happens?"

Mr. Heizerick came up to the counter and placed a dollar bill on the stained marble. I was startled. I had never seen him put down anything smaller than a ten-spot.

"Maw nickels," he said.

Across the stone face of the suffering saint, rolling the carved eyes down from their permanent glimpse of heaven, came a look of petulance. "Om tellinyuh what people do to other people," Abe Lebenbaum said bitterly.

"Maw nickels," Mr. Heizerick said.

"Only a dollar?" Abe said.

"Maw nickels," Mr. Heizerick said.

Abe shrugged, punched the *No Sale* key that clanked open the cash register, and clawed out a handful of nickels. A glance into his palm indicated that there were not enough. Abe pulled out a cylinder of nickels. He cracked the paper sausage-casing wrapper against the edge of the cash-register drawer as though it were an egg he was cracking open against the rim of a frying pan. The nickels showered out into the drawer and Abe started scooping them up and shoving them across the counter two at a time toward Mr. Heizerick.

"Ten, twenty, thirty. His mother it turns out, she's a bootlegger, that's what she is. Selling *schnapps* to weddings. Seventy, eighty, ninety, one dollar."

Mr. Heizerick swept the twenty nickels from the marble

counter into his cupped palm and slapped down another dollar. "Faster," he said.

"Ten, twenty, thirty," Abe Lebenbaum said, forking nickels
out of the pile with the forefinger and middle finger of the big
right hand that normally swung like a swollen pendulum
around his knees. "Forty, fifty, sixty."

"No," Mr. Heizerick said. "Fifty-five."

"What?" Abe said.

"Yirra nickel shawt," Mr. Heizerick said.

Silence in the candy store. Except for the hammering of my
heart. And the scrape of coins across the stained marble as Abe
counted again the nickels of the second dollar. There was
nothing I could do about my heart. It was banging against the
wall of my chest like a carpenter's hammer driving a nail. Why
not? I had thought getting the rent for my Aunt Sarah would
be easy. I had the two ten-spots Mr. Heizerick had given me
two nights ago for the bottle of Old Southwick. All I needed
was three dollars more. Circumventing Mr. Velvelschmidt's
threat about the *moof tzettle* had seemed a cinch. Abe owed me
a week's pay. All I had to do was pick it up. I had looked forward to seeing my Aunt Sarah's face when I came home with
the money. Benny the hero!

"You're right," Abe Lebenbaum said. "A nickel short." He
shoved out the nickel and continued forking out the rest, two
at a time. "So on account of this scout boy and his fancy
mother, I have to get the police today. Not even the police.
What police? They know me. They know I'm an honest businessman. They know with gangsters and *schnapps* peddlers
Abe Lebenbaum will have something to do like he'll have to do
with cancer. All day not the police. All day from the government in Washington, an Irisher with a name Kelly. That's all a
man needs. Irishers from Washington with names like Kelly.

All day questions. Who is this boy Benny Kramer? How long have you known him? How long has he worked for you? You should hear the questions these bestitts from Washington they ask. With yet that way they talk English. Like they were reading it from a subpoena. Ninety, a dollar."

Mr. Heizerick swept the new hill of coins from the counter.

I edged closer to the stained marble. "Mr. Lebenbaum, please give me my week's pay," I said.

With a certain amount of firmness, I must add. Just because my heart was trying to hammer its way out of my chest did not change my awareness that a scout was brave.

"I need the money," I said. "You owe me the money. Please give it to me."

The forefinger and middle finger of Abe Lebenbaum's right hand, which lacked the thumb he had sacrificed to the cause of peace and had been stabbing nickels out of the pile of coins on the marble counter, now changed direction. They stabbed at me. Like the tines of a carving fork. I ducked back just in time. But Mr. Heizerick was leaning forward to scoop up his third batch of twenty nickels. My elbow hit his arm. The nickels splashed down on the floor. Trying to catch them, Mr. Heizerick's body, encased in his natty tight coat, made several odd, spasmodic movements. The results were astonishing.

First, the pearl-gray fedora popped off his head, revealing that the zombie gambler was as bald as the moon-faced man in the Admiration cigar ads. As the hat went bouncing along the dirty floor, there was a long, ripping sound, and Mr. Heizerick fell back on his own hat. He made a series of funny noises while clutching at his middle. A couple of moments later I saw why. The buttons that held his natty topcoat so close to his body had torn loose, flinging the coat open and revealing that underneath the topcoat Abe Lebenbaum's most important customer was naked to the waist. In his long battle with the slot machine he had obviously lost his shirt.

"Git odda here!" he screamed. "Git odda here!"

I turned desperately to Abe Lebenbaum. "I need the money," I said. "You owe me a week's pay. Please give me my money."

"What I'll give you, you little bestitt," Abe shouted, "I'll give you a *killa!*"

A *killa* does not appear among the common human ailments listed in *Merck's Medical Manual*. It is the Yiddish word for a hernia.

"But, Mr. Lebenbaum," I said. "You owe me the money."

"Not to you!" he yelled. "To your mother. She always comes to get your pay. So tell her to come now. I'd like to see her. Tell her to come collect your pay. I'll give it to her, boy! I'll give it to her!"

The sound of his snarling voice drove me backward to the door like the blast of heat from a suddenly opened furnace door. My movement was hastened by the fact that Mr. Heizerick was beginning to recover. He reached his knees. He began to paw about for his hat. It seemed to me I'd better get out of there before the gambler's groping hands found the squashed fedora. As I stepped backward across the threshold of the candy store into Avenue D, I bumped into Abe Lebenbaum's mother. The little old lady was coming in.

"Benny," she said in English, "you're late."

13

THIS WAS NOT TRUE, of course. I had arrived in the candy store an hour and a half early. In the larger sense, however, Abe Lebenbaum's mother was right. Forty years later it occurred to me that the toothless little old lady's statement had been more than just another demonstration of her limited command of English. The old crone's words had been prophetic.

Walking out of the morgue in the Queens County General Hospital on that gray, cold Sunday before Christmas Eve when my mother died, I realized I was late again. In a way that, it seemed to me, could not fail to give any man pause. Not to mention the willies or even the screaming meemies. I was late for the identification of the body of my own mother.

"How'd it go?"

I looked down at the taxi driver sitting in the cab at the foot of the two steps that led up into the morgue. It occurred to me that he, too, must have had a mother.

"Not very good," I said. "I have to make another stop."

I opened the rear door of the taxi, humpbacked myself in, plopped down on the seat, and pulled the door shut.

"Where to?" the driver said.

"The year of Our Lord 1927," came to the surface of my mind as the only possible reply, but I did not utter the words aloud. I said, "You know where you picked me up?" I glanced at the clock. "About seven dollars ago?"

"Yeah," the taxi driver said. "I been thinking about that."

I pulled out my wallet, slid from it a ten-dollar bill, and pushed it across to him. "Let's start all over again," I said.

He took the bill, stared at it for a moment, then flipped up the flag of his ticking clock. "I didn't mean by what I said—" he said as the clock stopped ticking.

"I know you didn't," I said. "It's just that I need you more than you need me, and I don't want to worry about you worrying about me."

The driver started punching the keys of his coin box and fussing with his back pocket. "I didn't mean you should get the impression I don't trust you," he said again.

Who did?

"Don't bother with the change," I said. "That's your tip for round one."

The driver looked up into the mirror over his steering wheel. Startled. "Well, gee," he said.

Why not? I was not at the moment on the prowl for phrase-makers. "Forget it," I said. "It's Christmas." And I was on the trail of my mother's body. What a parlay.

"Well, gee," the driver said. That settled it. A phrase-maker he wasn't. "Thanks a lot, mister."

The witless phrase held my ear. One man's despair is another man's gratitude. I waited for him to ask the inevitable question. He did.

"Where to, mister?" he said again.

The beginning of the road. The start of the trip. The invention of the riddle. The initiation of the horror. But how would he know that destination? He didn't look any smarter than I did.

"One, three, eight dash two seven, Seventy-eighth Avenue," I said. "It's just off Main Street. If you know the general direction, I can guide you into the side streets."

"Do I know the general direction?" the taxi driver said. "My mother lives around the corner."

Why shouldn't she? All mothers live around the corner.

"Okay," I said. "Let's go."

I didn't really know where. Correction. I did know the precise address. I knew exactly how to get there. The way a jockey once told me a horse knows how to get back to the stable. But what was it I was getting back to? A modest three-room apartment in the Kew Gardens Hills section of Queens? Where my mother had spent the last of her eighty years? What was the point?

My mother was dead. I had to find her body. It had vanished somewhere between the Peretz Memorial Hospital on Main Street and the morgue of the Queens County Hospital on God forbid anybody should ask me what street. My mother's body was not likely to be in her apartment on 78th Avenue. Yet I knew that was my next stop.

"This it?"

I looked out the taxi window. "Yes," I said.

Yes, indeed. This had been it for almost a quarter of a century. How, I thought as I cringed under a sudden unexpected assault of terror, how was I ever going to get the hell out of it?

"Mister, I'm sorry," the taxi driver said. "I'm afraid I don't have the change."

I stared at the second ten-dollar bill I had handed over. It calmed me down. What in God's name was the matter with me? Had I signed onto some witless TV show to give an imper-

282

sonation of Diamond Jim Brady? Who was I to go around handing out ten-dollar bills to taxi drivers?

"That's all right," I said. "Keep the change."

Answer: I was a terrified fool confronted by the only experience nobody can handle in life: death.

"Jesus Christ," the taxi driver said.

"Yes," I said. "It's his birthday."

I got out of that cab fast.

My mother's apartment was one of about two hundred built around a courtyard in the form of eight two-story buildings made forty years before of red brick, gray plaster, and black iron window frames. Forty years had taken their toll.

On this dreary day before Christmas the red brick looked like carrots going bad on a vegetable stall outside a grocery store. The gray plaster was dripping away in unpleasant pellets. The black iron window frames were rust-pink. Fair enough. Scalps lose their hair. Muscles sag. Rear ends spread. Death shall have no dominion?

One of the nice things about the Borough of Queens, what makes the architectural pattern known as the development something that pleases the eye, is the arena it provides for children. Little children. Tricycle size.

The arena is always covered by pulped brown sod with enough peripheral fragments of green to indicate that once it was covered by grass. I have always liked places from which grass has been tramped away. Like Tompkins Square Park. Across the street from the Hannah H. Lichtenstein House. It indicates that people have been there.

In Queens the people are usually overweight young mothers with peripatetic children. Every Sunday of my life during the past years I had walked the gauntlet. From the curb to the entrance to 1-D.

283

The nice Jewish boy. The devoted son. Coming to make his weekly visit to his ancient mother. Carrying a shopping bag loaded with the items that any other mother could have purchased for herself during the past seven days in shops no more than three hundred feet around the corner from her front door: aspirin; bagels; toothpaste; whiskey; and of course mineral oil. My father left my mother a single legacy: the conviction that the human bowel is totally incapable of performing its function unassisted.

Over twenty years. Lugging bagels and mineral oil. Through clusters of gossiping mothers who should have been dieting, and whirling knots of screaming kids who should have been muzzled. Twenty-odd years of nodding and smiling, acknowledging the *kvelling* of the fat ladies who, like the Japanese, are ancestor worshipers. Adoring the weekly arrival of the successful son from downtown who turned his back every Sunday on God knows what enormously lucrative business deals in order to bring to the mother he loves her weekly ration of intestinal lubricant.

It had always been the toughest part of those Sunday morning visits. The adoration of those fat ladies reminded me of a poodle I had bought for my sons when they were very young. It was a mistake. I don't like dogs. But I had been boning up on how to be a good father. The books said the way to do it is to provide the kids with one of man's best friends. My sons didn't seem to know the rules. The poodle bored them. They paid no attention to him. My wife, a kindly girl, is also a tough-minded citizen. The dog had been my idea. It was up to me to take care of him. I did.

With an irritation that verged on repugnance. Not because the poodle was unattractive. On the contrary. The papers that came with him indicated clearly that he was a beauty. Our neighbors agreed. They petted him and made murmuring sounds of endearment that drove me to a hatred for Albert Payson Terhune that was thoroughly irrational. Terhune was a collie man.

The reason for my hatred made me feel like Jack the Ripper. The foolish dog loved me. He followed me everywhere I went. Even into the bathroom. I had to learn how to snap the door shut fast. When I wasn't looking he sneaked up behind me and licked my hand. Frequently, I regret to say, other parts of my body. When he heard my voice he came loping out to smother me with what I suppose must be called kisses. Boy, were they wet. And boy, did I hate them. And boy, was I going crazy.

Why? Because I don't like affection I have not earned. That dog loved me, sure. But I knew why. I was the only one in the family who would feed him. How could I not? What kind of person would allow a three-hundred-dollar dog to die of starvation?

Not a boy who went out to Queens every Sunday morning to bring his mother the toothpaste and bagels she should certainly have learned, after all her years in this country, how to purchase for herself. Especially since she was in perfect health, vigorous to the point of being a nuisance, and plentifully supplied with cash by guess who.

The poodle finally died. My wife and sons did not notice his passing from our family scene. I did not call his absence to their attention. Their indifference gave me a chance to live with the discomfort of my relief. I had not wanted the stupid dog to die. I'd had nothing to do with his demise. But his death took a load off my back.

Now, twenty years after the death of that dog, crossing the grassless square in front of my mother's apartment house in Queens, I faced a moment of horror. The parallel between the death of the poodle and the death of my mother made my stomach knot. I couldn't believe that such a detestable thought should have crossed my mind. But it had. It had. It had. And the only thing that saved me from being sick was the weather.

Today I did not have to nod and smile to *kvelling* fat ladies. Today I did not have to pat the heads of screaming kids trying to knock me down. Today was not tricycle or wading-pool weather. And it was only a few hours before Christmas.

The fat ladies and their screaming offspring were indoors. Probably eating their heads off. Nobody saw me as I crossed the hard grassless square of frozen sod to the 1-D entrance. Anyway, I didn't see anybody see me. It was a short journey. For years the distraction of the plump mothers and their maniacally active children had made it easier for me to walk the perhaps one hundred feet. Today, for the first time, as I pulled from my pocket the key to my mother's apartment, I was glad to be alone.

The feeling vanished as soon as I closed the door behind me. The smell almost knocked me over.

Let me say immediately that my mother was a neat housekeeper. Not sensational. But neat. I cannot say honestly that I would have wanted to eat off her floors. But that was not because of the way she treated them. My mother treated her floors as though they were an enemy who could be kept at bay only by constant sluicing and scrubbing. The reason why I would not have wanted to eat off my mother's floors is simply because she had spent her life on floors that were not made of the best materials. All the sluicing and scrubbing in the world will not take the smell of decay out of rotten wood. That's why my mother as a young woman always bought the strongest-smelling cleaning materials in the grocery store. I was raised on Fels-Naphtha. It is conceivable that this is why I have been totally bald since my twenty-third year. I consider myself lucky to have retained my teeth.

During the last days of her life my mother came to grumbling terms with detergents. She went at her floors with weapons that came in plastic squeeze bottles, later in spray cans, and were advertised on TV by fading movie stars and glowing quiz masters. As a result, her three modest rooms on 78th Avenue in the Borough of Queens always smelled like those tiny porcelain bowls in which my dentist's nurse mixes the stuff she uses to clean my teeth.

To combat this, I introduced my mother to one of the century's great inventions. The Open Window. She fell for it. My mother's apartment had two exposures, and so picked up the added benefits of cross ventilation. Soon after she discovered what fresh air can do to odors, my mother's home took on some of the qualities of those wind tunnels that families named Guggenheim are constantly presenting to universities for tax-deductible reasons and the study of aerodynamics. Summer and fall, winter and spring, whenever I came into her apartment on Sunday mornings I had to hold onto my hat.

That's why on this dismal day before Christmas I stopped short as soon as the door slammed shut behind me. My hat sat quietly on my head. There were no breezes. I realized that nobody had been inside these three rooms for thirty-two days. Since the Sunday morning when my mother fell and broke her hip.

Before climbing into the ambulance that was to carry her to the Peretz Memorial Hospital, I had gone around the apartment, carefully closing all the windows. While I had been shaving that morning the weather forecast on the radio had been unpromising. Barometer falling. Winds from the northeast. Precipitation possibility eighty percent. I had shut my mother's windows tight. Now, thirty-two days later, the air in my mother's apartment was no longer really air. It was a smell. The smell of death.

For a few moments I must have lost control. I think I went slightly crazy. I remember running from room to room, slamming the windows up wide. The needling winds of the rotten day came pumping in. Whirling the draperies in the living room. Flapping the curtains in the bedroom. Banging the Venetian blind in the kitchen. It didn't take long to get them all open. My mother had never had much. Not even windows. The number of places through which she could look out on the world had been limited. It was probably better that way. What she saw never pleased her very much.

Except once. Long ago. And those windows through which she had looked at that strange time had actually been portholes. But I'm not sure even about that one piece of her life which she might have enjoyed. I had not been with her on board the *Jefferson Davis II*. And she had never said a word to me about her voyage. It was her silence that had troubled me for forty years. I stood there, suddenly stunned by a thought that must have been stalking me all day: now that she was dead, her silence was final. Now I would never know.

Two things brought me up out of this dismaying thought. My hat, caught in a gust from 78th Avenue, went sailing off my head out of the living room into the foyer, and as I turned and ran to retrieve it, I heard the telephone.

I stopped and stared at it. My mind doesn't always function logically. Here I was, standing on the day of my mother's death in the foyer of her three-room apartment in Queens, and what was I thinking about? Sir Arthur Conan Doyle.

I was suddenly remembering that when I was a boy I had read about his will in the *American Weekly*. Or perhaps it was some other Sunday supplement. Or maybe not his will. It could have been a statement he had made to his family from his deathbed. It was a time when famous people always kept the hearse waiting until they thought up an appropriate exit line.

Anyway, I was suddenly remembering that Sir Arthur, in addition to being the creator of the greatest character in English fiction since Mr. Micawber, had also been a militant spiritualist. I recalled distinctly that he had promised his family he would communicate with them from what the *American Weekly* or its contemporary called the Great Beyond. Now I almost fell through the foyer floor of my dead mother's three-room apartment on 78th Avenue in the Borough of Queens. I was absolutely convinced the ringing phone was a call from my mother. Calling to tell me that you couldn't trust anybody any more. Not even the people who run hospitals. When she was a girl, and a person died, the people in the hospital at least knew where the body was. Why they let the person die in the first place—all right, we won't discuss that now. After all, what can you expect from doctors? Bills. What else? But once the person was dead, was it too much to expect from doctors that the son who came to the hospital he should be able to see his dead mother?

I figured to hell with my hat. I allowed it to go skipping across the floor of the foyer into the kitchen, and I grabbed up the phone.

"Hello?"

"Is that you?" said the voice of Herman Sabinson.

People do ask the damndest questions. Who else could it be? But the damndest questions do help. Like bicarbonate of soda. You don't want brilliant repartee. You want your heaving stomach to settle down. Herman Sabinson had always been able to settle mine.

289

"Yes," I said. "Herman, listen. Something terrible has happened."

"I know," Herman said. "Please stay there. I'm coming right over."

"Where are you?" I said.

"At the hospital," Herman said. "I stopped off to see Mrs. O'Toole and pick up the paper I asked you to sign, but she was gone."

"It's the day before Christmas," I said. "She won't be back until Tuesday."

"How do you know?" Herman said.

"I called the hospital from the funeral parlor." I looked at my wristwatch. "About three hours ago. When they told me I had to go to the morgue to identify the body. I called Mrs. O'Toole right away. To ask why. But she was gone."

"Well, you see, it's the day before Christmas," Herman Sabinson said. "She won't be back till Tuesday."

So I knew the trouble was worse than I'd thought. When Herman Sabinson is upset he doesn't listen to what you're telling him. He's tuning in on his own thoughts, trying to figure out what to say that will soothe you.

"I could grab a cab and meet you at the hospital," I said.

"No," Herman said. "I want you to stay there and wait for me. A few minutes, that's all. I'm coming right over."

"Herman," I said.

"What?"

"How did you know I was here?"

The astonishment in his voice came across the wire as clearly as a perfectly tuned TV picture. "Where else would you be?" Dr. Herman Sabinson said.

Well, I thought as I hung up, I'd had a pretty good year.

290

My wife and I had earned a winter vacation. If it hadn't been for my mother falling down and breaking her hip, I might have been on one of those hot islands in the Caribbean, rubbing myself down with dollar-a-bottle suntan lotion and trying to keep the frolicking jet set from kicking sand into my daiquiri. Or I might have been at home, helping my wife place the children's presents under the tree. And wondering, as I had wondered during every year of my married life, what Rabbi Goldfarb would have said if he had seen one of his old *cheder* students fooling around with a Christmas tree. Since I knew what he would have said, and I could see that old polished chair rung rising to the sky for a downward cut at my ankles, I came out of the past and back into the present.

It consisted of a windy foyer that had been cleansed of the smell of death. The place now smelled like all the rest of the Borough of Queens. An improvement, I suppose. I started moving around the apartment, shutting at a more leisurely pace the windows I had only a few minutes earlier so hysterically opened. In the process two things happened.

I retrieved my hat. And for the first time I took a good square look at the arena in which my mother had spent the last years of her life.

The word arena had never occurred to me before. Now that the defending champ was gone, I saw why. On the inside of her door, in addition to the double Segal lock, she had hung a chain bolt with links as thick as a salami. There was also a peephole, but my mother never used it. She answered her bell by pulling open the door as far as the chain allowed: three inches. Thus she could see not only the face of her visitor but also the visitor's legs.

"When somebody comes to steal your money," I remembered her once saying, "who cares about the shape of their nose or if they wear glasses? It's with the feet that they'll kick you in the *kishkes*."

All visitors were potential assailants. In my mother's strange view of life some things were diamond-hard. Profits were rare. Losses normal. You had to devote the main thrust of your energies toward taking precautions against loss.

I now noticed for the first time, even though it must have been there for years, that leaning against the wall in the corner of the foyer, just inside the door, was the fat bamboo pole of the Morse flag I used to carry every Saturday night from East Fourth Street to the meetings of Troop 244 in the Hannah H. Lichtenstein House on Avenue B. The sight made me remember something else my mother had once said.

It was during one of my regular Sunday morning visits. We were discussing a grisly New York *Daily News* murder in one of those high-rise apartment houses on the Upper East Side of Manhattan where the only people who seem to be safe are the landlords. Probably because they are always in the sauna bath at the Fontainebleau in Miami. The victim, an elderly widow, had admitted to her apartment a man who had claimed to be an upholsterer. When he came at her with a knife, the woman tried without success to defend herself by swinging at him a baseball bat her now grown and married son had used when he was in the Little League.

"A mistake," my mother had said. "When the murderers come, anything you have to swing, it's too late. A stick is better. A pole. Something you don't have to swing. Just poke. With the sharp end. If you know where to poke."

I did. It astonished me that she knew. During the war, when I was stationed in England, I had been ordered to take, as a preparation for D-Day, a commando course given by a British guerrilla officer who had been trained in Burma.

"What you want to do is forget the Marquis of Queensberry rules," he told us one morning on the lawn in front of our barracks. "What you want to remember is your life depends on putting the other bloke out of commission before he can do the same to you. The easiest way to do that is to get at what we might call his vital parts. Like this."

With a broom handle not unlike the bamboo pole that later showed up in the foyer of my mother's apartment in Queens, and without any swing or wind-up, he lunged forward, as though with a spear he were stabbing at a boar during a hunt in some Silesian forest.

"There, now," the British officer said as he straightened up. "There's one chap wouldn't be in a position to do any more procreating of his species, would he?"

Probably not. But at least he would have lost the capacity in an understandable conflict. A formally declared war. Between his country and a clearly identified enemy. With a name. And a flag. And a capital city. And field marshals whose exploits were described with foreign correspondent clarity in the daily press.

But who had been my mother's enemy? Against what had she chained her door? To fight off whom had she placed my old Morse signal pole at the ready?

Surely not against the rapists and murderers who had killed the woman in the high-rise apartment house on the Upper East Side. These creatures were a recent development. They had appeared on the scene since New York had become Fun City. That chain on the door, however, and that bamboo pole in the corner, these had been there from the day my mother had moved into this apartment. The day, or a few thereafter, when I had come home from the war and had helped move her into 78th Avenue. In those days New York had been safe for the residents of Queens. But not, apparently, for my mother.

I hooked the chain into place. She was dead. But her body was missing. I had a small boy's irrational but very real feeling that she might walk in at any moment. If she did, I did not want her bawling me out for not locking the gates of her castle properly.

I turned from the front door with the feeling I was turning from a portcullis, after making sure the drawbridge was up, to move on in my inspection of the castle defenses.

I didn't get very far. In the living room I realized that for thirty-two days, while my mother had been in the Peretz Memorial Hospital, I had refused to face what I now could not escape: the disposition of her possessions. Looking around, I could see that even in this area she had left behind her an irritating contradiction. So far as my mother was concerned all those TV commercials paid for by manufacturers of furniture wax and other cleaning products were a lot of malarkey. My mother's final word was spread all around me: nothing improves the appearance of old furniture so much as a thirty-two-day layer of dust.

I don't mean old furniture as in antique old. I mean old as in Grand Rapids old. Or wherever the furniture came from that used to stand around our tenement flat on East Fourth Street. Note the words: stand around. On East Fourth Street people did not decorate rooms. They filled them.

Where the stuff came from with which my mother had filled ours, I don't know. Some inexpensive furniture store on Avenue D, C, B, or A, no doubt. These thoroughfares were lined with them. And the stores were stuffed with pretty much the same things. Sets, they were called. Bedroom set: bed, bureau, two chairs, and a mirror. Dining-room set: table, sideboard, four or more chairs (purchaser's option), and a mirror. Living-room set: couch, known as a lounge or "lunch," two stuffed chairs with matching upholstery, a sweet table, later known as a coffee table, and a mirror. Kitchen set: not yet invented.

These pieces were placed around the appropriate rooms in accordance with their shape and the wall space available.

I was standing in the middle of her apartment on 78th Avenue, remembering the way my mother had arranged our dining-room set in the front room on East Fourth Street, when I realized I was staring at the pieces of the same set, and that they were arranged now, so many years later, exactly as they had been arranged when I first became aware of them as a boy.

Astonished, I saw that even the cut-glass bowl, from which I was once allowed to take fruit without asking permission, stood on the sideboard, to the left of the door. I walked to the bowl and picked up a dusty orange. Through the grit under my fingers I could tell it was wax. I poked about among the dust-covered apples and bananas and peaches. All wax. I did not understand why I had never before noticed that all these years my mother as an old woman had preserved here in Queens the appearance of the rooms in which she had lived as a young woman on East Fourth Street. I was asking myself why when the doorbell rang.

I went back to the portcullis and lowered the drawbridge. Herman Sabinson faced me through the open door. I wondered why a man in a heavy overcoat should looked naked. Then I noticed that Herman was not carrying his little black bag. Why should he? The patient was dead.

"You all right?" he said.

I gave it a moment of thought. The moment was unexpectedly filled by a recollection of my feelings years ago when I had learned the poodle had died. It seemed unwise to let my thoughts hang around in that neighborhood. "I'm fine," I said. It was better to lie.

"So why don't you invite a guy in?" Herman Sabinson said.

Herman was one of those strange kids who had come every day to Rabbi Goldfarb's *cheder* from below Delancey Street. He was not a part of my life on East Fourth Street. He had gone to J.H.S. 97 on Mangin Street. He had belonged to a scout troop in the Educational Alliance. We never really knew each other. Years later, visiting a sick friend on Central Park West, I stayed longer than I had been warned to stay, and so I met his doctor coming in. The doctor said he thought we had met before. I said I thought so, too. Thirty seconds of "Didn't you used to?" and "Weren't you one of?" and contact was established. There are no friendships so solid as the cemented friendships that never existed. And there is no cement so binding as the Lower East Side. Ten minutes after we met in my sick friend's apartment, Herman Sabinson and I were convinced that we had flown together in the Lafayette Escadrille.

I turned over to him all my insides. Then I fed my wife and kids into his professional orbit. My mother came last, but she got most of Dr. Sabinson's attention. Kids from 97 and the Edgie were helpless in the presence of old Jewish ladies. Herman revered my mother. I don't think Herman revered me. But I had an immediate feeling that he liked me. Perhaps what he liked was a recollection of the days when life was simple. When people were not yet dying. When people were not yet people. When his concern was for learning how to save the abstractions who some day would become people. Anyway, Herman seemed to like me. So I liked him back. Why not? What more can you ask? The time I spent with Herman always made me feel good. As I grow older these times become more important.

"What are the good moments of this life? They are like the good moments of an egg." The Duchess of Malfi. I don't quote her very often. But what the hell. It was the day before Christmas. And my mother's body had disappeared. And I was scared stiff.

"Sorry," I said to Herman Sabinson, and stepped aside. "Come on in, kid."

Herman came in. He took off his hat, started to slip out of his coat, then stopped. "Jesus," he said. "It's cold as a duck's ass in here."

"I had all the windows open," I said. "Nobody's been in the place for thirty-two days. When I came in, it really smelled."

"Thirty-two days," Herman said in a troubled voice.

He scowled down at the floor. Following his glance, I wondered if it was possible that the brown linoleum on the foyer floor had come, like the living-room furniture, from East Fourth Street. Then I remembered ordering it for my mother from Macy's when she moved into this apartment, and I knew the time had come to pull up my socks.

"Well, figure it out," I said. "She fell and broke her hip on November twenty-second. So that's eight days to the end of the month of November or the thirtieth. And today is December twenty-fourth. Twenty-four plus eight is thirty-two."

Herman Sabinson looked up with apparent reluctance from his contemplation of the ugly brown linoleum. The color had been my mother's choice. No, her insistence. All her life she had preferred not things that were pretty but things that "didn't show the dirt."

"You're right," Herman said. "Thirty-two days. What a

297

woman." He apparently felt this observation was either too
intimate or faintly disrespectful, so he corrected it immediately. "What a person," Herman Sabinson said. "What a
wonderful person."

The faint tremor in his voice was not unfamiliar. In tricycle
weather I had been hearing it for years every Sunday morning.
From the overweight young mothers who *kvelled* as they lay
back in their beach chairs while I ran the gauntlet of their
screaming children. On my way with my shopping bag across
the scrap of damaged lawn from the pavement of 78th Avenue
to the door of 1-D. The Japanese ancestor worship syndrome
ruled Herman Sabinson's life. Geriatrics was his trade. Most of
his patients were old ladies in Queens whose Manhattan-based
sons paid him a monthly fee to make sure none of their business
competitors could say they did not take good care of their
ancient mothers.

"Yes," I said.

Herman Sabinson looked at me with a troubled frown. I
sensed a note of criticism. As though he felt my comment was
inadequate. A man had just said my mother had been a wonderful person. With a throb in his throat. As though he were
delivering a eulogy in Riverside Chapel. And what had I said
in reply? "Yes." That's all. A simple, unadorned yes. Worse
than that. A noncommittal yes. As though I felt it was just
possible that she had not been a wonderful person. I could
feel Herman's distress. I wanted to get out of the orbit of his
emotions. I was having enough trouble with my own. I
wrenched the steering wheel.

"Listen," I said. "What the hell has happened?"

"Now, look," Herman Sabinson said. "I think you should
calm down."

The notion that I did not look or sound calm was distressing.

298

As though I had gone into a business meeting where it was important for me to give the impression that I was non-chalantly indifferent to the outcome, and one of the men at the other side of the table had made some nasty crack about the way I was biting my fingernails. The word aplomb does not cross my mind very often. Crossing it now, all I got from the brief encounter was the uncomfortable feeling that I must have lost it.

"I'm perfectly willing to calm down," I said. "In fact, I'm anxious to calm down. But you've got to admit this is a pretty terrifying mess."

"Now, look," Herman said.

"No, you look," I said. I could hear my voice rising, but I didn't care. It made me feel better. "You call me in the morning," I said. "You say you want to perform an autopsy. You ask me to go to the hospital and sign a paper. I say okay. I go to the hospital. First, this iceberg Mrs. O'Toole, she says it's no longer necessary to sign the paper. But I insist, as long as I'm here, I tell them, I might as well sign it, so she lets me sign it. Then I go over to Battenberg's to arrange for the funeral and they tell me I have to go to the morgue to identify the body."

Herman came in under my pause for breath with "Did they tell you to go today?"

I stared at him. Herman is one of those men who weigh in at about a hundred and forty-five pounds, yet look fat. It's the shape of his face. It is round and plump and sags down into a tiny button chin. He always looks as though he is trying to remember all the words of the Hippocratic Oath in Greek.

"What are you talking about?" I said.

"What they told you at the Battenberg Funeral Home," Herman said. "Did they tell you to go to the morgue today?"

"No, they told me to go tomorrow morning," I said. "But I figured as long as I'm out here in Queens I'll go over now. Which I did—and what happens? They tell me in the morgue my mother's body has disappeared."

Sharply, Herman said, "Did they use that word?"

"What word?"

"Disappeared," Herman said.

"For Christ's sake," I said. "I wasn't carrying a tape recorder. How the hell should I know what words they used? It was some guy named Bieber. Or Beybere, he wants it pronounced. He was in charge, and he said my mother's body was not there. In the morgue. He said her body was not there."

"Yes," Herman Sabinson said, "but did he say it had disappeared? Her body?"

Through my soiled anger, which was making me feel good, came a clean thought that made me feel less good. Herman Sabinson was not a fool. Just because he wore those narrow ties with small embroidered flowers under the knot and he fastened them to his shirt front with one of those gold things called a tie tack, that did not make him a fool. Herman Sabinson was trying to help me.

"I don't know," I said. "Probably this Mr. Beybere didn't use the word disappeared. Now that I think of it, I seem to remember all he said was her body was not there, in the morgue. Maybe I just assumed he meant it had disappeared. What else could it mean?"

Herman took my arm and led me into the living room. He looked around, obviously for a place to sit.

"Don't," I said. "Not until I get a cleaning woman in here. Just tell me, for God's sake. You can do it standing up. What's happening?"

"Well," Herman Sabinson said. He paused, as though to

make sure he had the right words. "There's an ordinance in this city that says no doctor can sign a death certificate for a person who dies as the result of an accident unless the body is first checked out by the medical examiner."

"Accident?" I said. "Do I have to tell you? You were there. You were with her. My mother died in a bed at the Peretz Memorial Hospital."

"As the result of an accident," Herman said firmly.

I had always thought accident meant being hit by a truck. Or gunned down while crossing a street on which a couple of rival mobs were shooting it out. Or passing under a paint scaffold when the ropes tear loose.

"What accident?" I said.

"She fell down right here in this apartment," Herman Sabinson said. He gestured toward the foyer. I had a stab of irritation. Did he think I had forgotten? Did he have to refresh my recollection? Didn't I know where she had fallen? Didn't I know where I had found her? "She broke her hip," Herman Sabinson said. "She was taken by ambulance to the Peretz Memorial Hospital. Thirty-two days later, this morning, she died. As the result of an accident. It may not make immediate sense to you, but believe me, it's the law. In the eyes of the law your mother died as the result of an accident. The accident of her fall out there in that foyer. Therefore, I cannot sign the death certificate until the medical examiner looks at the body."

"What's stopping him?" I said.

I hadn't really asked a question to which I expected an answer. I had merely exploded a piece of my irritation with a situation that was driving me crazy. It was the remark of a smart aleck. To my astonishment Herman Sabinson took it seriously.

"The day," he said. "That's what's stopping him."

"What day?" I said.

"What day?" Herman said. "You must be a little *farmisht*. Don't you know what today is?"

"It's the day my mother died," I said.

"It's also the day before Christmas," Herman said.

"What's that got to do with my mother?" I said.

"And it also happens to be a Sunday," Herman said.

Through my confusion I could feel the necessity to grasp at the role of the cool, unemotional man of reason. "Why should those two facts affect the disappearance of my mother's body?"

"Look," Herman said. "She was a wonderful woman, and I can understand your being affected by her passing, but you must bear in mind that she is not the only person who died today in the City of New York."

I must confess it was a thought that had not crossed my mind until now. "All right," I said. "I'll bear it in mind."

"Bear this in mind, too," Herman said. "People are dying in the City of New York every day. Seven days a week. Not only on Sunday. In every borough. Not only in Queens."

"All right," I said. "I'll bear that in mind, too."

"To handle a situation like that, the medical examiner has to work out a system," Herman said. "I mean, think about it. One man can't go running around all over the city and look at all the dead people that keep piling up every day."

I wished Herman had not told me to think about it. Into my head suddenly came the image of a man in running pants. A stethoscope in one hand. A pad of death certificates and a ballpoint clutched in the other. I could see him running down the streets of the city. Entering the doors of Bellevue at one side. Emerging moments later at the other. Racing for St.

Vincent's. Streaking through Mt. Sinai on his way to the Peretz Memorial.

"I assume he has assistants," I said.

Again Herman Sabinson gave me the precise little school-teacherly nod of approval that dug his button chin into the jowl to which, at his weight, he was not really entitled.

"Exactly," he said. "In each borough the medical examiner has an office and a staff. Every morning the hospitals all over the city call the medical examiner's office and report the number of deaths that took place in their hospital during the past twenty-four hours. Then a member of the medical examiner's staff comes over to the hospital, checks out the dead bodies, gives them the official okay, and the doctors involved in each case are in the clear to issue the death certificate."

"Why aren't you in the clear?" I said.

Again Herman looked troubled. He unbuttoned his heavy overcoat. He tapped first the knot in his tie, then the small embroidered flower under the knot, and finally the gold tack shaped like the sign of Caduceus that held the tie to his shirt. I had the wild feeling that Herman was thinking of himself as a cornet and he was tapping his keys to come up with the right musical answer to my question.

"Because the medical examiner has not yet seen your mother's body," he said.

Curiouser and curiouser, I thought, and wondered if under the circumstances a mind into which lines from *Alice in Wonderland* came flooding was not in danger of going off its rails.

"As I said before," I said, "what's stopping him?"

"He doesn't know where it is," Herman said. "Your mother's body."

"Then the word I used is right," I said. "My mother's body has disappeared."

Herman Sabinson looked around the room through the sort of scowl that occasionally crosses the face of a politician's press representative as he steps up to a battery of TV microphones and cameras to make an unpleasant but inescapable announcement.

"We don't know that yet," he said.

"Herman, for God's sake," I said, "what *do* you know?"

"That's better," he said.

"What's better?" I said.

"Your tone of voice," Herman Sabinson said. "Shouting at me is understandable under the circumstances, but not helpful."

"When did I ever shout at you?"

"You've been shouting at me ever since I came in here," Herman said.

"It's just because all the windows are closed," I said. "The place is just a great big sound box. Every word booms."

"My words don't boom," Herman said. "And now that you've got yours down to a rational tone, I'll tell you exactly what we know. This morning the clerk at the Peretz Memorial Hospital called the medical examiner's office, as he does every morning, and reported the number of people who had died at Peretz during the past twenty-four hours. There were four, among them your mother. Ordinarily the medical examiner's office would have replied okay, Dr. Soandso will be over sometime before noon, or between one and three, or whatever. But not today. You know what the guy at the medical examiner's office said today?"

"Herman," I said, "if I did, would I be standing here in this lousy apartment up to my knees in thirty-two days of dust, listening to you drive me crazy?"

"This happens to be a very nice apartment," Herman Sabinson said. "The sons of very few of my patients have provided their aged mothers with comparable accommodations. As for the dust, that's not your mother's fault. As I need hardly remind you, she has not been here to keep it clean."

"Then where is she?" I said.

"We will come to that," Herman said. "The man at the medical examiner's office told the clerk at the Peretz Memorial that he was alone in the office. It was the day before Christmas. It was also Sunday. And because of the lousy weather, his two assistants had called in sick. He was all alone. He could not leave the office to come over to Peretz Memorial to examine the four dead bodies. So the clerk at the hospital said what should I do with the bodies? And the man in the medical examiner's office said all I can do is send over the ambulance to pick them up and bring them over here to the morgue. So the clerk at Peretz Memorial said okay." Herman Sabinson's scowl was now directed at me. "I'm sorry," he said. "But that's what happened."

"The ambulance came?" I said. "They picked up my mother's body and the three other bodies? And they took them to the morgue?"

"Yes," Herman said.

I thought about it for a couple of moments. "I see," I said, although I wasn't quite sure what I saw. "It must have happened, then, between the time you called me early this morning, and the time I arrived at the hospital?"

"That's right," Herman Sabinson said.

I did some more thinking. "Wait a minute," I said. "By the

time I arrived, Mrs. O'Toole knew about it, because she said it was no longer necessary to sign the paper you asked me to sign."

"What happened was this," Herman Sabinson said. "After I called her and said you were coming in to sign the paper giving me permission to do the autopsy, she did a routine check to make sure they would have an operating room waiting for me. When they asked what for, she told them, and what they did was check the room in which your mother had died, just to make sure they would be able to move the body to the operating room for me. That's how they learned the body had already been taken away to the morgue. So they called Mrs. O'Toole and told her. She was upset, naturally, and she tried to reach me on the phone, but I was out on calls. It was at this point that you arrived at the hospital. After you left, Mrs. O'Toole called the morgue. They said the ambulance had not yet come back with the four bodies, but she'd better tell the next of kin of the four dead people they'd have to come to the morgue the next day to identify the bodies. Now, I want you to understand this. She's a very conscientious person, Mrs. O'Toole."

"I've seen her," I said. "She looks conscientious as hell. But she left her job around noon today. With four dead bodies floating around in an ambulance somewhere in the Borough of Queens."

"Well, for Pete's sake," Herman Sabinson said. "It's the day before Christmas."

"It's the day before Christmas for everybody," I said. "Including the next of kin of those four dead people. I assume your conscientious Mrs. O'Toole, before she left the hospital, she called the Battenberg Funeral Home and told them to give me the message about going to the morgue?"

"Of course she did," Herman Sabinson said. "I told you she's very conscientious. I don't know who she called about the other three dead people, because they were not my patients, and I'm unfamiliar with the details. But she knew you were a Battenberg customer because their name was on the papers involving the demise of your father last spring."

"As I understand it, then," I said, "Mrs. O'Toole now disappears from the story?"

"Story?" Herman Sabinson said.

"What would you call it?" I said.

"You're shouting again," he said.

"I'll stop when you tell me where my mother's body is," I said.

Herman Sabinson blew out his breath in a tired sigh. It made the small embroidered flower on his tie buckle. The sign of Caduceus, however, stayed put. My confidence in the medical profession took a step upward.

"We don't know yet," he said.

The word "we" was a jolt. In my youth it was the word Charles Augustus Lindbergh always used when he referred to himself and *The Spirit of St. Louis.*

"Who is we?" I said.

"Well, all the people involved," Herman said. "You see, what happened was, the two men on the ambulance, after they made their pickup at Peretz Memorial, they had three more stops."

Their favorite discotheques, no doubt.

"Three more hospitals?" I said.

"Of course," Herman said firmly, and then all the firmness seemed to drain out of him. Herman Sabinson looked as though he was going to cry. I glanced swiftly at his tie tack. The sign of Caduceus had buckled. My confidence in the medical profession took a nose dive.

"What's the matter?" I said.

"The ambulance," Herman said. "The two guys running it. I mean the driver and his assistant. They never showed up at those three other hospitals."

If I had been capable of thought, I would have taken a stab at it. But I didn't seem to be capable of anything. I was numb. My incapacity seemed to help Herman. At any rate, he didn't cry.

"I want you not to worry," he said. He came close to me and put his hand on my arm. "It could be at worst maybe one of these traffic accidents. Or they got lost. That's probably the explanation. They got lost."

"Two guys from the medical examiner's office?" I said. "Who pick up dead bodies at these same hospitals every day of the year?"

Herman nodded grudgingly. It was as though we were playing a game and he felt he had to acknowledge the fact that I had scored. What you learned at ten in the Educational Alliance on East Broadway you did not forget at fifty on 78th Avenue in Queens. Fair is fair.

"I know it sounds crazy," Herman said. "But a lot of things that go on every day in this city seem crazy."

Few things are more irritating than the incontrovertible statement that is also irrelevant.

"Herman," I said.

"No, wait," he said. "What I'm trying to say is ambulances don't disappear into thin air. This ambulance is bound to show up. It could be located any minute. We've got the cops on it. What I mean is, after all, what's the harm? Those four poor souls, nothing more can happen to them. After all, they're dead, aren't they?"

"I don't know," I said. "I never saw them."

It was not a kind thing to say. But I was not feeling kind.

"You mean you don't trust me?"

Herman Sabinson's usually steam-heated voice was all at once as cold as a popsicle. His hand, I noticed, left my arm like a pigeon taking off.

"Stop talking like an idiot," I said. "Of course I trust you. I'm just confused. I don't know what to do next."

"That's why I asked you to meet me here," Herman said. "I gave the police this number. They promised to call as soon as they got word about the ambulance."

He looked at his watch. For no reason that makes sense, I found myself wishing desperately that the timepiece was not fastened to his wrist with one of those gold-plated expansion bands that has imbedded between its links a tiny calendar.

"It could be any minute now," Herman said. "The cops are really very reliable. People are always rapping them. They're never around when you need them. They never show up when you call them. Maybe so. But one or two rotten apples in a barrel doesn't mean the whole barrel is rotten. They have good people, the police. They have feelings. A man's mother dies, her body disappears, the cops of this city will find her. Believe me, they really will. While we're waiting for them to call, there's a couple of things I feel I must tell you." Again Herman sent his troubled look around the room. He reminded me of those characters in gangster movies who hesitate and check their immediate surroundings on the brink of a crucial revelation to make sure there are no eavesdroppers. Herman Sabinson said, "Maybe we should have a drink, huh?"

I looked at my watch. The glance was not upsetting. No gold links. No imbedded calendars. Just a black leather strap that was beginning to look seedy. As a gesture toward stupid, brainfatigued normalcy, which suddenly seemed to me the most desirable state a human being can attain, I made a crisp mental note to buy myself a new watch strap. After the funeral, of course.

"Isn't it a little early?" I said. "It's only about three-thirty."

"I've been on my dogs since a quarter to six this morning," Herman Sabinson said. "It wasn't light yet, for Christ's sake. That's almost ten hours, Benny boy. My ass is dragging. A shot of the old elixir is just what the doctor has just ordered for the doctor." Herman laughed. Well, tittered. No. What in God's name did he do? It comes back. He giggled. And added, "As well as for the patient."

So I giggled, too. After all, it was what the doctor had ordered. "Let's see if I can get a couple of clean glasses," I said. I moved toward the kitchen.

"I'll get the hooch," Herman Sabinson said.

The word plucked at my mind. I had not heard the word "hooch" spoken aloud since the days on East Fourth Street when I first discovered that my mother was running the stuff for Mr. Imberotti.

"It's on the floor in the bedroom closet," I said. "In that little blue canvas zipper bag marked *Sabena*."

"I know," Herman Sabinson said as he walked out into the foyer toward the bedroom. Following him into the foyer on my way to the kitchen, I thought about that. He knew? How did he know? The question suddenly gave me a picture of Herman Sabinson's relationship to my mother. He used to come in to see her every Tuesday and Friday. Anyway, that's what his bills indicated. Somewhere between eleven o'clock and noon on those two days every week he would check her blood pressure, listen to the beat of her heart, examine the tiny veins in her eyes, ask her to cough, urge her to lay off the Hershey bars, suggest low-caloric cola drinks instead of Dr. Brown's Celery

Tonic, and assure her that for a woman of her years she was doing fine.

It had not occurred to me until this moment that some time during or after these items on the bi-weekly ritual were checked off, my mother and Dr. Herman Sabinson had shared a shot of hooch. I mean booze. I could see them doing it. I could see the picture in my head. Somehow, the picture cheered me. There had been very little pleasure in my mother's life. It was refreshing to realize on this terrible day that for years I had unconsciously helped provide her with two tiny islands of pleasure every week. My mother had always liked Herman Sabinson. I had always paid not only for his visits but also for the booze. Sorry, hooch.

I went into the kitchen feeling confident I would find something on my dead mother's shelves I had never found there during the last years of her life: two clean glasses.

It is a fortunate thing for those who guard and burnish the image of Benjamin Franklin that my mother had never heard of him. She did not trust electricity. I had, over the years, succeeded in shoehorning into her apartment an electric toaster and an electric heating pad. But that was as far as she would go with what Franklin brought into Western civilization when he went out into the thunder and lightning storm and flew his kite. Even with these two items my mother's distrust was obvious.

She was never satisfied that her toaster had turned itself off when the toast popped up. She pulled the plug out of the wall. My mother felt that as long as the plug was sunk in the socket, electricity, which she understood only in terms of dollars-and-cents figures on her monthly bill from Con Edison, was flowing out like water from a dripping faucet. I have often thought she was right. You should see some of my Con Edison bills. But

311

my mother was not right toward the end. When her eyes began to fail.

When I discovered my mother couldn't see what she was doing, I tried to put a dishwasher into her kitchen. She reacted like Horatius holding back the enemy at the bridge. Electricity to wash a glass? If I wanted to be crazy uptown where I lived, fine. That was my business. But not for her. She didn't need any help from Con Edison with the simple business of keeping her house clean. As a result, while she thought her glasses were spotless, the things from which she actually drank looked like just-emptied milk bottles.

I found two of them in the cupboard over the kitchen sink. I rinsed them carefully, dried them with a paper towel, then gave them a final rubdown with my handkerchief. Unsanitary, no doubt. But cosmetically more attractive than the last dish-towel my mother had used before she was carried to Peretz Memorial. It looked like the flag of Tripoli. That is, if the dominant color of the Tripolitan flag is still charcoal-black. Coming out of the kitchen with the glasses, I met Herman Sabinson coming out of the bedroom with the bottle of Cutty Sark.

"No dust on this stuff," he said.

When he is not talking about the health of his patients, Herman's conversation tends to be not unlike lettuce on inexpensive sandwiches. Filler.

"It's because of the way she kept it locked away in that zipper bag," I said. "You want any ice?"

"Not unless you do," Herman said. "Your mother and I always drank it straight."

"Was it fun?" I said.

The question seemed to take him by surprise. The surprise led to pleasure. Herman Sabinson smiled. "It sure was," he

said. "I used to look forward to my two visits a week here."
Herman took one of the glasses. We walked into the living
room together. He poured a couple of inches of hooch—no,
booze—into my glass, then took care of his own. "She was a
funny woman," he said.

A scream, as I recalled.

"In what way?" I said.

"When I used to come in?" Herman said. "Every Tuesday
and Friday? She was always sort of like tense, you might say.
You know? On edge? Everything I did, her blood pressure,
examining her eyes, the heart, every step, she watched me like
I was a butcher and she was buying a chicken and she was
damn well going to make sure I didn't put my thumb on the
scale while she wasn't looking. Then, when I'd give her the old
okay, when I told her she was fine, she'd smile and she'd say
in Yiddish: Another week, another *schnapps*. She'd go out in
the bedroom and get the bottle. Say, by the way, why did she
keep it in that Sabena bag?"

Why did she keep her tube of toothpaste in the cardboard
carton that had housed it on the druggist's shelves?

"My wife and I went to Europe a few years ago," I said.
"The first Sunday we were back I brought my mother the usual
stuff. Aspirin. Toothpaste. A bottle of what you call hooch. I
think a girdle, too. My wife bought it for her. Anyway, I
couldn't find a shopping bag to carry the stuff in, so my wife
said take the airline bag. I did, and my mother fell in love with
it. Damned if I know why, but it pleased her to hide her bottle
of booze in it. Well, here's to something or other, Herman."

I raised my glass. He tapped his against mine. We sipped.

"You shouldn't be upset," Herman said.

Of course not. Just as I shouldn't be bald. Nevertheless, I
was. "What do you want me to do?" I said. "Give a party?"

313

Herman's button chin dug into the jowls. "Please don't worry," he said. "They'll locate that ambulance. Honest, they will. That's not the point."

Oh, God, I thought, here comes one of those damned letters to the Corinthians.

"What is the point?" I said.

"The last few years," Herman said, "I saw her more often than you did. I know you called her on the telephone every night at six o'clock, no matter where you were, but you saw her only Sunday mornings. I saw her every Tuesday and Friday. She was ready to go."

Astonished, I said, "You're saying she wanted to die?"

Herman Sabinson took a sip and tapped the embroidered flower under the knot of his tie. "Put it this way," he said. "And let's leave it at that. She was ready to go. Period."

He could leave it at that. I couldn't. "How the hell do you know such a thing?" I said.

Herman Sabinson shrugged. "You're a doctor, you learn certain things," he said

"Like what?" I said.

"People don't die like cookies cut out from a piece of dough," Herman Sabinson said. "I mean people die different. Differently? Okay. People die differently. Everyone in his own way. If you're a doctor for old people, the way I am, you see the worst ways. It's not like accidents. Or heart attacks. Or strokes. Or even suicide. Sudden stuff. No. You have a practice like mine, mostly old people, you don't get a lot of sudden stuff. You get slow wearing out. Machines running down. Remember when we were kids? We used to follow the fights?"

"The fights?" I said.

Irritably, Herman Sabinson said, "Don't you remember the Dempsey–Carpentier fight?"

I certainly did. I'd heard it from a crystal set on Columbia Street. On the sidewalk in front of Rabbi Goldfarb's *cheder*. Chink Alberg brought the set with him from school. We met in front of the garbage cans. Instead of picking rocks out of the ashes for beaning the rats upstairs, Chink broke up the headphones and gave one half to me. We took the risk of getting our ankles broken for being late by Rabbi Goldfarb's chair rung in order to find out how Carpentier was doing against Dempsey. He did not do well.

"What the hell has my mother's death got to do with the Dempsey–Carpentier fight?" I said.

"Fighters get zonked," Herman Sabinson said. "A belt to the *kishkes*. A rabbit punch to the *playtziss*. Or the poor slob has a glass jaw and the other guy clips him. Whatever it is, he gets it fast, and he's finished. He doesn't have time to sound off with one of those fancy last lines."

I gave myself a couple of moments. All devoted to staring into my drink. Before I dared say what my startled mind was urging me to scream. "Had Sir Arthur Conan Doyle made contact from the Great Beyond as he had promised, but with the wrong family?"

"You mean last lines like Nathan Hale?" I said. " 'My only regret is that I have but one life to give to my country?' "

Herman nodded. "Sort of," he said. "Except not exactly. Nathan Hale was, I understand, a Yale man. Those Ivy League guys are not exactly typical. Most people, they're about to buy it, they just scream no, no, no, don't let me die. That's how most old people do. They don't think of anything except they're about to go, and they don't want to go. Younger people, they see the exit curtain going up, they try to think of something to say. Gallant like. You know? What the hell, sort of. Especially if they went to college."

315

"Like that guy to whom Nelson said 'Kiss me, Hardy'?" I said. "At Trafalgar?"

"Now, that's very interesting," Herman Sabinson said. " 'Kiss me, Hardy' is not true." He must have seen the puzzled look on my face. Herman laughed and said, "What Lord Nelson, when he was dying, what he is supposed to have said while Hardy held him in his arms, this 'Kiss me, Hardy,' you know, of course, it's been an embarrassment to the British Navy for years."

This conversation suddenly seemed singularly inappropriate to a couple of middle-aged men waiting for a call from the police about the disappearance of the corpse of one of their mothers.

"No," I said, "I didn't know that. Why should the British Navy be embarrassed because Nelson said 'Kiss me, Hardy'?"

"Well, I think if you think about it a minute you'll see it right away," Herman Sabinson said. "One man saying to another guy 'Kiss me.' It's sort of faggot stuff."

"Oh," I said.

I had never thought of Horatio Nelson as a faggot. I had thought of him as the insatiable lover of Lady Hamilton.

"So the British Navy did a little research," Herman Sabinson said. "And guess what they came up with?"

Jellicoe at Jutland.

"What?" I said.

"It wasn't 'Kiss me, Hardy,' " Herman said. "What Nelson said was 'Kismet, Hardy.' You get it?"

The word brought into my disordered head the vision of Alfred Drake in a turban singing his heart out to Dorothy Sarnoff in a veil.

"Not quite," I said.

This seemed to please Herman. He was ahead of me.

"The word 'kismet' means fate," Herman said. "Nelson was upset because Hardy was upset because Nelson was dying. So Nelson said, or wanted to say, he wanted to cheer Hardy up. He said don't knock yourself out, Hardy. Don't take it so big. We all have to die, Hardy, is what Nelson was saying. It's inevitable. It's fate. 'Kismet, Hardy.' Relax. It's just fate, Hardy. Kismet. It happens to everybody. Like today, to your mother."

I tried to equate Nelson's flagship at Trafalgar with the Peretz Memorial Hospital in Queens. No luck.

"Well," I said, "I'm certainly glad to learn that Nelson was not a faggot."

"It clears Hardy, too," Herman Sabinson said. "Boy, let me tell you, was that a relief to the British Navy."

Wondering why the phone didn't ring, I heard myself saying, "It's like Goethe."

"Who?" Herman said.

"That German writer," I said. "*Faust* and all that other stuff. You know."

"Oh, *Goy-teh,*" Herman said.

"That's what I said," I said.

"How is 'Kismet, Hardy' like Goethe?" Herman said.

Guiltily, I felt a stab of pleasure. Now I was ahead of Herman. "When he was on his deathbed, his last words," I said. "He was supposed to have said 'More light!' and then died. Everybody assumed he meant what he wanted, what Goethe had missed in life was not enough truth."

"About what?" Herman Sabinson said.

"Everything," I said. "Learning. Human beings. What the world is all about. Why we are born. Why we suffer. That sort of thing. So everybody assumed what Goethe meant by his last words, he wanted more, you could say, illumination on the great questions that have puzzled man from the beginning of time. More illumination on life."

"You mean Goethe didn't want more illumination on life?" Herman said.

"Maybe he did," I said. "But that isn't what he meant by his last words. What Goethe actually meant, the room was dark, or it seemed to him to be getting darker as he got closer to death. So he said to the maid, she was standing by his bed, he said 'More light!' All he meant, Goethe wanted her to draw the curtain aside a little further."

Herman Sabinson took a sip from his glass, replenished it from the bottle he still held in his hand, then started to laugh. "That's not bad," he said. "But you know the one I like?"

"Which?" I said.

"Lord Chesterfield," Herman Sabinson said. "You know. The guy who wrote all those letters to his son? Always blow your nose before it starts to drip? Never pick up a lamb chop in both hands? If a guy puts the bite on you for twenty bucks give him ten, on account of that's all he really expected to get in the first place? That sort of stuff?"

"What about him?" I said. "Lord Chesterfield?"

"He was lying there on his deathbed," Herman Sabinson said. "After all, you can't keep writing letters to your son forever. You either run out of ink or you run out of steam. Anyway, the old lord was lying there, getting ready to go, when the butler came in and said some guy was downstairs. I forget his name. Say Jones or something. Anyway, Jones was one of Lord Chesterfield's worst political enemies. So when the butler said Jones was downstairs, Lord Chesterfield said, 'Show him up. If I'm still alive when he enters, I shall be glad to see him. If I am dead, he will be glad to see me.' " Herman took another sip from his glass. "Pretty good, no?"

"Yes," I said, and then I had a delayed reaction. "You mean, Herman, my mother said something before she died?"

Herman nodded worriedly. "Yes," he said.

"Something she asked you to tell me?" I said.

The worried look sank more deeply into Herman's face. "I don't know," he said. "She didn't say I should tell you, but otherwise, why would she tell it to me?"

"Tell me what she said," I said. "We can figure out later who she meant it for."

"Well, there's something came first," Herman Sabinson said. "You know she developed this bedsore? Three days ago?"

"I think the nurses could have prevented that," I said.

"Probably," Herman said. "Then, probably not. I gave them instructions to turn her regularly, and I'm sure they did. But you get a person over eighty years old, they're immobilized for over a month, thirty-two days, there's some things you just can't avoid. Anyway, they'd been keeping her on her stomach to let the bedsore dry, and when I came to see her this morning, that's how she was. On her stomach. I sat down by the bed, and she recognized me, but I didn't do much. I could tell she was pretty low. I was wondering if I should call in a couple of nurses to turn her, when she opened her hand. Like this." Herman Sabinson set down the bottle of Cutty Sark, clenched his hand into a fist, then slowly spread the fingers wide. "When she did that, something fell out of her hand and bounced off the bed to the floor." Herman Sabinson pulled something from his pocket. "I picked it up," he said, "and my first thought was to give it back to her, but then I saw nobody was ever going to give anything back to her. She was, well, she was gone."

Herman put his hand out toward me. From his palm I took a small rectangular piece of cardboard. It was about three inches long and two inches wide. Then, as I felt the weight of the thing, I realized it was two or more pieces of cardboard pasted together. On the top piece was painted in long-faded colors the picture of a man and a woman in the sort of bathing suits we used to wear when I was a kid. They were sitting on the back of a grinning whale that was lashing its way happily through a piece of turbulent sea full of mountainous whitecaps. The bodies of the man and woman riding the whale had no heads. Where the heads should have been, two ovals had been cut into the cardboard. Into the ovals had been inserted snapshots of the heads of real people. The one on the left was a snapshot of my mother as she had looked on the night of the Shumansky wedding. The snapshot on the right was a picture of Walter Sinclair wearing his black turtleneck sweater. Both were smiling into the camera. Over their heads, in scroll letters that were outlined in pasted-on scraps of silver foil, were the words: "Coney Island, 1927." The edges of the pasted-together cardboard rectangles were badly worn. Two of the corners had apparently once separated. They had been carefully fastened together with Scotch tape.

"What I can't understand," Herman Sabinson said, "I don't understand how she could have held onto this thing. I mean, you know, when they check you into a hospital they take all your possessions. They lock them away downstairs in the safe, and you go up to your room balls-naked. How in the name of bejesus did she hold onto this thing for thirty-two days?"

"I don't know," I said.

It did not, however, seem to me much of an achievement. She had held onto a puzzling and unsatisfying life for nine-tenths of a century. By comparison, holding onto a dime Coney Island penny-arcade snapshot seemed a cinch.

"Does it mean anything?" Herman Sabinson said.

It meant two things. After all these years I finally knew

where the *Jefferson Davis II* had been holed up for at least part of the time after the Shumansky wedding. And why once several years ago my mother had asked me to add to the aspirin and mineral oil and other contents of my Sunday morning shopping bag a roll of Scotch tape.

"Probably not," I said.

"The girl, she looks like your mother," Herman Sabinson said. "When she was young, I mean."

"Could be," I said. "Like everybody else, she was obviously young once."

"What about the man?" Herman said.

I shrugged. "Just some guy riding a whale," I said. "Did she say anything? My mother?"

"Say anything?" Herman said.

"Like 'Kismet, Hardy'?" I said. "Or Lord Chesterfield?"

"Well, no, not exactly like that," he said. "I mean, what she said made no sense to me. But maybe it will mean something to you."

"Try me," I said.

"Your mother," Herman said. "Just before she died. Her last words. Your mother said: *I could have had a life if only the Melitzer Rabbi had stayed home.*"

14

S HE MAY HAVE BEEN RIGHT. But the ifs of history are like the anagrams in the morning paper. Even when you've worked one out, where are you? Waiting for tomorrow's paper.

The truth about the Melitzer Rabbi was that he probably would have preferred to stay home. Unfortunately, he had no more control over his destiny than my mother had over hers.

It was a time when the Jews of the Lower East Side were beginning cautiously to come up out of the storm cellars and take a look around. Everybody on East Fourth Street, for example, including my mother and father, had arrived from Europe in that universal vehicle of the persecuted: a crouch. Fleeing from Cossacks. Cringing from the knout. Looking backward with apprehension, forward with hope. Cowering in this new land behind locked doors to avoid *moof tzettles*.

Then came the war, and Woodrow Wilson's Fourteen Points, and some people started to earn a little more of the New World's coin of the realm than the amounts needed to pay for food and shelter. Not all, but some. And an odd thing started to happen. Like the passion for gambling in tulip bulbs that a century earlier had swept Holland, a passion for importing religious leaders swept the streets between Delancey and 14th, the avenues from Second down to the East River.

I have always had a feeling that the drive was not purely spiritual. The Rotarian overtones were obvious. If the people on East Fifth Street, most of whom were Austrian, chipped in to bring over a rabbi from some town near Salzburg, the people on East Sixth Street, who were predominantly Polish, would get together at once and raise the money to bring over a "bigger" rabbi from somewhere near Warsaw. The word bigger did not refer to the rabbi's height, weight, or girth. It referred to how close his European congregation had been located physically to a large city.

Perhaps this was why my parents did not seem to get caught up in the general passion. Even after all these years, and the investment of a modest sum in the publications of Rand Mc-Nally, I have never been able to find on any map the town of Berezna in Hungary where my mother was born. As for my father, his devotion to the Erste Neustadter Krank und Unterstitzing Verein seemed to exhaust whatever chauvinistic instincts he may have possessed. Rand McNally is no more illuminating about the province of Neustadt in Austria than it is about the town of Berezna in Hungary.

I cannot believe there were no rabbis in Berezna and Neustadt. It would be like believing that there were no midwives or *mohels*. Children must be assisted from the womb to the family bosom. Male offspring must be circumcised. The citizen's soul must have an intermediary with God. But I suspect that neither Berezna in Hungary nor Neustadt in Austria was located close enough to a large city to arouse the Rotarian instincts of the men and women who, like my mother and father, had fled a mapless dot to settle in the *goldene medina*.

A common enough trait. If you were born in Paramus, New Jersey, and under pressure from enemies, emigrated to Australia, would you devote much time, energy, or money to bringing over to Brisbane the math teacher who coached the basketball team at the Thomas Alva Edison High School in East Orange? I have noticed that the only people who boast they were born in Ride-It-Easy, Arkansas, are politicians, gossip columnists, actors, fashion designers, and orthodontists who have made it in the big time on our Eastern Seaboard. In 1927, on East Fourth Street, my parents had not.

Others had, however. Mr. Shumansky, for example. George Weitz's father, the doctor. Even Abe Lebenbaum. Or maybe it pleased them to think they had. I cannot remember which one started the ball rolling, or even if it was one of these three. I do know they were all deeply involved in the project known as "bringing over the Melitzer rabbi."

I use the word project in an attempt at precision. I am moved to make the attempt because I have been out of touch for some years with the process of bringing over to America rabbis from Central Europe. Times change. A man grows stale. I recall distinctly, however, that in 1927 the process was quite different from bringing over a beekeeper or a wheelwright. In those days you didn't move a rabbi the way you moved a member of his congregation. In those days you moved a rabbi the way the army today moves a division. Support troops must be transported along with the men who will do the actual fighting, or the actual wrestling with God. At the receiving end, in this case East Fourth Street, arrangements had to be made for accommodating not only the rabbi but his entourage. The arrangements included welcoming ceremonies appropriate to the stature of the spiritual leader. Melitz is a town not far from Berlin. The people on East Fourth Street who were in charge of bringing over the Melitzer rabbi decided that the appropriate welcoming ceremony should be a block party.

I had been aware in a vague way for some time that our block was about to receive a distinguished visitor from Europe called the Melitzer Rabbi. In an equally vague way I was conscious of the fact that a block party was being planned. My vagueness was not due to stupidity. Or lack of interest. It was simply that I was imbedded up to my epiglottis in a time of life when anticipation played second fiddle to reality.

The promise of an Eskimo Pie next Saturday was not unpleasant to contemplate. If you were the contemplative type, which I was not. But it was today's gum ball that made my heart go fast. Upcoming block parties for rabbis from places called Melitz were exciting to hear about. But it was the eliminations for the Boy Scouts of America All-Manhattan Rally that squeezed the juices of life so totally out of the present moment that you could die. I almost did. The night I tried to collect my salary from Abe Lebenbaum so I could give my Aunt Sarah the twenty-three dollars with which to pay our rent to Mr. Velvelschmidt the bloodsucker.

Nothing pulls the rug out from under the human spirit so successfully as defeat. If on that terrible night in 1927 I had collected my five dollars from Abe Lebenbaum, would I have gone crawling back to our tenement at 390 East Fourth Street, hugging the building lines to avoid being recognized by classmates and neighbors? Before I say no, which I will, note that I stop at classmates and neighbors and do not add friends. Since the night of the Shumansky wedding, when my mother had disappeared, the word friend had vanished from my consciousness. When the world turns against you, you don't look for help. You look for applecarts to tip, hides to claw, things to destroy, opportunities to strike back.

Abe Lebenbaum with five dollars a week had earned my devotion. When he refused to pay it, he earned my hatred. He had plucked from my grasp, willfully and—I think I was bright enough to figure out—illegally, the wherewithal to set my life back on an even keel. I did not understand what my mother was up to. I understood my feelings about Walter Sinclair even though I could not quite connect them with my mother. My feelings about my father stood in the way. But I understood clearly about my Aunt Sarah.

I had left our house with the certainty that I would bring back the money she needed to get Mr. Velvelschmidt and his dreaded *moof tzettle* off our backs. I came slinking home with the knowledge that I had failed. I had only Mr. Heizerick's two ten-spots. It was not enough. Is it any wonder that I stopped in the downstairs hall?

I stood there, examining my surroundings. Not because I admired or disliked them, but because I could not bring myself to push through the hall door and climb the stairs. As a result, I saw for the first time that the white marble floor and walls of the downstairs hall must have cost a lot of money. Certainly more than the brown stamped tin that lined the halls of the rest of the building. Even the panel of mailboxes set into the west wall of white marble seemed to me all at once a thing of beauty. I had never before given it a thought. Now it occurred to me that the broad sheet of brass, cut up into numbered boxes, must have cost more than the twenty-three dollars we owed Mr. Velvelschmidt.

I think what drew me across the hall to examine the mailboxes was a not quite clearly thought out thought. Brass was valuable. It was the sort of stuff Old Man Tzoddick brought back every day in his pushcart from uptown. Shiny metals were what I had seen him lugging from the pushcart down the stone steps to his cellar. Maybe I could tear this sheet of brass from the white marble wall and sell it to Old Man Tzoddick? Maybe I was going crazy?

This did not seem a dismaying or even remote possibility. I recall pretty clearly that when I was fourteen going crazy fell into pretty much the same category as going to Coney Island. All you needed was the fare. Just the same, how did one go about tearing a plate of brass mailboxes out of a white marble wall? The question must have been more than rhetorical.

If it wasn't, why was I suddenly running my hands over the metal? Clawing at the edges with my fingernails? Stopping short when I realized there was a flash of white paper showing through the grille of the box marked *Kramer*.

My first instinct, as always, was to turn and run. What stopped me was the realization that a scout who was trustworthy, loyal, helpful, all the way down to and including reverent, could not also be a fool. Whatever it was that showed through the grille of our box, it could not be the *moof tzettle*.

After all, the bloodsucker had made his threat only an hour ago. Perhaps less than an hour ago. In 1927 the mails were admittedly in sounder shape than they are today, and *moof tzettles* seemed to move faster through the postal system than any other form of communication, but even so, it seemed reasonable to a senior patrol leader, who had just assured himself he was not a fool, to assume he was staring at something else.

I picked the brass door open with my fingernail. No tenant in our building owned a key to his mailbox. Landlords like Mr. Velvelschmidt provided nothing for their victims that would have to be retrieved when they were thrown out for nonpayment of rent. From the mailbox I pulled an envelope. On the front, in penciled block letters, was a single word: BENNY.

I thumbed open the sealed flap and found a piece of paper folded several times around what felt like a wad of toilet paper. Spongy. I unrolled the paper. The wad consisted of two pretty ancient ten-dollar bills, a five, and five singles. On the paper, in the same penciled block letters, appeared the following message:

> YOUR MAMA SAYS GIVE TWENTY-THREE DOLLARS TO YOUR FATHER TO PAY THE RENT THE OTHER SEVEN DOLLARS FOR MR. NOOGLE TO LET USE EMPTY BATHTUB APARTMENT TWO NIGHTS UNTIL BLOCK. PARTY YOUR MAMA FINE DON'T WORRY DON'T FORGET MAKE DEAL WITH MR. NOOGLE.

15

IN YIDDISH the word *noogle* means nail. In our tenement the word *noogle* meant "the bloodsucker's apprentice." Mr. Noogle was Mr. Velvelschmidt's janitor.

He was also our landlord's brother-in-law. Which probably accounted for the dichotomy in Mr. Noogle's character that confused the tenants of 390 East Fourth. As a brother-in-law, dependent for his family's bread and butter on a bastard like Mr. Velvelschmidt, it was understandable that Mr. Noogle should be nervously relentless in carrying out the bloodsucker's orders about riding herd on the tenants. What was not so understandable was Mr. Noogle's foolhardy eagerness to risk making a crooked nickel behind Mr. Velvelschmidt's back. A cringing coward on the one hand; on the other, a courageous crook. You never knew which one to expect.

Mr. Noogle was tall, thin, chinless, and ageless. He walked as though he counted on his swinging arms to keep him from toppling forward on his face. Not unlike a skinny ape. His sad eyes hung out over sagging pockets of dark, bruised flesh in which any reasonable-sized kangaroo could have accommodated a set of triplets. He looked foolishly harmless and yet gave you the impression he was capable of malevolence. As though a basset hound, while staring up at you with a look of mournful devotion, was actually calculating how much he could get in a pawnshop for the gold fillings in your teeth.

When a tenant behind in his rent reached the end of a string of assurances, promises, lies, and pleas that led to the inevitable *moof tzettle* and the burly representative of the sheriff's office arrived—in years of intimacy with the species, I have never encountered an emaciated eviction officer—to dump the family's lares and penates on the sidewalk, it was Mr. Noogle who held the hand of the weeping wife, consoled the frightened children, and assured the mortified husband that he must not despair, because when you were flat on your back, things were bound to look up. On the other hand, it was Mr. Noogle, in a voice that would have been the envy of Gyp the Blood, who told you from the corner of his mouth that if you knew which end was up, you would keep your trap shut about the dime you paid him for the privilege of taking a bath in Top Floor Back.

Taking a bath on East Fourth Street was not an easy thing to do. The architects of the tenements had never taken scrubbing into consideration. Why should they? Their job was to provide as many scraps of space as possible in which human life could be maintained at a minimal level. Then the Top Floor Back on East Fourth Street was cleared out by a *moof tzettle*. And as a result Mr. Velvelschmidt was unexpectedly brushed by the bracing winds of progress. He tore out the gray cement washtub that occupied one quarter of the floor space in every kitchen on East Fourth Street and installed a *vonneh*.

This was the Yiddish word for the white enamel bathtub with a long slope at one end and four metal claw feet that finally invaded most of the Lower East Side. In 1927, however, at least on East Fourth Street, the *vonneh* to Mr. Velvelschmidt's tenants was a spectacular innovation. Nobody living in 390 East Fourth Street had ever seen one.

This was obviously the reason why Mr. Velvelschmidt felt his experiment would pay off. With a gleaming white *vonneh* occupying almost half the kitchen, he clearly felt it was a cinch to collect more rent for Top Floor Back than he had been collecting before. I still don't understand what was wrong with his thinking. If I had owned 390 East Fourth, and if I had been a bloodsucker, I believe I, too, would have felt that by installing a *vonneh* in Top Floor Back, I would have had the inhabitants of East Fourth Street beating a path to my door. They didn't.

Maybe what was wrong was the price. The rent on Top Floor Back in its washtub days had been nineteen dollars a month. With the *vonneh,* Mr. Velvelschmidt set the price at twenty-five. To his surprise, there were no takers. Six dollars a month on East Fourth Street in 1927 was more than the traffic in non-smelling would bear. An occasional dime, it was discovered, however, was not. Mr. Noogle made the discovery.

While the flat stood empty he got busy. Sloping along in his basset-hound style, he would approach tenants who were carrying down garbage or lugging up coal and offer to let them use the bathtub in Top Floor Back for a fee. In the beginning there was no time limit. You paid Mr. Noogle a dime and he gave you the key to Top Floor Back. You carried up your towel and soap and took a bath. When you were dressed you came down to his Ground Floor Back apartment and returned the key. Inevitably, the dime-payers soon discovered that two could bathe for the price of one. Before long, entire families were soaping themselves for a single fee. This improved the smell of the 390 East Fourth hallways, but it held down the amount of Mr. Noogle's extra income. He laid down a rule. For a single fee only one person could use the back bathtub, and the bather could remain in the apartment for no longer than a half hour. Mr. Noogle enforced this rule in person. He owned a dollar Ingersoll watch. From the moment a tenant carrying soap and towel handed over his or her dime, Mr. Noogle remained outside the door of Top Floor Back, watch in hand.

I did not know how many customers every day handed over their dimes to Mr. Noogle. I did know, however, from the note Walter Sinclair had left in our mailbox, that I had seven dollars with which to perform the task he had assigned to me. Thus I became involved for the first time in a lifelong and usually losing struggle with the complexities of mathematics.

The computation should have been fairly simple. The seven dollars were intended to carry me through to the night of the block party that had been planned to celebrate the arrival of— in Yiddish it emerged as "the coming of"—the Melitzer Rabbi. That meant I had to tie up the *vonneh* in Top Floor Back for at least forty-eight hours. Say fifty. Even Walter Sinclair, in whom my faith now unhesitatingly rested, was entitled to a margin for error. Indeed, my infatuation was such that I felt he was entitled to more than a margin. I decided to give Walter Sinclair the broad ribbon of an extra day. Seventy-two hours.

To do this properly, I started with the word "assuming." Thus: assuming that Mr. Noogle's customers purchased their half hours in the *vonneh* around the clock, at a dime for each half hour, his maximum take for the seventy-two-hour period could be no more than one hundred and forty-four half hours multiplied by a dime, or fourteen dollars and forty cents.

Trouble. I had only seven dollars. Back, therefore, to the word "assuming." It was clearly inappropriate. Who, after all, came knocking at Mr. Noogle's door at one or two or three o'clock in the morning to buy a crack at the *vonneh?* It seemed reasonable to conclude: nobody. How many hours, then, would it be reasonable to assume the *vonneh* was sought after? And by how many inhabitants of 390? My mind was not accustomed to the beat of the drummer who ultimately sent people like Einstein to the mathematical heights. I settled for a quick estimate. Half.

Thus the seven dollars entrusted to me seemed not inadequate. I shoved the pencil-lettered note into one pocket of my pants, the thirty dollars into my other pocket, and climbed the stairs. My Aunt Sarah was sitting at the kitchen table, as usual reading the *Daily Forward.* Studying it, anyway. From the bedroom beyond the kitchen came my father's rasping snores.

Looking back on it now, it strikes me as an eerie scene. The tenement kitchen. Lighted by a faint dot of flickering blue and gold and white flame at the end of the curved gas jet hanging from the ceiling. Sending shadows like delicate waves across the green corridor walls covered with my scribblings. The big square black iron stove banked for the night, smoking slightly. The beautiful fat woman in a coarse flour-sack apron bent over the newspaper. And the knowledge that she was there because my mother had disappeared. My heart jumped with excitement. My gut quivered with fear. My Aunt Sarah spoke.

"It says here a man named Greenspan died today in Washington," she said. "He owned a department store."

"A lot of people are dead," I said.

"Like Aaron Greenspan," my Aunt Sarah said.

"I didn't mean him," I said.

"He's the one the government they mean," my Aunt Sarah said. "In the paper, you read the paper, the government when they go after someone, they always catch people."

Not people like Walter Sinclair.

"They won't catch Mama," I said.

"You know where she is?"

"No," I said, "but I know she didn't kill Aaron Greenspan."

"Who killed him?" my Aunt Sarah said.

"Mr. Imberotti's son," I said.

I said it the way, if I had been asked the name of my scout-master, I would have said Mr. O'Hare. At that time, as I recall, life presented many difficulties, but no uncertainties. Facts did not have to be tested. All they had to be was accepted. There were no shaded areas between guesswork and evidence. Logic worked. I had heard Mr. Imberotti threaten my mother: Do not try to supply the Shumansky wedding. My mother had disregarded the threat. She had supplied the Shumansky wedding. Mr. Imberotti had carried out his threat. Not in person, of course. Nobody inhaling steam out of a teakettle on the Saturday night my mother and I had visited Mr. Imberotti could have been well enough on the night of the Shumansky wedding to carry a gun across from Lafayette Street to the Lenox Assembly Rooms. But Mr. Imberotti's son had been there. If the government was as good at catching people as the *Daily Forward* said it was, when Mr. Kelly caught the killer of Aaron Greenspan, he would not be catching my mother. Q.E.D.

"How do you know this?" my Aunt Sarah said.

"I know it," I said.

She gave me a long look. By long I don't mean she took a long time doing it. I mean my Aunt Sarah wrapped it around me, like a rope, tying me to the simple statement until she was satisfied I could not escape from it.

"All right," my Aunt Sarah said. "What should we do now?"

It was the moment when I crossed the line from boyhood

into maturity. In the complicated machinery that ran the world, I had suddenly been moved up to the control panel.

"Here is for Mr. Velvelschmidt," I said. I pulled the roll of bills from my pocket and counted out onto the blue-and-white checks of the oilcloth on the kitchen table two tens and three singles. "For the rent," I said. I then put down the two ten-spots I had received from Mr. Heizerick. My heart thumped as I said, "And this is for you."

My Aunt Sarah nodded. "And?" she said. She said no more. I knew she understood how I felt.

I counted out the five and the last two singles. They covered a large part of the kitchen table. In those days paper money was about the size of the pages torn from copies of *Boys' Life*.

"This is for Mr. Noogle," I said.

16

I THINK NOW that perhaps all our lives would have been different if those seven dollars had not been made available to *shmeer* Mr. Noogle. On the other hand, different does not mean better.

"It's like a horse, they put on those things to cover his eyes, and they give him a *shtipp,* and he starts moving the way the owner wants him to move," my Aunt Sarah said to me years later, on the day of my father's funeral. "The horse has nothing to do with it, and neither have we. We go the way we're fixed to go from the beginning. We can't stop it."

I've never wanted to believe that. I think as I look back on my life that there are places where I didn't have to go. I went because the way was open. Or easy. Or because it looked attractive. Or because someone I was stuck on wanted to go that way. The reasons are always reasonable. But not necessarily compelling. In every instance I know, now, that I could have gone up another street. But I cannot say that I would have ended up in a better place.

I can, however, say now what for years I refused to say even to myself: my mother went the way she went because she was trapped. I learned that the night of the block party for the Melitzer Rabbi.

One of the peculiar things about this block party is that nobody was sure just what time it would take place.

The project had started somewhere in the confused machinery that ran the synagogue near the Avenue D corner. The main reason for the confusion was that the synagogue had been built sometime between the end of the Grant administration and the beginning of the new century by immigrants from Melitz. They had made a mistake. Melitz was a town about sixty miles northeast of Berlin. The immigrants who built the synagogue on East Fourth Street apparently had good reason to believe that they were building their house of worship on what was going to continue to be a German block. They were wrong.

I don't know how the shift came about, but when my father arrived from Austria and somewhat later my mother arrived from Hungary, the Germans in the area had moved on and nested solidly on Tenth Street. Synagogues cannot be moved like other personal possessions. They can be sold, however, like other forms of real estate, and I understand that the German Jews of Tenth Street tried to sell their synagogue to the Austrian and Hungarian Jews on Fourth Street. No luck.

Fourth Street, my piece of it, anyway, was not a very prosperous block. I don't know what synagogues were going for in those days, but whatever the price the residents of East Fourth Street either could not get it up or were not interested in buying anything from Germans. I suspect the latter was the more compelling reason. I never heard a good word said on East Fourth Street about a German.

Not even on Saturdays when they came down from Tenth

Street in surprisingly large numbers to worship in the synagogue they had left behind them years ago. I never thought it odd, not in those years, anyway, that on the Sabbath, when the Germans came pouring into Fourth Street carrying the gold-embroidered green and blue and red velvet bags containing their *siddurs* and prayer cloths, the citizens of East Fourth Street poured out in other directions, toward synagogues that were housed in rented lofts in rat-infested structures like the one in which during the rest of the week Rabbi Goldfarb conducted his *cheder* on Columbia Street.

The parallel is not quite parallel, but the situation does remind me now of Berlin after the end of World War Two. The city sits in the Russian zone. By treaty we have access to it. But the access makes for uneasiness. Sometimes for ugliness. The period of the Berlin airlift was no fun. Here again the parallel is not quite parallel, but it is difficult to overlook. When the Germans of Tenth Street decided to bring over the Melitzer Rabbi and install him in their synagogue on Fourth Street, they were embarking on a complicated and dislocating venture in if not quite hostile then certainly unfriendly terrain. Who, on East Fourth Street, gave a damn about the coming of the Melitzer Rabbi?

The answer, surprisingly enough, was not only my mother. She had what might be described as the catering concession. But it takes—anyway, in 1927 it took—more than booze to make a block party. It took an exercise in tactical synchronization.

The block party was scheduled for a Saturday night. On Thursday morning carpenters and electricians began to arrive on East Fourth Street. German carpenters and electricians. The distinction is important for a curious reason: there should have been no distinction. There were no carpenters or electricians on Fourth Street. I mean the way there were grocers and butchers and tailors and blacksmiths—one blacksmith, anyway—and chicken merchants. Repairs that required carpentry skills were always made, rarely with skill, by the tenement janitors. At 390, for instance, by Mr. Noogle. As for repairs involving electricity, all the tenement homes on the block were lighted by gas. The only electricity on East Fourth Street came from the two lampposts on the Avenue D corner. The lampposts on the Lewis Street corner were still lighted by carbon arcs.

When the Avenue D lamps needed attention, the city took care of it. I cannot remember just how. Perhaps some minor official arrived when I was in school or at *cheder* and installed a new electric bulb. In those days they all had a sharp point at the bottom. We were told in J.H.S. 64 science class that this was caused by the men in the factory who wore asbestos gloves with which they sealed the bulb by twirling the hot molten glass between thumb and forefinger. Maybe they did. I have learned to doubt many of the things that were fed me as hard fact in J.H.S. 64 science class. Anyway, the electric lights at the Avenue D corner of Fourth Street were a minor puzzle to me. The carbon arcs at the Lewis Street corner presented no such difficulty to the mind of a senior patrol leader.

Every day, just before dusk, a man came walking down the block wearing a sort of almost black, certainly very dark gray, knapsack humped up between his shoulder blades and a shiny leather cap or helmet on his head. He carried a long stick with an odd trigger handle. It was not unlike the implements that became commonplace years later for reaching up, grasping, and bringing down boxes of corn flakes from the top shelves of supermarkets. The man would reach up with this stick, slide the head in under the glass dome on top of the lamppost, and do something to the triggerlike handle at the bottom. A tiny spurt of flame would dart up to the carbon arcs. The facing points would ignite. A lovely warm glow would pour down on the corner of Lewis Street and Fourth. The man would do the same to the other lamppost, and move on.

It was a small daily ceremony to which I had not realized I had learned to look forward until the Germans of Tenth Street sent in all those electricians and carpenters to set up the block party for the arrival of the Melitzer Rabbi.

At the end of two days of efficient hammering they had closed off our block with barricades at the Avenue D and Lewis Street corners. Across the block, from poles set on the facing sidewalks, strings of small red, white, blue, and green electric lights were stretched on black wires that soared like halved barrel staves up, over, and down to the other side of the street. The effect was to make the familiar block an unfamiliar sight. A long sausagelike cavern, like a loosely woven basket designed to hold loaves of French bread, that had been lowered over our heads.

I watched it take shape with astonishment. In the evening, when somebody threw the control switch inside the synagogue and all the colored lights came on with a noiseless explosion, my breath caught in a small gasp of pleasure. But I also had a feeling of uneasiness. Through the green and yellow and red lights I could see the man with the knapsack and the long pole poking his tiny jet of flame at the carbon arcs on the Lewis Street corner. He no longer seemed to be doing anything important. The Germans, intent on giving the Melitzer Rabbi an appropriate welcome, had taken the mystery out of the Fourth Street night.

The night they chose was a mistake.

340

Anybody on Fourth Street could have told them so. The Jews of Tenth Street, however, rarely listened to anybody but themselves.

Word had come through to them, presumably from the Immigration Department, that the Melitzer Rabbi, who was being processed at Ellis Island after leaving the ship that had brought him from Europe, would be free to leave on Saturday morning. The Jews of Tenth Street decided to meet him at the dock with an appropriate delegation. This, while a tribute to their devotion, was tactically dubious.

Saturday, any Saturday, is a day of worship. It was no day to shepherd home from the Castle Garden ferry at the lower tip of Manhattan a man who was touched by reverence and surrounded by an entourage of nobody quite knew how many members, all washed by the same glow of heavenly light. The trouble was that on Saturdays, Jews who were *frim,* meaning deadly serious in their devotion to the rituals and strictures of their religion, would no more think of moving about in any form of vehicular transportation than they would think of striking a match or even a wife. The trouble was complicated by the fact that the Jews of Tenth Street did not seem to be aware of the distance in terms of miles between their home block and the lower tip of Manhattan.

I cannot believe that the question did not cross their minds. Or the minds of their movers and shakers. Or surely the mind of one leader. They must have had at least one. Germans always do.

In any case, the Germans of East Tenth Street in 1927 acted in a manner that I suppose there will always be people like me to call typical. They divided their forces. Those who were most *frim* came down to the synagogue on Fourth Street carrying their gold-embroidered velvet prayer bags as they did every Saturday morning. The others—I later estimated that at the start there were easily a hundred—set out on foot for the Battery.

During the past many years I have given this one day in my life a great deal of thought. Perhaps more than it deserves. And yet, until the day my mother died and her body disappeared from the Peretz Memorial Hospital in Queens on the day before Christmas, the only concrete result of all those years of thinking was the conviction that my life would have been entirely different if the Germans of East Tenth Street had decided to meet the Melitzer Rabbi, and celebrate his arrival at the Fourth Street block party, on a weekday. They would almost certainly have used the subway. Or the Avenue B streetcar. Or even a few taxis. Money, after all, was not a prime consideration. My point is, that coming up from the Battery on wheels they would almost certainly have arrived on East Fourth Street before dusk. Walter Sinclair and I had assumed they would. Our plan, or rather his, was based on this assumption. That was why, on Saturday afternoon, following the *chulent* and during the *lunch,* I left our flat, climbed the stairs, and let myself into Top Floor Back with the key Mr. Noogle had given my Aunt Sarah in exchange for the seven dollars Walter Sinclair had left in our mailbox.

Chulent was the staple of the Sabbath meal, a thick, heavy, delicious stew made of meat, beans, potatoes, onions, and spices. Every housewife on the block made her pot of *chulent* on Friday. Before sundown every boy on East Fourth Street carried the family pot up the street and around the corner to Mr. Siegel's bakery on Avenue D. Here Mr. Siegel placed the pots in the oven to keep warm overnight. They were never labeled. Every family had its own special pot, and Mr. Siegel identified every one of them by their contours as readily as he identified the owners by their sons.

Saturday at noon, when the family heads started coming home from the synagogue, the sons headed back to Mr. Siegel's bakery. Here the *Shabbes goy*, a gentile who was paid to perform tasks on the Sabbath forbidden to devout Jews by Holy Writ, would remove the pots from the oven with a long wooden shovel, and we would carry them home, piping hot, for the midday meal. After every scrap had been eaten, the head of the household lay down for a postprandial nap that was known as the *lunch*.

The word came from the piece of furniture on which these naps were taken: a brown leather couch with a headrest at one end. In shape, the one we owned, which was exactly like every other on the block, was not unlike the object on which in popular paintings of the period Madame Récamier is seen receiving the guests in her salon. To every family on the block this piece of furniture was known by the word under which the manufacturers of Grand Rapids had sent the model out into the world of immigrant America: a lounge. On East Fourth Street the word was pronounced *lunch*.

I waited until my father lay down and covered his face with the black and red polka-dotted bandanna he had owned since his service as a conscript in the cavalry of Emperor Franz Joseph.

"You want help?"

It was my Aunt Sarah, speaking from the kitchen sink. I stopped on my way to the front door.

"No," I said.

"You sure?" she said.

I was positive. Walter Sinclair had laid it all out. "Yes," I said.

My Aunt Sarah addressed the big brown pot from which she was scrubbing away the last scraps of *chulent*. "Sometimes things happen," she said.

Maybe they did. But not when Walter Sinclair was in charge. My mind, dominated by visions of the *Jefferson Davis II*, corrected the image at once. I shouldn't have said not when Walter Sinclair was in charge. The correct phrasing was: not when Walter Sinclair was at the helm. I had just started to read Conrad.

"Nothing is going to happen," I said. What else do you say and believe at fourteen?

"I'm glad to hear it," my Aunt Sarah said. "Because tomorrow I have to go back to New Haven."

My heart jumped. During the few days since the Shumansky wedding, when my mother had disappeared, I had grown accustomed to the presence of Aunt Sarah in the house. I liked her better than my mother. I had extended this feeling into the certainty that my Aunt Sarah was going to be with us forever. I had conveniently forgotten that she had a family of her own in New Haven.

"You'll come back?" I said.

"If everything is all right," my Aunt Sarah said.

"In New Haven?" I said.

"No," she said. "Here."

That settled any lingering doubts I may have had about the day's plan. "Everything is going to be all right," I said.

"Good," my Aunt Sarah said. "But watch out for Mr. Noogle."

"Why?" I said. "You gave him the seven dollars."

"And he was glad to take it," my Aunt Sarah said. "But he's related to that bloodsucker, Mr. Velvelschmidt. For bloodsuckers taking is easy. Giving back, that's what they find hard.

Take care." It was her first reference to the fact that my part in the block party might be hazardous.

"I'll take care," I said.

It was more than a phrase. It was a promise. That's why, even though it was Saturday afternoon, I climbed the stairs to Top Floor Back on my toes. Every family head in the building was snoring through his nap. I could have gone clumping up those stairs, banging together garbage-can covers like cymbals, without fear of detection. But I tiptoed.

Inside Top Floor Back, I locked the door behind me and took a quick look around. There was not much to see. Kitchens in uninhabited tenement flats on East Fourth Street tended to look like my science textbook illustrations of lunar craters. My interest, however, was in the *vonneh*. It looked exactly as it had looked the night before when I had brought up from the dock the last delivery the *Jefferson Davis II* had made for the block party. I ran my hand over the burlap wrappings that shielded the bottles. The wrappings were still damp, but the river water had run off down the *vonneh* drain. Handling them would be no problem. I walked out into the front room. It was like walking out into a huge dirty cracker box. No furniture. No curtains. Nothing on the walls except long gray stains from old roof leaks creeping down the plaster like belligerent stalactites. The windows were gray smears. Crossing to them, the long strips of naked floorboard creaked under my then approximately hundred pounds. Through the cracks came the rich, ripe smell that hung over the Lower East Side every Saturday afternoon: the mixed smell of stale urine and fresh *chulent*. It was a setting that I now see must have been a horror. On that day in 1927, however, it was perfect. Top Floor Back was a corner flat. From the windows of that stinking front room I could see not only the dock, but I could also look down on all of Fourth Street. As soon as I looked, I knew something had gone wrong with Walter Sinclair's plan.

The plan had been simple. Since it was Saturday, the block party could not start until the Sabbath ended at sundown. However, Walter wanted the deliveries made before sundown.

"Get the dough before it gets dark," he had said to me. "Once the sun goes down you have to make tracks. By the time you do, and you're far enough away to feel free to count, you're too far away from where you got the money to do anything about it if the payoff man short-changed you. I want to be the hell and gone out of here before they start hoisting them for this boy from wherever it is he comes from."

"Melitz," I said.

"Yeah, well," Walter said, "get the money before he goes back home."

"He's not going back," I said. "The Germans from Tenth Street, they're bringing him over to live. I mean he's going to live here forever."

Walter Sinclair laughed. "They're in for a surprise," he said. "Nobody lives forever. You get your mitts on that money before this boy unpacks his bag. Your mama tells me they're going downtown to pick him up early Saturday morning. Seems to me we can count on the welcoming committee getting back here by let's say sometime in the afternoon."

I had counted on it, and I had made my plans accordingly. What I had not counted on was the distance between East Fourth Street and the Battery ferry that brought immigrants across from Ellis Island. Later, when I was putting together the pieces, I could not quite work it out in miles, but I learned it was a four-hour walk for the average citizen. I'm sure I could have made it faster by doing scout pace. The delegation from Tenth Street, however, did not know about scout pace. Even if they had, I am certain they would not have used it on a Saturday when they were heading toward a meeting with the spiritual leader of the European town from which they had emigrated to America. They most certainly would not have used it on the way back from Ellis Island.

As I was to learn during World War II, a convoy takes its speed from the slowest vessel in the group. The Melitzer Rabbi, as I was to learn somewhat earlier, moved at the speed of a power saw cutting through the trunk of a giant redwood.

Later I learned what happened that day. The Tenth Street delegation arrived at the Battery shortly after eleven in the morning. The immigration officials were not ready for them. By the time the officials were ready, the Melitzer Rabbi was not. It was, I gather, a matter of protocol. He did not feel that he and his entourage should share the ferry with immigrants of lesser distinction. He was, as I have said, a German.

How this problem was resolved I do not know, but from a member of the entourage it was learned that halfway across the bay from Ellis Island to the Battery it struck the Melitzer Rabbi that he was on board a vehicle driven by an internal combustion engine on the Sabbath. Some sort of scene took place. The issue was settled on the Manhattan shore. The Melitzer Rabbi conducted a religious ceremony on Bowling Green.

It was probably somewhat different from the ceremonies Peter Stuyvesant used to conduct in the same place, but the results were not dissimilar. Gorges that had risen, fell. Tempers that had flared, sputtered out. Hysteria that had reigned, was driven from office. Gastric juices started gnawing at the walls of empty stomachs. Prayers stopped. The march northward started, toward East Fourth Street and *chulent*.

I knew nothing of this at the time, of course. At the moment when I looked down on East Fourth Street from the filthy front room windows of Top Floor Back, the Melitzer Rabbi, his entourage, and the Tenth Street welcoming committee were plodding uptown with stately grace somewhere between City Hall and Broome Street. Below me their destination, East Fourth Street, was as deserted as the room in which I was standing. The street looked better, of course, because the dome of arched wires with dangling electric bulbs that had been built over the block gave promise of imminent festivity. But my problem was not cosmetic. My problem was to get eighty bottles of booze out of the *vonneh* behind me and up the block to the synagogue near the Avenue D corner.

If the Melitzer Rabbi and his welcoming committee had arrived when Walter Sinclair had calculated they would, the block below me would have been as busy as one of those slabs of honeycomb in the window of Mr. Lesser's drugstore. Nobody would have paid any attention to me as I moved back and forth, up and down the block, from Top Floor Back to the synagogue, carrying several bottles at a time wrapped in the old copies of the *Jewish Daily Forward* I had carefully accumulated beside the *vonneh*.

On a deserted street, however? Who knew what eyes were watching from what windows? *Chulent* caused some people like my father to snore insensibly through their naps. There were others on Fourth Street, however, in whom it was rumored *chulent* produced a fiercely dyspeptic insomnia. How did I know that it did not cause its victims to spend their hours of agony staring down into the street?

I didn't know. But I did know I could not turn to Walter Sinclair for advice. He had promised to bring the *Jefferson Davis II* into the dock just before dusk to collect the take. I also knew I had promised him I would have the money waiting on that dock.

Like better men before me, I rose to the occasion.

I left the flat, locked the door carefully, tiptoed down the stairs, and started up the block. I was engaged in what I learned later, during the war, to call a recce party. I wanted to see if the arch of wires and bulbs over the street was dense enough to conceal a senior patrol leader from the eyes of possible sleepless *chulent* consumers seething with heartburn. I never found out. Perhaps ten feet before I reached the entrance to the synagogue, a man stepped out in front of me.

"Well, well, well," he said. "An old friend. How are you, sonny?"

My heart did its irritating flip-flop. The man was Mr. Kelly.

"Hello," I said.

"Going anywhere?" Mr. Kelly said.

Once more I wish I did not have to say I thought fast. Nonetheless, facing Mr. Kelly on the sidewalk in front of the East Fourth Street synagogue on that Saturday afternoon in 1927, I did think fast. I had to.

"I'm going up to Sheffield's," I said.

"For a bottle?" Mr. Kelly said.

I got it faster than I used to get most things in those days. It is one of the disadvantages of sarcasm. It tips its mitt. Even fools grasp at once that someone is trying to make them look foolish. They react.

"Yes," I said. "Grade A."

I moved on up the block. I turned left into Avenue D and broke into scout pace. At the Third Street corner I turned left again. I belted down to Lewis, turned left a third time, and raced back to Fourth Street. I didn't stop for breath until I was up the stairs and into the long green tunnel decorated with my scrawls.

"Aunt Sarah," I said.

"Ssshhh," she called from the kitchen. "Papa is sleeping."

I came out of the tunnel, and stopped short. I felt exactly the way I had felt down in the street when Mr. Kelly had stepped in front of me. Unexpectedly, I was in the presence of an enemy.

"Hello, Ma," I said.

I had not seen her since the night of the Shumansky wedding. Since then Walter Sinclair, making his deliveries to me on the dock, had assured me several times she was all right. I did not know what the phrase meant. I knew, of course, that it was meant to be reassuring. But even today I feel about it the way I felt then: I don't quite believe it.

"Is that all you have to say to your own mother?" my mother said.

Most people, of course, lie to themselves. I am no exception. I'm rather good at it. I've been doing it for years. It pleases me to set down, therefore, a completely truthful statement. There was a time when I did not understand the wonderful therapeutic value of lying to yourself. To my mother's question—"Is that all you have to say to your own mother?"—the truthful answer was: "Yes." But who had the courage to say it? Especially at my age? My Aunt Sarah, who knew everything there was to know, stepped in.

"What else is there you want him to say?" she said.

"He could say he's glad to see me," my mother said.

I wondered if I was. My Aunt Sarah sensed, of course, that I was wondering.

"Say it," she said.

Getting through life consists of slipping out of tough spots. The trick is to find the way out. When somebody points the direction, I am grateful.

"I'm glad to see you," I said gratefully.

"Listen to the way he sounds," my mother said. "You call this glad?"

My Aunt Sarah said, "Do you care if he's glad?"

My mother, who was sitting at the kitchen table, looked annoyed. "When a boy sees his mother," she said, "he should be glad."

The young woman who now sat at our kitchen table seemed to have almost no connection with the person who only a few days ago had been my mother. She had yellow hair piled gaily, carelessly high on her head like the whipped cream on a charlotte russe. There was even a small comb fastening stabbed saucily into the top of the pile. It looked like a tortoise-shell cherry. She was wearing something that was known on East Fourth Street as a gamp. I learned later that the word was actually guimpe. A dress cut wide at the throat, with narrow shoulder straps, not unlike a man's overalls, to set off the fluffy blouse with long sleeves and many ruffles that was worn under it. I had never seen this sort of thing worn by anybody but young girls. I had certainly never seen one like my mother's. It looked like a holiday. Her guimpe was a beautiful soft pink. On East Fourth Street this was a totally frivolous color. The blouse was so full of ruffles billowing up around her neck that she seemed to be surrounded by smoke, like the girl with the Spanish combs in the Cuban cigar ads. Most important of all, though, was her face. There was no fear in it.

"Stop talking like a fool," my Aunt Sarah said. "Of course he's glad to see you. Maybe he's a little surprised, the way I was when you came in, but glad? How can you even say such a thing?"

"He doesn't look glad," my mother said.

My Aunt Sarah turned to stare at me, as though to check the accuracy of this preposterous statement, and then I could tell from her face that she had suddenly thought perhaps it was not so preposterous.

"Benny," she said. "What's happened?"

"The street is empty," I said. "They haven't come back yet. The Melitzer Rabbi and the Germans. The whole street is dead. Nobody. But in front of the *schul* he's standing there."

"Who?" my Aunt Sarah said.

"Mr. Kelly," I said.

"From the government?"

It was my mother's voice. High. Alert. Startled. So I knew she understood what had been happening. And at once I also knew how she had understood it: from Walter Sinclair.

"Yes," I said.

My Aunt Sarah nudged my shoulder. "Yes, what?" she said.

Thus I understood that she did not quite understand what my mother understood.

"Yes, Ma," I said.

My mother rose from the kitchen table. I don't like the verb, but I can't think of a more appropriate word. She didn't stand up. She didn't shove back her chair and push herself erect. My mother rose. Like Venus coming up out of the shell in the framed picture Miss Hallock, my R.A.1 teacher in J.H.S. 64, had hung on the inside of the door to the supplies closet. More clothes, of course. Venus was not wearing a pink gamp and a white blouse dripping ruffles. But the gestures, the movement, the flow were the same.

"You mean we won't get the money?" my mother said.

My mind had not gone that far. All I had been worrying about was how to carry out the part of the plan that Walter Sinclair had assigned to me. I saw now that this was not far enough. My reactions to financial problems had been picked up from the reactions of my parents. Particularly my mother.

Once a month, every month, we—actually, she—were on the brink. The moment we—she—got up the twenty-three dollars that held off the enemy, the threat vanished from my mind. I grasped now that it did not vanish from my mother's mind. It may have receded, but it did not vanish. The sigh of relief was to me the gift of freedom for a month, which at my age seemed forever. Not to my mother. The relief that came with paying the rent did not wipe out the terror that next month the enemy would be at the gates again. On that Saturday afternoon, at that strange moment, from the tone of her voice, for the first time in my life I had an inkling of what my mother was after: security.

"No," I said, and then I corrected myself. "I mean I don't know."

"Why don't you know?" my mother said.

Today a mother speaking like that to a child would provide Dr. Spock with the raw material for at least a fat chapter. Possibly a new career.

"Because Walter said I should start carrying the bottles to the *schul* during the *lunch*," I said. "Walter said all those people with the Melitzer Rabbi they'd be here after *chulent* and the street would be crowded. Walter said nobody would notice me. But the street is empty. The Melitzer Rabbi and all those people, they're not here yet. The only person down there in the street, it's that Mr. Kelly. Walter wouldn't want me to carry the bottles in the empty street, with Mr. Kelly watching. That's why I don't know if we'll get the money," I said. "If I get caught by Mr. Kelly we won't get the money. I have to ask Walter what to do."

"Who is Walter?"

I turned. My father was standing in the doorway from the bedroom. He did not look very good. Nobody looked good on Saturday after rising from his nap after *chulent*. But I had never seen my father look as bad as this. His face was the color of the stone sides of the Hamilton Fish Park Branch of the New York Public Library. His eyes had spidery red lines running in crazy little darts from both sides across the whites toward the pupils, as though they were trying to extinguish the bright gleam in the middle. It was not a very reassuring gleam. And I saw for the first time why my father was always so fussy about combing his hair straight back. It was tumbled forward now. The bald circle on top was clearly visible. My father was barefoot, but he still wore the pants and shirt in which he had gone to *schul* that morning. Except that he had removed the collar. The gold stud dangled from the unfastened neckband. The suspender elastic had slipped from his right shoulder and was slapping gently back and forth against his thigh. I hated the way my father looked.

"He's a man I'm in business with," my mother said.

"Business?" my father said.

"Business," my mother said.

"What kind of business?" my father said.

"None of yours," my mother said.

They were speaking, of course, in Yiddish. If their words lose something in the translation, I'm glad. Pure hatred is terrifying.

"I'm your husband," my father said. "Everything you do is my business."

"I paid the rent two days ago," my mother said. "If you want to make it your business, I'll take back the twenty-three dollars, please." She held out her hand.

My father came out of the bedroom doorway into the kitchen. "Where did you get the money?" he said.

"From a place where you couldn't," my mother said.

"You haven't been home since the night of the Shumansky wedding," my father said. "Where have you been?"

"Doing what you don't know how to do," my mother said. "Paying the rent."

My father gathered his spittle with a low, grinding roar and spat it in my mother's face. "*Koorvah*," he said.

My mother's hand came up, out, and down, as though she were waving bon voyage from a dock to someone at the rail of a departing ship. The result was astonishing. To me, anyway. By the time my mother's arm returned to her side my father was flat on his back.

"Don't you ever use that word to me again," my mother said. "Or you'll never speak another word to anybody again."

Her words emerged slowly, with precision, as though she did not want any of them misunderstood, and the decibels of sound on which she sent them out were not very high. But the effect in that tenement room—as I leaned back, terrified, against my own scrawls on the green walls of the hall, and my Aunt Sarah cowered back, confused and frightened, against the black cast-iron sink—was as though each of my mother's words was a nail, and she was hammering it squarely, neatly, securely into my father's supine body.

"When you've lived the kind of life I've lived," my mother said, "then you can talk, and then you can call names, but until then you hold your stupid filthy mouth shut."

My mother's voice stopped. Her breath was coming fast. She went to the sink and turned on the tap. She took a glass from the drainboard and let the water run into it.

"Chanah," my Aunt Sarah said.

My mother shook her head. My Aunt Sarah moved away, a few more inches, toward the far side of the sink. My mother took a swallow of water. She turned off the tap. My father seemed to come alive. Slowly. His body moved like a hibernating snake starting to uncoil. He turned on his side. He put one hand to the floor. My mother came back and stood over him. My father stopped moving. He remained on his side, one hand flat on the floor.

"I have a chance," she said. "For the first time in my life I have a chance to make things better. Not like it was over there." She gestured behind her, as though she were flinging away something obscene. I realized she was referring to Europe. "The way I was told it would be over here," my mother said. "And it never was. Never. But now I'm going to make it better. Now I know how to do it." She paused, and she took a sip of water, and she said to my father, "Don't you or anybody else try to stop me. You hear? Don't even try."

There was a knock on the door.

"Go," my Aunt Sarah said to me.

I ran down the green tunnel and opened the front door. George Weitz faced me.

"They're coming in," he said.

I stared at him. George was at the top of my list. What was he doing here? Then I remembered. I had hired him and Chink Alberg and Hot Cakes Rabinowitz to help me move the bottles from Top Floor Back to the *schul*.

"Wait," I said.

I slammed the door in his face and ran back down the green tunnel. On the way through the kitchen into the front room I saw that my father had come up off the floor, but I did not stop. At the front-room windows I looked down on Fourth Street. George was right. Dusk was beginning to clap down. The red and blue and green and yellow bulbs had been turned on. Under them I could see people moving. They were crowding around a tall man in a *shtrahmel,* a wide-brimmed black hat trimmed with brown fur. I could tell from the way he acknowledged what were obviously obsequious greetings that the Melitzer Rabbi had arrived. So had the time to get going. I ran back through the kitchen and to the front door and opened it.

"What the hell's going on?" George Weitz said.

Since the morning after the eliminations finals for the All-Manhattan rally, his position at the top of my list had never been challenged. I needed his help, and Walter Sinclair had authorized me to pay for it, but I didn't owe him any explanations.

"Where's Chink and Hot Cakes?" I said.

"Upstairs on the Fourth," George said. "Waiting."

"Okay," I said. "Come on."

They were waiting, all right. Outside the door of Top Floor Back. I opened the door with Mr. Noogle's key and led them to the *vonneh*.

"One bundle each," I said. "Wrap it in newspaper. Get going."

"Money first," George Weitz said.

I fished from my pocket three of the twelve quarters Walter Sinclair had given me. I gave a coin to each of my three fellow members of Troop 244.

"Next quarter when you come back for your second bundle," I said.

"Whatsa matter?" George said. "You don't trust us?"

"Chink and Hot Cakes, maybe," I said. "Not you. Get the lead out. I'll be here when you get back."

They pocketed the coins, took their bundles, and went out. I ran into the front room for another look down at Fourth Street. It was getting darker. The colored lights looked brighter. The people under them seemed animated. I turned and ran out of Top Floor Back. I locked the door and ran down to our flat. When I came into the kitchen my father was standing near the sink. My Aunt Sarah was on his left. My mother was at the kitchen table. For a few moments I couldn't understand what was happening. It was as though I had stumbled into one of those paintings where some action has been frozen for reproduction on canvas. Then I heard my father's voice.

"If I'm what you call me," he said, "it's because of this rotten country where everything was going to be better. Better? Sewing pockets in pants on Allen Street? Getting paid only those weeks when they have pockets to sew? Hiding in corners from bloodsuckers like Mr. Velvelschmidt? You think for me it's better than it is for you?"

"I'm not thinking about you any more," my mother said. "I'm finished with you," she said. "From now on I'm thinking only about myself."

Behind me the front door opened and slammed shut. I turned toward the approaching footsteps. Walter Sinclair came out of the green tunnel, and it was as though something had suddenly gone wrong with my eyes. I knew it was Walter, and yet I didn't seem to recognize him. I blinked stupidly at the blond hair, the tall slender figure, the easy smile, the black turtleneck sweater. All the pieces of the portrait, so to speak, were in place, and yet the total of all the pieces added up to something unfamiliar. I had the feeling that I didn't really know this man. He could have been an imposter. He didn't belong here.

"Benny," he said. "Be dark very soon. Your mama and I, we got to get the old *Jeff Davis* away from that dock. What's holding things up, Benny?"

"You know my son?"

Walter turned toward my father. So did I, and all at once I

knew what was wrong. The look on my father's face told me. It was a look of fear. For the first time in all the years since he had come to America, my father was seeing the face of the New World.

"I know Benny very well," Walter Sinclair said, and I knew why he had seemed out of place, why I'd had the feeling he was an imposter who did not belong here. He didn't. Walter Sinclair belonged to the open air in which I had met him. The dock. The barges creaking at their moorings. The smell and movement of the river. And the continent behind the river. The continent that had made a glowing promise to my father but had not kept it. The continent that did not have to keep any promises to Walter Sinclair. He was part of it. He owned it. He would always be out of place in a tenement kitchen on East Fourth Street. He was part of the fresh air of the New World. My father had never breathed that air. I could see that at last my father understood why. His face told me. I had never seen a human face look like that.

"You know my wife, too?" he said.

Walter turned toward my mother. His smile changed slightly. "Why, yes," he said. "She introduced me to Benny."

He came further into the kitchen, still smiling. Then I heard a slap and a thump, and the smile fell from Walter's face. He leaped forward. I turned, and for a frightened moment, I did not grasp what had happened. Then I realized my mother was shielding her face from another blow. Walter Sinclair reached her before my father's swinging arm did. Walter covered her with his left arm. With a short, hard, chopping movement of his right fist, he knocked out three of my father's upper front teeth. He went down clutching both hands to the blood spurting from his mouth.

"Sorry about this," Walter Sinclair said. "I always heard you guys from Europe were gentlemen, bowers from the waist and all that. Try to live up to what I heard. Don't touch that girl again."

The door banged open. Chink Alberg came running in. He was carrying the bundle wrapped in pages of the *Daily Forward*. "Benny!" he screamed. "Benny, they got George and Hot Cakes!"

Walter Sinclair stepped across my father. He grabbed the front of Chink's sweater. "Who got them?"

"Imberotti, from over Lafayette Street," Chink said. "I mean he's the only one I know. I recognized him. But the others, the other guys—"

Walter knocked the breath out of him with a hard shove. Chink staggered back against the wall. Walter stood there for several moments, scowling down at the floor. He was trying to figure the next move. I was watching him so closely that I did not see my father get up. He had reached Chink and pulled the package of bottles out of Chink's hands before anybody in the kitchen was aware of what was happening.

"All right," my father said. "All right." The words came spitting out on a spray of blood from his smashed lips. "I'm what you say I am," he said. "I'm a nothing. And now I'll show you what a nothing can do."

For several moments after he was gone I wondered stupidly why I seemed to be waiting for a familiar sound. Then I realized that with his hands full, my father had not been able to slam the door behind him.

17

FORTY YEARS LATER, in the Queens apartment out of which thirty-two days ago with a broken thigh my mother had been carried to the Peretz Memorial Hospital from which on this cold day before Christmas a few hours earlier her body had disappeared, I could still hear the deafening silence of that door being unslammed in 1927.

"He must have been crazy," Herman Sabinson said.

"What?" I said.

"Your father," Herman Sabinson said. "On the Saturday they gave that block party for the Melitzer Rabbi. Your father must have been nuts."

I stared at Herman Sabinson with a sense of confused astonishment. Until this moment I had not realized I'd been telling him about that Saturday in 1927. I had never told anybody else. Not even my wife. Why Herman? He must have suddenly found he was asking himself the same question.

"Look," Herman said. "I don't mean to be nosey. But we're a couple of guys having a drink. Killing time while waiting for a phone call. I think it's probably made you feel a little better, sort of eased the tension sort of, to tell me about it. But if you feel you've told me too much, forget it. I've got nobody to repeat it to, even if I wanted. The only time Sandra listens to me is when I tell her how much I'm depositing in her checking account. But if it embarrasses you, or sort of makes you feel, you know, uncomfortable like, like I say, forget it. You don't have to say any more. Us Jewish boys, boy, have we got memories."

I wondered where his had started.

"Yes," I said.

Yes, indeed.

"Just the same," Herman Sabinson said, "I can't help thinking, from what you told me about that day, the day of the block party for the Melitzer Rabbi, your old man must have been a little nuts."

I had always thought so. It had never occurred to me that anybody else might think so. I looked at Herman Sabinson in a way that it embarrasses me to confess was new: with interest. "Why do you say that?" I said.

Herman sloshed the drink in his glass. He looked uncomfortable. "Well," he said, "of course, I never knew your father in those days, but for a long time, the last dozen years before he died, he lived right here in this apartment." Herman looked around the living room hung with pictures of my youth as though to reassure himself that he was in the right place. "You see a man two, three times a week, maybe you think all you're doing you're checking his blood pressure, you're counting his pulse, and of course you're doing that. Just the same, you're also getting a picture of the guy. What he's like as a human being. You're absorbing it without knowing. You know what I mean?"

I didn't, but I nodded and said, "Sure." All at once I had the feeling that if Herman kept talking I might learn something. At my age, it was high time.

"The picture I got all these last dozen years," Herman Sabinson said, "the picture I got was a nice, sweet, gentle sort of person. Not on account of he was an invalid in a wheelchair. Believe me, I've got some patients, they're invalids in wheel-chairs, their characters, the way they act, believe me, they're giving Hitler a bad name. Some of the bastards I have to take care of, don't quote me, but wow!" Herman rolled his eyes to the ceiling.

"I'll bet," I said.

"But your father, no," Herman Sabinson said. "And I'm not saying that just because I'm talking to his son. He was one sweetheart of a guy, your old man, he really was."

I thought of the day after the Shumansky wedding. The day my mother disappeared. The day my Aunt Sarah came down from New Haven. The day Mr. Kelly visited us in our Fourth Street kitchen. The day my father belted me.

"Yes," I said.

"Just the same," Herman Sabinson said, "I never got the feeling of a very bright guy. I don't mean he was dumb. But let's face it. Einstein he wasn't."

Not Albert, anyway. "No," I said, "Einstein he wasn't."

"That's what I mean about the way he acted that day," Herman Sabinson said. "The day of that block party. I mean he must have known by that time what the score was. The government guy made that pretty damn clear, it seems to me. Your old man must have known your mother was running booze."

"Hooch," I said.

"What?"

"I liked it better before," I said. "When you called it hooch."

Herman Sabinson gave me a peculiar look. Who could blame him? He had just come to the conclusion that my father had been nuts. And having studied in a reputable medical school, Herman must have had some knowledge of the Mendelian laws.

"Whatever you call it," Herman said, "your father must have known your mother was running it, and he must have known that this was dangerous because that kid was killed at this wedding. That kid who was marrying the chicken guy's daughter? You know?"

"Aaron Greenspan," I said.

"Right," Herman Sabinson said. "Well, Jesus Christ, that was gang stuff. Those wops? You know the name?"

"Imberotti," I said.

"Those boys," Herman Sabinson said. "They made it perfectly clear they were not going to let your mother get away with it. Your father knew that."

The trouble was, of course, that he knew more than that.

"I don't think he was a very worldly sort of guy," I said.

"Worldly, shmerldly," Herman Sabinson said. "How worldly do you have to be to stay away from guys with guns?"

"I don't think that was on his mind," I said.

"Well, it should have been," Herman said. "That's what I mean when I say he must have been a little nuts. He knew these Imberottis, a few days, before he knew they'd shot up this Greenspan boy. Then he also knew from this kid, the one came running in with the bundle of bottles—"

"Chink Alberg," I said.

"That kid, yes," Herman Sabinson said. "We had a Chink at the Edgie. Chink Rosen."

"There's a Chink on every Jewish block in the United States," I said.

"On account of how his eyes slanted," Herman Sabinson said. "Chink Rosen. That's why we called him Chink. I imagine it was the same on your block. So when your father saw this kid come running into your kitchen, he knew the Imberottis were down there in the street. He knew they didn't go around slapping wrists. He knew those boys did it with guns. But in spite of what he knew, what did your father do? He grabbed the bundle of bottles from this kid, this Chink whatever his last name was, and your father he says he'll make the delivery to the *schul* himself, and he runs out with the bottles. Right into the arms of these guys with the guns, who shot him into a wheelchair for the rest of his life. You call that a sensible way to act?"

"No," I said, "I guess not."

"After forty years," Herman Sabinson said, "you're still guessing?"

I looked at him with renewed interest. Of course I was. That was the problem. The feeling that I might learn something grew stronger.

"Listen, Herman," I said.

He started to. I could tell by the way he tapped the gold sign of Caduceus on his tie. But just then the phone rang. I went out to the foyer.

"Hello?"

"Dr. Sabinson there?"

"One moment, please." I covered the mouthpiece and called, "Herman, for you."

He came into the foyer and took the phone.

"Yes?" Herman listened for a few moments, then said, "You sure?"

The speaker at the other end must have been. Because Herman kept nodding for several moments as he listened. Soaking it up, whatever it was. Agreeing.

"All right," he said finally. "Thank you." Herman hung up and turned to me. "Everything is okay."

He couldn't have uttered a more irritating phrase. I have learned not only to distrust it, but to be angry with people who employ it. Everything is never okay.

"Spell that out, please," I said.

Herman Sabinson nodded in a troubled way. He understood my irritation. "What I mean is," he said, "I mean I've got the facts."

"What are they?" I said.

"It's one of those dopey mistakes," Herman said. "The ambulance, the one they sent from the Queens medical examiner's office to the Peretz Memorial Hospital, the guy driving it, it turns out, he's new. They just hired him. Or he was just assigned to the job a few days ago. A Puerto Rican kid, I understand."

"What's that got to do with it?" I said.

"Nothing, I suppose," Herman Sabinson said. "A driver who is not a Puerto Rican would probably have made the same mistake."

"What mistake?" I said.

"He went to the Peretz Memorial Hospital and he picked up your mother's body around eleven-thirty this morning," Herman Sabinson said. "But he had two more pickups. The Evangeline Booth General down near Throg's Neck, and the Francis Xavier Special Surgery on Columbus Avenue."

"In Manhattan?" I said.

Herman Sabinson nodded. "That's what caused the trouble," he said. "On account of it's the day before Christmas, and a Sunday yet, too, they're short-handed all over town, so they gave him this Manhattan pickup. I mean, ordinarily he would have done only the Queens hospitals and gone back to Queens General. This pickup in Manhattan, though, Francis Xavier Special Surgery on Columbus Avenue, he got his signals crossed. The driver. He thought he was ordered to carry all the bodies to Francis Xavier. Which is what he did. You can imagine what a snafu that caused. Anyway, they've just got it straightened out. What they want you to do, you don't have to go to Queens General again. All you have to do is go over to Francis Xavier. You can identify your mother's body right there, in Manhattan. They understand it's their fault, the mix-up, I mean, so they're trying to make it easy for you."

Without warning I fell apart. It was as though I had been paddling along on a stretch of lonely but smooth water and been caught in a sudden squall. The sound of my own sobs terrified and disgusted me. It was like no weeping I had ever heard or heard described. I felt cheap and worthless. All at once, I saw no point to the half century through which I had managed to remain on my feet. It had always seemed to me terribly important to keep going. No matter what. Now I saw it had all been a waste of energy. For the first time in my life I wished I was dead.

I turned and walked out into the bedroom my mother and father had shared for the last twenty years. I did not realize Herman Sabinson had followed me until I heard his nervous little cough.

"Don't let it get you," he said. "When someone dies, people always cry. I see a lot of it. Honest, believe me, it's natural."

It was not natural for me. I had got through the death of my father without tears, and he had been a man I liked. Even after that day when he had belted me. But I had never known how I felt about my mother. Except for that one moment, the moment when we were sitting on the dock late at night, waiting for what I then did not know was going to be the *Jefferson Davis II,* and she had put her hand on my shoulder to reassure me against the shapeless threats of the river. She had been a source of irritation to me for so long. Why was I suddenly acting like a Hindu widow struggling to escape the clutching hands of relatives who were trying to restrain her from hurling herself on her husband's funeral pyre?

"Look at it this way," Herman Sabinson said. "It's better it should happen here in private. I mean in front of a friend. At least now you know you won't make a spectacle of yourself when you get there."

"I'm not going," I said.

Herman Sabinson walked around me as though I were a statue, moving with slow, deliberate, stalking strides until he was directly in front of my face.

"You don't mean that," he said quietly.

The horror was that I did.

"Herman," I said. "Can't you do it for me? You were her doctor for twenty years. You can identify the body better than I can. I've never asked you for a favor. We're East Side boys. We always stick together." I caught myself just in time. I had been about to remind him that we had flown in the Lafayette Escadrille together. "Please do this for me."

"There's things nobody can do for you," Herman Sabinson said. He added, not without irony, "It's against the law." He took my elbow. "Come on," Herman said. "Act like a guy who grew up on East Fourth Street. I've got the car outside. I'll ride you over."

18

HERMAN SABINSON drove the way all doctors drive. With very little regard for other vehicles on the street, totally absorbed in only one problem: finding a parking place. By the time we reached the hospital I was all right. That is to say, I was no longer shaking. How I felt was another matter. A matter in which I took no pleasure. But at least I looked the way any average citizen of middle years should look while entering a morgue to identify the body of his mother. If this does not provide a sharply etched picture, I am not surprised. I have never in my life seen a man of middle years while he was entering a morgue to identify the body of his mother. Francis Xavier Special Surgery on Columbus Avenue is not noted for a profusion of mirrors.

"I'll wait for you," Herman Sabinson said. Then he must have seen something in my face, because he added, "If you want?"

I did, of course. Which is why I had to refuse. "No, thanks," I said. "You told me to act like a guy who grew up on East Fourth Street."

Herman Sabinson tapped the knot in his tie, touched the embroidered flower under the knot, and tipped the golden sign of Caduceus that held the tie to his well-fed little belly. The three movements, like a flourish of small trumpets, brought a smile to his face. Herman was proud of me. He'd known all along that all he had to do was mention the code by which we East Side boys lived, and I would shape up.

"You've done more than enough," I said. Like many people my age I watch a great many World War II movies on the late show. I know the dialogue. " 'You have rendered service above and beyond the call of duty,' " I said. "I'll feel better if you let me take it from here alone."

"Okay, kid," Herman Sabinson said. "But if you want me, you know my number."

"Thanks, Herman," I said.

"I mean my number at home," he said. "Not the service. Sandra always knows where I am."

She did, indeed. Sandra's father had been a policeman.

"If I have any trouble," I said, "I'll call you at home."

Herman Sabinson patted my arm. "Just remember this," he said. "What's happened to you is upsetting, but it happens to everybody."

I wondered. A few minutes later I was seated at a desk in a room not unlike the one in which a few hours earlier I had met Mr. Bieber. Or had his name been Beybere? Already he seemed a shadowy creature out of a shapeless past that kept moving away from me.

"Yes, we have the body," said the man behind the desk. "Do you want to identify it?"

His voice was more harsh than Mr. Bieber's had been. Perhaps because Manhattan up around Columbus Avenue is a harsher part of town. I had never before thought of Queens as an outlying province.

370

"I was told I have to," I said.

"Yes, you have to be told that. But it's no more than a formality. I have all the papers." He tapped them. "Many people find it an upsetting experience. Everything is in order, I assure you."

I wished all at once I could believe his assurance. "You mean I don't have to actually—?" My voice drained away. I could not finish the sentence.

"No," the man behind the desk said. "All you have to do is sign here."

He pushed a paper across the desk and made a tiny X with his ballpoint next to a dotted line. I took the pen and hesitated. What would Herman Sabinson think of me? Or George Weitz and Chink Alberg and Hot Cakes Rabinowitz? I could see them on learning of my defection. Gathering around me slowly in the troop meeting room in the basement of the Hannah H. Lichtenstein House. Placing a loaded revolver in front of me at the table where as senior patrol leader I had helped them to grasp and believe that a scout is trustworthy, loyal, helpful, friendly, courteous, kind, obedient, cheerful, thrifty, brave, clean, and reverent. The cold eyes of Mr. O'Hare stabbed at me across their heads. They turned and marched to the door. As Chink opened it, Mr. O'Hare turned to give me a final glance. His eyes dropped to the loaded gun in front of me. The scoutmaster nodded compassionately but sternly. He knew I would do the right thing. The door shut behind them. I closed my eyes.

"Is anything wrong, sir?"

I opened my eyes. The man behind the desk was looking at me with a troubled frown. I shook my head. "No," I said.

To hell with George Weitz, I thought. Nuts to Chink Alberg

and Hot Cakes Rabinowitz and Mr. O'Hare. I signed. The man behind the desk looked pleased as he retrieved the ball point and the paper.

"Good, good," he said. I sensed a note of triumph in his soaring voice. He had achieved something I was not in a position to win. "Thank you," he said.

"That's all?" I said.

"That's all," he said.

About
The Author

JEROME WEIDMAN, who won the Pulitzer Prize for *Fiorello!*, has long been a distinguished novelist, short-story writer, essayist, and playwright. Among Mr. Weidman's seventeen novels are *I Can Get It for You Wholesale, The Enemy Camp, The Sound of Bow Bells,* and *Fourth Street East.* His successes in the theater include *Tenderloin* and *I Can Get It for You Wholesale,* which he adapted for the stage from his own novel of the same name. His courtroom drama, *Ivory Tower,* written in collaboration with James Yaffe, was the American Playwrights Theater selection for 1968 and won the National Council of the Arts Award for that year. He has also won the Drama Critics' Circle Award and the Antoinette Perry ("Tony") Award. His short stories—which have appeared in *The New Yorker, The Saturday Evening Post, Harper's, Esquire,* and every other major magazine in this country, England, Canada, Australia, Europe, and Asia—have been collected in seven volumes, including *The Horse That Could Whistle "Dixie," The Captain's Tiger,* and *My Father Sits in the Dark.* His best-known travel books and collections of essays are *Letter of Credit, Traveler's Cheque,* and *Back Talk.* His books and plays have been translated into ten languages.